The Woman in the Waves

Camille Booker

HAWKEYE

PUBLISHING

First published in Australia in 2025 by Hawkeye Publishing.

Cover Design by Anne Freeman

A catalogue record of this book is available from the National Library of Australia.

ISBN 9781923105362

Proudly printed in Australia.

www.hawkeyebooks.com.au

Praise for THE WOMAN IN THE WAVES

'The depth of characters, the atmospheric setting, and the wonderful storytelling makes *The Woman in the Waves* a must-read!'
Leanne Quinn

'That rare combination of lyrical prose with propulsive plot. The beauty and power of the landscape and Missy's stake in myth and legend will stay with me for a long time.'
Lindsey Armstrong

'This utterly compelling book has such a haunting, gothic atmosphere. I felt bewitched by it long after I'd finished reading.'
Lorna Peplow

'An eerie, beautiful book that transports you to another time and place. From the first page I knew I was in the hands of a great storyteller.'
Sophie Stern

'This unique story is so atmospheric and intriguing, it crept under my skin and stayed there long after I stopped reading. The author has drawn Missy in a perfectly imperfect way: naive but cunning, selfish but loving. Get ready to be mesmerised, wave by wave and chapter by chapter.'
Ike Levick

'Missy and Shaw are characters that continue to stick with me, long after first reading. This haunting novel is full of stunning prose, evocative of dark and disturbing shadows in a vividly written landscape.'
Rebecca Lewis-Smith

Praise for THE WOMAN IN THE WAVES

The Woman in the Waves is an atmospheric coastal mystery full of suspense and intrigue. Set in a small fishing town in 1920s Australia, Booker's beautiful prose and masterful storytelling bring the coast to life on each sea-drenched page. I couldn't put this down; the characters and evocative coastal setting haunted me afterwards.'
Fiona Clarke, winner of the Exeter Novel Award

'Booker is a master of gothic noir. Gripping, intriguing, evocative, *The Woman in the Waves* will sweep you away and leave you gasping for more, right down to the very last haunting breath.'
Skye Stranger

'A sublime novel, beautifully written with a real hint of menace. Booker's ability to create such a real sense of time and place is astonishing. It stayed with me long after I'd turned the last page.'
Sarah Lupton, finalist of the Exeter Novel Award

'The Woman in the Waves* is a mesmeric historical story written by a unique talent. Booker takes us back to a gothic 1921 on the east coast of Australia when a fisherman's daughter, Missy, stumbles upon a body. This vivid encounter sets up Missy's quest to understand the legends of the sea and the disappearance of her mother. With tight-lipped locals, a new detective on the case, and a lighthouse overseeing all, the stench and mystery of this eerie fisherman's village is spellbinding. I'm mad for this one!'
Kelly Sgroi

Salty, strange and haunting, *The Woman in the Waves* blends myth, legend, history and intrigue with just the right amount of darkness. Like a cold, cruel sea, this book will make you shiver."
Kell Woods, author of 'After the Forest' & 'Upon a Starlit Tide'

For John-John and Matilda.

These pages contain discussion and instances of self-harm, suicide, and mental illness
which may be triggering.

1

Segunda-feira

Widow's Peak, 1921
South Coast New South Wales
Sixty Miles South of Sydney Cove

A seagull's screech startles me.

The wet rope slips through my chafed fingers and plunges further into the blue. My palm opens and the rope releases, a blister rupturing like a gaping fish mouth. I curse under my breath: rough hands and vulgar language just two consequences of being a fisherman's daughter for nineteen years. My grip tightens and the rope halts. I heave it back toward me, tossing the coils on the deck. Judging by its weight we have trapped a good haul. Cray, perhaps lobster. Either way it will fetch a good price at the market.

I peer into the deep water and gasp, almost losing the rope a second time. There beneath me, just under the surface, is a monstrous octopus with a bulbous, reddish-brown head. My skin breaks out in gooseflesh. I've heard tell of such things, but never, not in all the time I have spent on the ocean, have I trapped one before. They live in the Midnight Zone, the deep dark waters of the ocean floor.

The trap jerks as it breaks the surface. It loses buoyancy and the weight of the octopus grows heavier. Tentacles sink to the bottom of the cage, its skin droops from its body like a pair of wet trousers. On breaking free of the waves, like a creature from an unknown world, the hideous thing unspools its arms, wide, pearly round suctions on all eight of them, and extends them toward the boat.

For a moment I am seized by the length of them, unable to pull the rope, unable to move, dumb-stricken. Eight thick arms speckled with two-inch-wide suckers ripple toward me, draw me in. The trap lowers onto the deck of the *Senhora ao Vento*. The octopus must be more than three yards in diameter, with all its tentacles spread, trying to grab hold of something, fighting to escape. The trap lid swings open and one of the arms unfolds from its metal cage.

I am at a loss as to how to kill it, and I don't have long to decide, so with two hands I grasp its enormous head and drag it across the deck, its suckers making it almost impossible. I rip at it, heave it, gaining traction. The head slides through my fingers, but I dig my nails in further, causing the creature to release its suction. Finally, I toss it into a crate then slam the lid down. Collapsing on top of the crate, my heart hammers inside my chest as I try to catch my breath.

The crate is made of wooden slats with open spaces between, but I figure they are too small for the octopus to squeeze through. So once my hands have stopped trembling, I leave the beast and return to our traps. A moment later I turn to see the octopus working its way through the narrow spaces.

Kneeling close beside the crate, I grimace then jerk away as its slimy arms reach for me. When our eyes meet, I know this animal is *thinking*. Its black horizontal pupils gaze at me, and I can feel it sizing me up as we both wonder: who is stronger? Smarter?

A single tentacle snakes toward me, slowly, sinuously, beckoning. *Touch me*, it says. I almost reach out my hand, mesmerised by its slimy beauty, its wily charm. Then four of its tentacles spill from the narrow spaces between the slats, while the others use their strength to pry open the lid. Its elastic head condenses and pours through like liquid. The octopus is on the deck, moving fast toward the gunwale.

I lunge at the octopus, spearing it through the head with the knife I keep in my belt. The knife slips through muscle and sinew. But the strength of the creature is such that even with the blade's point piercing through its head and entering the wooden deck, tentacles reach up and over the side of the boat. It heaves itself upwards, trying to pull itself over the side, desperate to escape.

The sharp end of the knife, dug into the deck with all my weight, leaves a trough half an inch deep. There is no turning back now. If I can put an end to this creature's suffering, I must. I use all my force to hold the octopus still.

Slowly it loses strength and dies. I gather the limp mess of tentacles and suckers in my arms, its skin slippery and velvety, then toss it back in the crate and sigh with relief. My heart beats erratically; I put my hand on my chest.

Growing up on a fishing boat, my father taught me to catch, trap, and kill before I had learned to read. Reading wasn't important. Fishing was. There's no malice in it. I like to believe the fish aren't aware of the net that tightens around their scaly bodies. Yet for some strange reason, and I don't know why, it felt like that octopus knew. It *knew* it was going to die. But can octopuses really know such things? With its horizontal eyes upon me, I saw its panic grow as it used its wits to escape. As though it were saying to me, *you'll pay for this, Missy Green. Just you wait.*

Fishermen are superstitious folk. No group of people harbour as many cautionary tales as those who live by the sea. And something tells me there will be consequences to pay for winning this battle. All that creature wanted, its dying wish, was freedom. I gave it a type of freedom, I suppose. There is freedom in death. There is freedom in oblivion.

Besides, killing isn't necessarily evil. Sometimes killing is a mercy. Sometimes killing is necessary.

When soldiers go to war, they are told, ordered, to kill men – mirror images of themselves – and when they return home, they are lauded for it. Medals pinned to their breast. It's exactly what that German philosopher, *Nietzsche,* means when he says nothing is right or wrong. There is no morality. It's about the will to survive, an animal's most fundamental instinct. And in that moment with the octopus, my will was stronger.

Still, as I catch my breath, I shudder at what consequences lie lurking for killing such an intelligent, mysterious beast. A creature that almost outwitted me. For if that animal did understand its fate, then I don't want to be the last thing it saw.

I crane my neck to check whether my father has heard any of the disturbance from inside the boat's cabin, but underneath his fisherman's cap, his face is serene. His brows are knitted in concentration as his fingers work their way through a knot in one of his nets. I'm not surprised he didn't hear the commotion with the octopus. That man seems to enter a different world when he's sitting with a net across his lap. When I was young, he could sit for hours detangling. He'd sit for so long that I would drape one around me just so I could have a chance to sit on his lap, too.

The islands we fish are about two miles off the coast of Widow's Peak. They are rocky and the vegetation is sparse, but the waters provide us with enough of a haul to get by. The islands are too small for anyone to live on, but they are steeped in myths, as old as the rocks and just as real, told and retold by the generations of fisherman families that have long worked this stretch of coast.

My own father would tell me bedtime tales of the West Wind. The West Wind lived up on top of Widow's Peak Mountain with his six daughters, Wilga, Lilli Pilli, Wattle, Clematis, Geera, and Mimosa. Mimosa, an unpleasant child compared to her sisters, was so disobedient and rude to her father that he snatched off the piece of mountain where she sat and threw it into the sea to cool her bad temper.

Shocked to discover she was trapped on an island without her family, Mimosa sat sulking for days and days, until she turned into a mermaid and slid into the sea.

Mimosa's fate should have been a lesson to her sisters, but after time, they too grew disobedient. One evening, the West Wind arrived home to find the remaining sisters lazing about on warm rocks. Their father's patience waned. Taking a deep breath, he blew all the rocks, except for one, out to sea, so that there were five islands, with five little mermaids sunning themselves. Geera was the only daughter who remained. From the mountaintop, she gazed out at the Five Islands for so long, she turned to stone. Dust and dead leaves fell upon her, grass and wildflowers grew over her, and she became the mountain, the shadow in which Widow's Peak lies.

What a strange thing to have so many sisters, I would say to my father in an attempt to stall his departure from my bedside. But he would bid me good night, huff out the candle, and leave me alone in the dark.

Seabirds circle Big Island – two islands joined like lovers. Depending on the weather and conditions, we fish anywhere from the sheer rocky side to the calm inlet. Our livelihood depends on this sea and the haul she gives us, so we always keep a close eye on the weather.

The West Wind barely whispers this morning. The shearwaters are moaning, and the waves lap quietly at the shore. We are immersed in nature here, far away from the rest of the world.

My father, Augustus Green – *Gust* – pours boiling water into two mugs from a coke-black iron kettle inside the small cabin at the helm. The stream of water threatens to soak the sleeve of his old blue jersey, but he has done this a thousand times, so it stays dry, and he fills the mugs to the brim. The loose tea leaves float to the surface like flood debris.

He reaches for my hand and places the scalding mug in it. I wrap my numb fingers around its smoothness, the blister in the cushiony part of my palm stinging on the hot surface. I inhale the floral steam then rest the mug on the controls and slip on my woollen gloves. The boat bobs up and down as we sip our strong black tea in silence, apart from the breeze, which is starting to pick up, the gulls, and the slap of the water on the hull.

'Swell's up,' my father says.

'Fog's coming in too,' I say in return.

'Mm,' he grunts.

My mug is so full that when a wave crashes into the side of the boat, hot tea sloshes over the rim and onto my hand. I lick my skin and taste the ocean. I don't mind, I'm used to the taste of salt. Salt has been a permanent residue my whole life.

The engine fires up. We chug ahead and the water tosses the boat around. The gulls trail our wake, their keen, red-rimmed eyes hungry for scraps. I'm drawn to the ocean. The colours, the cold, the animals, the atmosphere. I love it and there's nothing that can keep me away. Even my name, Missy, *Marissa*, means 'of the sea'. Though I suppose I never really had a choice, coming from a town like ours, the family into which I was born. And the mother who vanished when I was a baby.

My father steps out on deck, holding his tea with one hand and the port side of the boat with the other. He edges his way around, running his hands along the ropes as a merchant would caress a piece of finest silk. When he stops, he leans his upper body against the gunwale, pulls back the soft cloth of his fisherman's cap and turns his face to the predawn sky, his sun-lined skin creasing as he inhales the last of the twinkling stars. Spray lands on his cheek. He reaches up and brushes it away, leaving a wet smear on his face.

By five o'clock I find our usual place near Rocky Islet, where we usually net some decent-sized rock blackfish, and lower the anchor. My father helps me with the nets. Salt spray has accumulated in the bristles of his beard, but I doubt he would even see if I held a mirror to his face.

It is around this time the thick fog that has rolled down off the mountain advances over the ocean. It settles in around us and, in the distance, the foghorn begins to blare.

As we wait for the haul to be brought in, I sit on an upturned wooden crate, like the one I threw the dead octopus in, and gaze out as the sea and the sky are enveloped in white.

Soon there is nothing to see but fog, so I close my eyes. It's unnaturally quiet. The sound of the waves slapping against the underside seems amplified. Fog does this. Just the constant *slap-slap* of the waves with the occasional lonely moan of the lighthouse's foghorn.

Then there's another sound, underneath the slap of the waves. A deeper, more mournful sound, and it's not coming from the lighthouse. It's ominous, as sad as whale song and just as heavy. It penetrates deep into my bones. I get off my makeshift seat and step closer to the side of the boat.

Peering out to the horizon, there is nothing to see but white – the fog is so heavy. There is moisture in it, it makes my face wet to touch. My skin pricks. That noise is getting louder. It's coming from the waves.

'Missy?' My father's voice, absorbed in the fog, makes him seem closer than he is.

'What is it?' My own voice sounds muffled.

'Where were you?'

The fog is impenetrable. A sinking unease passes through me. Something tells me hours, not minutes, have passed since this fog enveloped us. My father's hand clutches my shoulder.

I gasp. 'Did you say something?'

'You ready?'

The foghorn blares.

I must have imagined the sound. Fog can do strange things to your hearing. Especially when you're out on the water. It can make you feel like you're in one of those padded rooms of an insane asylum. Complete whiteness, complete silence. No sharp edges. Nothing but the screech of seagulls inside your head, foghorns blaring, the heavy song of whales. I hum to myself to break the silence. The upbeat music that plays along to my favourite Charlie Chaplin film, *The Tramp*. I must have seen it at least five times. Each time I left the cinema with a secret wet patch on my trousers from laughing so hard. Nobody noticed.

We bring up the ropes together. The fingers poking out of the holes in my gloves are stiff with cold and the wet rope grates them raw. Spume flicks the side of the boat, spraying my face. I wipe away the coldness with my sleeve and, as I do, a bleached piece of driftwood floats past. A wave crests and then it disappears. Craning to see into the fog, there is nothing, just that sound coming from the ocean floor and drawing closer to the surface. The moan is deep and primal. It's coming up with the rope, with the haul. Soulful, sorrowful, it approaches and breaks free of the waves – the sound – but no vision of anything, and when it does break free, it dissolves into the fog.

I doubt my hearing.

I doubt my mind.

I wait.

The foghorn blares.

I am about to bring up another trap when the sound rolls again, muffled, and distant, but this time, different. It is a voice, certainly. A woman's voice. Hissing. The hissing elongates and when I hear it, it becomes my name, *Missy*. The rope slides from my hands and I lean forward over the gunwale, my fingers gripping the side of the boat, my hearing strained. She calls my name again, longer this time. *Missssssssy*, she hisses. *Misssssssss*. The voice calls my name, calls me.

Leaning further over the side, I call into the white, 'Hello?'

There is nothing but numb silence on the surface of the ocean. My ears hum. For a moment the fog clears, it swirls around me and something pale darts past in the water. A school of fish perhaps. Or perhaps it is bigger than that. A shark.

No, it's a body. A woman. Underwater, she comes into focus, her eyes are open, and her skin is as pale as seashells. Her long, dark hair undulates like kelp with the current. She glides past the boat, under the waves and, as she does, more details appear: scales, a fish's tail, silvery-green opalescence. I must be mistaken; it can't be a fish tail. Perhaps it is simply a woman going for a swim. But why is there a woman swimming this far off the mainland? Does she need help?

The foghorn blares.

I cast a glance over my shoulder at my father, but he is busy unloading the haul and, when I look back, the woman's head and bare chest have surfaced. She looks at me. Right at me. My body stiffens and the hairs on the back of my neck stand on end. Her face glistens in the fog and her hair spreads about her like frayed rope on the flat surface of the sea. Her mouth forms words, or perhaps a song, but I cannot hear her. I cannot and I do not think I want to. My heart pounds in my chest with fear and wonder. Looking around for my father again, I realise the man has deserted me. I turn back to the woman in the waves. I can't peel my eyes away from her, she is so lovely, so beguiling. A wild thought enters my head. Should I dive in? So easily I could slip beneath the ocean's silky surface; my father would not hear a sound. The thought escapes just as quickly as it appeared.

When I open my mouth to speak, the woman's face contorts hideously. She lets out a jarring, blood-curdling wail and I can't tell whether my ears ache from the sound or with cold. Through the screech, her eyes beg something from me. When the screech stops the shape of her body disappears beneath the crest of a wave, that silvery-green fish tail flicks whitewash into the air. She recedes into the blue depths, and I can't be sure I've seen anything at all, and even though I'm trying, I can't see her anymore. She's gone. The fog.

I stand on the deck for a moment, frozen by what I heard. What I saw. Did my father hear it? He certainly didn't see it. What was it that I saw, heard? A body? A woman? A woman with a fish tail. *Avó* would call that a mermaid. It makes no sense. Why did she look at me like that?

That seagull's screech echoes in my ear, trilling. It won't stop. I can't think. It's too close here, too silent. I need space, the roar of the waves. I need to walk. Walking will clear my head, help me think.

Dawn has broken but the fog completely chokes the sun.

My father's voice cuts through my thoughts. 'Bout time we be getting back.'

My father, ever the timekeeper. I head inside the wheelhouse in a daze.

The last of the haul is unloaded into the crates, the nips of their claws sound like teeth snapping and biting as we make our way back to the harbour through the gloom. We're on a nice stretch of coast, with the escarpment all around, but after so long, I hardly notice it.

As we round the headland, the cliff draws nearer. The lighthouse creeps out of the grey, like a slender white finger telling the ocean to go to Hell, its details visible even through the gloom: the red rust around the window like old blood, the narrow iron railing of the balcony at the lantern room. The lighthouse does not welcome people.

The White Widow, the locals call it, which makes no sense because it's a widower who's manned it for the past five decades. The dark figure of the man appears at its tip, an opaque shadow, a grey-blue. The light is still flashing even though it's morning now and it barely penetrates the fog. He'll turn it off soon.

'You think he sees us?' I ask.

My father, looking out to sea, doesn't even bother to turn around. 'He doesn't see anything beyond what goes on inside that tower.'

'He just doesn't like outsiders,' I say. 'It's how it should be for a lighthouse keeper.'

'That light's made him mad.'

A shiver runs down my spine as the mermaid's face floats in front of my vision, her flowing hair, dark as kelp. Her haunting eyes. That sound coming from her mouth. Cold hands wrap themselves tightly around me.

Widow's Basin comes into view, and with it, the harbour. Two walls made of huge rocks and boulders that don't quite meet, one set a little back from the other. My father used to say it looked like eyebrows on a face. I would joke that the rock walls needed to be closer together, or even touching, because I inherited the eyebrows of my mother's country, where they were as thick as caterpillars. Even though I know thin eyebrows are the current style, I have no time for that; no desire to pluck and draw them back on.

Through the fog, the harbour is alive with chugging boats. I navigate the *Senhora ao Vento* into Widow's Basin and turn left into the U-shaped harbour, pulling her up at the end of the wooden gangplank, next to the sandstone wall of the old port. Oil swirls on the water's surface, a pelican glides between the boats. I ignore the sneering looks of the other fishermen as they gather their nets and unload their hauls. My father doesn't notice their leering.

I jump up the gunwale and stretch my leg down so that the tip of my toe touches the sandstone step that disappears into the water. The boat wobbles and I momentarily overbalance. My boot slides across the green slime that lines the bottom step, and it rushes up toward my face. I brace for impact and feel confused when it doesn't occur. Rather than colliding with the sandstone, it's my father's arm I feel on my shoulder as he steadies me. I smile gratefully and squeeze his hand in thanks then clamber up the rest of the steps to the road level, leaving him to unload.

Passing the line of boats tethered to the harbour, a group of men unload their crates of fish from the decks. Their sleek silvery bodies gleam against the men's festering blackened fingers. The men snigger when they see me.

'Lost your sea legs there, love?' Old Gil Sanders laughs, throaty, deep, and the rest of them chuckle.

I glare at his blotchy, weather-damaged face, the dark green veins beneath the surface of his skin, his wide-open mouth, full of broken teeth, and keep walking. I may not yet be twenty, but I know more of this sea than they ever will. Bloody hire-a-hand bastards with no boat of their own and no loyalty.

I avoid the market area where the merchants are already calling to each other, unloading their boats and trawlers with haste. Despite his age, my father sells more fish than any of them. Experience has taught him well. I wonder how much that octopus will bring in.

From the harbour the sandy trail meanders along the shoreline, lined by long grass. Far behind me now, anchors and God-knows-what-else splash into the waters. The fog rolls thick, but I know this path blind. I climb over the grass hill, upwards past the shrubs, and hear the waves below, crashing into the rocks. The suck of the water. The woman's face flashes again in my head, the way she stared at me, the way her eyes harpooned right through me, like she was trying to tell me something. Warn me of something.

The tide sounds low. I'm high above the water level, along the grassy edge of the cliff, sheer and menacing. I peer over. The waves retreat to reveal glimpses of green algae clinging to the rock shelf. I walk higher and higher up the hill, over the small, yellow-flowered weeds that dot the grass.

The fog lifts slowly, and I gaze out at the coastline. The ridge of mountains, a long line that runs all the way north, is a dark purple silhouette. Ghostly shapes behind the curtain of fog. Seagulls flap overhead.

The grass becomes more windswept the higher I climb, until the White Widow comes into view. The lantern room first: domed like a soldier's helmet, the sun reflects the white mist off the dark windows, and the wraparound balcony, its once gilded edges corroded to rust with time and salt and ocean spray. A moment later, the rest of it appears, and I pause to take it in. A luminously white cylinder, broken only by the black door. There are no windows on this side of it, only one small circle, almost at the top, facing out to sea. It's isolated and colossal and overwhelming.

I'm a bit breathless from the climb because I'm walking at

pace and still haven't eaten anything, but it matters not, because I need to walk. The path veers off to the left, to the tower, to the office and the keeper's residence. Smoke feathers from the chimney of the cottage. Usually, I would visit my grandfather, but not today. I continue to the right, toward the surf beach, where there will be no people.

I need to walk.

The crash of the waves.

I need to think.

Descending the other side of the grass hill toward the dunes, the beach is deserted. A long strip of beige, yet to awaken. In the far distance, chimneys from the steelworks puff columns of white smog into the already white sky, like beautiful moths. Rusted needles with little fires burning at their tips.

My boots sink into the soft sand as I step off the grass and trudge down to the shoreline where the wet sand is easier to walk along. The waves break on the shore with rhythmic constancy. The Five Islands, where we just were, are dark lines on the horizon. Stepping stones, three of them clustered together, the two others further apart, some distance from their sisters.

I check over my shoulder. The lighthouse is perched high on the cliff behind me, windswept and raw. Its eye asleep now. The foghorn still thunders intermittently although I have grown accustomed to its wail. I walk at brisk pace along the shore for a long distance, far away from the harbour, from the town, from my father, so I can be alone. So I can think.

Something small juts out of the wet sand. It's smooth and pale, like the colour of that woman's skin, the woman in the waves. I bend down and unearth it from its nestled position and realise the shell isn't so small but about the size of my hand. It fits in my palm but it's heavier than its size would suggest. It is round and conical shaped, like a snail's shell, with a hole in one side and a sharp edge on the other. The spiral at its centre expands like the stairs to the lantern room. I pocket it and continue my walk.

That woman, in the waves, was she real? She reminds me of someone, someone close to me, someone I never knew. Seeing her this morning, with her beautiful fish tail and her mournful song, has awoken something in me. Something about my mother.

I remember my mother in pieces. That's a lie. I don't remember my mother at all. I was too young when she died. I remember her from the photograph we have, the only one of her, and in the memories of my father and my grandfather. I don't even know that much about her. I know her name. *Neve*, the Portuguese word for snow.

When I was very young, almost as soon as I could talk, I remember asking, 'Where is she?'

My father would answer, 'Not here.' The only answer I ever received.

'Why?' I would cry. 'Why isn't she here? Why won't you tell me?'

My grandfather, my *Avô*, pronounced *a-voh*, Edgar Coehlo, filled my head with stories about my mother to make me stop crying. Snippets of riddles and sea myths he would tell me, late at night, after the light had been lit. 'Your mother belonged to the sea, to the sea she returned.'

I learned to keep those stories locked away. To drag them to the bottom of my ocean. My grandmother, my *Avó*, I never met either. She died before *Avô* and my mother had left their village and sailed from *Lisboa* to make a new life for themselves here, in Widow's Peak. A hemisphere away.

Most of my younger years I spent alone. In tide pools, catching fish and crabs. Growing up without a mother to teach you the ways of women will do that. I knew I was different from the other girls, not only because of how I looked, with my hairy eyebrows, pale skin, and dark hair. Like all the women these days I keep it short – bobbed like the mannequins in glossy magazines. But, unlike all those other women, I keep it short out of convenience. Often, I forget to wash it and the fish-smell would accumulate with long hair, as thick and wavy as mine is.

But I was different in other ways, too, I couldn't say precisely how. I was strong: I could lift crates, wrestle huge fish into submission. I was fast: I could run and swim. I was not especially pretty or girly, though I wasn't ugly either. My eyes, like my mother's, dark, but too big and too sensitive. I was a mystery to myself and even more so to others. And the older I got, the more apart from everyone I felt.

After my mother's death, nothing changed and yet everything changed. Life continued, again and again, without concerns for our loss. The tide ebbed and flowed, waves rose and fell, boats left the harbour and returned with full nets, an unsinkable ship struck an iceberg in the Atlantic Ocean and sunk, a Great War waged.

So, I stopped asking. My mother became a secret. My father, whose silence has always been heavier than any haul, would not even utter her name in my presence. Whenever I asked him about her, he became much too busy with something to give me a proper answer. The pain, I assumed, was too much for him to bear.

That was all I knew of her until six years ago when I reached the age of thirteen and all that came with it: the bleeding, the swelling chest, and, most of all, the questions I'd never dared to ask before. I was old enough to start thinking about such things.

Horrible thoughts entered my mind. Frightening thoughts. Did I burst from my mother's body and kill her doing it? I did not want to be alone with my thoughts anymore.

She drowned, they told me then. That's all. She drowned in the ocean when I was one year old.

I think my father was relieved when he was called up and he didn't have to suffer any more of my questions.

A flock of gulls take flight as I approach, their red-rimmed eyes peer at me suspiciously. That seagull's screech has rung a note inside my ear since hearing it earlier this morning. I pull at my lobe and shake it, but the sound won't go away.

Shoving a hand in my cardigan pocket, I roll the seashell between my fingers. The soft pad of my finger presses against the tip. A painful thing that isn't quite painful enough. I force the edge of the shell to slice into my nailbed and the seagull's screech dims to a muffled whisper. Background noise. I exhale in relief.

Something thrashes along the shoreline up ahead, and when I turn to check how far I've walked, I immediately wish I wasn't so far from the harbour, from my father with his steady hand, his steady temper, his calm and rational mind.

At first, I see it as an old fishing net, rolled up in a knot at the edge of the waves being tossed about helplessly by the white water. But it isn't a fishing net. It is some sort of creature writhing on the shoreline. I edge closer and realise with horror that it is the woman from the waves.

My mouth slackens and my breaths become shallow.

The mermaid.

I squint and see her clearly, lying there, her tail flapping at the tips of the waves, long dark hair soaked down her back, beautiful fish scales muted in the weak light.

The world falls silent.

'Missy,' she hisses.

Time slows, the waves cease to roll to shore, and the breeze stops rushing past my ears. I stare, my eyes wide open. I cannot close them, and yet I cannot pull them away. Things are not always what they seem on this bewitching coastline, especially with fog. But I cannot be sure what I'm seeing is real.

'Who are you?' I feel foolish when I hear my voice, small and meek, swallowed by the fog.

'It's me.' Her scales shine like coins at the bottom of a murky puddle, smooth and wet and glistening. 'Your mother.'

A cold finger touches the base of my neck. 'You can't be. You drowned.'

She shakes her head; her lips stretch into a smile. 'I didn't drown, Missy. I'm alive. I promise.'

There is a long pause, it seems forever. I am frozen, rooted to the ground, slowly sinking into the sand. My heart skips in my chest, my stomach twists and churns. 'I don't understand. They told me you were dead.' Tears sting my eyes; the wind forces them out. 'You've been alive all this time?'

'I've been with the mermaids. And now they've sent me to bring you home. Don't you want to come and meet your sisters? Wilga… Lilli Pilli… Wattle… Clematis… Mimosa… Haven't you always wanted a sister?'

Wonder engulfs me. 'They're real?'

'Of course they're real. Come with me, I'll show you.' The

mermaid stretches its arms out to me. 'It's your turn, Missy. Come with me. I'll take you to them.'

'Where?'

'To the Five Islands.'

'That's where you've been all this time?'

The mermaid's lips curl into a smile and she nods. I am no longer descending into the wet sand but floating in the air. Joy rushes through me, and I could weep for it. I go to her outstretched arms. They wrap around me and suddenly I'm soaked. We embrace. We cling to each other. I press my fingers so deep they make indents on the mermaid's shoulder blades. I let her stroke my face, wipe the saltwater from my cheeks.

'Come with me,' she sings. 'I've missed you so much.'

'I've missed you, too,' I manage through sobs. 'You have no idea how much.'

I am wet and covered in the grit of sand because I have wrapped myself in the body of this woman who I have missed all my life. I bury my face in her neck and nod and whimper in her arms and tell her I'm ready to go.

'Don't cry, Missy.' She strokes the back of my head. She soothes me. 'I don't want you to suffer anymore. It's time for your pain to end.'

I pull away and look at her face. 'My pain?'

'You want to know the truth, don't you? I know there is a part of you, somewhere deep, that wants to know why I went away. Why I left you and your father. That's why you can't get on with your life, isn't it? And why, when you're feeling lonely, you sometimes wish you could join me. Follow me into the ocean.'

I stare at her desperately.

I nod.

She wipes away my tears with her cold fingers, unnaturally long. 'Ask him.'

I taste the salt as a tear slides into my mouth. 'Ask who?'

The mermaid turns and faces the cliff, far away in the distance. Her arm outstretches and her finger elongates. She's pointing to the lighthouse.

Avô?

Then her arms wrap around me, and I let her sway me back and forth.

'He knows the truth,' she whispers. 'He's hiding it from you.' I let her cradle me, while she rocks me back and forth, for how long, I couldn't say. Her voice becomes fainter and fainter. 'Follow me, Missy,' she chants. 'Follow me into the ocean. It's time. Time for you to join me. Join us.'

My eyes close, I inhale her, feel her cold skin against my own. The screech of a seagull snaps my eyes open. The mermaid's arms are suddenly heavy, like dead weights, like an anchor pulling me down.

And then I see clearly.

And I smell rot.

The rank odour enters my throat. I can taste it. It is mixed with a tinge of sweetness, like a putrid piece of meat with a drop of cheap perfume. The mermaid is not moving anymore, her swaying has stopped. I untangle myself from her pale limbs and stumble backwards. Clambering to my feet, I take two steps back.

I am chilled to the marrow of my bones.

There is a dead woman in front of me.

Her body lies in the early morning light, motionless, drowned in the ocean. Her hair – not long and dark, but short and blonde and crawling with sea lice – covers half her face. It is tangled in seaweed; her cheeks are coated with sand and drops of water have pooled in her collarbone. I watch, horrified, as a seagull lands and picks the sand matted in her brittle yellow hair, her eyes gaping blankly ahead.

I curse, my body shudders uncontrollably, and questions swirl in my mind like the foamy wake of a boat. Who is this woman? Why is it me who found her? And, more alarmingly, why did I imagine her to be a mermaid? What is happening to me? *Is* there something wrong with me? I doubt myself, my own mind. But that's nonsense. I'm not mad. I know what I saw…

And yet…

I look around but there is no use calling for help. Not here. I consider running over the dunes and waving my arms to attract attention, but it is unlikely anyone would be passing by, this far out of town, this close to the steelworks.

For a moment, for just a heartbeat, my chest swells with a memory and instinctively I place a hand over the dead woman's midsection. My fingers trace the sharp escarpment of her hip bone and stroke the cold curve of her belly as the slight swell of it rises under the thin layer of fabric, mottled, wet, and gritty with sand. My hand lingers there for one beat, two.

I wait, and listen, my breath suspended. Try not to think. Try to forget what I saw. But the image of the mermaid's face fills my mind, creeps in like fog. My mother. The appearance of her has filled me with longing. I'm gripped by it. Gripped by the desire to find out. I need answers. I need an explanation.

My father always said I had an overactive imagination.

I'm not mad. I do not believe in mermaids, or ghosts, or any such fanciful stuff. I know the difference between what's real and what isn't. I *know* mermaids aren't real – they're myths. But I also know what I saw. She was there, I saw her, heard her, felt her when she draped her cold limbs around me, her sand-coated fingertips scraped against my skin when she wiped away my tears. My face still feels raw where she touched it, like a burn mark.

I am rational, sensible.

Yes, the myths *Avó* used to tell me filled me with wonder when I was a child, but I also knew to dismiss them as just that – myths. Stories. But now, on this beach, in this fog, I *did* see a mermaid. She had been there, as solid and real as the dead woman lying here now.

Real, living, flesh and scales.

Clearly, certainly.

I do not believe in mermaids.

But what other explanation is there?

The seagull shrieks overhead. I jerk my hand away, wipe the grit from my face and stare for a moment at the ocean, its waves rolling to shore, as before, as ever, as consistent as a beating heart. Sitting on the wet sand in a trance, numb, unaware of everything except the tug of the wind at my hair. Listening, remembering, going over and over it all in my mind. Asking unanswerable questions about myths and reality and their edges, the borderlines between.

Rationalising. Logic, reality, common sense.

The woman I saw from the boat, the woman in the waves, wasn't real. It was just my eyes playing tricks on me. Or the fog. The mermaid I saw on the beach, the mermaid claiming to be my mother, was just my imagination – my subconsciousness – trying to tell me something. That it's time to find out the truth about what happened to my mother, to force it out of them.

Just try to forget. Try to forget what I saw.

But the image of her face still fills my mind, still creeps in, like this fog.

I take three deep breaths and count to twenty. The first thing I must do is notify someone about this body. Think, Missy, snap out of it. The police will know what to do.

I stand and shake the sand from my trousers. The waves hiss and foam along the shore, my eyes glide along the surface of the ocean, tinted black or silver, depending on the density of the fog. My gaze broadens, revealing the faraway cliff and the luminous white of the lighthouse, as though a dark cumulus gathers in the distance, like some kind of sinister creature. Wind howls, waves boom. The sounds transport me, building into an ululation of terror.

What makes this feeling so creepy is something else. The sense that, since killing that octopus, the world – once familiar – will never be the same again.

I must find out the truth. How did my mother die? They know what happened to her. And now I need to know. The truth. No more lies.

2

DETECTIVE Ronan Shaw rolled the nineteen-nineteen Model T Ford to a stop at the edge of the dunes, under a row of Norfolk Pine trees, and finished his cigarette. The car was donated to Widow's Peak Police Department by the folks up in Sydney six months prior. To control the increasing levels of crime, the Inspector-General had decided to introduce a motor vehicle to patrol the streets of Widow's Peak and neighbouring suburbs. The Model T was driven straight off the docks at the port to the station and now shared among the police officers there. It served its purpose and proved reliable.

Shaw stubbed the cigarette butt in the ashtray, almost full — apparently no one had thought to empty it from the day before. He got out of the car, trudged down the soft sand toward the shore and headed left, the steelworks looming behind him. He could just make out where he was walking to, despite the lingering fog.

His boots sunk into the wet sand, leaving a trail of puddled footsteps along the shoreline. His well-made coat kept out the cold wind, but the hem of his trousers was already soaked with seawater, the fine grey fabric more suited to an office than stomping along a beach.

A wave broke and water surged up the sand toward the roped-off area. A stench prickled Shaw's nose as he crossed the high-tide mark, littered with dried bits of seaweed and shells. He approached the two men guarding a stretch of canvas. One stood barely five feet high, tubby around the middle. The other was lean and wore a neat, pinstriped suit.

This was where the stench was coming from. It filled Shaw's nostrils and mouth with the taste of death. A smell he had come to associate with France. After the war, when Shaw had left Europe and sailed to Australia, everything had looked so simple: no barbed wire to crawl under, no Germans to kill, no shells to avoid. The war was over. At least, that's what he'd thought. When he went to bed, night after night, it started all over again. The barbed wire, the Germans, the shells.

When Shaw reached the cordoned-off area, a low humming vibrated from underneath the canvas. He took a small tin of Vicks from his coat pocket and unscrewed the lid then wiped some of the salve under his nostrils. The scent of death was quickly erased by a mixture of camphor, menthol and eucalyptus oil.

'Morning, Constable, Sergeant,' Detective Shaw said as he passed the two cops standing guard. The humming increased in volume the closer Shaw got to the body. As he ducked under the rope, the tubbier one with fair skin and freckles spoke.

'Good to see you, as always, Detective,' he said. Shaw recognised him as Junior Constable Lou Bowers. Bowers still showed signs of youth: a constellation of spots along his jawline, a roundness to his cheeks.

The other was Sergeant Hector Cole. Older, perhaps not in

years but in what he had seen overseas. War did that, it aged you, not just physically. Shaw had worked with Sergeant Cole at similar scenes in the past. He wore his dark brown hair parted deeply on the side with a fashionable wave at the front and boasted a lampshade moustache. Sergeant Cole reached into the leather satchel he carried, extracted a large camera and bent toward the covered body.

'Hope you've got a strong stomach,' he said.

Shaw kneeled next to the corpse, hidden by the large sheet. The humming was incredibly loud under there. Shaw focused his gaze on the stretch of canvas, and, when he did, something moved. Something small, but something definitely moved. He pulled back the sheet and a swarm of flies escaped in a black cloud, some attempting to make their way up his nose.

Shaw drew the cover all the way back and the head emerged, pale and snarling at him like an angler fish: mouth open and the bottom row of teeth bared. He turned his face and coughed into his elbow, took a lungful of fresh sea air then returned his gaze to the victim.

The pop of the flashbulb from Sergeant Cole's camera sparked and he leaned in for a closer look. 'Good God,' he said. 'Her eyes are missing.'

The white downy tip of a seagull's head appeared from under the canvas covering. The bird flapped its wings, opened its red beak and gave a short sharp screech, irritated at having been disturbed. It lowered its beak to the corpse's face and pecked. It had clearly been feasting on the woman's eyes. Now Shaw understood what he had seen moving under the canvas: an opportunistic scavenger eager to make a meal out of his morning discovery.

'Have you ever seen anything so revolting?' Sergeant Cole asked.

Shaw wished this was the worst thing he had seen. He wondered if Sergeant Cole had witnessed the delirium of men who suffered from typhus fever, the constant hacking through pneumatic lungs from the gas, men crippled by gangrene after standing eight days straight in rancid trench water, men who were silent from shock. The black blood, the blown jaws.

Steadying himself, Shaw leaned in for closer inspection. The eyes were indeed missing. Two red holes with flies buzzing all around. They had resettled on the body, busying themselves with finding the juiciest parts to pick at.

Shaw shooed the gull away, but the stubborn thing wasn't leaving without a fight. And the flies. The *flies*. He sighed deeply, looking at the body of the woman in the sand. The corpse, which lay on its back, fully clothed and covered in flies.

Moving around to the midsection, Shaw placed a finger under the armpit, feeling for internal temperature. Cold. He then checked for rigour mortis by lifting the arm and assessing its stiffness. Shaw squinted out to sea, calculating. Time of death could be anywhere between as few as two or three hours ago, to as many as twenty-four hours prior.

'She's been here a few hours, this one.' Shaw glanced across at Constable Bowers, taking in the gloomy look on his face, which had grown paler since peeling back the canvas sheet.

A wave crashed and white water reached the woman's toes, leaving foamy bubbles as it ebbed away. Shaw rolled the corpse over and noted her dress, with its fashionable mid-calf length, dry now but stiff from saltwater. Before the war, women wouldn't dress like this. But that war changed everything, didn't it? Changed the world.

He checked her back and shoulders before laying her down and carefully inspecting the face, opening the lips and checking the mouth. No cuts or bruises, no signs of foul play. Only a mass of tangled blonde hair and the holes in her face where the eyes were supposed to be. Behind him, Constable Bowers vomited into the sand. Sergeant Cole laughed.

Shaw looked up. 'Never seen a dead body before?'

Sergeant Cole slapped Constable Bowers on the back. 'Nah, Lou's a conchie,' he said. 'Ain't that right, Lou?'

Constable Bowers shrugged his hand away. 'Fuck off, Hec.'

There were no wounds on her arms, no bruising. Shaw examined the fingernails which had half-moons of sand wedged under each one. He pressed two fingers to his temple and drew circles to release the tension headache that was building. What was this woman doing in her final moments? Who was she with? And how did she end up here, on this beach, all alone? He decided to start with what he *did* know, as much for his benefit as for the others.

'Well, gentlemen, guessing by skin texture and teeth, I'd say she was in her early twenties. Face is in very bad condition.' Shaw stood and peered at the footprints around the corpse, noting their size and shape. Then he turned to the other two cops. 'Any missing persons reported?'

Constable Bowers sat in the sand, facing away, but Sergeant Cole stepped closer to Shaw, camera still in his hands.

'No, no one reported missing,' he said. His moustache twitched. 'What do you reckon, Boss? Late-night swim?'

'In all her clothes?' Shaw turned to look at the horizon. The waves chopped and churned. He took out a handkerchief from his breast pocket and wiped his hands. 'Besides, who'd want to go swimming in that? More likely she fell from a boat, out at sea.'

'Or she was pushed,' Sergeant Cole suggested.

Shaw eyed him, then finally said, 'Whatever happened, this doesn't seem like an accidental drowning.'

Even though there were no signs of foul play, Shaw wouldn't rule it out. He stared down the beach. Hadn't he visited here as a youngster? He had memories of digging in the sand and building sandcastles. Or had he? No, he was thinking of summers back in Ireland. The wild coasts of County Clare. Even the lingering fog transported him back to his childhood and the craggy, Atlantic coastline.

He noted the lighthouse in the distance, the waves belting against rocks below the cliff. A fall from that height could easily be fatal. But there were no signs to suggest that might have happened. And surely somebody would have seen or heard something like that. He would probably need to speak to the keeper, just to be sure.

Shaw put his hands in his coat pockets, fingered his cigarette case. 'It's surprising nobody came across her earlier. Though I don't suppose many people walk this far along the beach away from town so early in the morning. Who'd you say reported it?'

'It were that fisherman's daughter,' Sergeant Cole said. 'Up before the crack those type are.' He took another photo, a closeup of the face, what was left of it. After another *pop* of the flashbulb, Cole squinted at the corpse, lying in the sand. 'Hang on a minute,' he said. 'Isn't that… That's Sonny Fynn's girl.'

Shaw glanced at Cole. 'Sonny Fynn?'

'Sonny Fynn – the mobster. Scary guy. Never been right since Gallipoli.' Sergeant Cole pointed to the corpse. 'He goes with her. He does, I know it. What's her name? Lara something. She works at The Milk and Honey. A cabaret.'

Shaw raised his eyebrows. 'Cabaret?'

Sergeant Cole shrugged. 'Speakeasy.' He pointed to the woman again. 'It's her, Boss. I'm telling you. She's a cocktail waitress. Wears a little thing with feathers, isn't that right, Lou?'

Constable Bowers looked sharply away, suddenly transfixed at a point on the horizon. 'How would I know?'

'You all right, Lou?' Sergeant Cole called. 'You look a little green in the face, mate.'

Bowers stood shakily, grasping the rope that surrounded the crime scene for support. His fingers almost missed the line because his dark blue police tunic was too long for his arms. Shaw noted Bowers's jittery nature. Was he always like this? It could perhaps be why, in all his time with the force, he had never been promoted from Constable.

'I'm fine.'

The next wave came and soaked the woman's feet. As it retreated, some of the sand under her ankles gave way. Grains poured into grooves toward the ocean.

Constable Bowers took a step closer to Detective Shaw and crouched next to the dead woman, nice and close, and probed her arm as if to prove the sight made no impact on him. He looked up at Shaw, shading the glare from his eyes.

'Looks like she drowned if you ask me,' Bowers said. 'With the currents now, there're a lot of strong rips. You get caught in one, could take you far enough offshore and it'd be tricky to swim back.'

The water lapped at her feet, the sand pulling away in chunks from under her.

Shaw folded his arms, gazing down at Constable Bowers. He noticed the brass buttons on his uniform desperately needed shining. 'At this stage, cause of death is still under investigation, Constable.'

Bowers stood up, next to Shaw. 'What, so you think she was murdered? We've had the odd body in Widow's Peak before. Mostly drowned fishermen. Not murder. Just doesn't happen around here. You'd know that if you were local.'

Shaw retrieved the cigarette case from his coat pocket, opened it and placed a cigarette between his lips, tasting the paper and tobacco. He lit up, cupping the flame from the breeze. He'd been in this game long enough and he had very little time for shortcuts. Experience had taught him to do things right the first-time around. Shaw had no idea whether this woman met her end at the hand of another, or in the sea. And while he knew they could significantly delay the investigation; he would be remiss to make an assumption without a post-mortem examination. He paused to inhale deeply, then spoke.

'Wouldn't want to assume anything at this stage. And neither should you. If you wish to discuss the ravages of the sea, I'm sure the Surf Bathers and Life Saving Club down at North Beach would be only too pleased to share them with you. As policemen, it's our duty to uncover the facts and follow them up. Most important thing is to examine the physical aspects of the case. The knowable facts.'

Constable Bowers shifted his weight uneasily in the sand then glanced at Sergeant Cole, who snickered. 'Of course, Sir,' Bowers muttered under his breath.

Faster and faster the water rose, causing the sand to dissolve from under the woman's legs, lifting them up and down and threatening to wash her out to sea.

Shaw turned to Sergeant Cole. 'Get the undertakers out here to take the body to the mortuary before she goes out with the tide. Have the PM arranged as soon as possible.'

'Right-o.' Sergeant Cole leaned in to take another photograph. The flashbulb popped violently with a sharp streak of light and a puff of smoke.

As Cole took more photographs, Shaw turned to Constable Bowers. 'And I'll need you to arrange an appeal for witnesses. Put word out in the newspaper. Knock on a few doors. Someone must've seen something around here.'

'A young woman alone on a deserted stretch of beach?' Sergeant Cole interjected. 'Wouldn't think anyone would be here by themselves late at night.'

Shaw gave this some thought. He checked around the roped-off area and along the beach for footprints in the sand but found none. Either she was out for a solo late-night stroll, or she washed in with the tide. If that were the case, she could have been killed anywhere, and dumped out at sea. He decided to keep his musings to himself.

'But then this isn't just any young woman,' Sergeant Cole continued. 'This wouldn't have been the first time she's got caught up with the wrong crowd.'

Shaw gazed down at the corpse, finishing his cigarette. He wondered how well Sergeant Cole understood the strength and resilience of working-class women. He didn't see a ring on Cole's finger. The young men these days didn't seem to be in any hurry to be tied down. They'd rather spend their meagre wages at places like The Milk and Honey. On women who wore things with feathers.

Shaw glanced again at the corpse. Going by how she was dressed, he wouldn't want to assume this woman was common or not. But he doubted she had led a sheltered life, given that she ended up alone, dead on a beach. He rubbed his chin, clean shaven. Military habits. 'Who'd you say reported it?' he asked again.

'Young girl found her, earlier this morning,' Sergeant Cole said. 'She came to the station to report it around seven, seven thirty.'

Shaw flicked his cigarette butt away. 'Where is she now?'

Cole and Bowers looked around sheepishly.

'You let her go?'

'She wasn't under arrest.' Sergeant Cole pointed down the beach. 'After she showed us the body, she headed off in that direction.'

'Did you at least get her to make a statement?'

Another pause. The silence stretched on, interrupted only by the crash of waves. Shaw rubbed his forehead and sighed.

'You said she was a fisherman's daughter?' he said. 'Go down to the harbour, find her, and bring her down to the station. I need to ask her a few questions.'

3

Segunda-feira

THE dead woman's stench is all over me. My stomach churns from it as I hurry along the sandy path toward home. And, even though I know it's not real, I can't stop thinking about what else I saw on the beach. The woman with dark hair and a fish's tail. The mermaid. The *thing* that claimed to be my mother.

A question has bloomed inside me, like algae in the sea. How did my mother really die? The question reverberates within my body, living and breathing and moving inside me. It remains, endlessly rotating around, like driftwood in the ocean. Then a response whispers in the far corner of my mind, a response that's really another question. *Why don't I ask him?*

Some of the morning's fog lingers in the cold air but most of it has burned away, and the sky is clear with bright sunshine.

The path through the dunes is well-worn; it weaves through the clumps of slicing grass, toward the fishermen's huts that line that shore along Widow's Basin. My father and I live in the one furthest away because the rent is cheapest. It's draughty with two bedrooms and a common area where we sit and make small talk. The plaster is unpainted, the floors unvarnished, but there are two fireplaces that keep us warm, which is necessary because that's the only source of warmth to be found in our house. We rarely laugh there.

At least the lighthouse is white and bright inside. The silences don't seem to weigh so heavy.

The door's salt-rusted hinges groan as I heave it open, annoyed at my insistence, and I am hit with the familiar waft of smoked fish. I pass the fireplace, in the chimney hang strings of curing rock blackfish, like a washing line, and glance at the photograph on the mantle. The only photograph we have of her. The only one that exists.

I always picture my mother, Neve, as this woman in the photograph. Barely a woman, a girl, seventeen. Her dark hair almost covering her face from a gust of wind, caught forever in this image. That gust has probably travelled across the whole world a hundred times by now. I wonder if it has ever blown through my own hair. This is how she has stayed in my mind, over the years, frozen in a moment of happiness. In a gentle, vulnerable pose. I cannot imagine her aged.

Never have I seen what she looked like sad, or gloomy. Just that beautiful, sunny face, smiling at me when I come in from the harbour. I preserve her in my mind as this woman I see in the photograph every day. Before she died. Before she had me. Before she had even married my father. I wish I could tell her all the ways I need her. Important ways. Invisible ways.

There inevitably comes a time when a girl wants to know – *needs* to know – about her mother. A mother's life can be a good indication of a daughter's… whether she makes the same choices, whether she is defined by the same fate.

In the alley behind our hut where we wash our clothes and our bodies, I fill the tin bath by hand. It takes many trips to the second fireplace and waiting for the kettle to boil, but I am covered in sand, and I reek of the sea. It's in my clothes, the fish-stink and rot permeate my skin.

The back gate opens onto a small yard. A square patch of yellow grass sulks all the way to the lane, where our chicken coop houses our rooster and three hens, whose eggs make up half of our daily food. The rest comes from what we catch every morning and fail to sell.

I reach into my pocket, retrieve the shell, and set it on the lip of the bath, then strip off and throw my sand-heavy clothes into a wet pile in the corner. I don't have to worry about anybody seeing me. We fishing families keep to ourselves. Sometimes too much. Sometimes I can feel my loneliness. It's a thing I can locate with my fingers, and if I push on it too hard, it hurts. I do not know what to do with it. Sometimes I feel like I'm drowning in a world full of air.

Before I step into the steaming water, I stare into the small looking glass, pocked with age, that sits on the shelf next to my father's shaving things, untouched since his return from the war. I don't have Gust's light hair and green eyes. Most of me is hers. But my face, with its spattering of freckles against pale skin, is nothing like that smiling, carefree woman in the photograph. Neve's skin never had any freckles. It was pure, perfect.

My lips make me look like I'm always pouting, or sad. I attempt to smile into the glass, but it just feels wrong. My long neck makes me self-conscious because I am so often as tall as any man I stand next to, sometimes taller, and my hair, which falls in waves around my ears no matter how long I ignore it, never seems to grow past my jawline.

At present, it is dusted with sand and God-knows-what else. I tremble at the thought of touching that dead woman on the beach. What sickness might she have passed to me? The great epidemic may be over, but people still die of the Spanish Influenza.

Shaking the fish scales from my hair, I step into the large tin pot we call a bath and let the steamy water overcome me. I sink into it, the heat prickling all over my body, scrubbing myself clean to get the stink away until my skin is red and scraped. No more fish scales, no more fish-stink.

Once again, I see the dead woman's pale face, her sand-matted hair, the sea-lice crawling on her skin. I can feel them biting me. Phantom bites stinging my legs and arms. I scratch at them, rub them with carbolic soap.

My body slowly pickles in the warm water. I notice the shell, resting on the rim of the bath. Absentmindedly, I pick it up, rinse it with bath water and examine it. Turn it around in my hands, feel its smoothness, its curves, its edges. My finger traces its spiral.

My grip tightens around the shell as I submerge my head below the surface. In the silence I think about the shell's perfect spiral and imagine what it could be made from. A word swims to me under the water. From a book I read. Molluscs. Molluscs produce calcium carbonate from the mantle, laying down layers over their lifetime. Together, these layers form the seashell, its calcified layers building upon each other, over and over itself. A lifetime of layers to form its shape. Like hair, growing from roots.

I hold my breath for as long as I can and, when my lungs burn, I come up for a mouthful of air. I reach up to pull the wet hair off my face and when I do, I grab hold of something slimy like algae. Despite the hot water a cold shudder sweeps through me. My body tenses as I scratch at the spot on my scalp. Tiny flecks of shell come away onto my fingertips. It's not unusual to find sand or shell or scales in my hair, but this feels foreign, slippery, like a piece of seaweed. Pressure builds in my chest and my stomach hardens. I give it a firm tug. My skin crawls when I realise the seaweed is caught in my hair. I rip at it, but it is connected to my head, and it feels like I'm pulling out a chunk of hair but it's slimy and it stinks and my hair is clotted with seaweed and I want it away from me.

Finally, it comes loose, and a warm sensation trickles down the back of my neck along my spine. My hands shake as I flick the green slime on the ground and touch where the seaweed was, recoiling when I feel an open wound. My fingers are red, covered in blood. I touch the hole again. It doesn't hurt, but there's a thickness in my throat, nausea in my stomach. First the mermaid, and now this? What is happening to me? I dunk my head under to rinse the cut, then stand quickly and wrap a towel around my body. The towel is thin and full of holes, but it feels good to be clean.

Bending over to dry my toes, my calves, my thighs, I rub the towel between my legs, and that's when I notice the smell. The same cloying smell from the beach. From the dead woman.

Rot.

It's coming from me.

Disgusted, I throw the towel on the laundry pile, tug on a pair of trousers and pull a clean shirt over my head.

My father is in the room he calls the kitchen but that is more than it deserves. Two rickety chairs, a table that slumps in the centre, and a patch of damp by the window. He is seated at the table, up to his elbows in a tangle of nets.

I sit by the curtainless window where various shells and stones line the ledge. I add the spiral shell to the far end and put my feet up on the table. Reaching for the sharpening stone, I take out my gutting knife and rub it against the edge. We work together in silence for a while. A mass of crusted flesh, probably from the octopus, has dried between the teeth on the serrated edge of the blade. Using my fingernail I scrape at it, and it peels off in flakes.

This is why knives must be cleaned after each use. A fisherman's knife is a reflection of their state of mind. This particular blade has an almost razor-sharp edge, it becomes thinner and narrower all the way from the handle to the tip. This is what gives the knife the strength to cut through the heaviest bone structure, yet the flexibility to follow the skeletal patterns of fish. This type of knife cuts cleanly and evenly and can be resharpened quickly and easily. I bring the blade closer to inspect my work, but the light is so weak it's impossible to judge.

'It's dark in here. Should I light a candle?'

'Still foggy out?' my father asks.

I consider telling him what I saw on the beach. Then think better of it. 'Cleared up by now.'

'Enough for your grandfather to insist on that blasted horn,' he says.

My fists clench. '*Avô* says the horn keeps him company when I'm not there.'

A snorting sound escapes from his throat. 'That's what happens after being confined to a life of solitude. Start to crave the company of a foghorn.'

Anger pricks my fingertips, spreads up my forearms. I hate it when he talks about *Avô* this way. It takes a special temperament to be a keeper. They need to be all right with their own company. It doesn't mean they're mad. I try to send a barb over.

'A life of solitude? Like sitting alone in a dark room untangling fish nets?' The barb doesn't stick. My father continues his detangling. I send another. 'No wonder my mother disappeared.'

His fingers pause for a moment, then they find a new knot. He still doesn't bite. I'm fed up with his silences, so I decide to ask him outright.

'Tell me,' I say. 'Tell me how she died.'

'You know how. She drowned.'

'But she could swim, couldn't she?'

'People who can swim can still drown. Why these questions after so long?'

I shrug my shoulder. 'No reason. Just curious.'

My father eyes me suspiciously and I need to get out of here.

'I know it's hard—'

Before he can finish, I am out the door. I climb the hill along the hostile path, dodging the tufts of grass, still slick with dew. The snarling wind picks up the higher I climb, and I can hear the waves below.

At the top, I stand high above the sea, the lighthouse at my back, the gulls screeching overhead, and look over the edge. I breathe in the view, the unfathomable, beautiful view. The expanse of ocean, with all its deep, dark secrets, and the waves rolling below. The way it is never the same, it beguiles me with its many changing moods. It lures me with its salty beauty and fathomless depths. Any person who reaches those depths would be held down by the sheer weight of it until the water crushed them. It promises weightlessness, oblivion.

A thought creeps into my head.

If I wanted to, I could just jump.

Swim down to the bottom of the ocean and feel the entire weight of it crush me. I take one step closer to the void and feel the wind gust against my face. It would be so easy to step over the edge. Weightlessness. Oblivion. I turn so I can't see the sea anymore. Such melancholy thoughts will be the end of me.

Behind me, a match strikes.

'Been a long morning,' *Avô* says as he puffs on his clay pipe, his smoky-grey hair flapping in the breeze, nearly fossilised it is so dry. 'Drop of coffee'd do us good.' The words coil out the side of his mouth with the smoke.

We walk side by side to the small, sun-bleached cottage located next to the tower, the keeper's residence, *Avô's* home. It's a low building made from local stone and a corrugated-iron roof.

Avô's weatherworn face casts to the ground, the chapters of his life written there for anyone to read: years of sleepless nights, toiling on the light, days filled with hard labour in rough winds, storms, and beating sun. Memories of lost loves, loneliness. Except that nobody does read those chapters. Nobody comes here at all. With his musty clothes and short temper, he does his best to repulse visitors. He has become a recluse. I don't feel sorry for him because he wouldn't want me to.

Inside, the cottage has an institutional feel, with boot-scuff-stained floors, which is fitting I suppose, because apart from attending classes at the local school, this was where I did most of my learning. Right at this table. School was a waste of time anyway. I never learnt anything useful there. There's nothing a teacher taught me that I couldn't have learned from a book, or from the world itself.

Besides, people didn't like me much in school.

I was the odd girl who attempted to start conversations with interesting facts about sea animals. *Did you know that seahorses are the only animals where the male, not the female, gives birth to and cares for their babies?*

I don't think anyone was very interested in the fact that sea slugs can change from one gender to another and back again, depending on which is best for mating, either. I would come home in tears most days because the girls kept calling me Sea Slug.

One girl started a rumour about me. It's been years now and I still don't know what it was, but her mother talked to all the other girls' parents and told them I was not a child fit to be associated with, even if their mothers bought fish from my father. I try not to think about it.

The windows in the keeper's cottage are so small that the room is dark. The world, far away. The carpet in the living room is worn down to the threads. I don't need to walk down the corridor to know the bedrooms smell of tobacco and mildew. They've always smelled like that. It's the reason I made up the room in the tower, on the highest landing, just under the lantern room.

One creaky old bed and a few blankets, but it's right by the window shaped like a porthole. I like to watch the waves far below. Even when I was a child, I remember lying awake, my eyes glazing over while the waves hypnotised me as they rolled in and crashed on the rocks. They would rush forward without fear. I would imagine their coldness, hear their rhythmic thunder, taste their brine in the back of my throat.

The fire crackles as we sit at the small table, *Avó* and I, and sip our coffee by firelight. The cutlery tinkling on our saucers is the only sound in the quiet, until a loud groan from above cuts through the stillness and it's all I can do not to shield my ears.

Avô's eyes, blood-flecked and as blue as veins, shoot up past the ceiling, stained yellow from the coal he uses on the fire.

'The lamp,' he says. 'She needs oil.'

'Gust thought you were blaring the foghorn all morning,' I say. 'You want me to help you oil it?'

He exhales. 'Got no coal. My delivery driver didn't show up this morning. Look,' he gestures toward the fireplace, 'I'm burning firewood.' A log snaps in half and collapses in a flurry of embers. 'You hungry?'

For the second time this morning I realise my stomach is empty, apart from the tea on the boat, and the few sips of his coffee. 'What have you got?'

With knotty, gnarled hands he places his coffee mug on the table, stands and enters the kitchen. He rummages about the pantry, opening cupboards and drawers.

'Why not?' I call to him.

He stops his rummaging and cocks his head at me. '*Why not* what?'

'The delivery driver,' I remind him. 'Why did they not show up this morning?'

Finally, he finds what he is searching for. A beaten-up saucepan. He fills it with water from the pump and sets it on the stove.

'Beats me. Every morning for as long as I've been a wickie I've been getting a delivery from the Blue Mile Coke Company. For some reason, the driver didn't show up this morning.' He pats down his pockets and pulls out a box of matches, striking one up. He holds it to the stove. I hear the *woosh* of the flame as it catches. He eyes me. 'You can drive, can't you?' He possesses a hard stare, my grandfather.

'Yes, I know how to drive,' I say.

He tumbles a few potatoes into the pot of water. 'And you can lift a sack of coal.'

'I'm sure I'd be able to do that, yes.'

He stands by the pot as the water slowly begins to steam and, after a few minutes, I hear the potatoes simmering. My eyes grow heavy so I lower my head onto my arm, resting on the tabletop, drawing in long, slow breaths, feeling my stomach eat itself. When *Avô* returns to the table, he's carrying a plate of boiled potatoes and a fork.

'Job's not that hard. You could nip over to the tram line after you dock at the harbour. Truck'd be waiting for you. I can arrange for it.'

I take the fork and tuck in, ravenous. 'So, you're asking me to drive a delivery truck to the Blue Mile, pick up a sack of coal and bring it to you? How often?'

'I need a new one every morning.'

'Before I agree, I need to ask you something,' I say.

He eyes me, wary. 'About what?'

I wonder how to proceed. Cautiously, I conclude. 'About the sea.'

He frowns. 'The sea?'

'About what's in it. *Who* is in it.' Now he truly is uncertain of me, but I press on. 'You've always said that my mother was called by the sea. Gust says she drowned. Either way, the ocean is where she died.'

'*Sim.* And things have a way of returning from the bottom of the sea, don't they? Even the heaviest items sometimes float back to the surface.'

Avô always believed she would come back. That's why he never left. Why he climbs those stairs to the lantern room, night after night, refills the bath with mercury, polishes the brass until he sees his face reflected in it. He's waiting for her to return.

'When I was younger, you told me there were mermaids living close to the islands.'

He nods. 'Sirens do live in those waters.'

'But how can that be true? There are no such things. Are there?'

'They're sea legends. Myths. Just because you've never seen one, doesn't mean there are no such things. Myths have to come from somewhere.'

'Are they dangerous?'

'*Sim*, well, *sereias*. It's what they do, isn't it?'

'What do you mean?'

'Beckon, beguile, bewitch. *Lure* sailors to their watery deaths. Mermaids, they grab you using their hair.'

A shiver jolts down my spine. I remember the woman's hair, frayed liked rope, on the surface of the ocean, shrouded in mist. I think of the slimy green seaweed that I pulled from my own scalp, the wound that opened up. I swallow a lump of potato, dry and thick. 'Their hair?'

He nods. 'Watch out for their hair, or they will take you under the water,' he says. 'Especially out on the boat. Once, when I was much younger and I was on the sea, our engine got tangled. The captain told us not to look. But I saw something that I can't explain. It was very quick. There was a lot of movement. And it wasn't fish.'

'What was it?'

'Hair. Long, dark hair.'

'Today, out on the boat, I thought I saw something,' I say. 'In the water. A woman.'

'What woman?'

'A pale woman. With dark hair and a fish tail. She looked like… my mother.' My grandfather scoffs. 'You don't believe me?'

'There are some things I've learned in this life, girl. If you look at something long enough, sometimes the mind conjures up images. Same thing happens with the ocean. When you're on the sea every day, it takes whatever's inside you, and shows it back to you.'

'It was *her*,' I say. 'She spoke to me. She told me she was alive and living in the sea. Gust says she drowned. But I know she could swim. What if the myths about mermaids really are true?'

Avô runs his gnarled fingers across his chin, rough with white coarse stubble. 'Whether she drowned or not, your mother's life ended in its depths, one way or another.' His eyes travel over me with such caution that I don't know what to do; I'm frozen. He clears his throat. 'Could be that father of yours had a hand in it. Just like the West Wind blew his daughters out to the Five Islands. Ran out of patience with her. Got fed up. Took a big breath and blew her out to sea.'

My heart's pounding in my ears is deafening. Gust would never do that, I tell myself. Would he? Either way, I know better than to talk to my grandfather about my father. I change tack. 'Could she have…' I swallow a lump of potato. It sinks slowly down my throat. '…turned into a mermaid?'

He looks at me, his face full of scorn. 'The sea took your mother. It's not for me to say whether she turned into something or not. The sea is full of mystery. Now, are you going to drive or not? Because my light needs coal.'

I take the last few sips of my coffee, cold and gritty now, but still bitter and strong. 'Don't you have anyone else who can do it?'

Avô shakes his head. 'No one I trust,' he says. 'Do this, and I will tell you about Neve. I will tell you about your mother.'

My heart skips. 'You'll tell me how she really died? You promise to tell me the truth?'

Avô peers at me through those watery, distrustful eyes. 'Why is it you want to know this so suddenly?'

'After this morning, I have… questions. It's like a great gap has opened up. Questions that, if I don't find answers to… if I don't find out the truth about her, I'll go mad.'

He grunts and takes my empty coffee cup to the sink. I know by his silence we have a deal. How does a woman disappear into the ocean? Never to be seen or heard from again? I need to find out. I'm going to find out what happened to her. Just wait and see, old man. Just wait and see.

I race back down the hill, over the familiar ruts and grooves, avoiding the clumps of grass. The dew lingers so my boots threaten to slip but I know this path at midnight.

I pass the fish market. Only a scattering of vendors remains, most are packing up for the day. The lack of breeze down here does nothing to dissipate the smell of rank seawater. Usually I am immune to the smell but after this morning and all the strange happenings – first the octopus, then the mermaid and the dead woman on the shore, the seagull's screech that has been reverberating inside my ear, the seaweed in my hair and that hole, that wound, opening up on my scalp, the rotting smell – it's all too much; it sets my nose and stomach on edge.

Turning the corner from the harbour toward the line of fishermen's huts I stop dead. Parked outside our house, stark against the watery light, is a large black car with four white wheels, its headlamps shining weakly onto the sandy road. I walk slowly nearer, my eye drawn to its black paint, sun-bleached with age.

The car is as subtle as a foghorn, and just as welcome.

4

Monday

DETECTIVE Ronan Shaw shivered as he sat at his desk, filling in a form with the few details he could recall about the dead body that had washed up on the beach.

The police station at Widow's Peak, like many of the buildings in town, had been built out of the local sandstone, which meant it blistered like a bonfire during the summer months and froze like the Arctic in winter. Through the open window, the church bell tolled eleven times.

The door to his office creaked open and a slender young woman carrying the scent of saltwater emerged. Shaw flipped the file closed and stood to welcome her into his cramped office. She was tall with a mess of dark, chin-skimming hair, and, it might have been the way she moved in those trousers, but she approached his desk with a self-assuredness that took him slightly aback.

'Good morning, Mrs…?'

The young woman looked at him with big doe eyes, rimmed by eyelashes like black feathers. 'Green,' she replied.

'Please, have a seat.' Shaw motioned to the chair in front of his desk. 'Tea?'

She sat opposite and crossed one leg over the other. 'Thank you.'

Shaw called to his secretary, Midge, who appeared in the doorway. 'Shall I pop the kettle on?' she asked.

'Yes, thank you.' Shaw shot an awkward smile across the table. The young woman failed to notice as she was glancing around the small room which, Shaw suddenly felt, could do with a tidy-up. He took the opportunity to scrutinise her, to work out what sort of person she was likely to be. Was she trustworthy? Or a liar? Someone who attempted to conceal the truth? After years in the job, he considered himself adept at reading people's faces, scrutinising their expressions for the truth. A person's face could betray them. Even the best liars cracked briefly, allowing displays of true emotion to leak out.

Shaw studied the young woman's gaze and posture. She showed no signs of stress; her eyes did not avoid his, her feet were not tapping, and her hands were not fidgety.

Midge reappeared carrying a tray with a teapot, two cups on saucers, and a jug of milk. Setting the tray down with a clatter in front of Detective Shaw, she poured tea from the teapot with shaking, arthritic hands, and sat at a small desk behind a typewriter, ready to type the statement. Midge had been Shaw's secretary since he arrived in Widow's Peak. Every year he expected her to hand in her notice of retirement, and every year she surprised him by clinging on to her position.

'Milk and sugar?' Shaw asked.

'Milk, no sugar,' the young woman replied.

Shaw added a splash of milk and handed her one of the teacups. As she reached across and took it from him, the subtle scent of sea spray and salty fish glided across the desk. She must have come straight from the harbour, Shaw thought. Although she had the face of a deer, there seemed to be nothing dainty about her. Her limbs were long and sinewy, and her hands seemed made for work.

Shaw leaned back in his chair, mirroring the young woman's body language, and took a sip of milky tea, considering his first move: ask questions to build trust. 'Will your husband be joining us?'

The young woman's expression betrayed nothing. 'I don't have a husband. I live with my father.'

The clunky sound of the typewriter started up and the young woman jumped slightly in her seat. Midge's bony fingers continued to thump the letters, oblivious.

Shaw placed the teacup aside and knitted his hands together in front of him, leaning forward reassuringly. He could see that she was slightly jumpy – justified, he gathered, given that she found a dead woman on a beach earlier that morning. He knew, in order to put her at ease, he needed to comfort her, and he knew he could do this easily by addressing her using her name. What was it again? He glanced at her. Green – like the ocean. 'Now, Miss Green…'

'It's Missy,' she corrected.

'I'm sorry?'

'Call me Missy. That's my name.'

Shaw raised his eyebrows. 'Very well.' The mistake most cops made when eliciting information from people was focusing on which questions to ask. Shaw knew questions were important, but what he didn't say was just as important as what he did. He knew he had to get the young woman to open up, to tell her own version of events.

'Missy, I've been led to believe you were the one who discovered the body of the woman on the beach earlier this morning.'

Missy nodded; silence descending the room. Shaw did not attempt to fill it. He removed a cigarette from his silver case and balanced it between his lips, struck a match, and lit up. He inhaled, then spoke, waving the match in the air to put out the flame.

'Can you tell me, in your own words, how you came across the body?' he finally asked.

Missy looked up at the ceiling, recollecting her thoughts. And, in a flash, there it was: the crack, the betrayal. A frown appeared on her face, and she shut her eyes for a moment. With a shaking hand she placed her cup of tea on Shaw's desk, the teacup rattling in its saucer. 'I'm sorry, I…'

'It's all right.' Shaw rested his cigarette in an ashtray, filled with half-smoked cigarettes poking out at all angles, and took out his notepad and fountain pen. 'When you were on the beach, did you see anyone else there going to or coming away from the place you stumbled upon the body?'

Missy shook her head. 'No, there was no one on the beach that close to the steelworks.'

Shaw's pen scratched across the notepad. 'What were you doing that far up the beach?'

'I was walking,' she said. 'I needed to walk, I…' Missy looked into her lap.

Shaw's pen continued scribbling. 'Did you move or touch the body in any way?'

Missy hesitated. She slipped a lock of hair behind her ear. 'Yes, I did. I thought…'

Shaw looked up from his notes. 'You thought…?'

'I don't remember what happened.' Shaw continued to look at her. Missy glanced at Midge typing up her words, then let out a breath and shook her head. 'It sounds stupid.'

Shaw leaned back in his chair and rolled the pen between his fingertips. 'No stupid answers here, Miss Green. We're just trying to gather any information we can at the moment. And since there were no witnesses…'

Missy glanced at Midge, then back at Shaw. 'All right,' she said, 'but I'd rather tell you alone.'

Shaw's secretary looked up from her typewriter, her beady eyes enlarged by the spectacles sitting on the round tip of her nose. He nodded and she stood and slipped out the door.

Detective Shaw gazed at the young woman sitting opposite him. Despite her shabby, masculine clothing, Miss Green was quite striking. It was uncommon to see women with such dark hair and eyes, almost unusual, in this part of the world. And the pout of her lips was quite distracting. The hairline at the back of Shaw's neck prickled with heat. Someone must have lit a fire in the other room. Or perhaps the tea was hotter than he had realised.

He cleared his throat. 'All right, Miss Green,' he said, leaning forward. Placing his pen down and clasping his hands in front of him, he looked directly into her eyes. 'What is it you'd rather tell me alone?'

Missy chewed her lip. She looked up at Shaw. A warm feeling washed over him. 'Do you promise you won't laugh?'

Shaw hesitated. He hadn't been expecting that. 'All right,' he said. 'I promise I won't laugh.'

'The dead woman… I… I thought she was a mermaid.'

A pause.

The cigarette smouldered in the ashtray.

Missy shook her head and looked at the window. 'I told you it sounded stupid.'

Shaw nodded, reached for the cigarette, tapped off the excess ash and took a drag, eyeing Missy. She did not avert her gaze, showed no signs of deceit, no perspiration coated her forehead. He could not tell if she was lying, or whether she actually believed what she was telling him. He wanted to be reassuring, to show agreeability. If she was holding back, he needed to unlock her thoughts.

'Reminds me of the story of Niamh and Oisin,' he said. 'In Irish mythology, Niamh was so sad about losing Oisin, she gave herself to the sea.'

Missy raised her eyebrows and widened her eyes. 'She drowned herself?'

Shaw shook his head. 'No. She's immortal.' He cocked his head at her. 'But why would you think a dead woman was a mermaid?'

'My father and I fish the shores around the Five Islands. This morning, on the *Senhora ao Vento*, I saw a woman in the waves.'

Shaw nodded. He still had no idea whether this woman believed what she was telling him, but head nodding was the universal sign of agreement, and it would keep her talking. 'The *Senhora ao Vento*?'

'That's the name of our boat,' she said. 'A fishing trawler.'

Shaw nodded again. 'I see. And did anyone else see this… mermaid?'

'My father was there but he… he didn't see the… the…'

'The mermaid?' Shaw repeated.

'She was in the waves. But it wasn't. It can't have been. It was a fish. Or maybe a shark. My father and I net all manner of creatures from those waters.'

Shaw laughed but soon stopped when he noticed Missy was serious in her claim. Again, he leant back in his chair, picked up his cigarette, and took another deep drag. He realised with annoyance that his own leg was tapping under the desk. Was this woman actually telling the truth? He certainly was not in the mood for this. 'You thought you saw a mermaid swimming amongst the waves, but it ended up being a shark? Surely you don't believe that, Miss Green?'

Missy stiffened. 'You make it sound like I'm mad,' she said. 'I'm not crazy.'

'I speak to a lot of people in this line of work, Miss Green. Very few of them are actually mad.' He eyed her. 'Most of them are liars.'

'I'm not lying either. Ask any sea-faring person in this town. There are myths… legends about mermaids swimming in those waters. Have been for centuries. My grandfather…'

'Your grandfather?'

'He's an old sea man. He tells me stories.'

'Stories about merfolk?'

'That's right. Myths. Legends about the sea. He mans the lighthouse. I lived with him there while my father was away… at the war.'

Shaw stubbed his cigarette in the ash tray. He continued to stub it even after he knew the tip had been extinguished. He glanced up from the mess of ash and cigarette butts. 'Where did he fight?'

'France. He doesn't talk about it much.'

'Nor do most of us,' Shaw said. He reached for his cigarette case and held it open for Missy. She took one in her long fingers and placed it in her mouth. Shaw did the same, then lit a match and held it across the desk. Missy leant forward, cupped the flame, and inhaled the tobacco. Shaw lit his own and drew in deeply, his eyes settling on a filing cabinet in the corner of the room. Lost in a memory.

His eyes found Missy again. She sat cross-legged, leaning back casually in the chair. He glanced at his notepad and noticed that pen ink had smudged in blue blotches across the page from his sweaty hand.

Shaw shut the notebook and tossed it in the desk drawer beside him. He knew what he should do next. He'd done it dozens of times. Hundreds. Missy had opened up; she'd revealed something vulnerable. And now it was his turn. He knew the more he shared, the more open and trusting the other person would become. This was the perfect moment, to build trust, to elicit the actual truth from her. And yet, he could not bring himself to open the door to those locked-away memories.

Finally, Shaw let out the smoke in a long stream of liquid white. 'It's best not to dwell on it. Plenty of men've turned useless that way.'

Shaw noticed Missy glance at his wedding band.

She brought the cigarette to her lips and blew smoke at the ceiling. 'Does your wife ask you about it?'

Shaw waved the question away. 'It's nineteen twenty-one. Been three years since most men returned from the war. People know by now not to mention it.'

Missy shrugged. 'I think you ought to talk about it.'

'I think we'd rather forget.' Courage in silence and all that,

Shaw thought darkly.

'So, who was she?' Missy asked. For a moment, Shaw thought she was still talking about his wife. 'The woman, on the beach?'

Shaw flicked ash into the tray. 'Conditions were treacherous at sea last night. High tides. Although I don't suppose I need to tell you that, what with you being a fisherman's daughter. Nevertheless, we're having a little problem with identification. And thanks to a certain seagull, her face is quite damaged. Nobody's registered a missing female in the last twenty-four hours. But one of my men seemed to recognise her as a waitress from The Milk and Honey.' He added, 'A local cabaret.'

'Cabaret?' Missy said. 'Sounds like a speakeasy.'

Shaw took a deep breath, raised his eyebrows, and nodded. 'Seems like everyone in town knows about it except me.'

'You need to have been born in Widow's Peak to know all of its deep dark secrets, Detective,' Missy said, and Shaw swore he saw her lips flicker into a smile. Heat throbbed in his ears and his eyes glanced over the paperwork on his desk, suddenly at a loss for words.

He nodded, placed the cigarette in his mouth, and shuffled the papers into a neat pile, regaining his composure, his focus. 'So everyone feels compelled to remind me this morning, Miss Green,' he said, with the cigarette dangling from his lip. 'Still, I should probably follow up on that lead.'

Missy reached over Shaw's desk to stub her cigarette out in his ashtray, embarrassingly full. As she leaned, the billowy cotton shirt, too big for her slender frame, gaped slightly open at the front and Shaw was obliged to avert his eyes, to fix them to the neat pile of papers.

'I don't think the Madame will let you in,' Missy said as she sat back in the chair.

Shaw nodded; composure restored. 'No, she knows I'll shut her down.' He eyed Missy for a moment. Had he gleaned enough information from her? The more this young woman spoke, the more mysterious she seemed. Perhaps he should keep her close, get to know her. An idea floated to him. 'Unless we go together?'

Miss Green's lips curled into a slight smile. 'Why would we go together?'

Or was it more than that? Did Shaw feel an innate need – *desire* – to protect this alluring, vulnerable, perplexing, young woman? He tossed his half-smoked cigarette in the cold, milky tea.

5

THE tangy stink of piss and liquor invades my nostrils as I walk with Detective Shaw along the cobblestones of a brick alleyway. The laneway is empty, apart from the garbage awaiting collection. Rotten mounds crowd our path: mouldered meat, soiled sanitary napkins, piles of empty wooden crates, an abandoned bicycle with its front wheel missing, bottles of sour milk residue. I slip on a haggard leaf of lettuce, so thin it's almost translucent. Two large wine barrels guard an unremarkable doorway, like sentries on duty. On the opposite brick wall, large red painted letters tell us we are standing in a tow away zone.

An oily rat skitters along the gutter matted with decomposing leaves. I jump at each noise; my nerves are on edge and I have that familiar sting of needing the outhouse. Taking a step closer to the doorway, I notice something stuck to my foot. It's a pamphlet of some kind; the ground is littered with them. I lift my boot, peel the paper from the bottom, minding not to get any of the garbage water on my hands, and read the title: *Medley of Meat Recipes*.

Detective Shaw futilely rattles the padlock on the door then glances back down the alleyway, right then left. I'm half a head taller than him and I can tell by his salt-and-pepper hair that he is older, perhaps in his late thirties. His cold blue eyes, slightly sunken, seem to miss nothing.

'Wait here.'

His Irish accent lingers in the putrid air as he strides off toward the police car that brought us here, his coat flapping behind him in the chilly breeze. A hiss of steam bursts from a grate. It ascends like a ghost, skirting the face of the crumbling brick wall, to the sky. In the rectangular space above, between the two buildings that make up the alleyway, exposed wires dangle perilously low. Why did I agree to this?

When Shaw returns, he is holding a crowbar. I take a step closer to him to watch how he does it. His nostrils flare slightly, and suddenly I am conscious of the fact he may be able to smell the wound on my head. The festering hole that opened up when I ripped out a clump of my own hair trying to rid that seaweed. The smell of rot and dead fish has stayed with me ever since. These strange occurrences have shifted something within me. I can't be sure that what is happening to me is real. I can't be sure that anything is real, but to be safe, to be sure it is the putrid garbage he is smelling and not me, I take two steps away.

Detective Shaw positions his body close to the lock, parting his legs slightly. Sliding the crowbar through the padlock, he wedges it against the door then applies a small amount of pressure. The lock buckles. He drives it down with considerable force, pushing away. After a moment, the padlock snaps and jangles to the cobbles. Resting the crowbar against the wall, Shaw nudges the door. It swings open. He holds it open for me, but I hesitate. Dank air curls out of the darkness and smells stale and putrid and of dread. I wish I had not agreed to this. I wish I was holding that crowbar.

With trembling hands, I step inside, and Shaw follows. The door slams shut behind us. It takes my eyes a moment to adjust to the dim light. I take a few steps forward and put my arm out in front of me in case I bump into something. Shapes begin to form in the darkness. I blink. Blink again. Pale shapes, with limbs and torsos. Rows of them. Dozens of them. My stomach muscles clench and the hairs on the back of my neck stand on end.

Naked bodies hang upside down by their legs, the joints at their hips straining unnaturally. My heart quickens and I feel lightheaded. They have been cut open, exposing their rib cages like the keys of a piano. Patches of dried blood coat the stone floor, brown like rust, and the metallic iron smell in this warehouse is worse than the alleyway. My stomach clenches and I clasp my hand over my mouth to stop myself from bringing up my breakfast.

Pig carcasses.

Detective Shaw looks at me. 'What's wrong?' he says. 'Haven't you ever had pork roast before?'

I frown at him. 'No.'

He smiles. 'Really?' With a smile like his, he makes this putrid place seem bearable. 'I'll have to make it for you some time. Few roasted potatoes. It's a real treat.'

I'm too nervous around so many dead animals to think of anything witty to say so I remain silent and keep searching for what it is we are looking for.

One of them swings on its hook. The screech rings out through the warehouse. Was it the screech of the hook or was it the seagull? They sound the same. It is still quite dark, and I cannot make out much. I step in a puddle of blood, not dry as I expected but sticky black.

Shaw disappears behind a row of pigs and a moment later he calls to me. 'Miss Green? Come and have a look at this, would you?'

I follow the sound of his voice, pushing past the dead weight of a carcass, the pig's bristly skin brushing against my fingers. Shaw is wearing dark clothes, but I can just make him out. The door he stands before is large and made of some sort of metal. He bangs upon it with his fist. Nothing. He tries the handle, and it opens.

A blast of cold air hits us. It's pitch-black inside. I hear him rummage in his coat pocket and retrieve a box of matches. I know it is his matches because one drags across the striker and a flicker of light illuminates his face, creating dark shadows along his high cheekbones which are so sharp they could slice through fish skin. We are standing close together; I can smell the woody scent of his cologne and make out the light spray of freckles on the bridge of his nose.

He holds the flame up and we follow a few shelves loaded with large blocks of ice to the far end of the cool room. The quiet *drip-drip* from things unseen and Shaw's deep breaths is all I hear. It's so cold in here my own breath escapes in a cloud.

Shaw glances at me, then inclines his head toward a creamy-white cabinet with silver metal hinges and a latch handle.

'What is it?' I ask. The word *Kelvinator* is scrawled in black across a metal plaque.

Shaw stares at it. 'An electric household refrigerator.'

'I've never seen one before,' I say. 'Have you?'

He nods. 'Once. In England. I got invited to a swanky party at some rich fellow's country estate. He'd shipped it back after a visit to America.' He knocks on the small door; the clang reverberates in the small space. 'This one doesn't seem to be running.'

'How can you tell?' I whisper.

'Listen.' We put our ears to the cold porcelain door. I breathe in his cologne. 'Do you hear that?' he asks.

'Hear what?' In this confined space I suddenly feel very conscious of the silence surrounding us.

'Exactly.' Shaw steps back. 'It's too quiet. The one I saw was as loud as a steam train.'

I leave my ear pressed against the door of the refrigerator. 'Wait,' I say. 'I *do* hear something. Footsteps on the other side. They're coming closer.'

The wall around the small refrigerator pulls away and the backlit, scowling face of a woman appears.

'Afternoon, Ma'am.' Detective Shaw beams a charming smile at her. 'My name is Robert Harvey.' His Irish accent suddenly disappears, and, in its place, he speaks pure Cockney. The woman in the doorway eyes him up and down. Shaw gestures to me. 'This here is me sister, Melinda Harvey. Our parents sent us. We're looking for our other sister. She didn't come home this mornin'.'

The woman places a hand on her hip. 'Who is it yer lookin' for?'

'Our sister. Lara Harvey.'

I peer at Shaw then. So *that's* her name? The name of the dead woman. Is this really the first time he's mentioned it? Lara Harvey. The woman on the beach. The woman I wrapped myself in. The thought makes me shudder. Or is it just the cold?

'Lara never mentioned any family,' the woman says.

'We're from out of town.'

For the first time, I wonder if he carries a gun. I also wonder at Detective Shaw's intention to drag me along to this place. When he explained that we would charade as the dead woman's siblings to gain entrance to the speakeasy, I had thought he was pulling my leg. But I could see now why he thought having me with him would decrease the proprietress's defences. His keen eyes watch her as though they can see her thoughts. Still, the woman frowns, unconvinced.

'You say Lara's your sister? You don't look nothing like her.' She points at me. 'Your hair's as dark as the soil in my vegetable garden. Lara's blonde.' I jerk reflexively and feel my face and neck flush at the insult. I pray that Shaw doesn't notice. No, he won't, not in this dim light.

'She's our stepsister,' I say, surprised at how easily the lie peels from my lips.

'Has something happened?' the woman asks.

'That's what we were hopin' you'd be able to help us with, Ma'am. We'd like to speak to Mrs Wendy Jenson. I understand she runs this establishment.'

The woman keeps a firm arm on the doorway, blocking anything behind her. 'What establishment would that be?'

'That bar you're hiding behind you. Would you mind asking Mrs Jenson to speak with us?'

She folds her arms across her chest. 'You're speaking with her. Now tell me what this is about, or I'll ask you both to leave.'

'Mind if we come in?'

The woman glances over her shoulder, seemingly displeased with the thought. 'Whatever questions you want to ask, ask 'em here.'

Shaw sighs. 'I thought it might come to this.' The stark planes of his face are cast in shadows as he reaches into the pocket of his trousers and retrieves his badge, presenting it to the woman. Her eyes widen when she sees it, and she attempts to heave the door shut, to slam it in our faces, but he has his boot wedged in the opening. 'We have some questions for you, Mrs Jenson. It might be easier if we come inside.'

'You're not here to shut me down, are you?'

'That depends how cooperative you are. Just a few questions, then my associate and I will be on our way.'

The woman sighs. 'All right. Come in.'

She ushers us through a dimly lit corridor to a tiny space filled with worn leather furniture, arranged as if in a living room, with an air of polished reserve. At the far corner of the room, stairs lead to a small round platform, which I assume acts as the stage for the cabaret. The bar is fully stocked with bottles and crystal glassware, a row of stools waiting patiently for the arses of men who seek to disconnect from the outside world.

'Have a seat,' the woman says. 'What is this about?' The woman lowers her backside onto the small table. It creaks as her weight comes down on it.

I sit on one of the leather sofas to the side and Shaw remains standing. He leans his upper body against the wall, casually folding his arms and crossing his legs at the ankles. The woman, Mrs Jenson, looks up at him.

'So, you do have a woman employed here by the name of Lara Harvey?' he asks.

The woman glares at Shaw, hesitating. Finally, she says, 'Yes'.

'How long has she worked here?'

'Lara's been with us now about eighteen months.'

Shaw nods. 'In what capacity?'

Mrs Jenson swallows, the bulge in her neck bobs up and down. 'Cocktail waitress.'

Shaw narrows his eyes. 'Do you mind my asking, Mrs Jenson, what sort of duties fall under the banner of a cocktail waitress?'

The woman clears her throat. 'Serve drinks to our customers.'

'That's all?'

'Well, some might provide light entertainment, depending on the mood of the night, and how much the customer is willing to pay.'

As I watch their conversation unfold, the questions and responses shot back and forth, I become more and more uneasy. I shouldn't be here. I should leave. I feel like an intruder, and I have no right to be listening. I'll stand up, excuse myself and walk out. Outside. They probably won't even notice my absence. I'll wait for Shaw in the alley. Anything's better than feeling like this. Like those creatures that cling to others for survival. Like a tongue-eating isopod. They attach themselves to a fish's tongue, sever it, then nestle into the space vacated by the missing flesh, allowing the fish to carry on its daily activities, all the while feeding on its blood. I don't want to be Shaw's isopod – I'm going to stand up in three seconds. Three… two… –

Shaw nods. 'When did you last see Lara?'

'Last night, during her shift. Why? What's this about?' The woman is growing irritated.

'How was she when you last saw her?'

The woman shrugs half-heartedly. 'Her usual self. A little quiet, perhaps, but we don't usually get time to sit down for girly gossipin'. We're running a business here. Listen, Mister, Detective, whoever you are, you'd better tell me what this is all about or I'm not answering any more of your questions.'

Shaw pauses, takes a breath. The silence between us rings like a siren in my ear. 'I'm sorry to inform you, Mrs Jenson, but sadly, Lara has died.'

The woman's hand flies to her mouth. 'Lara's dead?'

'We're still in the process of identification. But if our line of inquiry turns out to be correct, I'm afraid so.'

Mrs Jenson stands, jolting the small table backward with her backside. She walks in small circles with one hand on her hip and the other at her mouth. 'Dead? How?'

Shaw walks deliberately, slowly, toward where I sit. Reaching into his coat pocket, he fishes out his cigarette case then sits on the arm of the sofa, right next to me. He crosses one leg over the other and I feel the warmth from it, from his body. He opens the case and offers me a cigarette, which I accept because I don't know what else to do and I feel like I need to keep my hands busy.

'We're still investigating the circumstances,' he explains. 'Her body was found early this morning on the beach near the steelworks.'

He strikes a match and I lean in. The smoke relaxes me a bit and I start to feel more comfortable observing the scene.

Mrs Jenson stops halfway through one of her circles and turns to Shaw. 'Was she violated?'

'We don't suspect anything of that sort,' Shaw says. 'Now, would you mind if we ask you some more questions about her? To help with the investigation.'

Mrs Jenson reaches for the armchair opposite and sinks into it, her wide hips squeaking against the leather. 'I can manage that.'

Shaw rests his cigarette between his lips, takes out his pen and notepad from his coat pocket. 'How long have you known Lara?'

I watch the cigarette dangle from the cushiony corner of his mouth as he speaks. I watch the smoke curl. And the lips, and the way the words leave the lips, and the way the words sound, too.

'Since she started working here.'

'Did she seem happy to you?' Shaw rests the notebook on his knee and his pen scratches across the paper.

'Happy?'

He stops writing and looks at Mrs Jenson. 'Was she the type of person who might have hurt herself?'

Mrs Jenson leans forward. 'You mean suicide? No, not Lara.'

Shaw continues scribbling his notes. 'You said Lara was working here last night?' Mrs Jenson nods. 'What time did she finish her shift?'

'We close around two.'

'What time did she leave?'

'She usually leaves with her fella, around two-thirty. Sometimes three in the morning. But I can't be sure exactly… whether she stayed until close last night… it was late… and my memory isn't what it used to be…'

'Lara was seeing someone?' The cigarette wobbles up and down with his words.

'Well, yes,' Mrs Jenson says in a tone that implies it should be obvious. 'She was engaged to be married.'

'And what is the name of her boyfriend?'

'Fiancé,' Mrs Jenson corrects Shaw.

'I'm sorry?' Shaw uncrosses his legs. The leather armrest squeaks.

'The gentleman she's engaged to. He's…' Shaw stares at the woman, waiting, smoke swirling from the tip of his cigarette. 'Sonny Fynn.' Mrs Jenson folds her arms.

Shaw nods, adds to his notes. 'Did Lara complain of anyone recently?'

'What do you mean?'

'Have you noticed her receiving any unwelcome attention here?'

'She wouldn't have told me that.'

'Do you know of anyone she might've had a quarrel with? Anyone who might've wanted to hurt her?'

'You don't mean, Lara was murdered?'

'Cause of death is still under investigation. We can't be sure Lara was murdered. Yet. Have you seen anyone behave in a threatening way toward her?'

'She wasn't the sort to have arguments with people. Though I suppose someone might have been having a go at her about Sonny.'

'Her boyfriend?'

'Her fiancé.'

'Because he's a gangster?'

Mrs Jenson shifts in her chair. 'Some might call him that.'

'Was there anyone who had been bothering her about her fiancé, the gangster, Sonny Fynn?'

'I don't like to get caught up in the girls' private lives. We're a professional place, here, Mister.'

'Did anyone have a romantic interest in her, apart from Sonny Fynn?'

Mrs Jenson cackles. 'This is a cabaret house. All the gentlemen have romantic interests in my girls. It's how I put food on the table.'

As Shaw nods, he drops his pen, and it slips between us. He reaches down to retrieve it and his hand grazes mine. The knuckles, the soft hairs on the back of his fingers, their warmth against my skin. My breath quickens. I feel a pang, a quickening, a fluttering deep within, as though I have leapt off a cliff and am falling, down into the abyss. That moment, right before I hit the ocean, when I'm suspended in the air, and I've left my stomach behind.

Sounds soften as blood rushes to my head and my own fingertips tremble, as though electricity passes through them. As though I've swallowed a hundred moths and they are trying to escape the cage of my ribs, flying around, flapping their wings against every organ inside my body.

Weightless, silken wings.

Delicate, pale bodies.

Nocturnal dust.

This feeling I've never felt before — these moths undulating in my guts — is intensely uncomfortable, but there is also a deep, underlying exhilaration.

My knees pull together, my muscles contract, my hands clench into fists, and suddenly I am painfully self-conscious that Detective Shaw will notice my strange behaviour. Does he know my body is reacting this way? Can he see how hot and flustered I've become? How shallow my breaths? I try to swallow, but my throat has thickened, and what if it sounds too loud? I know it won't, I'm sure. Still, I worry: my body — my stomach, my heart, even my breaths — are making so much noise. All the normal human things I usually do have deserted me because all I can think about is impressing this person. To prove to him that I'm capable, that he was right to bring me here, with him.

That he *needs* me.

'Did Lara leave any personal effects here?' Shaw asks, returning me to the moment, here, with him.

Mrs Jenson motions toward the bar behind us. 'All our employees got their own locker behind the bar.'

Wiping my sweaty palms on my trousers, we follow the woman to the bar, and she gestures to an area in the narrow space behind it. Next to some bottles of unlabelled liquor, three separate trays of trinkets sit, each filled with slightly different contents: coins, a lipstick, handkerchiefs, a key. She picks up the middle tray. 'This one's Lara's.'

Shaw retrieves the shiny metal object and examines it. 'What's the key for?'

'I assumed it was a spare. For her apartment.'

'We'll need to take this. Evidence.'

Mrs Jenson snatches the key from Shaw's fingers and shoves it in her breast pocket. ''Fraid not. I said I would answer your questions but as *you* said, Detective, the identification process is still underway. Lara might very well still be alive. She be coming 'ere tonight and asking me why I be giving away her spare key to strangers claiming to be police officers.' Then she eyes me. 'I still haven't seen your badge, miss.'

Before I can answer, Shaw changes the subject. 'Did Lara ever speak about her family?'

Mrs Jenson lets out a long sigh. 'Hasn't got none. Far as I'm aware. That's why she was so struck with her fiancé. Promised her the life she never had I 'spose.'

The woman exits the narrow space behind the bar, squeezing

past me, and my arm brushes against her side. I simultaneously bump the woman's hip and touch her shoulder with my left hand. Meanwhile, my right hand reaches into her breast pocket, grabs the key inside, and slips it into the back pocket of my trousers. This all happens so quickly, in one fluid motion, that she barely has time to register. I look at her, clear my throat, beam my most polite smile, and mutter, 'Excuse me.'

She stares at me, confused, and I wait for what feels like the longest five seconds of my life. My adrenaline rushes, but then she continues walking, and I follow behind. I half do it to impress the man. Since he laughed at me back in his office, I've had the insatiable desire to prove to him I'm not mad.

'Bit of a catch then?' Shaw says.

'What is?'

'Sonny Fynn? He's a bit of a catch? Did Lara have any other boyfriends, or does she just have a thing for gangsters?'

'All women have their secrets. It's not my place to pry.'

'She didn't say anything to you? About being in any trouble?'

'Nothing to me.' Mrs Jenson stops talking, as if a heavy thought occupies her. 'She's really dead?' she finally asks.

'Seems that way, Mrs Jenson.' Shaw gestures to the alcohol behind the bar. 'Who supplies the liquor?'

Mrs Jenson shifts her weight uneasily. 'Sonny Fynn supplies all our gin.'

'I see, Sonny Fynn. And where does he get it from?'

Mrs Jenson cackles again. 'Detective, even if I knew, do you really think I'd tell you? Sonny Fynn keeps this business afloat. Besides, haven't you ever heard of bathtub gin? Anyone can make it these days; out of anything they can get their dirty old hands on.'

Shaw clears his throat. 'Anything?'

'Anything that ferments. Corn, sugar, beetroot. Even potato peelings.'

Shaw thanks her for her time and we leave the bar, back through the illusion of a door, through the cool room and the warehouse. As we pass, I try not to look at the pig carcasses swinging on their hooks. I wonder whether Shaw is disappointed with the information we gleaned from Mrs Jenson, whether he is disappointed that he asked me to come along, to help him. And then I remember the silver key in my pocket and a smile creeps across my face.

Detective Shaw swings the front door to the warehouse open and the air in the alleyway is as fresh as the sea compared to the stale stench of death inside that murder house. The lane is basked in the sunshine of the afternoon, red bricks emanating warmth. Shaw's dark hair, streaked with silver, glimmers in the light.

'I could go for a bite to eat,' he says. 'How 'bout you?'

I glare at him in disbelief. 'How could you possibly think about food after what we saw hanging in there by their trotters?'

'Come on, I know a great little deli nearby…'

Worry stirs in the pit of my stomach, that someone should see us together. Should see me unchaperoned, with Detective Shaw. The golden band on his finger glints in the sunlight.

'Your wife will not accompany you?' I ask.

He pauses. A frown sweeps over his face as he stares at me. 'You are very direct,' he says and turns to walk down the alleyway toward the car.

The laughter of children brings Shaw to a stop. The children huddle around a ball, legs kicking, arms pulling at each other. A dark-haired boy wearing spectacles waves his hands, trying to attract the attention of his teammates, failing miserably.

'Pass!'

The boy runs toward the scuffle but trips, falling face down into the cobblestones and swallowing a mouthful of dirty water.

The ball hits the tow away zone wall with such force that it rebounds off and into Shaw. Except Shaw flicks his right foot, balances the ball on the toe of his boot, and sends it straight back through the air, to the boy with the spectacles.

The boy traps the ball, dodges the oncoming children and sprints toward the road. He pauses, dribbles the ball around, faces the oncoming opposition, lines himself up and takes a shot. The ball soars through the air. There is silence, followed by the tinkling of broken glass, and immediately the children scatter. Within seconds the alleyway is deserted.

'What was *that*?' I ask as we make our way down the cobblestones, back to the car. He opens the door for me, and I slide into the front seat.

'What, that?' he laughs. 'My brothers and I played a lot of football growing up in Dublin.'

The passenger door clicks shut, Shaw walks around the front of the car and opens the driver's door. The car tilts as he steps onto the running board and climbs inside. Placing his hands on the polished wood steering wheel, he looks out the front window at the street, watching absentmindedly as the straggling children scatter and scream. I can see his mind ticking over.

'What are you thinking?' I ask.

'I'm thinking Lara Harvey got caught up with the wrong crowd.'

'You think someone from there murdered her?' I ask. 'Who?'

'Her boyfriend, Sonny Fynn, springs to mind.'

'*Fiancé.*'

His eyes meet mine and we smile.

'But what's his motive? Without a motive, there's no suspect.' Shaw sighs. 'I wonder if he has an alibi.' He turns on the ignition and the car rumbles to life. 'After that,' he shrugs, 'I've got nothing.'

'No,' I say. 'Not nothing.'

He looks at me. 'What are you talking about?'

From my back trouser pocket I pull out the key and hold it in my open hand. It glints in the sun beaming through the windshield.

'You magpie,' Shaw laughs, and the lines at his eyes crease together. He holds my gaze for a moment too long. Never in my whole life have I seen such a strong jaw and wide cheekbones. Eyes so blue they could ice water.

I look away, embarrassed, and toss the key to him. 'She compared the colour of my hair to shit.'

Shaw glances at the wisps of dark hair hanging in front of my eye, and smiles at me. 'No, not shit. *Soil.*'

My stomach leaps from my body, as though I'm falling from the cliff again. My eyes dart around uneasily, unsure, unable to land on him, unable to settle upon anything, so I look outside, to the street, only to find that the children have disappeared, as though they were never there.

6

DETECTIVE Shaw pulled the Model T to a stop at the kerb. The tightness in his jaw twinged as he strained to look through the front windscreen. A dark brick facade with a large sign read 'Phone TOMORROW For Your COAL TODAY'. The building stood next to a large entranceway, over which another sign, 'Morrow's Coal & Ice' told him he'd found the right place.

Shaw rotated the key between his fingers. He hadn't noticed the engraving at first. A small inscription in cursive at the base of the key was all he had to go on. The word *Morrow* could have meant anything.

After giving Miss Green a ride to the harbour, chance had seemed to intervene. On his way back to the station he had passed a delivery truck, stacked with sacks on its trailer, 'Morrow's Coal is the Best' painted in white on its side.

Detective Shaw opened the car door and approached the large entranceway that opened onto an empty lot, the gravel crunching beneath his boots. The ground was stained black and dotted with dark pools of water. Several trucks, just like the one he had passed on his way, were lined up on the periphery, shaded by makeshift awnings that bowed at the sides. A number of chutes extended from a hopper type building; a pile of empty sacks piled in a heap below.

'Help you?'

Shaw turned. A middle-aged man in dusty overalls was wiping his hands on a filthy rag. Shaw approached him and offered his hand. 'Detective Ronan Shaw.'

The man flung the rag to the ground and accepted Shaw's handshake. 'Bill Morrow,' he said. 'What can I do for you?'

Shaw retrieved Lara's key and tossed it to Mr Morrow. 'This look familiar to you, Mr Morrow?'

Mr Morrow's face didn't budge. 'Got my name on it.'

Shaw took the cigarette case from his jacket pocket. 'Mind if I ask you a few questions?'

Mr Morrow looked suspiciously at Shaw. 'What's this about?'

'Do you have a woman in your employ by the name of Lara Harvey?'

Mr Morrow shifted slightly. 'What if I do?'

Shaw clicked open his shiny case, revealing a row of perfectly white cigarettes. Bill Morrow glanced at them, then licked his lips.

'Well, if you do, Mr Morrow, then I shall have a few more questions for you.' Shaw offered the open case to Mr Morrow, who accepted and stuffed one in his mouth and another behind his ear. 'Now,' Shaw continued, 'it's a simple yes or no question. A woman, in her twenties, blonde, petite. Goes by the name of Lara Harvey?'

'Miss Harvey in trouble, is she?' When he spoke, the dried-out saliva that had formed in the corner of his mouth cracked.

Shaw held out the flame and lit Mr Morrow's cigarette. 'So, that's a yes?'

Mr Morrow inhaled and gazed at the entranceway to his depot, avoiding eye contact. 'That's a yes.'

Shaw left the cigarette in his mouth and took out his notepad and pen. 'Can you tell me anything about Miss Harvey's movements in the past week or so? Did she have any arguments with anyone?'

Scratching at the stubble on his chin, Mr Morrow said, 'I should say, nothing out of the ordinary. Why d'you ask?'

'Mind if you tell me a bit more about her responsibilities here?'

'All my drivers got the same responsibilities. Don't matter if they're male or female. Each of 'em got a job to do.'

'What would that entail, Mr Morrow?'

'They pick up their quota, bring it back here for sortin', then make their deliveries. Not that difficult. Simpleton could do it. She surprised me that one. Thought she was doin' a good job holding her own against all me other workers. They seemed to leave her alone. Although it might have something to do with that fella she goes round with.'

Shaw's pen scratched across his notepad. He looked up and eyed Mr Morrow. 'That being a gentleman named Sonny Fynn?'

'Aye, you've heard of him, then?'

Shaw nodded. 'How long has Miss Harvey been working here?'

'Nigh on two years now, I should say.'

'How many deliveries does she make a day?'

'Oh, I'd say, about ten or so.'

'Where to?'

'Different places, around town.'

'Homes?'

'Homes, yes. Businesses.'

Shaw sensed Mr Morrow stalling, or perhaps he was hiding something. Was everyone in this town in the pocket of Sonny Fynn? Either way, this could take a while. 'You said each of your drivers picks up their quota. Where do they pick it up from?'

'Blue Mile.'

'Blue Mile?'

'That's the name we in the coke business like to call the tramway what runs from the mine to the harbour. My drivers pick up their stock from the wharfies who work the Osborne-Wallsend Coal Company. Most of the stuff gets loaded onto ships, but people in this town'll pay good money for quality product, and Osborne-Wallsend coal is as good as it comes. We pay the wharfies a little extra to make sure Widow's Peak is well supplied.'

'Have you ever met Miss Harvey's boyfriend, Sonny Fynn?'

'Don't know nothing about boyfriends. Don't know nothing about people's private lives. We keep to ourselves 'round here.'

Yes, Shaw concluded, perhaps most of the people in this town *were* in the pocket of Sonny Fynn. 'Thank you for your time, Mr Morrow.'

Shaw flicked his cigarette butt into a murky black puddle and crunched back across the gravel toward the street. The weak winter sun sank low in the sky. It would be dipping behind the escarpment soon and Widow's Peak would be plunged into darkness. He wondered if he had enough time. There was still one person he wanted to speak to before the day was over.

The Model T Ford rumbled through town and down the hill toward the harbour. The blue curve of the sea came shimmering into view. The lighthouse glowed bright white on top of its grassy hill in the late afternoon, like a stick of chalk. Shaw passed the narrow strip of beach with the tram tracks running parallel and parked the car near the loading docks. When he opened his door, a gust of wind blew the pungent smell of fish and seaweed into his face.

Shaw ambled along the harbourfront, passing fishermen mending nets like old ladies in knitting circles. Gulls squawked overhead and swooped for any scraps the fishermen pulled out and tossed into the oily water.

Shaw's breath caught in his throat as a wave exploded like a bomb against the harbour wall. Some children watched the spray of white water, shouting in awe after each crash. He could never escape the crashing sound of bombs. It was usually followed by the phantom smell of cordite invading his nostrils. It returned every night. In the darkest hours, when the world was silent, the earth would shake beneath the thunder of machine guns, and he could feel the wet cold of mud all around him, as if he were back in the trenches. The earthy, shitty smell of it. Every night he fought in those trenches, the ones still in his head. He huddled in that hole in the earth, holding his ears against the blasts of artillery. The crashing of bombs. The smell of cordite. He'd become tired. So tired.

Darkness descended quickly over the harbour, and the weak glow of the pier lights created a pathway along the waterfront. Shaw headed around the horse-shoe bend, toward the bustling wharves, stinking of long-dead fish and exhaust fumes, as decrepit fishing boat engines started up and chugged out to sea. He walked along a gangplank, dodging rotten lobster traps, trying to make out the names of each of the old boats as he passed.

The last of the light drained away, casting shadows of holes in the timber planks below his feet. He walked on, forcing his eyes to adjust to the dull light. A figure approached, along the gangplank. He heard the footsteps coming closer but for the life of him he could not see anything. The footsteps stopped. Just as he stumbled over a nest of old rope, her face materialised from the darkness, and he was caressed by the scent of sea spray.

Missy Green carried a large barrel of fish heads. 'What are you doing here?'

'Evening, Miss Green,' Shaw said, dusting off his suit. 'I've come to have a chat to your father. Can you tell me where I'll find him?'

'My father? What do you want to talk to him for?'

'Few questions.'

A flicker of suspicion crossed Missy's face – even in the darkness Shaw caught the slight narrowing of her eyes, the frown. He could feel her mind working, sizing him up. She chewed her lip, then turned and gestured for him to follow her.

She led him to the end of the timber pier to the *Senhora ao Vento*, the Lady in the Wind. It was a shabby old thing, modest in size compared to the other vessels that bobbed nearby. The bow stood very high out of the water, but the sides of the boat sloped down. Poles jutted out at odd angles with ropes and pulley systems attached. For the nets, Shaw presumed.

'Gust,' Missy called. 'There's someone here to speak to you.'

Missy's father emerged from the small cabin at the front of the boat, where a faint glow of lantern light spilled onto the deck. His broad shoulders blocked out the orange glow and made his olive skin appear even darker.

Shaw extended his hand. 'Evening, Sir. You're Missy's father?'

'That's right,' he said. 'I'm Gust.' He wore an old fisherman's cap over a thick head of pale hair, a tattered, knitted pullover, soiled trousers, and black rubber galoshes.

'Detective Ronan Shaw.'

Shaw felt the coarseness of Gust's hand when he shook it, as though it was coated in sand. They were aged hands, older than his face suggested – which, Shaw guessed, was probably around fifteen or so years older than him – and scattered with scars all the way along his wrist and under his woollen sleeve.

Gust motioned to the boat. 'Sorry about the light,' he said.

'Don't mind him,' Missy called from behind Shaw. 'My father likes working in the dark.'

'Weren't you on your way to the tower?' Gust said to Missy.

The black water slapped quietly against the Greens' boat.

Shaw cleared his throat. 'Mind if we have a chat, Mr Green?'

Gust rubbed his bearded chin. 'All right with me.'

Shaw glanced at Missy standing on the pier in the dark, then lowered his voice. 'Not here,' he said. 'Let's take a trip. Do you mind?'

'We usually lay the traps at night. Pick 'em up the next day. Was just about to head out. You ever skippered a trawler before?' Gust asked.

'I've done my share of time on boats.'

'Fisherman, are you?'

'Some,' Shaw lied.

'Hop aboard.'

The timber deck creaked as Shaw stepped over the side and put his weight on the boat. There wasn't much room on the deck. He made his way to the front, dodging nets rigged up to various contraptions, stepping over coils of wire rope, bundles of more fishing nets, piles of crates stacked in neat rows and metal traps, brown and mottled with rust.

Gust held open the door to the small cabin that housed the steering station and motioned for Shaw to step inside. It was not much warmer inside than in the biting night air, and the smell of fish made it almost impossible to breathe.

Shaw cast his eyes over the engine controls and the steering wheel. Off to the side a small sink with a gas stove and two chipped enamel mugs hanging from hooks made him picture Missy and her father standing here sipping tea each morning at daybreak. The thought of being in this room drinking tea made Shaw's stomach lurch. He could not get past the rank smell of fish.

Gust started up the old engine then said, 'Leave you to it,' and returned to the crowded deck. The boat chugged and spluttered as they set off from the harbour with Shaw at the wheel. As he pulled the boat away from the pier, he noticed that Missy had already disappeared. They headed out past the rock wall, beyond the calmness of the harbour, leaving behind the glow of the pier lights, and into the open ocean, the darkness, and the wind.

Behind him, through the window crusty with salt, he watched Gust at the stern opening the traps, filling them with fish heads and setting them aside in stacks. Gust re-entered the cabin and Shaw coughed at the smell of him.

Gust laughed and patted Shaw on the shoulder. 'You get used to it after a while. Barely smell it anymore. The fish're always gutted on board. Usually the gulls are eager to pick up the scraps, but they don't fly at night.'

Gust stood next to Shaw, his steady stance reassuring Shaw's inability to see much past the front of the boat except the white foamy water at the stern.

'Where are we headed?'

'Just hug the coast south for a while. Then make your way out to the islands.'

They chugged along in silence and in darkness. The waves bounced the boat steadily up and down. Gust's quiet breathing and the chugging of the engine filled the small space. Shaw focused on the black ocean in front of them, sinking into his own thoughts, and waited until he could make out any sign of land. After a while, Gust stepped outside and busied himself with uncoiling a line of rope.

The first sliver of island came into view, appearing like a vision in the water, its dark mass of grass invisible against the night sky, but the shoreline was jagged and the current swirled in white all around the rocks outlining the land. Seabirds perched along the uneven ridge of the rocky shore, their white feathers ghost-like against the darkness.

A bang on the window from behind caused Shaw to jump. He turned to see Gust making a gesture with his hand across his neck that suggested he should cut the engine. Shaw shut it off and opened the door to the cabin with a click. Freezing sea spray stung his face. The invigorating smell reminded him of when Missy had walked into his office earlier that morning. He wondered what it would be like to see her working alongside her father on deck.

'Are we dropping anchor here?' Shaw called as he rubbed his hands together to fight the cold.

Gust shook his head as he unwound the rope. 'No anchor,' he said. 'We drift.'

Shaw stood a moment as Gust worked his way around the

boat, so familiar, so assured. He had been monitoring Gust's facial expressions since he climbed aboard. He needed to work out if, and *how*, Gust concealed information. But first, Shaw needed to establish Gust's baseline. He'd lure him into familiar topics he'd have no reason to lie about.

'Do you catch much around these waters?' Shaw asked.

'Most fishermen go out before dawn and return around midday,' Gust said. 'We don't need that much. We get by.'

Shaw joined him at the stern, stepping around empty crates and a dented tin pail. 'What do you use to catch the fish, not those traps?'

As the boat drifted, it rocked gently along the surface.

'Traps are for smaller catches, but it's the smaller ones that fetch the bigger price tags, so it's worth the trouble.'

Shaw flipped open his cigarette case, pulled one out and placed its papery end between his lips. He cupped the flame from the wind, lit up, drew in the smoke, and leaned against the back of the boat, watching Gust work. The creaking, groaning sound of chains unfurling on a massive spool punctured the otherwise silent evening, and Gust lowered the trap over the back of the boat, letting it plunge into the black waters.

How easily he threw those traps overboard. He could just as easily throw a body, Shaw mused. One as petite as Lara Harvey's wouldn't take much to lift over the side. But with Missy on board, he wouldn't have managed to do it.

Shaw had taken note of how Gust held himself, the sound of his voice, and his facial movements and gestures. Now that he had gained an understanding of Gust's cues, it was time to switch tack.

'Is Missy always on board?' Shaw asked, keeping the inflection of his voice as neutral as possible.

Gust sat on a crate with two lengths of rope in his hands. 'She's helmsman,' he said. 'She drives the boat.' He leaned back casually, his gesture reminiscent of the languid way Missy had sat in Shaw's office that morning. Showing no signs of distress, Gust's hands continued to work the rope. His movements were effortless, elegant, as he twisted the two ropes to become one, coiled one free end twice around the other and passed it back through the inside.

'What's that you're doing there?' Shaw asked.

Gust leaned in. Shaw noted the lack of distance between them; significant considering a person uncomfortable with lying would usually take a step back, not closer.

'This here is the double fisherman's knot,' Gust said. 'Lot of fishermen believe it's the best fishing knot. When tied properly. Impossible to untie once tightened. Problem is, most fishermen don't take the time to tie it properly.'

Gust looped the rope over itself in the other direction, his scarred fingers working almost as if they had minds of their own. He passed one end under the other, forming two neat knots, tugged at the ends, and held it up for Shaw to see.

'You don't use rods?' Shaw asked.

Gust shook his head. 'Trawling's the most common way of fishing in these waters,' he said. 'We use nets, like this one here.' He held up a wet web of white rope. 'Drag it through the water, or along the bottom. We hurl the trawl over the side. Usually takes a large crew but we manage by using a smaller net. Normally these nets trawl the seabed, some crew manage to get thousands of pounds of fish.'

'What sort of fish do you catch?' Shaw asked.

'Oh, anything really, in these waters. Snapper, bass, blackfish. But we also get shark, sometimes ray.'

Shaw could see his attempts to crack Gust were not working. He tried again. 'So, if you can do… all this… on your own, why drag Missy along?'

Gust eyed Shaw. 'Superstitious man, are you?'

'What do you mean?'

Bending over the stern, Gust dropped another trap. It hit the water with a splash. He righted himself. 'A woman on board's bad luck. You'd know that if you were a fisherman.'

Heat rushed up Shaw's neck. In his attempts to catch Gust in a lie, he had instead, embarrassingly, found himself caught in one. 'I'm not a superstitious man, Mr Green. But my question still stands. Why does Missy come?'

Gust pursed his lips. 'Grew up in a fishing family,' he said. 'Fishing's all I know. I raised her here. Just the two of us. So, Missy grew up with it too, I guess. And she loves it. Plus, Missy coming along gives me company, I suppose. Sea's a lonely place for those with battle scars. So, I suppose I encourage her. It's… selfish, maybe.'

'Your daughter said you were stationed in France?'

Gust straightened up, gazed at the water. 'The Somme.'

'Is that what caused the…?'

Nodding, Gust continued with the traps. 'Hmm. Shrapnel. They told me I'd be fine unless infection set in. And then of course, it always did. A shell exploded and the trench collapsed. I was buried… under half a tonne of earth it felt like. 'Cept it wasn't dirt it was… bodies… my friends… soldiers… dead horses.'

Gust lowered the trap over the side, stood and stepped closer to Shaw. Leaning against the stern, he folded his arms. Shaw continued to listen, smoking the cigarette down to the butt.

'Took two days to dig myself out,' Gust continued. 'When I finally did, I couldn't feel a thing. I was helped to the dugout and managed to carry on for some days. Only after that did someone explain to me that a shell had landed quite close. Gouged a hole in the earth as big as a room. Of course, I remember nothing of it. Now I wake up in the middle of the night suffocating under all that earth and mud.'

Shaw flicked cigarette ash into the black water. 'Can always tell a man who was at the Somme. Not by their wounds or the haunted stare in their eyes. By the drowsiness that follows them during the day. Of all those men I've met, not one of them has enjoyed a full night's rest since.'

Gust bent to pick up another trap. 'Where did you fight, then?' he called over his shoulder.

Shaw clenched his jaw. 'Not far from there. Cambrai.'

Gust handed the last trap to Shaw. 'I dare say the poor souls at Cambrai faired not much better than those at the Somme. Go and drop that over the gunwale, would you, mate?'

Shaw moved to where he had watched Gust drop the traps and followed suit. The metal cage landed with a loud splash as it hit the water and the chain rattled over the side, leaving a small, white flotation device bobbing on the surface.

'So,' Gust said as he wiped his hands against his trousers. 'What brings you on board my fine vessel this evening, Detective? It wasn't just your intention to dredge up old war memories, was it?'

'Missy came into the station this morning,' Shaw said. He watched Gust's face for any change in his facial expression, any hint of knowing.

Gust raised his eyebrows and widened his eyes. 'Ahh, so that's how you two know each other.'

'I wanted to talk to you about her.'

'About Missy? Why?'

Shaw hesitated. 'Have you noticed anything the matter with her lately?'

Gust's eyebrows drew together, the skin between them beset with wrinkles. 'Why would you think something was wrong? Did something happen?'

Shaw cleared his throat. 'She found a dead woman on the beach.'

Gust's eyes opened wider; the whites visible. 'Who did? Missy? When?'

'She didn't mention it? This morning,' Shaw said. 'She came to the police station for an interview.'

'The police interviewed her? Why would they do that? If she was just the poor child who found it? She didn't have anything to do with it.' A pause. Gust inhaled deeply, allowed his shoulders to relax. 'Come inside,' he said. 'Come in and I'll make us a cup of tea.'

Shaw followed him inside the cabin. Gust opened a small cabinet to reveal tin jars of different sizes with no labels. He felt each of them before placing his hands around a small square-shaped one. Opening the lid, he brought it to his nose, sniffing its contents. Satisfied, he heaped two large spoonfuls into the kettle, filled it and rested it on top of the stove. Gust's finger padded the surface of the stove, brushing over the gas ring. He struck a match, lit the stove, and stood there, looking down at the kettle, waiting for the water to boil.

When the kettle whistled, Gust unhooked the two enamel mugs and poured tea into each, then handed one to Shaw, who sipped the scalding liquid and nodded appreciatively. He took another sip. Bits of tea leaves washed into his mouth and stuck to his tongue and he supressed the urge to spit them out. The cabin was thick with the smell of salt and fish and tea and disquiet. He wondered how to broach the topic of Missy again.

'Mr Green, some people, when they experience trauma, like Missy did this morning, discovering the dead woman, they can go into a state of shock.'

Gust's face sagged slightly. 'Aye, she's sensitive, that's all,' he said. 'Nothing's wrong with her. She can get a little moody sometimes, but that's common for girls not yet come of age.'

Shaw's mouth went dry, despite the tea. 'How old is she?'

Gust sighed and said, 'She'll be twenty in a couple months. That's why she… well her mother died at the age of twenty. So she's been acting especially… sensitive about it I suppose. She has a tendency to be a bit melancholy at times.'

'Missy's mother died?'

Gust nodded.

'Mr Green, what's happening to Missy seems to be a lot more serious than just melancholy or sensitivity. Some people… when they're in shock, they can experience hallucinations, delusions… psychosis. Has Missy ever mentioned seeing mermaids to you?'

Gust prickled. 'Psychosis? Mermaids? What are you talking about?'

'I don't mean to upset you, Mr Green. Really, I don't. But Missy mentioned she saw a mermaid this morning, before she found the dead woman.'

Gust drained his tea and propped his mug on top of the

controls. 'You don't look like someone who believes in those types of tales.'

'I told you, Mr Green, I'm not a superstitious man. But I am concerned about your daughter. And I think you ought to keep an eye on her.'

Gust shook his head. 'It's her grandfather, the lightkeeper.' He exhaled and took his fisherman's cap into his hands. 'He's a bad influence on her.'

'How so?'

Gust looked far away. 'You know what happens to an apple left to rot? The rot spreads onto the next apple. He's been a wickie too long. It's done something to his mind.'

Shaw drank the bad tea just to keep his hands busy. 'Done what?'

'It's the mercury,' Gust said. 'If it can decay the prisms, imagine what it does to the brain. That's why light keepers are all mad. Affects women worse than men.'

'What does that mean?'

Gust looked at Shaw like he'd forgotten he was there. 'It's been said that women who live in lighthouses suffer from a melancholy disposition. And she spends an awful lot of time in that tower. Too much time, if you ask me. And it's my bloody fault.'

'How do you mean?'

Gust sighed deeply. 'I left her. I chose to leave. To fight. I left her alone. She had nowhere else to go, so she went to live with her grandfather. For four years. For four years she lived in the one place that's not safe.' Gust banged his fist against the side of the boat. 'I never should have abandoned her. I should have left her grandfather to rot, alone in that place.'

'You two don't see eye to eye?' Shaw said.

'After my wife died… Well, let's just say I've learned to keep my distance. He likes it better that way, anyway. He's a recluse.'

'The idea of manning a lighthouse seems like a lot of work. Why doesn't he employ an assistant?' Shaw asked.

Gust scoffed. 'He doesn't need one. He has Missy. Besides, he doesn't let people into the lighthouse if he doesn't have to. That man's temper is a sight to behold.'

'Look, I think Missy's been affected by what she saw this morning. She needs rest. Peace and quiet. And she should probably keep off the boat, for the time being.'

Gust hooted. 'I don't think she'll take too well to that idea. What she needs is to be kept away from that tower. Maybe you could keep an eye on her for me.'

Heat spread up Shaw's neck. 'Me?'

'Why not? It'll keep her away from the lighthouse. I'll agree to keep her off the boat, if you agree to keep an eye on her.'

Shaw hesitated. He had very little experience with young women, especially those with so-called moody dispositions. 'Who will you get to replace her?'

'The *Senhora*? Every seaman in Widow's Peak is looking for a way to make money. Plenty of men for hire at the harbour. I'm sure I'll be able to rope some unlucky bastard with a crab claw or two.'

Shaw sighed, resigned, then shook Gust's calloused hand for the second time that evening.

When they returned to the harbour, he left Gust and the *Senhora ao Vento* to dock. It was only as he walked back along the timber gangplank in the dark that he realised he still needed to unclench his jaw.

7

Terça-feira

BRIGHT light pours through the window, and it takes a moment for the fog in my mind to lift. I am not used to the feeling of waking up in such brilliance. My legs are twisted in the blankets, and I kick them off a bit too aggressively so they fall in a heap on the ground. Even though it was a cold night my undershirt is damp from sweat, and I must have kicked my socks off in my sleep. The sheets rustle and I find one, then the other, and put them on my freezing toes.

My brain struggles with effort as I grab the trousers that hang over the bed and pull them on, leaving the belt undone. Sitting on the edge of the mattress I try to work out how I could have overslept and why my father didn't wake me like he has done every morning since he returned from France.

Something is wrong. I feel it in my marrow.

My hand clasps my mouth as realisation hits and my heart flutters so fast, I feel dizzy. Something's happened. Gust has had a heart attack in his sleep. He's lying dead in the room next to mine. The wound in my head pulses with the beating of my frightened heart. I feel the gash with my fingers and recoil when I touch the crusty scab, calcified in small rings around the

94

opening, like a barnacle on the underside of a ship. I spread my hair so that the wound is covered and hope nobody notices the rank smell emanating from my barnacled head.

A seagull shrieks. I look through the window, at the world outside. Nothing. No birds. I hear it again, so clearly, I flinch. Somehow, I know the sound is not coming from outside.

My thoughts are frozen. How can I find my father like that, cold and dead in his own bed? I stand but my feet are numb from the cold and my legs are weak and shaky because my heart is still beating like a lunatic. I grab the bed post for support and take a slow, measured breath.

The floorboards creek under my feet as I take two tentative steps toward my bedroom door. Opening it a crack, I call out, 'Gust?'

No answer. Nothing. Not a sound. My chest tightens. I suck in breath. I can't believe this day has come. My brain still won't accept it. I can't imagine my life without him.

Opening the door fully, I move toward his bedroom. The light is yellow, the sun has already risen, it must be about seven or eight in the morning. Across the room I see something that doesn't make sense. His bedroom door is ajar. It was closed when I came in last night, wasn't it?

'Gust?' I call again, louder this time.

My pulse thumps like a drum in my ears and through it I hear the morning creeping in from outside: the lap-lap of the waves, the birds chirping from their nests. No seagulls though.

I take a few more steps, around the corner to my father's bedroom, and push open the door. My eyes peel over every detail before I cast them down to his bed.

His empty bed.

Relief floods my veins like a torrent. But the brief reprise subsides, and I feel the first twang of confusion, anger even. If he's not in his bed, then where is he?

I race to the front door, swinging it wide open, and grab my boots from the front porch. Running along the sandy road, I stumble and hop on one foot to pull them on. Toward the harbour. I must see if the *Senhora ao Vento* is docked.

'Where were you?'

Gust stands at the end of the pier, unloading the crates from the *Senhora*. He throws a crate full of crabs down next to my feet, then straightens his back and adjusts his fisherman's cap higher on his head. 'Morning to you, too,' he chimes. The nerve of the man.

'Answer the question. Where were you?'

Gust shrugs. 'Took the boat out this morning.'

'Without me? Why?'

He hands me a line of rope. 'You seemed a bit tired yesterday. Thought you needed some rest.'

My emotions threaten to surge out of me. 'I thought you were dead.'

He barks laughter. 'Can you tie off that end, or are you gonna make me do it?'

I tie the rope to the pier, tethering our *Senhora* to the land. 'What time did you leave? Why did you go without me? Who *drove* the boat?'

'You're not going to keep going with this all morning, are you?'

I stop dead, sensing movement. Hearing shuffling. Only then

I notice another person on the boat. Someone standing in my position, inside the cabin. Someone who is not welcome.

I shake my head. 'Not him,' I say through gritted teeth. 'Gil Sanders? Bloody Gil Sanders?'

Old Gil steps out on deck, his beady eyes lost in the wrinkles around his sockets as he squints from the glare off the water. 'Morning, Miss Green. Fine morning out on the water.'

This lousy, good-for-nothing hire-a-hand has no business on my boat.

'What are you doing here?' I snap.

Gil passes the rest of the crates from the deck to my father. I notice they are not quite as heavy as usual.

'Your father asked me to help him out for a while. Seems you might have a chance to steady your sea legs after all, love,' he cackles.

Nerves tingle along my arms. The desire to hit this man crashes over me like a wave. I want to scream. To throw myself at him. Turning to scold my deceiving father, I realise he is already making his way down the wooden jetty toward the market. I pursue him down the jetty, then along the harbour front.

'What were you thinking offering that slimy, tongue-eating louse work on our boat? How bloody dare you?'

I want to yell that he's gone mad, that I hope he might've died out there this morning, in the deep, betraying bastard that he is.

Gust ignores me.

I fight to keep myself from seizing him by the arm, balling his shirt in my fist, but his face is set so stern, I don't dare to. We near the market yard. It is still early, but the market has already come to life.

'Look,' I say, my voice higher than I intend it to be. 'Stop. Please, stop. For a minute. Just… talk to me.' It is as if my boat, the *Senhora*, is slipping away. As if, my whole life, all those hours spent on her, on the ocean, never took place. I can't let that happen.

Gust places the crate of crabs, still alive and nipping at each other, on the stone counter and pumps water to hose them down. He gives me a knowing look.

'That detective mentioned something interesting last night.' My back molars clench together at the mention of Detective Shaw. He went out with my father last night to lay the traps. I'd forgotten about that. 'Said you found a dead woman washed up on the beach yesterday morning.' Staring at the ground, scattered with fish scales and guts, I hear a popping sound as my teeth grind against each other. 'Why didn't you say something, Miss? Why didn't you tell me?'

I shrug dismissively. 'I didn't want to bother you with it.'

'Bother me with it? Missy…' he shook his head. 'Don't you think discovering a dead person is something you ought to tell someone?'

'I did tell someone. I told the police.'

'Ah, the police,' he says, nodding. 'Well, that policeman also mentioned you saw something else on the beach. A mermaid?'

My body heats with anger and embarrassment. 'I know what you're thinking. But I also know what I saw. It wasn't human. It had pale skin, and a fish's tail.'

Gust scoffs. 'A fish's tail? Missy…'

'What?' I nip.

Gust's face is placid. 'Maybe Detective Shaw…'

'Maybe Detective Shaw *what?*'

He sighs. 'Nothing.'

'Maybe he was right? Maybe I *am* imagining things?'

'I didn't say that.'

'No, but it's what you're thinking? Is that why you left this morning without me? Because Detective Shaw told you to?'

'I'm trying to do what's best for you.'

'I'm not a child.'

Gust looks at me cold. 'Let me tell you something, Missy. It is very well known, especially by people like us, that there are strange things in the ocean. But these are stories. Mermaids do not exist, do they? They don't exist. They're stories.'

I stare at my father, stare right through him, right through his disbelief. 'You don't understand,' I whisper. 'It was *her*.'

'Who?'

I inhale a breath. It tastes of fish and decaying seaweed and the chalkiness of seagull shit. 'Neve.'

'Listen to me,' he grips my arm. 'Missy, listen. After your mother died, I saw her too. And I heard her. I didn't know what was real. And then I realised it was all in my mind.'

I shake my head. 'This is different. Why won't you believe me?'

'I want you to feel better,' he says. 'I do. But we both know that you've always had a vivid imagination. I'm just asking you to listen to yourself.'

'You're just going to pretend like she didn't exist?'

We go back and forth in this way for a while, and none of his answers are ever enough. But I refuse to give up. In the end, tired of his avoidance, I ask the biggest question of all. 'How did she die? Tell me.'

There is a long silence. Just the lapping of the waves and the splash of seagulls diving for fish. My father shakes his head as if he is guilty of something he doesn't want to admit.

'Your mother,' he says. 'She drowned.'

'That's not what *Avô* says.'

'Your grandfather believes what he wants to believe. That's just how he copes. It's too overwhelming. He refuses to see that the most obvious, simple answer is the truth.'

'But she could swim. And *Avô* said her body was never found. Was it?'

'He says that so there could be a chance of her coming back. We know she's not coming back, right, Miss?'

'Why does he say the sea took her?'

'People deal with things in their own way. Your grandfather lost his only child. You can't tell him how to grieve. Your mother drowning is the only explanation. If you don't agree, then you're opening yourself up to his mad stories of sea monsters.'

'It doesn't make sense. How could she disappear? Something must have happened to her…'

'What are you looking for? What do you expect to find? Stop torturing yourself.'

I feel the slap of accusation in what he says. 'Perhaps you *do* think I'm going mad.'

'I think it's not healthy for you to be spending so much time at that lighthouse. Frightening yourself with imaginary things.'

'You know why I go to the lighthouse? It's because I feel her there. More than I ever felt her in that shack you call a house.'

'I think it might be best I go out on the *Senhora* with Gil for a while. You stay back, keep your feet dry.' He says the words to offer me comfort, but they come from a cold place, of anger and bitterness. We glare at each other for a moment, beyond words.

'Fine,' I say. 'I've got to go. I've got a job to do.'

My father frowns. 'A job? For whom?'

I storm off and utter the words under my breath as I leave, 'For *Avô*.' I don't even bother to look at my father's reaction. Let the man do as he pleases.

Back at the harbour, a large, black truck with white letters painted on the side, is parked along the foreshore. I poke my head through the door and examine the cab. Dust prickles my nose and the leather seats don't look very comfortable. The steering wheel sits high up but I shouldn't have too much trouble working the gears.

The large rectangular tray is empty, for now, but it looks like it could carry a fair amount of coal. The door squeaks open and, stepping up on the running board, I climb into the cab, grabbing the steering wheel. My boots tap the pedals. I turn the key in the ignition and the truck sputters to life. It has been a while, but the intuitive movements return almost instantly and before I know it, I'm rolling along the dirt road toward the tramline.

Wharfies busy themselves at the dock, loading carts and laughing with each other, probably about nothing deeper than the futility of women. The truck rolls to a stop and I yank the handbrake. When I step out, the men gaze in my direction.

I approach one of them. He's dressed in long blue overalls and a felt cap, not overly clean. He's shorter than the rest of them, younger. He smiles at me. His teeth look dazzlingly white against the black coal marks smudging his face.

'So, you're the new delivery girl?'

'Guess so.'

'Aren't you cold?' He looks me in the eyes but points down to my crotch, and adds, 'Your belt's undone.' My face flushes and my hands shake as I fumble with the buckle. 'Don't mind me,' he laughs. 'I'm a braggard.'

I follow him to the huge pile of coal, where two sacks of the stuff are lined up, ready to go. 'What's a braggard? A type of beggar?'

'It's what people call a joker.' He sticks his hand out to me. 'My name's Flea.'

I shake it. 'Missy Green.'

A rat scurries by. I flinch.

'What's the matter?' Flea asks as he bends to heave one of the sacks onto his shoulder. For a little guy, he is strong. 'Afraid of catching the plague?'

I bend to lift the other sack of coal. 'Aren't you?' The sack is heavier than it looks, weighs a tonne. It's lumpy and awkward in my arms.

'Not all rats carry plague, you know. Need a hand?' His voice comes from behind me, and I turn my back so he can't see me struggling.

'I'm fine.' The sack slips from my grasp and topples to the ground.

Flea laughs.

'Did I say something funny?'

'You sure you don't need a hand?' He looks over his shoulder at me.

I grit my teeth. 'Yes, I'm sure.' Using the strength in my legs to lift the sack, I carry it a few yards then slam it onto the back of the truck. My heart rate increases, and I've broken out in a sweat.

'See you tomorrow, Missy Green,' Flea says as he salutes me. 'That's it?'

'How much coal do you think one lighthouse needs? You're coming back tomorrow, aren't ya?' he calls over his shoulder as he rejoins the other wharfies at the dock.

I climb back into the cab and start up the truck's engine. The gears grind as I accelerate and circle around, away from the docks and back along the harbourfront toward the hill. The incessant rattling throbs my ears and the dust wafting in from the road stings my eyes. I must get my hands on a pair of driving goggles.

When I reach the base of the hill, I put the truck in first and take the incline steadily, trying to understand its limit. Slowly the gleaming white tower appears from over the ridge, and I pull up outside the keeper's cottage. A thin trail of grey smoke puffing from the chimney tells me *Avô* has run out of patience for this morning's coal delivery. My pulse quickens in my neck. I'll blame my lateness on Gust and his betrayal. I don't want to do anything that will upset *Avô*, I need him to keep his end of our agreement.

Avô piles a plate with steaming potatoes, carries it to the table and places it in front of me. He sits at the other end, pats his pockets, and retrieves his pipe. 'Right, girl. What is it you want to know about her?'

I fork a lump of boiled potato into my mouth as I ask my first question. 'Everything. I want to know what she was like when she was young. About when she was born... How she looked and sounded and behaved. I want to know how she really died, and, if it's possible she could still be... I don't know, out there, somewhere.'

Avô taps out the old tobacco from his pipe, flicking the tiny bits of ash to the ground, and stuffs it with fresh. 'Still alive, you mean?'

'Well, maybe not alive, but…'

'Where do you want me to start, child?'

'Start from the beginning.'

Avô squints, lights his pipe, puffs, and sits back in his chair, letting it rest on the table in front of him, smoke coiling from the end.

'From the beginning you say? Well, your mother, Neve, was born in the mountains. That's where we were living, my wife and I, when she was born,' he says. 'That's why we called her Neve. Portuguese for snow. I never really liked the name *Neve*.' The smoke from his pipe obscures his face. 'I always thought it sounded too little-girlish. But your grandmother chose it. I was hoping for a boy, so when she popped out a girl, I let her choose the name.'

Staring into the potato steam, I think about my grandmother, the woman I never knew, and wonder about my own mother's bond with her.

'She was a beautiful baby, your mother. Almost never cried. Easy to take care of even though life in the mountains was rough. I moved to *Foz do Douro*, a small town on the Atlantic Ocean, on the outskirts of *Porto*, when your mother was two years old.' His face lights up. '*Farol de Felgueiras*. What a beauty she was. Made me fall in love with towers, she did. Built in eighteen hundred and eighty-six. Thirty-two feet of raw stone granite, beautiful red lantern, right on the breakwater wall.'

Anticipation ripples through my body. Never before has *Avô* spoken so many words about my mother. At this moment, they mean more to me than air. I am greedy for more. Give them to me in huge lungfuls, my chest pleads. But I am conscious that once he sees how desperate I am, he will cut them off.

'Just you and her? *Avó* stayed in the mountains?'

Avó's gaze drifts to a faraway place. 'My wife never saw the sea.'

I wonder what that would be like, to have never beheld its vast blue depths. To have never even stood on the shore and have the waves break upon your bare feet. Unfathomable.

'What happened to her?'

Avó shakes his head. 'Another time, girl.' He continues, 'Neve was a well-behaved child. Obedient. Until she turned twelve or thirteen years old. Then her rebellious streak came out.' He smiles. 'I guess that's where you get it from. She was never a bad girl, you understand. But she did require a heavier hand. Then she turned sixteen, and… in came the boys.'

'My father?'

Avó reaches across the table for a fork, digs into the soft potato and shovels some into his mouth. 'By the time we had taken up residency here, your mother had no time for life in the lights.'

Avó finishes the plate of potatoes and pushes it away. He leans back, places his hands on his belly. 'She did everything she could to find her way out of it. I told her to slow down, she had plenty of time. But she got married to your father and, not long after, she got pregnant.'

'How old was my mother when she met my father?'

'She was just nineteen when she had you. Count backward nine months.' *Avó* leans his forearms on the table, shakes his head. He picks up his pipe, relights it and inhales. 'She was just a girl,' he says, almost to himself. 'I told her, if she wanted to get rid of it, I would have supported her.'

All the moisture drains from my mouth. I stare at him, unblinking, trying to process what I have just been told. Finally, I say, 'You would have aborted me?'

The old man waves his hand dismissively. 'Oh, please, girl. Don't be so melodramatic. You're here, aren't you? Besides, Neve was in no shape to take care of an infant. Living in that shack your father calls a house.'

I slump in my chair. My grandfather wounds me with my own insults. This conversation is more painful than I had anticipated.

8

Wednesday

The sky beyond the bedroom curtains was tar black. The rain started around five o'clock in the morning while Shaw was in bed, trying to find sleep. It began as a whispering in the air then the clouds coughed out great beads of water that beat down against the pane of glass. The apartment was cold, but even still, he felt suffocated under the bedsheets. Sweat coated his back, he rolled from side to side, until eventually, he sat on the edge of the bed with his head in his hands and a tightness in his jaw from the constant clenching.

Early rising was habitual for Shaw. A legacy of his childhood, burdened with the daily task of fetching the family's water because the pipes in their building were home to a large quantity of maggots and the water was filthy and unsafe for drinking. His brothers were too young, their arms too skinny, to carry more than one bucket between them. Shaw had the advantage of age: those few extra years allowing that teenage muscle to develop in his forearms and shoulders that his Ma made sure were being put to better use than down the boxing ring. Early rising didn't bother him. He had learned, over the years, to accept it. In fact, during the war it had been an advantage. What annoyed him now was that sleep never found him in the hours preceding.

His apartment was on the third floor of an Art Deco block in the heart of Widow's Peak. Beneath were two floors of identical apartments with identical layouts. The front doors all opened around a central foyer and afforded very little privacy, but he only rarely interacted with his neighbours. One was an elderly chap who seldom left the apartment, and the other, a mysterious one-armed fellow who often departed on business even earlier than Shaw.

Shaw lit a lamp and made his way to the dresser. He poured water from the pitcher into the basin and slapped some of it on his face, its iciness trickling down his back. Picking up his shaving soap and brush, he began a lather and applied it to his face. Gripping his blade at an angle against his skin, his hand moved in short, controlled strokes, passing it over his face twice then rinsing off the foam in the wash basin. Wiping the residual soap from his face and neck with a towel, he splashed on some cologne then dressed in a fresh three-piece suit and laced up his boots. From a shallow dish on the bedside table, he collected his wedding ring and wristwatch. He paused when he noticed his wife's gold wedding band, stared at it for a moment, then left the apartment.

Despite the grand marble entrance, polished brass railings, and modern design, the apartment block had been an unhappy compromise between Shaw and his wife, Mary. It aroused, as she put it, absolutely no emotional reaction. He agreed it was not a building that provoked strong affection, but for Shaw, as soulless as the block was, its dark brick exterior was at least architecturally inoffensive and quite a few steps up from where he had grown up. At least there was no lead in the pipes.

They had moved in three months before Shaw joined the police force and it could not have been more different from the home Mary had imagined: a cottage or some such, with a large garden and far too many rooms than they could ever find use for.

An opening had sprung up at Widow's Peak hospital and Mary was quick to apply. Though she was young and relatively new to the profession, with her field experience, compassionate nature and nursing instinct, the job was hers before she even had a chance to charm the pants off the doctors who interviewed her. So it was that they moved from her parents' mansion in Sydney's Rose Bay and relocated with their scarce belongings to the coastal town of Widow's Peak.

Shaw opened the door to the street and put his head down against the stinging rain. In these early hours of the morning, before sunrise, Widow's Peak seemed a lonely city, especially when he walked through it alone. No wonder, Shaw thought, who walks alone in the streets at night?

The sad, the mad. The lost, the lonely. The homeless. The sleepless.

The buildings, bathed in rain, pulsated mysteriously in the spectral light. Shaw wrapped his coat tighter as he passed the isolated streets, the closed businesses, the absence of people, the gleam from the streetlamps offering little consolation. In the alleys and street corners, darkness seemed to collect in a solid mass. A cat slinked across the muddy road in front of him. It paused and gave Shaw a hard stare, bothered at being caught in its attempt to pillage scraps from unattended garbage bins.

Fifteen minutes later, Shaw kicked the mud off his shoes at Widow's Peak Police Station. He marched through the empty rooms, heading straight for his office. Removing his overcoat, he collapsed in the chair behind his desk.

Midge popped her head in. 'Would you like some tea?' As early as it was, he could always count on Midge being there before him.

'I'm all right, thanks,' Shaw said, brushing water from his hair.

Midge pointed to the ceiling. 'He's expecting you,' she said. 'But he's in one of his moods.'

Shaw sighed and stood up.

Inspector-General James Mitchell had come to Australia from Scotland and joined the New South Wales Police service in 1884. His marked ability in his duties had earned him rapid promotion, and he was appointed Inspector after only fourteen years. In 1920, he departed on six months leave of absence, to investigate new methods in crime detection in America, England and the rest of Europe. Shaw's boss possessed an unashamed obsession with his search for new, modern police methods.

Shaw opened the door to Mitchell's office. The buzz of electric lamps filled the room. Mitchell was a man of tall build and was presently reclining on his chair, his long legs resting on his desk. As Shaw entered, Mitchell returned his feet to the floor and stood to greet him.

'Morning, Inspector,' Shaw said, sitting down opposite his boss. 'How was the trip?'

Inspector Mitchell's light brown hair appeared greyer since Shaw had last seen him. He had always kept it short, but it was starting to thin out too.

'A great success, Detective. I learned quite a bit about what our compatriots are doing.'

Shaw nodded. 'I gather this isn't a social meeting?'

'Indeed, Detective. I'd like to ask your opinion on something.'

Mitchell was dressed, as he always was, immaculately, in suit and tie. His shoes, polished to a shine, glinted the warm yellow glow of the electric lamps as he walked to the liquor cabinet against the wall. He poured liquid from two separate bottles into two cut crystal glasses, one as clear as water, the other slightly golden. He handed the latter to Shaw.

'Are we celebrating?' Shaw asked.

'Just taste this,' Mitchell replied. Shaw brought the glass to his nostrils and inhaled sweet notes of caramel and vanilla. He took a swig. 'What do you think?'

Shaw held the glass out and examined the contents. He smacked his lips. 'It's good,' he said. 'Why? What is it?'

Mitchell held out the other glass. 'Now try this one.'

Shaw accepted the glass of clear liquid. He dipped his nose into the glass, but it was without fragrance. He sipped. An immediate burning sensation entered his mouth and seared the lining of his throat as he swallowed. Shaw coughed.

Mitchell laughed. 'Wouldn't exactly liken it to fine French cognac?'

Shaw glanced up at Mitchell, handing him back the glasses. 'What do you know about France, you war-shy bastard?'

Inspector Mitchell laughed. 'The liquor you've just sampled is part of an import drive,' he said as he placed the two glasses of liquor on the desk between him and Shaw. 'You've heard of our fine nation's capital, I assume?'

Shaw nodded. 'When you indecisive Australians couldn't decide between Sydney or Melbourne, Canberra was chosen as a compromise.'

'Contrary to that belief, the site was in fact chosen because of its cool climate.' Mitchell pushed the glasses of liquor to one side and spread open a large map on his desk, shifting it so that it aligned with the edge of the desk, and pointed at it with his finger. 'Here it is. Canberra. A hundred and fifty miles inland from Widow's Peak. Should take you about five hours to get there. If you leave now, you'll arrive in time for the afternoon drop.'

Shaw cleared his throat. 'The afternoon drop?'

Inspector Mitchell sat back in his chair. 'Thanks to the liquor laws, these days Canberra is more dry than wet,' he said. 'But the laws don't stop the capital from finding a way. Especially when it's full of thirsty politicians.'

Mitchell reminded Shaw about the politicians preventing the granting of liquor licences. He told him the laws meant that it was impossible to obtain a licence to open a bar, but bringing alcohol into Canberra and drinking it there was not a problem. All over the Federal Capital Territory people were making their own booze. In bathtubs. But the wealthy in Canberra, and in Parliament, were still paying a lot of money for the real stuff.

Shaw pulled his cigarette case out of his jacket pocket and lit up. 'You want me to find out who's responsible for bringing bathtub booze into the FCT?'

Inspector Mitchell leaned forward, clasping his hands on top of the map. 'For the time being, Canberra looks likely to remain dry, unless someone builds a high wall across the border, or unless King O'Malley's idea of introducing the sale of liquor under Government control is put into operation.'

Shaw drew back on the cigarette. 'King O'Malley, the politician?'

Mitchell nodded. 'Minister of State for Home Affairs. Quite a colourful character. Very influential.'

Mitchell told Shaw that King O'Malley was responsible for having the legislation passed to prohibit the granting of liquor licences in the Federal Capital Territory. That temperance advocates in Canberra were now campaigning for a total ban on alcohol. And O'Malley was urging total prohibition in place of the present law.

'His views are likely to carry considerable weight, when Parliament gets down to the question,' Inspector Mitchell said. 'That means he'd have total control over the liquor trade. Which means he's about to become a very rich man. And Prohibitionists are keen to get his views nation-wide.'

'It was my understanding that the laws only prevented the *sale* of liquor, not its transport and consumption,' Shaw said.

Mitchell nodded. 'For the time being, there's nothing illegal about bringing it in. As I said, the pollies down there are thirsty buggers, Detective. And I'm not just talking about booze. They want to control the trade in order to funnel money into building their new neighbourhoods. And King O'Malley is not happy with the current state of affairs. To the public, it's because he believes the liquor business has increased intemperance, but between you and me, it's because he believes there is a competitor down there who is monopolising the liquor trade, which, according to him, should be his. This competitor, his rum is far superior, as you can taste. And he's selling it to the pubs for a much lower price. King O'Malley wants it to stop. That's where you come in, Detective.'

Shaw exhaled smoke.

Mitchell rubbed a hand across his clean-shaven jaw. 'And

here's the kicker: I received a tip off that the supply is coming from Widow's Peak.'

Shaw nodded, leant forward, and crushed his cigarette in the ashtray on Inspector Mitchell's desk. 'I believe I may know who this competitor is.'

Mitchell raised his eyebrows. 'You already have a lead?'

'I think it may have something to do with the woman who washed up on the beach yesterday morning.'

Mitchell nodded, waiting. 'I see. What are we doing about that murder?'

Shaw cleared his throat. 'Sir, we still haven't established that she was murdered.'

'Well, consider it established, Detective. What can you tell me about our mystery man, this bootlegger?'

'Sonny Fynn,' Shaw said. 'Nothing much. Apart from what's in the war registers. No records. No priors. He was also the dead woman's husband to be.'

'Have you got a photograph of him?'

'We have his military ID photographs. He won medals.'

Inspector Mitchell clapped his hands together. 'So, you've got his photograph. You know what he looks like. And if he shows his face in Widow's Peak, you bring him in. All right? Now, I've agreed to send my best man to Canberra to sort out this rum-running fiasco.'

'Sir, you're asking me to go to Canberra… today?' Shaw could feel the pounding of an oncoming headache. A body to investigate. A mystifying, nineteen-year-old fisherman's daughter to keep his eye on. And now this. He bit his tongue.

Inspector Mitchell gave Shaw a hard stare, just like the cat he had interrupted earlier in the dark alley. 'If we do this, Detective,

King O'Malley has promised to fund my proposal.' Shaw had heard about Inspector Mitchell's proposal for a new force that dealt with serious crimes, using all the mod cons from Europe. Mitchell raised his eyebrows. 'How'd you like to lead a team like that?'

Shaw nodded, considering. Finally, he asked, 'Why me?'

'You want to move up here, right, Detective? Think of it this way… you're going to be my eyes and ears down there. Besides, you Irish are a race of drunks, are you not?' Inspector Mitchel held up the glass of clear liquor, the one that had seared Shaw's throat. 'You'll be able to sniff out the real stuff from this.' He stood and walked to the potted fern in the corner of his office. 'You've got two days to bring him in.'

Shaw shook his head. 'Two weeks.'

Inspector Mitchell poured the glass of clear, bathtub gin into the soil. 'One.'

Shaw sighed, resigned. 'Agreed.'

Shaw stood and they shook hands. He turned to walk to the door.

'Oh, and Shaw?'

Shaw glanced back at Inspector Mitchell. 'Sir?'

'Take the car with you. Unless of course you Irish still prefer the horse and buggy?'

9

Shaw checked the petrol tank under the front passenger seat and placed four extra cans in the boot. After swinging open the driver's side door, he removed his jacket, laid it on the back seat, and climbed in behind the wheel, stashing his gun in the glove compartment behind a pair of leather driving goggles. He turned the key in the ignition, and the Model T cranked to life. The tyres made their monotonous hiss over the rain-washed road and deserted backstreets until he came to the main road through town.

The rain had eased by the time Widow's Peak disappeared from his rear mirror, but the dirt roads had already turned to muddy strips. Shaw wound his way along the narrower trails that headed south along the coast, then took the left-hand turn at Kiama. As he drove, he considered Inspector Mitchell's proposal and promise of promotion. Perhaps this was his chance to move up in his career. After all, this is what they had wanted.

He, and Mary.

As young couples do when they're in love, with life, with each other, Mary had cast off her upper-class roots in the service of her career, but not before her parents' social connections secured Shaw an interview with Inspector Mitchell at the Widow's Peak Police Department. It was all thanks to his wife's family connections, and his time fighting in service of the Crown. No one in his right mind would give a blue-collar job to an Irishman of absolutely no social standing, even if the number of capable Australian men had significantly dwindled since the war. Most of them had returned with shattered bodies and shattered minds and were shoved aside.

As a new recruit, he had trodden carefully at first, knowing that he was on a probation more rigorous and protracted than any provisional assessment from the senior officers.

He had hoped, if not to earn the respect and acceptance from his peers, then for their tolerance. But he was aware that he was regarded with wariness. That was three years ago, now. Thanks to the wholeness of his body, Shaw had walked in on his two legs, and kept on walking, up the ranks, without much resistance.

His first case had been a test, which he had successfully passed. He had hoped that promotion to detective would have helped alleviate the cultural divide, and in many ways, it had. He now commanded the respect and obedience of the junior officers, as well as the thugs and criminal underworld of Widow's Peak. But Australians had their ways, and they were firmly set. Now Shaw's boss was offering him the chance to move even further up the ladder. But with this promotion came a career bedevilled with politics. Top level policing always was.

Shaw pulled the Model T to a stop on the side of the dirt track, a few yards from the sheer fifty-foot drop to a small inlet of churning sea. He refilled the petrol tank then stepped closer and peered over the ledge. The water was bounded by high sandstone cliffs on each side, tangled with bushes. The drop stretched away from him; his vision blurring momentarily. A strong gust of wind lifted his body and suddenly he felt as though he was going over.

Shaw's legs buckled and he staggered backward, gripping a shrub for support. He told himself to snap out of it, he was safe, but another part of his mind felt – *knew* – the ground was going to crumble away from under his feet. He took three deep breaths to calm his pounding heart and wiped a sweaty palm on his trousers.

Back in the car, with shaking hands, he lit up, the smoke and tobacco coursing through his bloodstream steadying his nerves. Heights. Fucking heights. As he smoked, he thought about the dead woman, Lara Harvey, about her death. How did she end up on that beach? Did she fall? From a height? Was she pushed? Or did she jump? If she did fall to her death, or if someone dumped her body out at sea, either way her last moments would have been cold, frightening, and lonely.

It was a thirty-minute drive inland along the banks of the Minnamurra River and through bush to Jamberoo Mountain Road. This section of the roadway was steep, containing several hairpin bends through dense rainforest. Shaw took the hill in first gear but when the Model T stalled and skidded on the greasy wet road, he realised it was much too steep. The reverse gear was lower, and going backwards meant the gravity-fed petrol could reach the carburettor, so he turned the car around and ascended the slope in reverse. The track cut through forest abounding with every species of prickly bush and bramble. The vines were so thickly entwined around the huge trees, any light from the sky was obscured. He progressed slowly through the rainforest, passing waterfalls, along the ridgelines, toward the very top of the escarpment.

Upon reaching the apex, Shaw stopped at a lookout to refill the fuel tank, but the cloud was so thick up there, he could not see anything. He passed through the town of Robertson, a village with a few buildings; a school, a church, a post office and a butter factory. Just a collection of sandstone buildings lining a muddy street at the edge of a rainforest.

Shaw focused his attention on the changing scenery, which still felt alien to him. The air that made its way through the car was not fishy or salty, but meadow-sweet and all around were intensely green fields. He passed potato farms and lush pastures with contentedly grazing cows until the road finally brought him to Moss Vale.

It was another two hours through farmland and forest until Goulburn and, after several hundred miles of mostly bad roads, tiredness caught up with Shaw. He could manage tiredness, but what he longed for was rest. Peace, quiet.

Surrounded by distant hills, an expanse of land stretched before him that may have once been a lake but had long since dried out: a vast body of invisible water butting up against the federal highway. A memory. A ghost.

Finally, the Model T swooped down a hillside, and, sensing that Canberra must be somewhere near because of the fine tarred road, Shaw accelerated along the highway. A row of tin sheds flashed past, a string of cottages on the left, a big building on the right, then into what seemed like open country again. Was that Canberra, he wondered. Had he missed it?

Shaw took a sharp turn to the right which brought him to the crest of a rise. Several buildings loomed; the squatting shapes appeared to be isolated. Then suddenly, right before him, was Parliament House. He recognised it from a photo in the newspaper. It covered acres, rising up two stories, with surrounding manicured gardens, like a sprawling white palace.

So, this was Canberra, the capital of his adoptive country. But where? Unless someone explained it all to him or thrust a map of the city in his hands, he would have to assume all of its residents dwelled in holes. Nothing like the ramshackle urban centres of Dublin or London, or even Sydney. In this widespread valley, the dominating impression was of open space. Nothing but a few public buildings sprawled across a grassy plain.

Shaw circled back around Parliament House and came out at the rear. He branched to the left, followed the road beside Capitol Hill and found a main road.

Little more than a large village, all built to a plan, a mathematical equation. And hundreds of acres of space reserved for future buildings. Maybe *this* was what Mary had in mind when she said she wanted a cottage with a garden. Maybe they should have moved to Canberra. But why build a city in no-man's land, so far away from everywhere? Why lavish thousands of pounds upon it? Hundreds of thousands. Why choose *this* location, where its chances of success were less assured than if it were a seaboard city in some prosperous industrial or farming area? There must be more sinister reasons than its cool climate, as Inspector Mitchell had suggested, surely? Australians did not make much sense. Shaw felt as though he had found himself among a race of lunatics with a mania for town-planning.

A little further along, he passed a hospital and, curving to the right, came upon several small businesses, a newspaper office, a laundry, a cordial factory, bakeries, and the like. He parked the Model T in front of a small grocery store, grabbed the empty cans from the boot and stepped inside.

The clerk eyed him suspiciously. 'Can I help you?'

'Good afternoon,' Shaw said as he held up the empty cans. 'Would you have some petroleum to fill these?'

The clerk nodded and motioned for Shaw to follow him to the rear of the store. They exited a back door into an open space. Shaw handed the cans to the clerk and waited as he filled them, a slight breeze whispering through the trees across the street. A branch bowed and let off a loud rumble that seemed to be coming from further along. The rumble intensified, drew nearer, and it took a moment before Shaw realised it was not the tree that was rumbling, but something entirely different.

Then he saw it.

When Shaw had set off for Canberra on Inspector Mitchell's goose chase, he did not know what he was, in fact, chasing. But when he saw it, so out of place, it hit him like a bolt of lightning. Blood and adrenaline rushed through his limbs.

MORROW'S COAL & ICE.

A truck. A delivery truck, the white painted letters clearly on its side, filled with crates of liquor on the back shelf. The truck was heading east, out of town. He forced the panic down, and then he moved.

Shaw raced back through the grocery store, with no time to apologise for almost knocking a gentleman over as he passed. He scanned the street for movement. None. The wind died, the leaves stopped rustling, even the man cursing Shaw for running into him had calmed down.

In those frozen seconds, Shaw heard the rumble of the truck on the road behind the newspaper office. Before he could react, the truck was off. Shaw swore when his own clumsy attempts at opening the Model T's door slowed him further. When it finally flung open, he threw himself inside and revved the engine.

Weaving dangerously out of the parking space and along the main road, he pushed the car to its limit, over fifty miles an hour. Catching sight of the delivery truck on the highway, heading east toward Queanbeyan, he floored the pedal.

His heart raced; his arms tingled. Canberra disappeared and the highway transformed into isolated, winding back roads. Twilight was falling and the mean crescent moon cast almost no light at all. The Model T shook violently, the mechanical symphony of the engine, drivetrain whine, and tyres at the edge of adhesion all worked together to propel the car forward. But driving fast meant accelerating hard, braking late, risk taking.

The ear-splitting bang of metal against wood vibrated through Shaw, and he watched in horror as the tray of the delivery truck slammed into a tree. He pumped the breaks and the Model T rolled to a stop on the side of the dusty highway. He opened the glove compartment, pocketed his gun and jumped from the driver's seat.

Shaw ran along the road through the long grass and saw the driver attempting and failing to start his stalling truck. Shaw reached his arm through the partly opened window and clamped his hand over the driver's knuckles, crushing his fingers and ripping the keys from the ignition.

The driver raised his arm and elbowed Shaw in the face. Shaw recoiled, blood gushing from his nose. While he attempted to stem the flow, the driver opened the passenger side door of the truck and launched himself out. As soon as his boots hit the ground, he climbed over a wooden fence and fled into the surrounding shrub.

Shaw shoved the gun into his belt and gave chase, blood dripping from his nostrils onto his shirt. He scaled the fence. A jarring pain shot from his ankle to his knee. *Fuck.* Twisted ankle. His heart raced but he knew he had to keep going. Limping over loose rubble, he tumbled down a steep rocky slope. He pushed forward, the scrub scratching his face as he ran. His breath came in small spurts, hot and nervous. At his sides, his fingers curled into sweaty fists, swinging forward as if to make him faster.

Feet slipping, Shaw grasped at branches to steady himself. His lungs screamed and he willed his muscles to go far beyond his usual demands. The driver's boots crunched over the stones further along, over Shaw's own furious, rasping breathing.

Branches attacked him, sticks snapped under his feet, and huge grey rocks seemed to appear out of nowhere as if to try and stop him. His suit was shredded to rags, dirty and tattered. His throbbing ankle made his legs feel like lead, but he was closing the gap between them.

Then Shaw stopped.

The driver crouched low behind a bush, attempting to hide, not five feet away.

'*Freeze!*' Shaw yelled, gun drawn, safety off. 'Put your hands in the air.'

'Or what?' the driver said. 'You're going to shoot?'

'Aye, I'm going to blow some daylight into that head of yours.'

The man made a break for it. Shaw lunged, pinning him to the ground. Mud smeared the man's face and dripped from his matted hair. Shaw could smell him – the stench of his sweat. It conjured up images of mud-spattered soldiers in deep, waterlogged trenches.

Shaw shook the image from his mind. 'Widow's Peak PD,' he said. 'Don't move.'

There was silence. Then the man's head tipped backwards into the mud, allowing the tension in his body to ebb away. He let out a snort, then the laughter couldn't stop. He was choking on it.

Shaw released his hold and let the man sit up. 'You find something funny, arsehole?'

'Did you say you were Widow's Peak police?' the man said. 'Get off me, man. I didn't do anything illegal.'

'So why'd you run?' Shaw asked, still breathless.

'I thought you were one of O'Malley's boys. They shoot without asking,' the man said, still out of breath himself.

Shaw wiped his nose on his sleeve. The blood had finally stemmed. Either that or he couldn't make it out against the thick black slime smeared all over his arm. 'You did a number on my nose,' he said.

The man laughed, clapped Shaw on the shoulder. 'Can't blame a bloke who was fighting for his life, can you?'

Inspector Mitchell had warned Shaw that there was nothing illegal about bringing booze across the border. And this guy wasn't going anywhere, not after that chase, and out here in the middle of nowhere surrounded by thick shrub.

They sat side by side in the mud. Shaw retrieved his cigarette case and offered one up to the man. Shaw stuck one in his mouth, struck a match, and both of them lit up. They smoked silently for a while, gazing up at the trees, almost impossible to see now the sky above was dark. Listened to the calming wash of nocturnal sounds: the rhythms of frogs, the hypnotic calls of chirruping crickets, the buzz in the air.

Finally, Shaw spoke. 'Why go through all this if all you have to do is drive across the border and carry back as much as you want? Why go to the trouble of bringing it all the way from Widow's Peak?'

The man took his time to answer, drawing back on his cigarette, the orange tip the only thing visible in the dark. 'That scatter of cosy houses with their pretty little gardens you passed nearly two miles back? That's the suburb of Eastlake. And that big building on the right was the King's House. King O'Malley. Further over, a mile or so beyond Eastlake, more are forming the beginning of future suburbs.'

In his hurry, Shaw had overlooked those.

The man shook his head. 'The King. He runs this whole place, mate. He says he's for prohibition, but reality is he has a monopoly over the entire liquor trade. Why do you think we take the trouble to bring superior quality booze all the way from Widow's Peak?'

'So you *do* work for Sonny Fynn?'

The man grinned. 'You've heard of him?'

Shaw nodded. 'I'm trying to track him down. He's suspected of killing his girlfriend. Why would you protect a murderer?'

'You let a man like King O'Malley loose in Parliament, there's no telling what powers he will unleash. He wants to control the whole country. Sonny Fynn is making sure that doesn't happen.'

Shaw drew back on his cigarette, the paper making a satisfying sizzling sound as it burned. His body was abuzz with nicotine, with adrenaline. Finally, he flicked the butt into the soggy ground. 'Any idea who supplies it to Mr Fynn?' he asked.

'The rum?' The man shook his head. 'I'm just a delivery driver, mate.'

The buzz faded from Shaw's body, and, in its place, a heavy fatigue enveloped him. His eyes cast to the ground. His body ached, his limbs twitched, heavy, weary. 'Didn't think so.'

10

Quarta-feira

MY hands are covered in blood and algae and bits of broken shell. The first thing I am aware of is the pain. It feels as though my head has caved in on itself. The throbbing. Even as I consider it, it aches. It takes all my energy to lift my head from the pillow.

Rain drums against the small, round window and I realise I've slept the whole morning. My breath comes fast as fear takes over and worms its way through me.

I don't want the wound in my head to get worse. I don't, I don't, but I can't make it stop. I cannot get the smell off me. I've tried scrubbing my head raw and pulling out strands of my hair by their roots, but still, the stench clings to me. That wound has become a part of me, like my shadow. The air is constantly thick with the pungent stench of rotten fish, the metallic smell of blood. I will never be rid of it.

A few moments pass before my breathing calms, and I realise it doesn't matter. It's there, and I can't make it go away. But maybe I can stop it from festering. My instinct is to run, but I can barely lift my legs. Besides, I have no desire to move from this bed. It is safe and warm, and strangely quiet in this muted tower. No wind. The lantern prisms aren't turning. Just the constant, muffled, patter of rain. White noise.

My head decays around me as I remember back to yesterday. A wave of anger washes over me like a breaker. I dive below it and let it roll me over. My father abandoned me. Again. Cast aside, just like the West Wind blew his daughter out to sea.

I've never thought about it much, but when he went away to war, that's what he did then, too. Cast me aside. Chose war over me. Now he chooses Gil over me. He kept me away from the boat, from the water, the only place I don't feel alone, the only place I feel any sense of joy or happiness. He stripped me of it. I prefer anger to pain, or fear. At least the anger distracts from the pain in my head. It helps me focus.

Hot shame spreads down my neck as I remember that my father spoke to Detective Shaw about me. The heat ripples from my neck and settles into my chest. When I think about Detective Shaw, my pulse races. I don't know why I care so deeply about what that man thinks of me. What does he see when he looks at me? A lonely fisherman's daughter with no friends, no prospects? And what is it about him that causes me to feel this way? I'm sure many women have been struck by his handsome face with those eyes, the smattering of freckles along his cheekbones, the hairs on the back of his hands. But there is something endearing about his composure, something beguiling about his thoughtful silences. He is a man that could take care of a woman. Protect her. I curse my father for whatever he said to him about me.

My father. I keep asking, *why would he do this to me?*

I'm just so angry all the time. There's this knot in my chest and my father's betrayal has worsened it. I feel it getting tighter and stronger, like it's choking me.

He won't tell me the truth about my mother. He is hiding it from me. He wants to keep me away from the boat, from the ocean, from *Avô*, from the lighthouse. I hate him in this moment. Even more than that, I hate myself for letting him do this to me.

Yesterday at the market I let my anger control me. From now on I will be in control of it. Channel it. I clench my fists as I realise with cold horror what I want.

Revenge.

I want to bring him down, strip him of everything he loves and holds dear. Punish him. I want him to pay. I think about what I could do to inflict a small amount of pain on the man. Nothing serious, just enough to get under his skin.

The idea strikes me. And now I know what I'm going to do.

I rush down the spiral staircase, barge through the lighthouse door into the rain-soaked day and practically slide down the hill to our fisherman's hut. The door is wide open, probably because my father has just arrived home from the harbour.

Slamming the front door, I stand over the fireplace and warm my fingers over the embers. Even when I stare down at their glow, anger slithers like a serpent into my mind and lies there, tightly coiled, waiting to strike. I hear him moving about his bedroom. I poke the fire with the stoker, disturbing the precarious glowing formation. A smouldering lump drops and rolls across the floor. The hot ember touches my bare foot, but I don't register the pain. I am frozen in place.

My father pretends he is not a superstitious man, but like all fishermen, he can't help it. If there is one thing he never leaves home without, it's his cap. If there is one thing that would drive him mad, it would be to go out on the *Senhora* without it. And it is my desire to hurt him where it hurts the most.

I wait for him to stop making noises from behind his bedroom door. I know he keeps his cap on the drawers, inside his wardrobe. The last place I want to be is in the same room as that man, but I force down my pride and creak the door ajar.

He is in his bed. Rain lashes against the window and his room is full of shadows. The sheets have fallen halfway off his body, and one of his legs dangles off the edge, as though he fell asleep a moment before his body was horizontal.

I slide in and, as I glance around the room, notice his wardrobe doors hang open and almost all of his items of clothing are spilling out of drawers, like entrails spilling from a soldier's stomach, as though someone has been rummaging through them. The thought that his cap might not be among them makes my mission more urgent. I don't want to be in here any longer than I need to be. I tiptoe to the wardrobe where I know he keeps his cap. It usually sits right on top of the drawers.

It's not here.

When I turn to look at my father, he's staring at me.

Breath catches in my throat.

I blink. Peering closer at his face, I step to him, hold my hand up, wave. Even at the height of day, with the rain thundering against the window, with his eyes wide open, he manages to sleep like an infant.

My eyes squeeze shut. I sneak back out, go to the fireplace to grab a match, but then I notice my collection of shells and stones on the windowsill, and something catches my eye. A glint of the knife. Take me, it says. Like the octopus, it beckons me to reach for it. Only this time, I *do* extend my hand. Before I know what I am doing, or why, my fingers grasp the handle. There is no turning back now. Something is telling me to end him.

Back in his bedroom, my father is now awake and sitting up in his bed. I close the door calmly and slowly turn around, take one step closer to him. He shakes his head. I had to, he says. He holds up his hands. Please, don't hurt me. Let me explain. The panic makes his weathered face appear at least ten years older.

'Don't hurt you?' I laugh. It comes out more maniacal than I intend. I can hear the anger in my voice. The hysteria.

My father attempts to leave the bed, but I don't allow it. I grab him by the arm and yank him back. Cover his mouth with the hand that is grasping the knife.

He struggles. Kicks his legs. I hold him down. Hold him still. Wrestle him into submission.

My other hand reaches up and forms a crescent. It encircles his throat. I am on top of him. His arms are caught beneath my knees. His legs, trapped under the sheets, try to break free. He wheezes. I refuse to let go of him. A tear escapes his eye and rolls down his temple. He gags, chokes, it goes on and on, unending. Then the sudden, ear-splitting shriek of a seagull snaps me out of this moment, and my eyes shoot to the left, and I am standing in my father's bedroom, staring down at him. He is sleeping peacefully in his bed. My right hand, held aloft, still grasps the knife.

The smell is different when my eyes regain their focus. So is the light. I realise it has stopped raining and the sun is making its slow descent. I'm not confused about where I am; I know I'm in my father's room. I just… don't know how I got here. Or for how long I have been standing here, brandishing a knife above my father's sleeping body.

Out of fear he will wake, out of fear I will do something I have no control over, I decide to give up my search. Right when I reach for the door, I notice his cap on the floor. I grab it and bolt through the door, my heart heavy in my stomach. The door clicks shut and relief spreads through me.

In our sitting room I sink to the floor, my whole body trembling. Now, I know. I know for certain: I need to stay as far away from my father as possible.

11

Thursday

THE purple sky paled as Detective Ronan Shaw drove the length of the Blue Mile tram line. The tracks ran on a strip of gravel along the shore toward the harbour, waves crashing on one side, shrubs strangling the other. He followed the line to the docks, where it came to an end. The water in the harbour was as grey as a newspaper, the sea not yet blue.

Shaw yawned. The drive back from Canberra through the night had taken its toll, all the while he wondered if his troubles had been worthwhile. When his head had hit the pillow sometime after three in the morning, sleep had found him for the first time in a long time, but he was paying for it now.

He jerked the car to a stop and yanked the handbrake. Stepping out, he rubbed his hands together. Winters here were nothing like those in Ireland, but somehow Shaw still shuddered from the bitterness in the air. He walked briskly to the Blue Mile docks where wharfies were shovelling piles of coal from carriages into crates, then loading them onto the boats. The air tasted musty, of soot, like the chimney in the tenement building he grew up in on O'Connell Street.

The slums of Dublin were worse than those in London or

Glasgow. Mortality rates through the roof. Shaw's family was one of the lucky ones. They only had to share their one room between five people: himself, his parents and his two younger brothers. Some families shared single rooms between ten. Such were the consequences of devout Catholicism and child-rearing.

His Ma bore the brunt of the poor housing conditions, having to cook over open fires, fetch and carry water from distant communal taps, up several flights of stairs, all the while attempting to keep draughty rooms warm, and wrangle three hyperactive sons. His Da, at least what remained of Shaw's memories of him, was often unemployed, or drunk, or both.

Shaw's ears pricked up. A voice he thought he recognised made his heart dive down into his stomach. He rounded a corner then stopped in his tracks, his body stiffening. Missy Green, barefoot and dressed in long-johns with only a thin cotton shirt, the curves of her body outlined through the fabric, was laughing with one of the wharfies. Shaw gazed in awe at her, this alluring young woman so at ease with herself, with her body. Her short dark hair fell in waves as she threw her head back and chortled. Carefree, seductive, and a bit wild.

Shaw was compelled to examine her further. Missy Green did not seem to care what men thought of her, she wasn't aware of the state of herself. This lack of self-awareness was incredibly arresting. He'd never seen it before. All of the women he'd met always seemed too preoccupied with what men wanted from them, they always seemed to question, somewhere in the back of their thoughts, what they could do to please a man. With Missy, there seemed to be none of that. She was just herself. She didn't care. She had no idea the effect she had on other men. On *him*.

She was casually at ease with the wharfie, and Shaw felt a

twinge of bitterness swell inside. The wharfie appeared younger, probably closer to Missy in age. Closer than who? Than *him*? Why the hell was he wondering whether he was too old for her? Shaw tried to banish the thought from his head, but he could not peel his eyes away from them.

Missy was a woman made up of contradictions. Her long slender fingers and trimmed nails were covered in the muck of dead fish. Her elegant neck and dark eyes competed with her nest of wind-whipped hair. Her beauty was disturbing. *She* was disturbing. He should have found her repulsive, with her rough edges, her saltiness. Instead, Shaw worried he'd become lured by it. By her. This girl, this woman, this… outcast.

Missy followed the wharfie to a pile of hessian sacks and bent to pick one up. Her long, lean arms cradled it with ease, and she carried it to the truck that was parked nearby. The truck with *Morrow's Coal & Ice* painted in white on the door.

Shaw steadied himself and walked toward it. 'Miss Green,' he said. 'What are you doing here?'

When Missy caught his eye, he could have sworn he saw her blush. A smear of dried brown dust cracked across her cheek as she smiled. 'I'm picking up some coal. For my grandfather.'

'Do you mind if I ask why you're driving Lara Harvey's delivery truck?' he asked, lighting a cigarette.

Her eyes widened. 'The dead woman? This was *her* delivery truck?'

Shaw pointed at her with his cigarette. 'You've got dust all over your face,' he said. 'Don't you own a pair of motoring goggles?'

Missy wiped her face with her sleeve. 'No, why, do you?'

'As it happens…'

The wharfie appeared between them and loaded one of the sacks on the tray. Missy motioned to him. 'This is Tommy Mathieson,' she said, elbowing him. 'He's a braggart with the plague.'

Shaw nodded. 'Bubonic or pneumonic?'

The wharfie nudged Missy in the side. 'Bubonic.'

Missy grimaced.

'How long have you been a wharfie, Mr Mathieson?' Shaw asked.

'What, me? Been working here almost a year. Trying to earn enough money to get out of town.'

'Why would that be, son?'

The young wharfie smiled. 'Mister, have you seen this place? It's where people come to die.'

Shaw glanced at Missy, then returned his gaze to the wharfie. 'Mind if I ask you a few questions, Mr Mathieson?' He offered him a cigarette. The wharfie looked at it warily but accepted. Shaw reached across with a match and the wharfie drew back and nodded.

'It's Flea by the way,' he said.

'Don't you know why I'm here, Flea? A woman's body washed up on the shore two days ago. Sometime between ten pm and two in the morning. I'm trying to locate anyone who might've had contact with her, leading up to her death.'

Flea's face was suddenly serious. 'Who was killed?'

'A woman by the name of Lara Harvey.' Flea looked down at the ground and nodded slowly. 'You knew her, then? You two were pals?'

Flea looked straight into Shaw's eyes. 'Let's get one thing straight about Lara Harvey,' he said. 'I might've known her, but she was nobody's *pal*.'

Shaw cleared his throat. 'What do you mean by that?'

Flea smirked and shook his head. 'Look, I'm not saying what happened to her was all right, but I won't make excuses for her. Lara wasn't a nice girl.'

'Did you see her the day she died? Did you see or hear anything unusual?'

Flea took a drag of his cigarette. 'In what way?'

'Did she seem upset to you?'

Flea shrugged. 'Last time I saw her she was her usual self. What are you getting at?'

'Was she the type of person who could've jumped?'

'Lara? Kill herself?' Flea shook his head. 'Doesn't seem likely to me.'

'Are you acquainted with her fiancé, Sonny Fynn?'

Flea laughed. 'Mister, everyone 'round here has heard of Sonny Fynn.'

'Did Lara ever talk to you about him?'

Flea snorted. 'She mentioned all the fine things he bought her.'

'Did she ever talk about having arguments with him?'

'You think he did it?' Flea asked.

'Piecing together a victim's final moments is very important,' Shaw said. 'What she was doing… Who she was with… With enough patience, you eventually come across a lead. Now, Sonny Fynn – did Lara seem afraid of him?'

'He's a scary bloke. You'd be a fool not to be afraid of him.'

'Do you know anyone else who might've wanted to harm Lara?'

'She wasn't too friendly, but I don't know anyone who had

any grudges against her.'

Shaw handed Flea his card. 'If you remember anything, you can reach my office on that number. Call anytime.'

Flea saluted him then winked at Missy. 'See you tomorrow, Miss.' He turned and walked away.

Missy's smile spread across her face as she watched Flea disappear into the crowd of men. There it was again. The bitterness scraped its finger along Shaw's stomach, green-eyed and irrational. She turned to Shaw with her doe eyes and her pouty lips, smelling like the ocean.

'You think it could be him, her fiancé?' she asked. 'Sonny Fynn?'

Shaw lit another cigarette, nodding. 'He's a strong suspect. Trying to find evidence against him's a priority right now.'

Missy opened the truck door. 'I've got to get this load up to the lighthouse.'

'I'll come with you.' Shaw regretted the words the second they left his lips. The feeling in his stomach had made him edgy, eager.

'What? Why?'

'I'm retracing Lara's steps,' Shaw said, walking around to the passenger side door. 'If she came into contact with your grandfather the day she died, I'll have a few questions for him.' He opened it and climbed into the truck's cab.

Missy's lips pouted even more. 'He doesn't like strangers,' she muttered.

12

THEY pulled up outside the lighthouse, at the top of the grassy headland. Missy's grandfather was standing in front of the door to the tower, out of the blast of the wind. When Shaw jumped out of the truck, the roar of waves crashing against the rocks below the headland was deafening.

The lighthouse keeper stood with one hand resting in the pocket of his navy-blue double-breasted coat, five large gilt buttons on each side, and the other hand clasping a clay pipe to his mouth. He had Missy's dark eyes and thick eyebrows, his cap covered a nest of wiry grey hair, and his expression was as welcoming as the weather.

Shaw adopted his most charming smile. 'Top of the morning to you, Sir.' He extended his hand. 'Detective Ronan Shaw.'

The lighthouse keeper's grey whiskers twitched. 'Thought you might be along.' The old man made a deliberate show of removing his hand from his coat pocket and shaking Shaw's. 'Edgar Coelho.'

Behind him, Missy revved her truck.

'You've come about the young woman on the beach, am I right?' Coelho said.

Shaw nodded. 'You've heard about the incident?'

'News travels in this town.' He nodded at his granddaughter, who had dumped the sacks of coal and sped off back down the hill. No doubt to return to Flea at the docks for more playful flirtations. The lighthouse keeper puffed on his pipe, letting smoke escape from the corner of his mouth. 'Although I thought you'd be here sooner than this. Have you discovered how she died?'

There was authority in his voice, tinged with something else. Anger? Yes, that could be anger.

'I'm trying to work out how she ended up on that beach, so far out of town.' Shaw said. 'What she was doing in the water in the first place. It takes time. We're following procedures. One of the first things we do is seek information from the known contacts of the victim. I know she worked for *you*, Mr Coelho.'

'That's right. She delivered the coal for my lamp.'

'When was the last time she did this?'

'Oh, I should say, day before yesterday.'

'So that would make it Monday?'

'If you say so.'

Shaw hesitated. Missy had discovered Lara's body, washed up on the beach, early Monday morning. From his observations of her corpse, he estimated Lara had been dead for at least a few hours. Coelho was hiding something. 'Did she say anything out of the ordinary to you that morning?' he asked.

Coelho paused a moment, puffed on his pipe. 'Nothing strikes me.'

Shaw wondered why Coelho would have something to hide. How well did he know Lara? 'How long had she been making this delivery of coal to you?'

'Every morning now for a couple of years.'

'Were you fond of her?'

Coelho grunted. 'Barely knew the girl. Although she seemed nice enough.'

Shaw smiled. 'Strange you say that, Mr Coelho. I've heard she wasn't a very nice person at all.'

Coelho glared at Shaw. 'Like I said, I barely knew her.' He turned his back, said over his shoulder, 'I've got work to do. Prisms need polishing.'

'Mind if I tag along?' Shaw said. 'I just have a few more questions for you, Mr Coelho.'

Coelho grunted, opened the door, and motioned for Shaw to step inside the lighthouse. Shaw stood outside for a moment and craned his neck to look up at the immense tower. He stood there, fighting the gusts of wind, and absorbed the immensity of it; its striking bold whiteness, the huge plates of cast-iron secured together with giant bolts.

When Shaw entered the engine room, it was dark and dank and, underneath the faint scent of old smoke, it was filled with a familiar, pungent earthy aroma, almost musty, like mould. He knew that smell anywhere. As an Irishman it was as familiar to him as babies to mother's milk. His thoughts were drowned by a loud clunking.

'She was built in eighteen ten and she's still standing, tall and strong over a hundred years later.' Coelho was forced to shout over the noise of the gears.

Immediately to the left, the staircase wound elegantly upwards inside the curved wall of the tower, up and up, smaller and smaller all the way to the top. Shaw felt his heartbeat quicken as his eyes followed the dark metalwork of the handrail, tightening into a spiral and disappearing into the distance. He couldn't peel his eyes away from the top, through the tenebrous light, as though the lighthouse itself was drawing his gaze upwards.

'How tall is the tower?' Shaw asked.

Coelho picked up a lamp and pulled a box of matches from his pocket. 'Just over one hundred feet.' He struck a match. 'Nearly five hundred feet above sea level.'

The lines on his leathery face were momentarily exaggerated, like trenches, as he lit the wick inside the lamp. 'One hundred and twenty feet from the bottom inside the shaft.' He tapped his boot on the stone floor under their feet. 'The floor below us here goes down twenty extra feet, so the distance to the summit is at least a hundred and twenty.'

'It's hollow below the floor here?' Shaw asked. 'Wouldn't it be safer to fill it in?'

'She's made of solid iron walls, Detective. Four feet thick. A tower such as she is safe under any circumstances.' Coelho began the slow climb to the top.

'Can you show me?'

Coelho paused, said over his shoulder, 'When we come back down.'

Shaw's chest tightened. 'We're going up?'

'I told you; prisms need polishing. If you want to ask me questions about the dead woman, you'll need to come along.'

Shaw followed, and slowly they climbed the staircase with its gentle curve and broad steps, to the lantern room. As they ascended, their footsteps echoed on the metal grille of each stair.

Shaw's hands trembled the higher they went. He slid his left hand against the smooth cold wall to steady it. Their shadows grew and shrank, giant and grotesque, against the painted white of the curved walls, which dripped with condensation.

The staircase seemed to go on forever, and, adding to the

swoon of climbing to such a height, the gaps between the stairs seemed to widen and accentuate the long drop to the bottom of the lighthouse.

'You'll notice the tower sways when the wind gets bad,' Coelho said. 'If she didn't, she'd snap.'

Shaw came to a halt. The stairs continued unrelentingly upward. A wave of queasiness rocked him, and he was forced to grip the railing, squeezing his eyes closed. Even though he kept reminding himself that the tower was made of solid iron, its brilliant whiteness made him think of chalk. And the chalk his school master used always snapped in half at the slightest touch.

When he opened his eyes again, Coelho had turned and was staring at him. Light-headedness made Shaw sway like the tower in the wind. He bent over and inhaled deeply to catch his breath.

'Out of shape, are ye?' Shaw noticed how high they were through the gap in the stairs and felt his stomach go. Coelho laughed and patted him on the back. 'You get used to it.'

The cylindrical tower creaked and groaned. Shaw righted himself and nodded. 'So everyone keeps telling me.'

To take his mind off the climb, Shaw counted seventy-six remaining steps. His calf muscles burned. Eventually they reached a landing almost at the top of the tower, where an iron-framed bed was perched like a bird's nest under a small, round window, the only portal that offered a tiny glimpse of the blue world beyond.

An old desk stood next to it, cluttered with papers, maps, and a pair of old binoculars. And there were books. Books piled on every surface, from the bed to the shelves and the desk. Some as thick as dictionaries, others as battered as ancient texts. From where Shaw stood, he could read *The Collector's Encyclopedia of*

Shells on top of the pile on the desk. On the wall hung marine charts and a small barometer. Tins lined a shelf, along with more books, a length of rope, and other odds and ends.

'Commonwealth Lighthouse Service Notice Under Lighthouses Act of nineteen hundred and eleven says we're not supposed to have anything reclinable,' Coelho said, gesturing to the unmade bed. 'We do most things by the rules here. Others, we bend slightly.' He brought out his pipe from his coat pocket. 'Besides, it's my granddaughter who spends most of her time here.' He lit the pipe and gazed at the round window. 'We used to watch the whales migrating together. Of course, she prefers to be on her own these days.'

Shaw crossed the room in three steps. He picked up one of the books from the bed: *Beyond Good and Evil by Fredrich Nietzsche, Bilingual Edition English-German*. A knot formed in Shaw's chest at this small glimpse into Missy's world, her mind.

Natural light squeezed through a trap door above them. Coelho climbed a small ladder and opened it. Shaw followed him into the lantern room, full of the smell of gas and something else; tobacco.

The black curtains were drawn, increasing the stuffiness. An enormous prism of cut glass loomed in front of him, like a beautiful sculpture of ice; the lenses the height and width of a horse. Shaw shakily held on to the steel railing that ran along the inside of the round room and marvelled at the lantern.

Coelho blew out the candle from his kerosene lamp and set it on the ground next to the mechanism. 'Weighs four tonnes. Beautiful, isn't she?' Shaw had to admit the whole mass of glass was mesmerising. 'Every lighthouse in the world is unique, did you know that?'

Shaw raised his eyebrows. 'That so?'

'Each has a different sequence, so ships know where they are. Mine's fifteen seconds. When she's lit, she's visible in clear weather for nearly forty nautical miles. So bright you can't look at her. Lest you want to lose your sight.' Coelho opened a small door which led outside. 'Care to stand on the balcony?'

'Five hundred feet above sea level?' Shaw shook his head. 'I'll pass.'

'It's a keeper's duty to go on the balcony and check for vessels. Every hour. Come on, I won't bite.'

Coelho disappeared out the doorway. Shaw reluctantly followed him. The wind whipped his face as he stepped onto the slim balustrade balcony that looped around the top of the tower and seemed so frail and exposed, as though it could plummet to the ground at any moment. He gripped the chest-high railing, his knuckles turning white.

Coelho stood with his pipe in his mouth, eyes focused on the galloping ocean. 'Nothing to see today, not even with a telescope, except ocean and sky.'

Shaw cast his eyes over the immense view. The sheer expansive wildness of it. Gradients of blue filled his vision, and a line of fluffy clouds bulged along the horizon. He peered over the rust-spotted railing at the waves washing in and out over the rocks directly below and his brain did a forward flip. Taking a deep breath in, a deep breath out, he managed to let go of the railing long enough to extract his cigarette case and light up, despite the wind and his trembling hands. The tobacco soothed the queasiness gurgling in his guts.

The ocean below was dark, and the wind made small white caps on the waves. The sheer cliff down to the water was jagged and dotted with gnarled shrubs. The tide was out this morning and the rock shelf, dotted with shimmering concentric circles, shone like black squid ink. A small strip of sand butted against the bottom of the cliff wall, like a white crescent moon. Shaw wondered again if anyone could survive that fall. He thought not.

'What are you running from?' Coelho's voice, full of crag, sounded in Shaw's ear. He turned and frowned at the old man. 'That was the first question they asked when I took the job on this light, halfway around the world. On the edge of civilisation.'

Shaw squinted against the wind. 'What *are* you running from?'

'What all of us are running from, Detective.' Coelho opened his eyes wide. 'Ourselves.'

'Must get lonely sometimes.' Shaw said, watching the horizon. 'Isolating.'

'Life in the lights finds your weaknesses. It can overcome you if you let it. But if you're suggesting that I'm missing something by avoiding people and their intolerable gossip… You won't find any sentimentality in me if that's what you're hoping for.'

Shaw drew back on his cigarette and turned his gaze to the old man. 'I'm just wondering what kind of person it takes to run a lighthouse.'

'The kind that prefers a solitary life. Most wickies fall into three categories: romantic, pioneer, isolationist.'

'Which one are you?' Shaw asked.

Coelho turned his fierce gaze to Shaw. He reached his hand up to his mouth and held the clay pipe there for a moment. Finally, he took it out and uttered, 'Guess,' then disappeared back inside the lantern room.

Shaw flicked his cigarette into the wind.

It was warm inside, and the glass of the giant prisms glinted in the sunshine sneaking in from the flapping curtains. Coelho took out a rag, spat on it then rubbed the glass in tiny circles.

'You do this every day?' Shaw asked.

'Every day the prisms need polishing. So does the brass. Grass needs cutting, weather measuring, gears oiling, coal restocking. Must do all the chores before you get your forty winks.'

'Seems like a lot of work for one man. You never thought to hire an assistant keeper?'

'I told you before. It's my desire to be alone. Come now, Detective, you're costing me sleep. What is it you wanted to ask me about the dead woman?'

'Lara Harvey.' Shaw wondered again why Coelho might have lied about seeing Lara Harvey on Monday morning. He decided to play along. 'Can you say what time she arrived here, the day before yesterday?'

'Usual time. Round about six in the morning.'

Shaw took out his notepad and pen and jotted down the time. 'Do you know of any enemies she may have had?'

'So, got caught up in some trouble, did she?' Coelho asked.

'That's what I'm here to find out,' Shaw replied.

'It was quick, was it? He didn't make her suffer?'

Shaw raised his eyebrows. 'Who?'

'Her fiancé. That's who done it, isn't it?'

This surprised Shaw. It seemed like an intimate sliver of knowledge for someone claiming not to have known Lara very well. 'You knew about her relationship with Sonny Fynn?'

'I did.'

Edgar Coelho's contradiction was not lost on Shaw. Still, he played along. 'You think he could be responsible?'

'Let's just say I don't think she did this to herself. But maybe you ought to ask him.'

'I've heard that Mr Fynn is a difficult man to get hold of. Because of his line of work.'

'I'm not sure Mr Fynn works regular hours, like you and me, Detective. But I've heard tell that if one wanted to, one might find him doing business at the docks most nights. Round midnight.'

'Is that so?' Shaw said. Was now the right time to find out what Coelho was hiding? How well did he know Lara, really? Why would he hide that? Either way, it suggested he was guilty of something. *Probe*, Shaw thought. 'Lara told you those sorts of things, did she?'

Coelho paused rubbing the prism. 'It's a funny thing,' he said. 'You ever find yourself opening up to strangers? Confiding in them things you would never trust with your closest relative?'

Probe further. 'I thought you said you didn't know her?'

'She trusted me to keep her secrets. So I knew I could trust her with…'

Further. Shaw stepped closer, closing the distance between them. 'With?'

Coelho seized Shaw's arm and yanked him back. 'Watch yourself!'

Balls of silver trailed along the ground from the giant glass mechanism toward the toe of Shaw's boot. Shiny, silvery globules. He kneeled for a closer look. His face was reflected, distorted in the substance. 'What is it?'

'Mercury,' Coelho said. 'It comes out of the turning mechanism. The prisms sit in a bath of it, helps them turn smoother.' Coelho turned a small faucet and a drop of mercury dropped onto his finger. He held it up to Shaw. 'Every few weeks

I drain it, filter any stray oil from the lamp, clear out the debris.' Shaw marvelled at the way the silver sphere wobbled at the tip of Coelho's finger, encrusted with dirt. 'I top it up every now and then because it evaporates. Breathe it in, I suppose.'

The silvery substance shone in the light under the glass prisms. Shaw recollected Missy's father's warnings about the dangers of mercury. 'Is it deadly?'

'Many a keeper's lost their mind to quicksilver. Sent them leaping to all kinds of deaths.' For a moment, the trenches in Coelho's forehead disappeared, his demeanour softened, and his blood-flecked eyes seemed to float away. 'I can still hear my wife's voice, you know. Still hear it when there's nothing but the *woosh* of the light over my head. Plain as day.' He dropped the globule back into the bath and wiped his hand on his coat. 'But this stuff won't kill you. Not straight away. Won't even make you unwell. Unless you ingest it.' He nodded. 'Ingest a spoonful of this and you'll be wishing for death. Acute exposure. Knock you around a bit.'

Coelho opened the hatch door in the ground, and they exited the lantern room through the manhole, descending the short ladder to the landing.

Shaw peered at the staircase, coiled symmetrically down to the bottom of the tower. As they descended the one hundred and twenty-five steep steps, Shaw considered what the lighthouse keeper was hiding. What secret did he share with Lara? The echoes of their boots and their shadows followed them down the slow toil to the bottom.

'I just have one final question before I leave, Mr Coelho.' Shaw said once his feet hit solid ground. 'Can you tell me about your movements on Sunday night?'

'You want to know where I was? Have I failed to impress upon you the level of maintenance required of a one-manned lighthouse? Lighthouses are proper work. Solid, day in, day out work.'

'Is that why you use your granddaughter, Mr Coelho? Extra pair of hands?'

The vein in Edgar Coelho's forehead bulged. His eyebrows drew together, dark eyes glaring. 'Do not speak to me of my own blood.' Specks of spit flicked from the narrow line of his mouth. 'You ask how I stand the isolation? Missy helps by filling the silences with a bit of conversation. Makes the darkness a bit brighter.'

'You say Missy comes here to ease your loneliness? What about her, Mr Coelho? Do you ever stop to think about how it might be affecting *her*?'

Coelho stepped closer to Shaw. 'What are you talking about?'

Shaw didn't budge. His voice remained steady, unwavering. 'The stories you tell her. She believes them. She came to me yesterday talking of sea myths and mermaids. Not to mention the mercury. Do you ever stop to think about the damage it could be doing to her? You know her father doesn't want her to come here at all.'

Bitterness seeped from every dark pore on Coelho's face. 'Her father? You mention that man's name in my presence and you'll be sorry you ever set foot inside my tower, Detective. Now, if that's all you've come to ask me…'

'Aren't you forgetting something?' Shaw said. 'You said you'd show me the hollow bottom under the floor here.'

'You've cost me too much of my time this morning. Now get out before I lose my temper.'

Shaw nodded. 'I *do* know about your temper, Mr Coelho. I just wonder if you lost it the last time you saw Lara Harvey.'

The bulging vein in the lighthouse keeper's forehead darkened. His eyes bore right through Shaw. 'You've no right to make an accusation like that.' He opened the door and said, firmly, 'Now get out.'

Yes, Shaw decided as the piercing wind cut right through him, the lighthouse keeper was definitely hiding something.

13

Quinta-feira

I'M a prisoner inside my own mind.

I know before I wake that I am dreaming. It's one of those dreams where I'm fully aware that I'm asleep and my mind tells me I'm dreaming. It tells me to calm down, this isn't real. But then it betrays me and won't let me wake up. Watching the dream as if in a movie house, Charlie Chaplin in black and white, making me laugh so hard I leave the cinema with a secret wet stain on my trousers, tears stinging my eyes and I wipe them away, embarrassed at showing so much emotion.

So it is that I feel the hand lift the front of my thermals. It crawls its way down past my stomach and finds the warmth between my legs. The fingers are thick, solid, they are not rough, so when they begin to move and rub in slow-motion circles, rather than pain, I feel the warmth between my legs get hotter. What starts as a sensation of pressure quickly turns to a pleasant feeling just above my oyster-shell opening. The fingers are drawn inside me, they are searching, looking for something. For the little pearl, the hard, glistening ball buried within soft tissue. The fingers have tasted it before, and now they are searching for it, from their memory of ocean and brine. Past the layers of sargassum, inward, toward wet rock and seafoam. I quiver as one finger slips inside and reaches in deep, penetrating me and filling my cave with waves so heavy they shatter me. So blue they could ice water.

When the fingers come back they are wet; warm and wet. They search again and make tiny circles which sends pleasure further within me. I want more but how can I tell the fingers to move faster, move deeper, if they are not even joined to my own hand? I move my body in time with the circles, undulating my stomach like waves rolling in with the tide. The wet fingers move faster, and my body moves in rhythm with them. I fear at any moment the fingers are going to stop, to stop now when I am so close to reaching my crescendo.

My own hand extends to grasp the wrist and force it to stay. The hairs on the back of the hand are as soft as sea oak. My fingers work their way down further and I press their tips on top of the hand that is bringing me such ecstasy and on one of those fingers I feel something metal and cold. A ring. A thin wedding band on the fourth finger. The wedding band, the one I couldn't stop staring at. Detective Ronan Shaw's face flashes in my mind and I know it is his hand that I am holding, that I am forcing to tunnel deep inside me until I climax.

I release the hand and bring my own to rest on my stomach but what I feel instead is the slimy cold tentacle of an octopus. I watch in horror as I bring it to my face and realise that my own fingers have transformed into bestial tentacles with tiny suctions running along each knuckle.

A sharp breath rips into my lungs. My eyes open and I call for help and the next thing I know I am sitting up, drenched in sweat, and screaming. I am alone. The moistness between my legs is warm and I wonder if it is sweat or something else. I touch it and feel around but pull away in disgust.

Something wet and dangly threads through my fingers, something that feels like seaweed. It comes loose. It comes out in my hands. Long strands, intensely green, separate from their roots and stick to the spaces between my fingers.

Algae.

I try to get it off me, to flick it away, but it continues to come, it pulls out so easily. I can't stop pulling at it. I want it all to come out. I want to be rid of it.

My fingers move down and, suddenly, they come across quite a different texture. Underneath the fronds of algae there is something solid underneath. A very small round object with a sharp edge, hard, like coral. I run my finger over the surface. Explore its outline. There's more than one. Concentric circles emerge from the edges of the opening between my legs, just like the ones in the gash on my head. I move my hand around, trying to get a sense of what these things might be. A shock runs through me. They are barnacles.

A loud noise, like an explosion, jolts me and, breathing hard, I look around and feel for something, anything, to confirm that I am awake. The bed. The sheet is twisted around my legs and my pillow has fallen to the floor. I feel the draught through the windowpane. I know it is not early because grey light already creeps through the round window, it must be eight o'clock. I also know this dream is going to cling to me, and unless I get outside and wash it from me, I'll be carrying its shadow around all day.

Pulling on a shirt over my long-johns, I begin the decent down the spiral staircase, running my hand along the cool surface of the curved wall. The tower shakes slightly so I know the wind has picked up overnight. Outside, I cut across the sloping grass toward the dunes. Although it is morning, and my mind feels vulnerable from the dream, the sound of the sea fills my ears, and the rush of the ancient tide fills my lungs and I want to swallow a gulp of sea.

I make my way over the dunes and through the slicing grass, windswept and divisive. The sand is soft but wet and freezing, still untouched by the sun. It sticks to my bare feet, the cold numbing them.

My feet stagger down to the water's edge and along the shore in the direction of the steelworks. The breeze coming across the ocean brings the smell of salt. The sky is a pale purple but there is no fog, and the fires burn fiercely from the chimneys at the steelworks.

As I walk, my mind floats over all the strange things that are happening to me. The dream. The wound in my head, the barnacles between my legs. The dead woman. The mermaid. The octopus. I can't ignore the vulnerable feeling that somehow, they are all connected.

My eyes cast to the sand, at the phantom shoreline where shells and other debris mark the spot where the ocean abandoned them, scanning the fragments as I walk, until I notice the dull, striated exterior of an abalone shell. I kneel to it, cradle it in my palm, flat and oval-shaped, like a small shield. Turning it over, it reveals its iridescent nacre, shimmering silvery-white. Green-red and deep blue. It reminds me of the mermaid's tail. The mermaid that I stumbled upon, right here on this beach. The mermaid that swims through my thoughts, my dreams. The mermaid who was in fact a corpse.

I tremble at the thought of what I found here, three mornings ago. The image of the dead woman returns to me; her skin, pouncing with sea-lice, her blonde hair caked in sand. Her glazed-over eyes, like a fish at the market. *Deadeye* we call it. A tell-tale sign that a fish is in bad condition.

Now, it seems after that dream, hers is not the only face that haunts me. Why must I be encumbered by these feelings for Detective Shaw? He is married, he is much too old, he would never be interested in someone like me. And suddenly and out of nowhere an anger rises inside me, raw, bestial anger, and I need to be as far away from here as possible. I pocket the abalone shell, stand, and sprint along the beach, back toward the lighthouse and the waves crashing against the exposed, slate-black rock shelf below it.

The wind is at my back, pushing me along the beach, away from the site of the dead woman and I arrive, breathless and wild, at the cliff base. Rolling up my long-johns I slosh through the shallows and when I can no longer feel my feet, I climb up onto the rock shelf, stumbling across it in the weak light, the barnacles and pointy limpet shells stabbing into the heels of my feet. Coming to stand next to a moon-shaped crater filled with black water, I gaze out to sea. My fists unclench as I breathe in the morning air, crisp and clean and fresh. It calms my racing heart, eases my mind, filled with faces of the dead, of the unreal.

Behind me, at the base of the sea cliff, a narrow beach is hemmed in on both sides by the outcrops. A flock of seagulls huddle together on the sandy beach that stretches in a crescent, squabbling over something unseen, their white heads and grey feathers blowing against the breeze. The birds scatter and squawk at one another. The sudden boom of a wave against the rock causes the flock to fly off in a flurry of white and screeching, colliding with each other to get away.

All except one. One seagull remains on the sandy shore. It thrashes against the jagged rock shelf, trying to launch itself away from the path of another incoming wave. It beats its wings and hops on one skinny leg, red like boiled crab. The other leg has been lost. The gull doesn't lift off in time and the water breaks over it. When the wave retreats, the seagull is left washed up on the wet sand, a mess of broken wings and feathers. I clamber over the rocks toward the sand and reach down to the bird. It kicks its one skinny, red leg in the air.

Still alive.

The seagull flounders, trying to right itself, then stares at me, with its red-rimmed eye. It opens its tiny beak and screeches. Another wave breaks on the rocks and surges toward me on the patch of sand. I cradle the seagull in my arm like a baby as the water reaches my legs and then retreats. The bird struggles in my grasp, screeching, as it tries to break itself free. To fly away with the others who left it, abandoned, to the ocean. How could they forsake it like that? The anger returns, full force. Like I want to tear out the pages of a book. Like I want to smash something.

The bird looks up at me, totally trusting in my ability to make it better. To take the pain away. I know what I must do. It's cruel to leave it alive. I pick up a rock and place the bird in the sand. It pleads with me; one last screech, but I turn my head the other way and repeat to myself that this is the right thing to do. I'm putting it out of its misery. It's a kindness. With my right hand I bring down the rock sharply and firmly. The crack of rock against its tiny, feathered body is louder than I expect. Hot blood splatters up my wrist like port wine and a strange energy fills my veins. I feel the anger inside me tempering. The bird's webbed talon curls into a little C and I hear its screech but it's distorted now, blown away with the wind. Tossing the limp bird into the ocean, I head back toward the dunes.

At the harbour, I find the delivery truck waiting for me. The door squeaks open and I climb inside, prop myself up behind the steering wheel. I open the throttle and step on the self-starter pedal with my bare foot and turn the switch to start the engine. The truck rumbles and the engine idles. I throw out the clutch, place the gear lever in reverse and engage, gently trying the reverse, letting the clutch in slightly. Just enough. Now to low. Good. Now to second. Now to high. Fine. I place both hands on the wheel and ease down on the pedal and it is only then that I catch my reflection in the mirror. I am concentrating so hard that my face looks like a frozen corpse. I try to imagine something to take the tension off my mind. Shaw's piercing blue eyes glimmer in my vision, his distractingly sharp cheekbones and unconventional handsomeness.

The thought of his hand in my dream causes my palms to coat the steering wheel with sweat and the rumbling of the truck burns a warmth between my legs. I lean into the rumble and imagine Shaw's hand, imagine his large fingers slipping inside me. How his voice sounds inside my head, which is a nice break from the screech of that dead seagull. And despite myself, the corners of my mouth creep outward. Despite my bad mood and the faces that haunt me, I smile.

Pulling the truck up next to the loading dock, the wharfies look busy with their clumps of coal. When I climb out of the truck, Flea waves to me. He wanders over, his hands, blackened with coal and dirt, hang so casually by his side.

'Mornin',' he beams.

'Good morning,' I say.

He grabs onto my arm and pulls me toward him. 'Come here and have a look at this.'

I follow him to the end of the tram line. We pass a load of coal sitting in a huge tray and he jumps down onto a ledge just above the water level. He motions for me to follow, and I do.

'Look,' he says with his huge smile spread across his face.

My eyes follow his finger, which is pointing into the darkness underneath the dock. I blink a few times to try and make out what is under there. Scratching and squeaking and rustling noises draw me in. My eyes finally adjust, and I recoil, almost lose my footing. A nest of baby rats huddles together in the darkness.

'Why would you show me this?'

'Thought they were cute,' Flea says. 'Besides, I wanted to show you they weren't diseased.'

I hoist myself back up to the road level.

Flea pulls himself up. 'Did you hear about the rat problem at the church?'

I brush the gritty sand from my hands. 'No.'

He nods, and we stroll toward the sacks of coal bound for the lighthouse. 'The church didn't want to kill the rats, so they trapped them, and released them far away. But the next day, they came back.' Flea bends to one of the sacks and I pick up the one next to it. Flea continues. 'Next, they asked the rats politely to leave, but still… they wouldn't budge.' Flea hoists the sack up onto his shoulder. 'Finally, the priest had one last idea. He baptised all the rats.' We walk toward the truck, sacks loaded in arms, and lay them on the tray. Flea looks at me, grinning wide. 'Now they only come at Christmas and Easter.'

I can't help myself. I am helpless with laughter. The anger I felt earlier melts away and I am flooded with a sense of well-being. Tears sting my eyes.

'What are you doing here?'

I startle at the voice, deep and intimidating, and I can't be sure I didn't hear it inside my head. When I turn around, my heart leaps. It's him. He's really here, standing in front of me in his dapper three-piece suit, his pellucid blue eyes penetrating my soul. Desire swells between my legs and begins to throb. I suddenly feel very underdressed and masculine in my night shirt, long-johns and bare feet. I mumble something about my new job delivering coal for my grandfather's lighthouse and he looks at me like I've just stuck a needle in his eye.

Shaw and Flea eye each other so I introduce them and listen as Shaw asks questions about the dead woman, trying to distract from my thoughts of his hand between my legs. When they finish talking and I walk to the front of the truck, Shaw looks at me with an expression of such surprise, such confusion.

'I didn't think you were so old fashioned.' I smile. 'This might come as a surprise to you but it's the twentieth century. And women can drive trucks.'

'That's not it,' he says. 'Why are you driving Lara Harvey's delivery truck?'

There's that name again. For a moment I'd forgotten there were other women in Shaw's life. His wife. And Lara Harvey. I'd forgotten she even had a name. She was a real person. She had a life. Friends, probably. I didn't know I was driving the dead woman's delivery truck.

'This was *her* delivery truck?'

'That key you found yesterday,' he says. 'It belonged to one of these trucks.'

I stare at the truck, painted black with the words *Morrow's Coal & Ice* in white lettering on the door. 'Did it?' I'd barely noticed it. I open the driver's side door. 'My grandfather…'

'The lighthouse keeper?'

'He asked me to do it after his driver didn't show up, that's all.'

'His driver, Lara Harvey? Lara Harvey worked for your grandfather, delivering coal to the lighthouse?'

'I suppose.'

'Up until she died?'

'What are you getting at?'

He glances behind the harbour wall, toward the hill, where the lighthouse looms behind its grassy ridge. 'Nothing. I might have a few questions for your grandfather, though. Do you mind giving me a lift?'

'To the lighthouse?'

Detective Shaw walks around the front of the truck and opens the passenger side door.

'You know, he doesn't like outsiders,' I say through the open front cab.

'That's why you're taking me.' He climbs in and pats the driver's seat, right where my arse sits. 'Come on, I want to see a woman of the twentieth century drive this truck.'

I climb into the seat and start the engine. Shaw lights a cigarette and I am enveloped in his smoke. I drive us along the harbourfront toward the bottom of the grassy hill. The closeness of the car, the sweet prickle of his smell, overwhelms me, and I can do nothing but stare, mutely, straight ahead. Shaw's left hand with the wedding band is holding the cigarette but his right hand is close to mine and, as I change gears, I can almost touch it. If I extend my pinky finger, reach my hand slightly to the left…

'You're not one of those feminist types, are you?' he says. '*Votes for women* and all that?' He turns his body toward mine, one arm resting out the window.

I side-eye him. 'You don't think women should be given the vote?'

'Oh no, I think women should be given the vote. I just think that, once given the right to vote, they'll vote the way their husbands and their fathers tell them to.'

'You think all women do what men tell them to?'

A pause. I feel his eyes on me. 'Not all, no.'

'Do you think *I* seem like someone who does what a man tells her to do?'

He draws back on his cigarette and turns to look out of his window. 'No, Miss Green. You seem like the type of woman who would do the opposite of what a man tells her to do.'

I glance at the hand resting on his upper thigh and the words form in my head. I have to force myself not to say them aloud: *I suppose it would depend on the man.*

We reach the bottom of the hill and I take the incline slowly so as not to lose any of the sacks of coal off the back of the truck. We hit a bump and I grind the gear because I don't account for the extra weight of the load. The truck stalls. We roll backwards for one second, two, and my face prickles with embarrassment. I let out the clutch and put the gear into first, find the sweet spot and we lurch forward. I take a deep breath of Shaw's smoke and feel my breathing slow as we chug steadily up the hill toward the lighthouse.

'You're suspicious of him?' I ask.

'I don't know that I am, but something happened to Lara Harvey. And I need to consider all possibilities.'

We pull up in front of the tower, the wind up here is fierce, and it rattles the truck. *Avô* is there, standing at the bottom of the tower with his pipe in his mouth. He's heard our approach. Shaw gets out and walks straight over to him, leaving me behind, abandoning me, like the seagulls who abandoned their own kin to the cruelty of the beating waves.

When I open the driver's side door, wind whips my hair and bites the skin through my thin cotton shirt. I go to the back of the truck and unload the sacks of coal, dumping them on the grass beside the truck. I stare at the sacks, wondering what to do, cursing my grandfather's betrayal. Cursing them both. Let the old man come and fetch them himself. I've had enough of men and their nonsense for one day. Climbing back inside the cab I rev the engine hard.

Shaw follows *Avô* inside the lighthouse, and I watch him. As my grandfather is swallowed by the darkness of the tower, Shaw looks back in my direction. My heart skips a beat. Then he disappears inside.

I drive away, biting the inside of my lip, fighting back tears. I thought I knew solitude. But Shaw and his indifference proves I had no understanding of loneliness before. Now I am alone. I wonder for a moment about jerking the wheel and steering the truck toward the cliff for no reason at all.

My mind plays out the scene of what would happen if the truck went over. What it would feel like to plunge through the air and land at the bottom. No, I would never do that. I *know* what would happen if the truck went over. But still, the voice inside my head tells me to think about doing it. A piercing

whisper, a silent cry of desolation. But I hear it, clear as day…
'Go!' it says.

Then, just as suddenly, the voice disappears and I am completely within my wits, at least I think I am, and I think of *Avô*. He's relying on me to deliver his coal in this truck and not to drive it off a cliff. I have always felt the need to protect him. Because he lost both his wife and his daughter, I have always felt the most enormous and oppressing responsibility for his happiness.

When I see him sad or lonely, I feel it acutely in my blood. I don't know why I feel it so strongly, I just do, and so is my need to fix it. What he needs from me is reliability. Compliance. A granddaughter who doesn't create any problems. I can't fix what happened to cause his loneliness, but I can make sure he never has to feel it with me. I have to prove that with me, he can feel sure that I won't abandon him.

I remember years ago, when I first went to live with him in the keeper's cottage, he raised his voice at me. I was devastated. I must have been twelve or thirteen years old, when Gust was away at war, and I'd rushed in after school one afternoon.

He was drinking coffee, as he always did, and I still remember the bitterness of it on his breath. I burst in through the door, causing his coffee to spill. He bellowed something about being careful and calming down. Being an inconvenience, a momentary hassle, reduced me to tears for over an hour.

So I do now what I did then. I retreat into my shell. I listen to the waves, and I pine for someone to come into my life and take away the loneliness. I think about my mother. How I wish I had her, someone to talk to about the ways of men, how they make me feel; intimidated and wishing to please.

I park the truck at the dunes and leave it there. Take the winding trail down to the beach. When I get there, I freeze, confused by what I see.

A massacre.

Hundreds of seagulls, on the sand, not moving. Other birds, alive ones in the sky, move together in an otherworldly formation, like a school of fish. They dart and dive in the air, land, and peck at the dead ones on the sand. I wonder if it is possible that this is another hallucination. Or if I am dreaming still. If this whole morning has been a dream.

I turn and run back up the beach to the winding trail, to the truck, because I can't be sure that the massacre of birds is real or something that my barnacled mind has conjured up. Wrench open the door and slam it shut. Rev the engine and reverse, away from the massacre, whether it is real or inside my head, whether I caused it by killing that seagull or not, I need to get away.

Returning the truck to the harbour, I hurry home. My father looks up from his fishing net when I barge through the front door. My stomach drops and splatters to the floor.

'What are *you* doing here?' I ask.

Fish smoulders in the fireplace.

'Not much to sell this morning. Brought most of the haul home for us.'

I realise that our argument has been washed away like fish guts, discarded and forgotten. He will not speak of it again. All my questions will remain unanswered. Frustration and anger swell inside me, like the tide. I inhale the fishy smoke that fills the room and slow my breathing, slow my heart rate. 'Gil Sanders isn't pulling his weight?'

He gives me a measured stare then returns his focus to the

net. 'Gil's a hard worker. Just a bit of bad luck. Have you seen my hat? I can't bloody find it. That's the trouble. Don't like to go out without it.' My father would never admit he was a superstitious man. His head turns and he glares at me. 'What *is* that noise?'

I realise I've been grinding my teeth. I release my jaw and sit next to the window. In my pocket is the abalone shell, which I place on the windowsill next to the others, and then when I reach in deeper, there is something else in my pocket. Something hard and cold. My fingers shake as I pull it out.

The rock.

A single grey feather sticks to it, in a smear of blood. It weighs heavy in my hand, like a murder weapon. I place it carefully down at the end of the line of shells and catch my face in the reflection of the glass. No longer a frozen corpse, but alive and windswept and wild. Unhinged. Sometimes I frighten myself.

It takes my breath away.

14

Thursday

HUNDREDS of dead birds darkened the shoreline, their wings poking out at unnatural angles. Detective Ronan Shaw herded the crowd of onlookers behind the police tape. Some tried to crawl under to get a closer look at the mass of feathers and blood.

'Would you keep those people away?' Shaw called to Constable Lou Bowers.

Constable Bowers plodded laboriously up the soft sand, attempting to hold the crowd behind the tape. Even though he was overweight, his suit hung on him as though it was still on the coat hanger. His flushed cheeks and fair skin, already scorched in the late morning sun, suggested he may not be up to the task.

Shaw rubbed his eyes with his thumb and index finger. He already had enough on his plate, now he was dealing with the matter of these birds. He returned to face Henry Barkley, a local fisherman who had made the discovery earlier that morning.

'So, again, Mr Barkley,' Shaw said, taking out his pen and notepad. 'You say you saw them drop out of the sky?'

Henry Barkley wore a checked shirt and trousers, held up by a pair of suspenders. His cheeks were creased with deep, vertical wrinkles, as though someone had taken a ruler and pencil and etched thick lines down each side of his mouth.

Barkley chewed a hunk of tobacco. 'Like I said,' he spat a glob into the sand at his feet. 'I heard a bang and then a load of birds landed on my boat. When I pulled up on shore over there, 'round nine this morning, I came across this.'

Shaw gazed at the massacre of dead seagulls, and at the small fishing vessel tossing about in the waves near the shore. The line of birds stretched along the beach from where they stood, as far as he could see into the distance, toward the steelworks. The air was remarkably foul.

Barkley continued. 'Didn't want to hang around. Was such an eerie sight. Dead birds everywhere.' He lolled the tobacco around with his tongue, his hands on his hips. 'So I went down the police station to report what I seen.' He lifted his hat slightly, shook his head. 'Reckon at least a dozen landed on the boat. It's like there were hundreds of 'em in the sky and, all of a sudden, they just died and fell to the ground. It was quite surreal to be honest. Not something I ever seen before.'

The smell had to be one of the worst things Shaw had experienced, and he had experienced a lot of death in his thirty-five years. He wasn't the only person to notice it. Three women had made their way down to the shoreline, holding their noses. He called over to Constable Bowers.

'Get those people *back*, Constable.'

Bowers nodded but he was clearly having trouble maintaining order. He ushered a few people back, gesturing with his hands. The women took a few paces then, when Bowers was distracted, they hurried forward.

Shaw had no idea what could have caused such a scene, he had never seen anything like it, but if it was some sort of disease among the birds, he knew there was a possibility that it could spread to humans, too. He shook his head, tucked his notepad and pen into his pocket, and made his way over to Constable Bowers, whose face was shiny with sweat.

'See these ladies off the beach, would you, Constable? It's rancid.'

'Yes, Sir,' Bowers said and escorted the women up the sandy slope toward the road.

'So, what do you think's killed 'em?' Henry Barkley asked when Shaw returned.

Shaw gazed at the ocean. 'Could've been a storm out at sea.'

Barkley shook his head. 'I was out there, Detective. Didn't see no storm.'

'They could've been chased by a larger bird,' Shaw said.

Barkley spat a brown lump of tobacco into the sand. 'Doesn't explain the loud bang I heard though, does it?'

'You mean… like lightning?'

'Nah. This was more like… like something unnatural. Not quite as loud as lightning but similar.' Barkley pointed down the beach to the steelworks. 'Every now and then you hear loud noises coming from that power plant or whatever it is down yonder.'

Constable Lou Bowers returned, puffing, and stood between them. 'You think maybe they ate something that didn't agree with them? Something from the steelworks?' he interjected.

'Could be,' Henry Barkley replied. 'But you don't see no oil or nothing now, do you?'

'There's no clear indication to the cause of these deaths,' Shaw said. 'I'll have the incident reported to the Public Health Authority. Either way, get those people back until we know more. It may be some kind of outbreak.' Shaw pointed up the beach. 'Constable, get some fuel, get them in a pile with some sand round them, and burn them in case there's disease, all right?'

'Yes, Sir,' Bowers said and plodded off.

Detective Shaw, his shirt sleeves rolled to the elbow, his suit jacket long since discarded, had now been on this stretch of beach for several hours, dealing with the mass of dead seagulls.

After the initial excitement and the many failed attempts at holding them back, the onlookers had grown bored or disgusted enough to allow Shaw to get on with the task of cleaning up the mess.

Wispy clouds stretched across the clear blue sky and waves sloshed against the cliff below the lighthouse. The tide was high; the crescent strip of white sand had disappeared. The lighthouse stood high above, an erect column of white, the glass windows at the top dark and unblinking in the afternoon.

Detective Shaw wondered whether Missy was up there, in the tower, gazing out that small, round window below the lantern room. Or perhaps she was in the keeper's cottage with her grandfather. He cursed under his breath. Adrenaline spiked in his bloodstream as he realised he had completely forgotten about his deal with Augustus Green: he was supposed to be keeping an eye on her. Keeping her away from the lighthouse. He'd been so damned distracted by Inspector Mitchell's wild goose chase, Sonny Fynn and his illegal booze, and now these bloody birds.

Shaw felt a blast of wind against his face. He gazed up at the clear blue sky. Perfect kite-flying weather.

'Light them before the weather turns nasty,' Shaw called to Constable Bowers.

He lit a cigarette as he watched Bowers set fire to another mound of the dead seabirds. Thick black smoke spread down the beach and over the dunes, taking with it the acrid smell of burnt feathers and flesh. At least the fire would stop any risk of disease spreading, even if that didn't explain the loud bang that Mr Barkley described.

Shaw coughed as the wind changed direction and blew smoke right down his throat. He took a few steps up the slope and stood among the long reeds of dry grass, looking down at the beach and the smoking bonfires.

Orange flames licked the air. Small hissing sounds carried along the breeze as the droplets of moisture were forced out of the birds' bodies. In the trenches, they used to make piles like these and set fire to them. Of rats. The number of rats they added daily was unimaginable. Great pyres would burn with rats, gunpowder, piss, oil, and anything else they could throw on there to keep them alight. All mixed into one foul cesspit of burning fur and rot.

Then, like a wave had broken over his body, a great rush of peace, the clean scent of the ocean pierced through the stench of death and Missy appeared next to him.

'I saw the smoke.' She tucked her dark hair behind her ear and her warm, brown eyes glinted in the afternoon light. 'What's going on?'

Shaw inhaled deeply, breathing in her freshness. Being beside her made him feel clean, restored. He drew back on his cigarette then held it between his fingers. 'We've got a bit of a bird problem.'

'What happened?'

Shaw shrugged. 'Dead birds dropped out of the sky and ended

up along the shore.'

Missy gazed down the beach at the mounds of bonfires dotted along the shoreline. 'How many?'

Shaw offered Missy a cigarette. She accepted one and placed it between her lips. He struck a match and held it out for her, cradling it from the wind with his hand. 'Hard to tell. Two or three.'

Missy grinned. 'Two or tree,' she mimicked his accent, teasing.

'Sorry, I meant to say *th*ree,' Shaw repeated, poking his tongue out between his front teeth to emphasise the *th*, teasing her back, then wondered where this playful mood had crept in from.

Missy drew on the cigarette, exhaled, and asked, 'Two or three birds?'

Shaw sat in the soft sand, resting his elbows on his knees. 'Hundred. Two or three hundred.'

Missy sat next to him, digging her feet into the sand, her toes buried then re-emerging. They sat side by side, smoking, watching the plumes of black smoke coil into the sky, listening to the loud pops of exploding birds.

'Are you going to burn them all?' Missy asked.

'Makes sense,' Shaw said. 'They could be diseased.'

Missy stubbed her cigarette in the sand. 'Well, I'm glad you're cleaning it up. The whole harbour smells like death.'

The harbour. Shaw had thought about going alone to see if he could find Sonny Fynn, but perhaps he could find a way to uphold his end of the agreement *and* keep an eye on Missy.

'I'm afraid I must ask another favour of you, Miss Green,' he said. 'I need you…' All the moisture in Shaw's mouth drained away. He coughed, spluttered, then cleared his throat. 'I mean, I need your help. At the harbour. Will you meet me there? Tonight?'

Missy looked at him with those big doe eyes. She nodded.

Shaw stood and wiped the sand from his trousers. He took two steps toward one of the piles of flaming feathers and wings, his boots sinking into the soft sand, then stopped and turned back to Missy. 'Stay away from them,' he called. 'I don't want you catching anything.'

Missy grinned. 'Do I seem like someone who does what a man tells her to do?'

Shaw laughed, shook his head. 'No, Miss Green,' he said and continued backwards down the slope. 'You seem like the type of woman who would do the opposite of what a man tells her to do.'

15

Widow's Peak Harbour was dark, except for the glow of kerosene lamps burning on boats conducting night business. The *Senhora ao Vento* was one of those boats.

Detective Shaw bobbed quietly at the stern. The freshness of the night was muddled with the smoke from his cigarette as the cloud floated steadily across the deck. The door to the cabin creaked open and Missy made her way to him, placing a mug of tea in his hand. She lit another lamp, hooked it to the stern of the boat and peered down into the murky water.

'What time did you say he would arrive?' she asked.

Shaw checked his wristwatch. 'Around midnight.' He inhaled deeply through his nostrils, filling his chest with the cold, briny night. With Missy's scent, of tide pools and vast windswept beaches. 'Do you smell that?'

Missy shifted. 'Smell what? The dead birds? Or rotten fish? Because I've tried to scrub it out of the boat but it's…'

'No,' Shaw interrupted. 'The ocean.' He sipped the scalding brew. The tea leaves left a pleasant, floral taste on his tongue. 'As a child, even though we had very little money, we would spend every summer in Lahinch, a wee coastal town in the west of Ireland. That was the smell of holidays, of summer. The smell of the ocean reminds me of my childhood. Of my brothers.'

174

'You mentioned them before.'

'Aye. Patrick and Micheál.' Shaw smiled sadly. 'As youngsters, we used to fly this kite. I could never get it to do anything. But Paddy, he could make it dance in the wind. Whip it back and forth. I would watch him do that for hours. The smile on our faces. So carefree. We practically grew up on that beach. God knows where our parents were. Da was probably at the pub and my Mam was probably taking a break for the first time in months, but I can't remember either of them ever being there. The smell of the beach still reminds me of my childhood.' He brought the cigarette to his lips. 'Must be one of my favourite smells.'

'Where are they now?' Missy asked. 'Your brothers?'

Shaw offered Missy the cigarette and took another sip of tea. She held it loosely between her slender fingers, placed the papery end between her lips and took a long drag.

'Paddy was fifteen the last time I saw him. Micheál was twelve,' Shaw said. 'I left Dublin in nineteen fourteen. Enlisted in the British Army. We were poor, you see. My father's drinking didn't help. He could never hold down a job. My Mam, she was a strong woman but... well, I thought I could enlist, earn some money to send back home. It's what a lot of men my age were doing.'

'So, they're still there, in Dublin?' Missy asked, passing back the cigarette.

Shaw drew on it, the paper burning back like a wick on a stick of dynamite. When he spoke, his voice sounded thick, full of smoke, and regret. 'They were killed. While I was away. The Easter Rising in nineteen sixteen. After that, I suppose I was disillusioned with Ireland. When the war was over, I felt no connection to Britain, the country I'd fought for. So, I vowed never to return.'

Missy put her hand on his arm. 'I'm so sorry.'

Shaw flicked the butt over the back of the boat. It hissed as it hit the water. He gave her a dark look. 'I should never have left them in the first place. At least they never had to see the horrors of war. All that dust, mud, fucking… blood.' He glanced at Missy, then shook his head. 'Sorry, Miss Green. I shouldn't have said that. I was being crass.' He tipped the rest of the tea into his mouth and swallowed the hot liquid, the pain in his throat searing away the ache in his heart.

Missy removed her hand. 'I told you, call me Missy.' She looked into her tea. 'I suppose it's normal for someone like you to be crass about death. You've seen more of it than most.'

'Aye, Missy,' Shaw nodded. His eyes scanned the darkness around them, at Missy's face, lit with the dim light emanating from the lamp. It reminded him of a Caravaggio painting he once saw in a gallery in Rome, the one where the widow Judith decapitates Holofernes with his own sword. A shiver rolled up his spine. 'I don't think it ever becomes normal for anyone, but I suppose you learn to cope with it by detaching yourself.'

Missy stared at him, uncomprehending.

'Detachment. It's a defence strategy we were taught in the war. Detach yourself from the trauma of horrific events in order to endure. In our case, to continue operating in battle.'

'A coping mechanism.'

Shaw nodded. 'Isolate the memory, put it behind a door, close that door and open the next one. Keep all the bad thoughts locked away in different rooms. And carry on.' Shaw gazed at the darkened harbour, lost in faraway thoughts. It had been some time since the war ended. Except it never did, just as the memories never faded. 'But then being called to a homicide case, like Lara Harvey's, just opens another room inside your head. Another room, another door. Ad infinitum.'

'Homicide? So she *was* murdered?'

'We're still waiting on the autopsy but we're calling it murder because circumstances indicate it's a high probability. And there's really no other logical explanation. Everyone who knew her said she wasn't the type of person to hurt herself. So, how'd she end up in the water if she didn't jump? Was she pushed?'

'Would this be motive we speak of?' Missy asked.

'It would. So now we just need to find the guilty party.'

'Is that what we're doing here at the harbour, in the middle of the night?'

Shaw placed another cigarette in his mouth and struck a match then nodded, exhaling smoke. He offered the open case to Missy who took one and put it to her lips. Shaw lit another match and held it for her. Missy brought her mouth close and inhaled. She sat next to Shaw against the stern. In the mesmerising darkness the smoke twirled between them. Missy swirled the silvery-blue tendrils between her fingertips.

'It's pretty,' she said. Shaw looked sideways at her. 'The smoke, I mean. Looks like Cirrus clouds.'

'Cirrus clouds?'

'They're those wispy, feathery clouds that appear in the sky when the weather's about to change. They're made entirely of ice-crystals.' Shaw stared into her eyes and said nothing. She blushed and looked away, drawing back on her cigarette. 'But I don't want to bore you.'

'You're far from boring,' he said.

'Oh, please. You don't want to hear pointless facts about clouds.'

'Do you know any more pointless facts about clouds?' Shaw asked.

'I could tell you a thousand pointless facts about clouds. But to a lighthouse keeper, they're not pointless. Reading clouds can be quite useful for predicting the weather.' Missy gazed into her lap. 'Sorry. This was why I never really had any friends,' she said. 'None of the girls at school were particularly fond of me.'

'Why?'

Missy shrugged. 'I was different to them. I was taller. Stronger. A fisherman's daughter with no mother to teach me how to be a girl. I suppose that's why, when I got a bit older, I tried to befriend some of the boys.' She held up the cigarette, peered at it. Then she laughed darkly. 'We got caught smoking in the schoolyard once. I told the teacher they were my cigarettes. That I'd stolen them from home and brought them to school. I thought if I took the blame, those boys would like me. Want to be friends with me.'

'And did they?'

Missy shook her head and took another drag. 'I got the cane. In front of the whole school that bastard forced me to stand with my skirt pulled up above my head, bent over his desk. It was… humiliating. I can still hear the whistling sound, and then the crack, as it landed on the back of my legs. For about two seconds there wasn't any pain. It just felt like a light thud. Then it really hurt. After that, I stopped talking to people. I was sure that if I pretended I didn't exist, then people wouldn't notice me. I tried to become invisible.'

A loud shot rang out, piercing the stillness of the air. Missy jumped. Her hand flew out and landed on Shaw's arm and she peered behind her. 'What was that?'

Shaw covered her hand with his. 'A car backfiring?'

He stood. Placed the empty enamel mug on the stern of the boat. A truck drove slowly past, its headlamps illuminating the space like owl eyes. Exhaust wafted behind it, filling the air with thick diesel fumes. On the tray at the back of the truck, crates were stacked in neat rows. Glass bottles jingled as the truck rumbled over the uneven surface of the road along the harbourfront, toward the docks.

Hands linked, Shaw and Missy clambered over the gunwale and followed the truck on foot to the end of the Blue Mile tramline where it was stopped under the single bare light bulb of a streetlamp. They slid into the narrow space behind a shipping container. Like sardines in a tin, they stood sandwiched between the container and the stone wall, wet with algae. Just Shaw and Missy shrouded in darkness. As though no one else in the world existed. They stood side by side, clasping each other's hands, peering out as the truck idled under the yellow glow.

The idling stopped and the truck fell silent. The driver's side door opened, and a figure climbed out and leaned against it, as though they were waiting for something, or someone.

A loud crack rang out, and a pile of coal tumbled from a broken crate above Shaw's head. It clattered to the ground, showering both him and Missy in black dust. Shaw inhaled the powder, and it tickled his throat. A coughing fit threatened to overtake him. Missy covered her mouth with her hand, trying to hold back any noise.

Shaw coughed silently into his elbow until the coughing fit passed. When the air cleared, and they could breathe again, Shaw glanced at Missy. He gestured toward his own cheek and said, 'You've… here.' The words seemed to escape him. 'On your cheek.'

He pulled out a handkerchief and reached to wipe the smear away. His fingers brushed the side of Missy's neck. He left them there, perhaps a moment longer than he ought to, then held the handkerchief up for her to see. A black smear across the fabric.

A ridiculous wave of shyness came over him. 'Are you hurt?'

Missy checked her arms and hands for any marks. There was a scrape across her wrist. 'Just a scratch,' she whispered.

Shaw smiled then peered around the corner at the truck, but the figure had disappeared. He swore under his breath, cursed himself for being so easily distracted. The crates were illuminated, and he could see that they were identical to the ones in Canberra. Someone was producing and distributing bathtub gin in Widow's Peak, but where? And who was making the booze?

Crunching dirt under tyres came from behind and another car pulled up next to the truck. It was a silver Rolls Royce with tinted windows: luxury compared to the PD's Model T Ford. A tall man got out, closely followed by two shorter, stockier men. Sonny Fynn and his cronies, Shaw assumed.

Sonny Fynn was dressed in a smart, black suit and carried a large briefcase. The yellow glow cast moving shadows over his pockmarked face. His slicked hair glistened like the shine of a Sergeant Major's polished shoes.

The truck driver reappeared and suddenly Shaw recognised his slim build, his long blue overalls and felt cap. The black coal marks that smeared his face.

'Isn't that your friend?' Shaw whispered to Missy.

Missy's eyes bulged and she peered around the corner of the shipping container for a closer look.

Sonny Fynn stood opposite Flea under the streetlamp. Shaw positioned himself in front of Missy to get a better view of the exchange.

'You got the money?' Flea's voice sounded.

'If you've got the stuff.'

Flea gestured to the crates he'd been guarding at the back of the truck.

'Good,' said Sonny. 'We can proceed.'

The mobsters opened the car boot and began unloading the crates from the truck.

Sonny opened the briefcase on the truck's bonnet. 'In light of recent events, I'm renegotiating,' he said.

'Come again?' Flea said. 'My employer has set the price. He doesn't renegotiate.'

Sonny closed the suitcase and clicked the locks. One of Sonny's henchmen approached Flea. Sonny waved him away. 'Don't mind him, Lloyd. He's just marking his territory.'

'Is that what I'm doing?' Flea laughed. 'Let's get one thing straight, Mr Fynn. I don't work for you.'

Sonny smiled maliciously. 'That so?'

'A dog have you as a child did it? Gave you a good shake? Done something to your hearing?' Flea said. 'The money, Mr Fynn. The full amount.'

'A dog,' Sonny Fynn laughed. 'Very funny. I do know a thing or two about dogs.' Out of nowhere, Sonny lunged for Flea. He grabbed his head and held his face to the ground. 'You know, if you want to make sure your dog obeys you, you need to show it the stick. You work for me now, understand?'

Flea didn't move.

'Nod if you understand.'

Flea nodded.

'The police… Did they come asking questions? About Lara? Nod, dog.'

Flea nodded again.

'Do they have any idea who did it yet?'

Flea mumbled something.

'What was that, dog?'

'I don't know!' Flea yelled. 'I don't think so.'

Sonny turned to his cronies, who were standing a few feet away. 'Incompetent pigs.' He motioned for them to put the rest of the crates in the car, then returned his attention to Flea.

'I've got something I need you to do, and I want to impress upon you the seriousness of my intent. I'm about to give you an instruction. You do as I say, your face remains intact. Fail, and I will send my boot through your skull and into the road below it.'

'I'll do whatever you want.'

'When that Irish copper comes back, tell him I want to speak with him. You hear me? Only information leading to the son-of-a-bitch who killed Lara will save your face from becoming Irish stew, understand?'

'I understand.'

Sonny pressed his boot down further onto Flea's face then released it. He nodded to his men, then climbed back into the Rolls Royce. As the car drove away, the light from their headlamps pierced the shadow behind the shipping container where Shaw and Missy hid.

So quickly did this happen that Shaw, standing in front of Missy, was forced to press himself into her to avoid being seen.

His whole body leaned against hers, against the side of the shipping container, his palms at her shoulders, flat against the corrugated metal wall.

With this sudden invasion of space, Missy sucked in her breath. The scent of her neck sent shivers through Shaw's whole body. He looked down into her eyes. She looked up at his. A heartbeat, two. The sound of the tyres screeched along the harbourfront and then, silence. Their breaths synchronised in the darkness. Their heartbeats synchronised. He opened his mouth to say something, but he had no words. Shaw peeled himself off her and stepped out from behind the shipping container.

Flea turned at the sudden appearance of Shaw. 'Who the fuck are you?'

'Detective Ronan Shaw, Widow's Peak PD. We met the other day.'

Flea's face blanched, despite the blood oozing from the fresh scrapes. 'What are you doing here?'

'You want to tell me what that was all about?' Shaw asked.

Flea spat pink saliva then walked to the driver's side door of the delivery truck. 'You saw that whole thing?'

Shaw stood with his feet apart, his hands in his trouser pockets. 'So, Sonny Fynn has a message for me, does he?'

Flea opened the door to the truck. 'Look, man. This was Lara's thing. I don't want any part in this. You heard that guy. I'm just the middleman. I never asked for any part of this.'

'Where does the booze come from, Mr Mathieson?'

Flea stepped up onto the running board. 'You want answers?' He pointed to Missy, standing behind Shaw. 'Ask *her*.'

Shaw glanced across to Missy, then back to Flea. 'What do you mean?'

'Check her sacks. You might find something other than coal among her delivery load.' Flea got into the truck and drove away, roaring out of the harbour.

Shaw turned to Missy. Could she be involved somehow? He scrutinised her face, which seemed to display genuine shock. 'What do you think that was about?'

Missy stood stunned. 'I have no idea. What did he mean, something other than coal?'

Shaw reached into his pocket and pulled out his cigarette case, then offered one to Missy. He struck a match and held the flame to her, then lit his own, considering the likelihood of Missy's involvement, and what Flea could be hiding.

Missy puffed at the cigarette. Bearing in mind she'd only started driving Lara's delivery truck this week, he doubted Missy and Flea were in cahoots.

'One thing is for certain,' Shaw said, exhaling smoke, 'Sonny Fynn is certainly capable of murder. But why would he kill Lara? And why did he threaten Flea?'

'If Flea does know something, why not tell the police?' Missy asked.

Shaw shrugged. 'He works for Sonny Fynn now, I suppose.'

Missy half smiled. 'Like me, working for you?'

Shaw smiled, wordless, breathless, and nodded.

'You know… I like working for you,' Missy said. 'I've learned a lot, actually.'

'Oh?' Shaw said. 'What have you learned?'

'How to lie, how to steal.'

Shaw kicked a stone, sending it shooting into the darkness. 'Excuse me? I'm not a thief, nor a liar.'

She laughed. 'So, tell me something truthful, then.'

Shaw stepped closer to her. He reached out and held her arm. 'You always smell so good. That's the truth.'

Missy glanced at his hand, resting there, then back at his face. She cleared her throat. 'Your wife must be wondering where you are,' she whispered.

Shaw took another step closer, inclining his face toward hers. His hand moved from her elbow to her cheek, thumb running along her jaw. The coldness of her skin under his fingers sent a shudder up his wrist. Missy's eyes were closed. He bent to kiss her. Their lips touched, barely, before he pulled back. The kiss didn't linger, he had barely graced her lips. He wanted to be sure.

When Missy opened her eyes, her eyebrows knitted together and she backed away. She took one step, two, glaring at him. Shook her head. Shaw stood there, frozen.

'Your *wife*,' she said, then turned and ran. Her footsteps echoed as loud as a coal train in the dead of night. Even as the echo of her footsteps vanished, the briny scent of her lingered. Shaw called her name, but she had already disappeared into the gloom.

16

Sexta-feira

I DREAMT about him again. His dark hair, sprinkled with silver. My legs stretch on the too-short, too-narrow bed and I stare at the ceiling. I have slept late, and the day is already half gone.

When I think back to last night at the harbour, moths appear inside me, fluttering their velvet wings. A little voice in my head tells me I imagined it, that I am making such a fuss over nothing. But then I remember the weight of his body pressed against mine, the smell of his breath when he bent to me and the look in his eyes when I moved my mouth away. Afterwards, I returned to my room in the tower, alone. Alone like always. And now I wake, alone.

I pull back the sheets and roll on to my stomach. I reach my hand down the front of my long-johns to the warm part between my legs and think of him. The swollen chunk of flesh throbs under my fingertips. My breath quickens. I take my time. My feet stretch and I spread my toes until they curl inwards involuntarily, and I exhale and release.

Afterwards, I lie there, staring at the floor, the waves of my longing bouncing against the white, curved walls.

Why must I be so lonely?

The wound in my head has started to fester and the rot is spreading like a virus through the rest of my body. I shiver as if a fever has taken hold. Like a parasite it has infiltrated me, and it will spread. It will infect all of me. There are crusty formations of barnacles at its edges, and I feel the same thing happening to the gash between my legs. I scratch at it gently, shedding scales and bits of shell on the bedsheet in the process, then examine my nails. I scrape the scales from my fingers and waves of sickness crash through me, spin in circles like the silent glass prisms above me, it makes me angry and sick and sad. I curse at myself. None if it helps. Sometimes, I can't see the possibility of a way out.

I know that I need to do something physical with my body. I need to feel alive in my arms and legs, my muscles and bones. I want to wash away the rot, and my father always says that saltwater cures everything. The sky is clear and blue through the circular window, but the spray off the waves suggests there's a southerly that would make a swim at North Beach unpleasant.

I know that *Avô* will be wanting to fuel the lantern, but I don't have the energy to rush down to the docks. I don't have the strength for people today. And I cannot face Flea. Not after last night and his accusations. But I also don't have anywhere in particular to go, and if I don't get out of the tower, if I don't move my body, I'll go mad.

Shoving my feet into my boots, I lace them up, but they still feel so heavy, as though sand fills them. Pulling on my ripped wool cardigan, I reach for my father's cap that I stashed away in a drawer. The cap sits low on my head, covering my face. Then I stomp down the stairs and out the door into glaring brightness. Smoke from the keeper's cottage chimney tingles my nose. A distant bell tolls over near the harbour. And the ever-present screech of seagulls.

The sky is clear but it's cold out here. Meandering down the grassy slope, the feeble warmth of the winter sun thaws my skin. Down to the harbour, avoiding the docks, clomping along the road parallel to the Blue Mile tramway. I walk as fast as I can along the far side of the dock, eager to avoid the gazes of the wharfies, their questioning faces; *There's the delivery girl, why hasn't she come to pick up her load?*

Whirling around a corner, a heavy mass hits me, and the air is forced out of my lungs. My body swings over it, and I hit the ground hard.

'Are you all right?' the voice says and I shudder. It's at this moment that I know who I have crashed into. The one person I was trying to avoid. Flea holds his hand out to help me up. The left side of his face is grazed pink and angry where it scraped against the road, held down by the underside of Sonny Fynn's boot.

I gather myself with some difficulty and rub the sand and grit from my hands. 'I'm fine.'

'Where were you this morning?' he asks.

My hands are shaking from the collision. 'What?'

'You didn't show up in your truck.'

'Oh, I um… I overslept.'

Flea regards me with a strange grin. Stranger than usual, and I realise he is looking at what is on my head.

'What's with the hat?' he asks.

'What, this?' I say. 'It's my father's.' I shrug him off and continue walking along the harbourfront, away from the dock, with my head down, staring at the street, at the dirty sand, laced with weeds peppering the road.

Flea trails me. 'Are you incognito?'

'Am I *what*?'

A wagon passes us. It rattles and jolts along the tracks, carrying a large load of coal toward the dock. I continue walking, following the line north.

'Incognito,' he says. 'It means undercover. Concealing your identity.'

'Yeah well, I don't speak that language. And no, I'm not hiding anything.'

Halfway along the tram line, when I can no longer hear the noises from the harbour, I feel it again. The familiar lure of the ocean. It is a strong pull in my centre. The tide tugs at my mind, my heart. I cross over the tracks and walk down toward the water's edge.

It is late morning, and the wind off the ocean bites. Standing at the edge of the water, I cover my sleeves over my fingers and let the waves stroke the toes of my boots. I gaze out past the breakers, out to the horizon, where, on a sparkling sea, a boat slides along it. It is too big, this ocean, too beautiful. It fills me with a strange sense of foreboding. Tips of seaweed fronds peek through the blue surface, curling their fingers. They beckon me. The hiss of the waves against the shore whispers my name. *Missssssy.*

'Where are you off to in such a hurry?'

I flinch. 'Nowhere.' I march along the sand, hoping he will get the hint and leave me alone.

Flea holds up the lunch pail in his hands. 'I'm just on smoko.'

'I told you; I don't speak that language.'

Flea follows. 'Smoko? It's wharfie slang. Means I'm on my lunch break.'

'So?'

A little farther on, I stop to investigate a washed-up fish skeleton and bend to pick up a scallop seashell, shaped like a fan. Leaving the bones, I stuff the shell in my pocket.

'So, let's go somewhere.'

The tram line snakes away from the shore, disappears under a wooden bridge and heads inland, toward the mountain, half a mile to the mine entrance. I gaze back down the beach; in the direction we came. 'Actually, I think I'm going to head back home.'

'Come *on*,' he pleads.

I sigh. The wind is too cold for a beach swim, but the iciness of the water would numb this feeling inside me. I wonder whether Flea can be trusted to keep a secret. 'I do know a place and I haven't been down there in a while. I could show you. It's a bit of a walk though.'

Flea smiles. 'I'm sure I can keep up.'

'Fine,' I say, and kick my boots off. 'Follow me.' Without warning, I take off.

'Hold your horses,' I hear Flea call.

We run until the wind picks up and whips my hair around, the shoreline starts to curve, and the surf becomes a lot rougher. Flea is behind me, only a few paces back.

'You're not that fast, you know,' he yells. He catches me up and I slow my pace. 'Got you,' he says, reaching out and grabbing my arm. He swings me around to face him.

Frowning, I prise his fingers from my wrist, remove his hand from my arm. 'You did.'

A moment passes between us, as I attempt to catch my breath. His eyes linger over my heaving mouth. Then I break away. After that, we walk in silence, beyond the last remaining roads that border Widow's Peak. The paved track becomes dirt, lined with shrubs. Flea asks, 'Where are we going?'

'I told you it was a bit of a walk. Head back if you want.'

The shrubs and their peppery scent thin out the further we walk, and the sounds of the ocean grow louder. We continue on until the land beneath our feet begins to incline. Away from the town, away from people, a self-assurance overcomes me and I feel bold enough to broach the awkward topic we have both been avoiding since we collided with each other.

'How's your face?' I ask. 'Looks like it might be getting an infection.' Flea grunts, so I try again. 'What was all that talk last night about checking my sacks for something other than coal?'

Flea sighs. 'I thought you'd bring that up.'

'Well, you left in too much of a hurry to ask you last night. So, why did you try and get me in trouble?'

Flea stops walking. 'Look, I'm sorry about what I said. I'm sure your sacks are filled with nothing but the best coal the Osborne-Wallsend Coal Company digs up.'

'So, then why say it?'

'I guess I was having a hard time thinking clearly after Sonny Fynn stomped on my face.'

I eye him curiously, but I let it go. Beyond the shrubs, the headland emerges, sitting high above the ocean. Giant boulders topple down to the shore. There is no one in sight.

'That's the *Peak* of Widow's Peak,' I say, pointing to the headland. 'The green pool is down there, behind those big rocks.'

Flea peers down at the grey boulders. 'They look like they should have mermaids sunning themselves on them.'

I turn to him, eyes narrowed. 'What do you know about mermaids?'

He shrugs. 'Just what my mother told me. Bedtime stories.'

My eyes don't leave him.

'What?' he asks. 'You've never heard stories about mermaids? You work on a fishing trawler for God's sake.'

'I mean… I have. Of course, I have,' I say. 'But they're just stories. Mermaids aren't real.'

'Stories come from somewhere, don't they? Haven't you heard the story about the fisherman who caught one in his net? The mermaid warned him not to over-fish and all that. Just take what he needed. Enough to feed his family. But the fisherman didn't listen. And so, the mermaid drowned him.'

I screw my face up at him. 'Who told you that?'

'No one. That's the point. It's just a story. I was brought up on stories about the Likanaya and the Yawk Yawks.'

'Yawk – *what*?' My face is tense, my voice untrusting. 'You and your fancy languages.'

'They're the freshwater kind. Except they're mean and ugly and… tricky. But they all mean the same thing. Young girl… fish's tail. Same as a typical, saltwater mermaid. Except she has seaweed for hair.'

'*Hair?*' I remember what *Avô* said about mermaids luring sailors to their deaths, grabbing them, using their hair.

'You know that seaweed that floats up to the water's surface? It's said to come from the head of a Likanaya.'

'What else do you know?' I ask as I walk.

Flea's voice comes to me on the wind.

'Long, long ago, natives believed they instructed women in ceremonies.'

'What sort of ceremonies?'

Flea shrugs. 'I don't know. Women's business. Had to do with fertility and all that.'

I glance at him.

'Having babies,' he says.

'What do mermaids have to do with having babies?' I ask. Fertility? Babies? I was only a baby when my mother disappeared. When she was called into the ocean. I wonder if it could all be connected.

'In native culture, water is a symbol for women. It's taken from the idea of the sea being like a woman's…' he glances at my stomach, '…womb.' I feel my face flush with heat. 'And anyway,' Flea continues, 'children have gills before they are born, you know. It's how they can breathe inside.'

We take the trail toward the cliff and do not stop until we reach the tip of the headland, where a drop of about one hundred feet connects the Pacific Ocean to the sandstone boulders under our feet. There, we pause at the edge of the continent and feel the wind rush up from the sea. There are no people here, and no boats either.

'So, you think they could be real?' I ask.

Seagulls flap and screech overhead.

'What, mermaids?' says Flea. 'I don't know about that. All I know is my mother told me those stories at bedtime to get me to fall asleep.'

I think about the mermaid I saw from the *Senhora*. And on the beach. The mermaid claiming to be my mother. She seemed as real as the rocks under my feet. But the more time has passed, and the strange things that have happened since, the more I have convinced myself it was all in my mind. My imagination.

The ground below me tilts and suddenly the whole horizon is on an angle. My mind splinters and two voices sound in my head, one that tells me yes, give it a try, see what happens, and the other that shouts at me to turn around, you are mad, utterly crazy.

'Have you ever stood on a ledge and thought, *If I wanted to, I could jump?*' I say to no one in particular, although I know Flea is standing quite close to me. 'I think about it sometimes. There's nothing stopping me from leaping from this spot. Absolutely nothing. No one.'

Flea grunts. 'Yeah, those're called suicidal thoughts.'

I shake my head. 'No, this is different. It's not necessarily a suicidal thought. My mind plays out scenarios of what might happen if… It's like my rational brain *knows* what would happen, but that urge… that urge just pops up sometimes.' I lean over, craning my neck. Below, water laps the thin strip of sand, and the waves are calm and consistent, all the way to the irreproachable horizon.

'It's as though I could do it, but I don't actually want to, and I know I won't do it. It's just, if I wanted to, I could. It's within my power. My control. The thought lingers at the back of my mind. It doesn't just happen at the edge of a cliff. Any reckless impulse to do something self-destructive: swerve my truck into the harbour wall. It's not a desire to die. More a will to live. I am aware that I can easily jump off this cliff – all it would take is a single step. It's as though I know I won't really do it, and that choice… that freedom of choice… is staggering.' I look at Flea then, and my thoughts twist like a rope. 'That never happens to you?' He is staring at me with an expression of something between horror and awe. He shakes his head, his mouth agape, and I laugh it off. 'You ready?'

'Wait, what? We're going down?'

I grab his shoulders and give him a shove but pull him back from the ledge just as quick. The look on his face. Pure terror. I break out in laughter and point to the bottom of the cliff.

'See that gnarled finger of rock jutting out to sea there? The green pool is behind the row of boulders, just on the other side of that channel of water. You can only go when the tide is low, which it is now. See how there's only a thin strip of water flowing through? But we'd better be quick because I don't think it will be like that for much longer. Stay if you want, but I'm going down.'

I make my way quickly down the path and Flea clambers after me. On the descent, I look out at the water, trying to make out any signs of boats. The cliff path soon gives way to the huge boulders that we are obliged to climb over.

'Careful you don't twist your ankle,' I say as I step out along the finger of rock. 'You don't want a messed-up face *and* a crippled foot.'

He hurries after me. 'So, why can we only get there when the tide is low?'

'The thing about this pool, and why no one really knows about it, is that you can only get to it when the tide is low enough to get over the channel that separates the rock shelf from the ring of boulders.'

'How do *you* know about it?'

We rock-hop along the pointy end of the finger toward the circle of boulders, behind which the waves slosh and swirl.

'My father and I have come past this point a million times. At both low and high tide. When the tide is in, the channel overflows with water. If it comes in without warning, it can suck you out to sea. And if you're not a good swimmer, you don't really stand a chance.' I size him up. 'You can swim, right?'

He nods. 'I can swim.'

The channel separates us and the row of boulders, but at this moment, its width is only about two feet; one big step across the water to the rocks on the other side. I pause and tilt my head toward the sound.

'Stop,' I say. 'Listen to the sound the water makes.'

'I don't hear anything,' Flea says.

I nod. 'That tells us it's safe to cross. When you jump, land on one of those rocks on the other side, leave yourself enough room to get your foot in so you can pull yourself up and over the top, all right?'

The water washes in and out of the channel, slow and steady, as I leap across. Flea nods then steps over and lands on the rock on the other side without an issue and I smile at him. I climb up, take his hand, and help him up, and we stand side by side.

Glimmering black rocks slope into the water, creating a deep, dark, green pool. The boulders surround us and waves crash up their other sides.

'Wow,' Flea breathes.

'On a clear day, when there's no wind, you can see all the way to the bottom.'

'It's really beautiful,' he says.

'It's deep too.'

Beside the pool is warm, the boulders absorbing the heat of the sun. I toss my father's cap to the side, undo my belt, wiggle out of my woollen cardigan, and throw them all into a pile. I stand there for a moment in my long-johns, then, with a loud splash, I jump in. The water is freezing and clear as glass, the coldness steals my breath. Allowing myself to sink, immersed in the water, my thoughts steady. I descend, I relax, I unravel. At the sandy bottom I open my eyes and gaze up through the water, wait until my lungs burn, then push off and burst through the surface.

'Don't you feel the cold?' Flea calls.

'Course I do,' I call back and splash him. 'I'm just not a baby about it.'

I dive under again. My body stretches underwater, and my arms reach in front of me. Two large strokes. Gliding to the outer edge of the rockpool, I relish the feeling of the cold water around my body. In this silent world, all my worries melt away: the mermaid, the festering wound in my head and the yearning one between my legs, my father, Detective Shaw and my feelings for him, my loneliness. They are sucked out with the undertow. I surface, then I float face down, bubbles and blurry water swirling below me.

There is nothing like the weightless peace of floating, of freedom. The incredible calm of being in a world underwater. I used to be obsessed with the idea of living under the sea. I wanted to swim in its depths, feel the velvety sand with my bare skin. I learned never to share these strange thoughts with anyone. Not even my father. Even he would look at me in a way that suggested these thoughts were not normal.

Coming up for air, I hear another loud splash. Flea has finally dived in. I pull myself up and out of the water then lie down with my chin resting on my arm on the warm rock, basking in the sun like a skink and picking at the striped barnacles that crust the sides of the pool. The salt dries on my skin and makes me feel light and prickling with life. I lie there, watching Flea in the water, making a little pile of those triangular shells.

'So,' Flea says, 'what's it like being the lighthouse keeper's granddaughter?'

I shrug. 'Nothing special, I guess.'

'But you get to see that enormous light up close. Must be pretty special?'

'People always assume the light must be huge. It's not. The actual light comes from a tiny flame of vaporised oil that burns in a mantle. It gets magnified and directed through the prisms. The Fresnel lens bends the light into a beam so intense, ships can see it more than thirty miles away.'

'Still, it'd beat working the docks all day.'

'You don't work the docks all day. It's barely midday and you're lazing about in the sun.' Flea splashes me. I pretend to cower. 'Why don't you get a different job if you don't like it?'

'Easy for you to say. You got to go to school. I've been working since I was eight years old.'

'I hate to be the bearer of bad news, but school isn't all it's cracked up to be. At least not in my experience.'

'You didn't like school? What, didn't you have any friends?'

I shake my head. 'I used to cry about it, sometimes.'

There is a long silence between us. I remember back to the day I realised crying was pointless. So I just remained inside my own head. I made friends with the sea creatures I found in rock pools or along the shore. Anemone, hermit crabs, starfish. Things got worse for me when my father left and I went to live with my grandfather. I began to have conversations with them inside my head. *They* all found me interesting. After a while, I needed their little voices. Without them I was actually alone.

I laugh light-heartedly. 'Even now, it catches me off guard when people smile at me. When they include me in their conversations. When they remember who I am.'

Flea pulls himself out of the water and sits next to me, splashing his feet. 'I wouldn't worry about people remembering who you are. You and that detective seem pretty friendly.'

My ears heat at the mention of Detective Shaw. 'I barely know the man.' My response comes out in a rush.

Flea nudges me. 'Seems like he has a thing for you.'

'He's married.'

'So? You've noticed how he looks at you, surely?'

My neck tingles and I feel my face flush. 'I don't know what you mean.'

'Yes, you do.'

I suddenly need to dive under the water again. 'I don't.'

Flea stands up then. 'If you say so.'

'Besides, he's at least ten years older than me.'

The surface of the pool swirls and the sounds of waves hitting rock seem to be coming in a little faster and stronger. Flea climbs up one of the boulders and I gaze over at him. He's staring down. He curses. I hear the panic in him.

Scurrying over I hear the deep sloshing noise of the channel even before I peer over the edge. Scrambling to pull my boots and clothes back on, I heave myself up next to him, look to where he is pointing. A stiff wind pierces through my body and a shudder runs through me. The channel is a deep dark trough, swirling with white water. The surface of the rock finger is already submerged under two or three inches.

'Follow me,' I say and twist around to slide down the rock face. 'Quick, Flea,' I call over my shoulder. Waves are coming in at chest height but there is no other way across.

I lower myself down to a ledge that remains clear of water and wait for a break in the waves. 'Listen,' I call to him, trying to keep the panic out of my voice, 'I'll go in the next break, then you follow me over.' He nods; his carefree smile has disappeared. 'Move down to the ledge when I'm over and wait for me to tell you when to go.'

The water surges out furiously, and the tip of the rock finger is under at least a foot of ocean. I take a deep breath and leap over to the rock. Before I land, I know my foot won't hold. It slips across the wet surface, my already heavy boots even heavier now that they are filled with water. I throw my arms out so that at least I will fall on to the rough rock finger on the other side and not into the gushing, sucking water.

Flea swears and calls my name. I grit my teeth as I hit the rock. My boot finds traction and I shift my weight forward. My palms graze across the rough surface, but I remain upright. I look back across the channel at Flea, waiting on the rock ledge.

'I'm all right,' I call.

All the colour has drained from his face.

Steadying myself, the waves crash against my legs, up to my knees. I wait for another break in the waves, hoping for a sign that a smaller one is on its way. Flea is losing patience, panic beginning to overcome him.

My eyes flicker down to the channel, the narrow opening where water sucks in and out, and I am certain a body would fit through that space, and if it did, how quickly it would be dragged out to sea.

'Now?' he calls.

I scan the channel and out past the break to see what is

coming. I know he won't last much longer so I nod and yell, 'Go! Now!'

He leaps from the ledge across the channel. His boot lands with a little splash as it hits the rock under the water, and he smiles at me. He wipes his brow theatrically but at that moment a rogue wave knocks him sideways. He loses his footing and gasps as he falls back, toward the channel. He goes under, his arms flailing. His hand reaches out and grasps for the same surface I crashed into, searching for the rock and for me.

Crawling to the edge of the rock finger, rocked by the incessant waves, I plunge my arms down. I feel his body being dragged in one direction – the wrong direction. I grab his clothes and wrench him back up.

Flea breaks the surface and coughs and sputters. I feel lightheaded with relief, and we clamber backward, away from the channel, the feeling of firm rock under us.

Now that we are across, a surge of excitement sweeps through me. My heart beats faster, and I feel wild with the proximity to danger. I laugh uncontrollably.

Flea's face is grey. 'Remind me never to follow you anywhere again.'

After our swim and brush with watery death, we hurry back to the harbour where I leave Flea at the dock. I pick up the truck and load the sacks onto the back. Tossing my father's cap on the front seat, I drive the loaded truck up the hill to the lighthouse.

'Took your time today, girl,' *Avô* says. 'Where have you been?'

'None of your business,' I say, almost to myself.

He eyes me. 'Want some coffee? Or maybe something a bit stronger?'

I drop a sack of coal at his feet and wipe my hands against my trousers. 'Like what?'

He turns to walk toward the cottage. 'Nothing,' he grumbles.

Outside the keeper's cottage I stop to fill the pail from the water tank. He holds the door open for me and we head inside. *Avô* puts the kettle on the stovetop, and I pour the water into it from the pail. Black dirt entrenches the old man's fingernails.

'I've been thinking, *Avô*,' I say as I take a seat at the kitchen table. 'I want to know more about my grandmother. About *Avó*.'

Avô sets the table with plates and cups then sits in the chair at the other end. He lowers his head. 'It's a sad story.'

'I need to know.'

He brings his pipe out of his pocket. 'Why do you want to expose painful and shameful memories, girl?'

'We have a deal, remember? I drive the truck; I get to ask the questions. Why did she not come with you and my mother to the port?'

Avô pauses. 'There's nothing more to tell,' he finally says. 'She was troubled, that's all. It happens.'

My hands prickle with sweat. 'Troubled? In what way?'

Avô sighs. 'It started not long after your mother was born. It was a dark time, very dark. Small things at first. I'd find her wandering off with the baby along the cliff paths. They were so common in those mountain villages, I never thought anything of it. She'd just be standing there, at the edge, staring off into the abyss.'

He stuffs his pipe with tobacco, strikes a match and puffs at the end. 'People in the village started taking turns, watching out for her. Helping with the baby.' *Avô* scoffs. 'Didn't do her any good. After she cut open her wrists, I took her to see one of those fancy doctors in the city. But she would rather have died than be locked up in that soulless place filled with mad people. So, I decided to keep her at home.'

He takes a deep puff on his pipe and holds in the smoke, slowly releasing it as he speaks. 'Over the next few months, it was like her mind just closed off. She wasn't herself anymore. Then, one day, my dear wife was found at the bottom of a cliff.'

The kettle whistles, *Avô* stands and goes to the kitchen to pour the coffee. I gape at the vacant space he leaves at the head of the table, considering all he has just told me. My heart pounds but I wonder why I am not more shocked at this revelation. It is as though it has dislodged something within me, confirmed something I already knew, deep down inside.

'After the funeral I took your mother off the mountain and found a job as a wickie in *Rio Duoro*. Then we left that cursed land for good and sailed all the way here. Ran away, as far as we could. Of course, your mother grew up knowing all of this. I never kept any of it from her.'

Avô hands me a mug of coffee and I hold it in both hands. I am a whirl of emotions. I need to ask more to confirm whether knowing this information outweighs what has been missing from me.

He sits again, drags on his pipe. The sour tang of his body mixes with the sharpness of the tobacco. 'Missy, you inquisitive little eel. You said you wanted to know. There's your answer.' He squints at me through pipe smoke. 'You understand this more than you think you do. You're a lot like her, you know. Even when you were little, I saw things in you. Parts I'd hoped would be spared.'

I stare at the grains of wood in the tabletop. My mouth has

gone dry. I swallow a mouthful of bitter coffee, so I can speak. 'Like what?'

His voice is barely above a whisper, but I still hear him. 'Dark things. She felt everything too much. She had a penchant for melancholy.'

My head hurts. I need fresh air.

Standing, I leave the table, open the cottage door, and drift across the lawn toward the tower. I walk around its huge base to the cliff on the other side, and stand at the foot of the lighthouse, looking out to the horizon.

The wind whips my hair around me. At the top of the cliff, with the waves way below, surging blue and immense, I close my eyes, inhale the smell of the ocean. A crash, a boom. Screeching.

Scraping hair from my eyes, I open them, and notice something moving down on the rock shelf. The rocks and sand are shifting. But I am too far away to see in any detail. I peer over the edge of the cliff. The tiniest sound escapes my mouth. My hand begins to tremble, and I almost drop my coffee mug, but I manage to steady myself. Inching closer to the edge, my eyes widen in terror.

It isn't the rocks and sand that are shifting. It's what's *on* the rocks and sand. Crabs, thousands of them. Sand crabs, rock crabs, even a few lobsters. They scuttle over the porous surface of the rock shelf, the entire mass moving together as one. An octopus slithers across the sand, its bulbous, reddish-brown head inclines toward me. *The* octopus, from the *Senhora*. No, it couldn't be. I killed it.

Didn't I?

Its black, vengeance-filled eyes recognise me, and my flesh crawls. This creature has returned from the watery depths to take its revenge upon me. To make me pay for what I did to it. Little does it know that since our battle, I have been paying in more ways than I thought possible. First the mermaid, then the dead woman, the barnacles, the rotting of my mind. Since I speared my knife through its bulbous head, since it died in my arms, I have been paying the price. I wish we had never trapped that cursed creature.

At the water's edge, fish flick their bodies in the waves as if they are trying to come ashore. Seagulls circle overhead, curious.

Out in the water, something else moves. Something pale. Not driftwood, nor a shark. Breath catches in my throat. The coffee mug slips from my fingers and shatters on the rocks below. I cry out but I cannot move my arms or legs. I am in a state of total terror. And then I see her, the top of her head.

The woman in the waves.

The mermaid with salt-bleached skin and a silver-green fish tail. She's in the water below me, in all that mess of surf. I cannot look away. She is rolling in the white foamy waves; her dark hair tangled with seaweed. Her huge tail, as long and as curved as a shark's, thrashes about in the waves, its gleaming wetness reflecting the light in a beautiful, oily rainbow.

I want, I *need*, to know that I see her, that she isn't just some apparition, some hallucination, conjured up by my diseased mind.

Then there is a voice. A call. From the ocean. I want to hear more so I take another step forward. And listen. Another step closer. I stumble and lose my footing then realise with horror that if I take another step, I will go over the edge.

I locate the path down to the bottom, but something draws my attention. Every fibre in my body freezes.

Hands.

Pale hands rise from the water. They grip the jagged rocks, and then the mermaid hauls herself onto the rock shelf. Hair that could be seaweed hangs dankly around her face.

The mermaid's head turns and looks straight up at the lighthouse, at me. Or she would have, if she had eyes. At this distance, it is difficult to tell, but they look like empty, black pits.

She waves at me, and, after a moment, I raise my hand to wave back. I take a deep breath. Seagulls circle closer. The blanket of crabs scuttles from the rock shelf, up the path, between the tuffs of grass and shrubs that cling to the cliff wall. The octopus glides along with them, and my stomach trembles with fear.

It *is* the same woman. Neve. Her dark hair, her elongated paleness. Holes for eyes. Seeing her brings up a cold melancholy in me and I am taken over by it.

Now, I do believe.

The mermaid has returned. My mother has come for me, again. She reaches for me. She says, *come to me*. I feel that cold finger touch the base of my neck, a little more firmly this time. She calls again. Her dark mouth pulls me toward the ocean.

I sink, falling.

Down the path, I try not to squash the hundreds of crabs under my boots. When I make it to the bottom, I step along the jagged rock shelf, toward the water's edge, where the mermaid now sits on a large rock, calling, waiting, her fishtail shining in the bright sunshine. I stand before her. Her cold limbs, those of my watery mother, wrap around me. Her embrace, like a wave, crashes over me. Her tentacle-like fingers grip me and suck me and pull me to her. We look at each other.

She smiles. 'Did you ask him, Missy? Did you ask him to tell you the truth?'

I nod. 'He said you drowned. That you drowned in the ocean.'

Her fingers touch my face, their bone-white skin is as rough as dead coral washed up on shore. 'But that isn't the truth, is it?'

I breathe shakily. 'What *is* the truth?' I ask. 'Did Gust blow you into the ocean? To the Five Islands? Is that what happened?'

'Did he tell you that?' Her lips curl into that sharp-toothed grin. 'It's a lie. That's why he feels such guilt. Why he hides from the world. That is why I'm here, Missy. To help you find out the truth. He cannot lie forever.'

A tear escapes. 'But you're not really here.'

'Oh, but I am, Missy. I am. And you cannot hide from me. I'm your mother. There is a sickness in you,' she says. 'You feel it rising up like the bile that leaves a bitter taste in the throat. I know because it was in me, too. No more lies. No more hiding. You belong here, with me. Come…'

But before I can say *yes, take me with you*, she turns sharply away, as if she is called by someone, something from the deepest part of the ocean. She releases me and dives into the water. Her forked tail fin thrusts her through the wave and white spume flicks into my face. Then she disappears under the crest.

The tide tugs. Every nerve and cell in my body entices me to go in after her.

A gust blows across the ocean. It bites my face, stinging from the sea spray. I feel the bone-dry rock where she sat. Even the briny smell of her has vanished. But still, I call to her. I call her name, *Neve*. There is nothing. Only the slap of ink-blue water against jagged rocks.

The sounds around me — the waves launching themselves against the rocks, the wind whistling past my ears, the gulls screeching high above – all become faint and distant, then they suddenly boom. A wave crashes above the rock shelf and the rush of water knocks me over. My feet slide from under me, and I fall heavily against the rocks and, all at once, I come to my senses.

I wipe my palms on the sides of my long-johns and clamber upright, stumbling to the safety of the cliff base, gripping the rocks for support. Gone are the crabs, the birds no longer circle overhead. The octopus has disappeared. I breathe deeply, regaining my thoughts, willing the fog of confusion to lift.

I look back to where the mermaid was, and then I see him. My hands tremble, and I turn my face away in horror. I count to ten and then force myself to look.

The feet, Missy, just look at the feet. That's what I say to myself. The feet are covered in boots, and boots are ordinary things. Brown, scuffed up, leather boots. Then I look further up, at his legs. Trousers. Made of some rough fabric. Dirty, wet. Dark blue. His legs are tied together with rope. And then things become bad.

His shirt is torn, and so is his body beneath. But it's not a shirt. It is the same fabric as the trousers. It's overalls. There is a head, not a face, because that is gone. No eyes. No nose. The man has been carved to pieces.

My hand covers my mouth and I notice it is still trembling. My mind blanks. I can't think of what to do.

It is not my mother, and it is not a mermaid.

My heart stops dead in my chest.

It's Flea.

17

Friday

The thick, antique door heaved open and the musty yet perfumed smell of beeswax and incense entered Detective Ronan Shaw's nose. The stale odour of sanctity, the familiar fragrance of faith. He thought back to the last time he had set foot in a church. The vows he had made to his wife. Forsaking all others, in sickness and health. He had declared – he had promised – to live out his intent. Some promises, he realised, were impossible to keep forever.

Shaw passed the stoup and resisted the urge to cross himself as he entered the nave, an action as impulsively reflexive as sneezing into his elbow or stepping aside to let somebody pass.

He scanned the church. A lady clad in black, her face hidden behind a dark veil of lace, was folded over an altar with burning candles and arranged flowers, mourning her lost husband. Or perhaps her sons. A priest and an altar boy stood together in the far corner of the Gospel side, under a statue of the Blessed Virgin Mary. The Immaculate Mother, draped in blue, her serene face tilted toward Shaw, her outstretched palms inviting him to return to the house of God from which he had walked away many years ago.

The priest whispered and the altar boy nodded intermittently. The lad looked the same age as when Shaw's younger brother, Micheál, became altar boy at St. Saviour's. Mickey had always been the most loved son. The youngest. The doted upon. So, it became his nature to do things that pleased their Da. Shaw and his brother, Paddy, received nothing more from their religious upbringing than expulsion from Sunday School and a clip around the ears for bad behaviour.

A few people were scattered among the polished pews, some quietly talking, their whispered voices echoing in the chamber. Shaw glanced at the confession booths. The curtains were drawn back but both were empty. He scanned the room again, only this time noticing the gentleman sitting in the row closest to the altar, his dark hair, deeply parted and glistening with pomade, and his snappy black suit.

Shaw's footsteps carried outward as he made his way down the aisle toward the front of the church. High, stained-glass windows cast kaleidoscopic patterns upon the stone floor. He stopped at the second row and sat behind the man, restraining a cough at the pungency of his cologne as he slid along the smooth pew.

The man in the front row stiffened. 'You're a difficult man to get hold of.'

Shaw cleared his throat. 'When I heard you wanted to speak to me, Mr Fynn, I did my best to make myself available.'

Sonny Fynn spoke without turning around to face Shaw. 'I appreciate that, Detective. This is a matter of urgency.'

'Best be quick, or I'll be missed. You mind telling me what this urgent matter is about?'

'I understand you're the detective on Lara's case,' Sonny Fynn said. 'I want to know everything you've got on her killer so far. I want to know everything you know.'

The arrogance of the man. Shaw had assumed there would be a level of egotism, but he had not expected this. He leant back against the pew, stretching out his arms. 'Why do you need to know, Mr Fynn? What would you plan on doing with that information?' Sonny Fynn turned his face, his profile visible for the first time, the craters along his cheek emphasised in the diffused lighting. 'Besides,' Shaw continued, 'you must know I can't divulge anything to you. I've heard some very bad things about you.'

Sonny Fynn scoffed. 'Such as?'

Shaw maintained a business-as-usual expression. 'Oh, this and that. Can you tell me where you were on Sunday evening?'

'I can. Can you tell me why you still haven't caught the son-of-a-bitch?'

Shaw crossed his legs. 'Would you outline your movements to me please, Mr Fynn?'

'I wasn't anywhere near Widow's Peak.'

'So, you were where?'

Sonny Fynn shrugged. 'I have businesses to run.'

Shaw nodded theatrically, looking around the church. The priest and the altar boy had moved to the ambulatory. 'And business is booming, I hear. A little birdy down in Canberra told me there are some people there who'd like to put a stop to that.'

'You suggesting I should be afraid of that orange-haired Yank, O'Malley?'

Shaw shook his head. 'You served, right?'

'The war was over a long time ago.'

'Tell me this, Mr Fynn: did you and Lara have any arguments

this week? Any disputes?'

Sonny Fynn peered around at Shaw, his dark irises, almost as black as his pupils, glistened in the flickering candlelight. 'What are you suggesting?'

'Just asking routine questions.'

Sonny Fynn's jaw tensed. 'You still think it was me?' he spat. 'Why would I kill Lara? We were engaged. I wanted to marry her.'

'When did you last see her?' Shaw asked.

Sonny Fynn's nostrils flared. 'Not that day.'

'Was she avoiding you?'

'No.'

'I don't suppose she was seen with any other men recently?'

The skin on Sonny Fynn's neck flared red. He turned front on to Shaw; his lip curling back. 'Enough.' He breathed hard.

Shaw pushed further. 'Anyone at The Milk and Honey showing her a bit too much attention?'

Sonny Fynn's voice was loud, too loud for this quiet space. 'I said *enough*!'

The priest shot barbs through them. '*Shhhhh*!'

Sonny Fynn sucked air through his teeth. 'I'm not accustomed to being spoken to like that.'

Shaw raised his eyebrows. 'Your reputation precedes you, Mr Fynn.'

'Underestimate me, Detective, and see how it goes.'

'I've no time for macho bravado this morning, Mr Fynn. I responded to your invitation because I wanted us to understand each other. You want something from me, and I want something from you. You are a businessman. So, I have a business proposition for you. A deal. Soldier to soldier. You want information on your girlfriend's killer, and I want to know who your supplier is.'

Sonny Fynn scoffed. 'And what do I get in return?'

'I can offer you a new relationship with the police. We could turn a blind eye to all of your operations. Including those across the border in Canberra.'

'Why are you doing this? I don't think the police would look too kindly upon Irish scum going against the rules.'

'I'm not here to be liked. I'm here to solve a fucking murder.'

'So, all this, just for a name?'

'The name of your supplier, yes.'

Sonny Fynn tightened his mouth and stared at Detective Shaw. 'Let's get one thing straight, Detective. If you find the son-of-a-bitch who murdered Lara, you'd better tell me first. I mean *before* you make any arrests, agreed?'

'Agreed. I'll even hand him over to you personally, Mr Fynn,' Shaw said. 'Tell me the name of your supplier, and we have a deal.'

Sonny Fynn hesitated. He turned and pointed his finger at Shaw. 'If you fail to tell me who it is, and arrest the guy, your days are numbered, you got that?'

Shaw held out his hand to Sonny Fynn and he shook it.

'You're a brave man, Detective,' Sonny Fynn said. He took a handkerchief from his breast pocket and wiped his palms. 'My supplier desires to remain anonymous. But it wouldn't take a genius to figure it out.'

'The name, Mr Fynn,' Shaw said.

'You saw those birds yesterday morning? Hundreds of 'em, lying dead on the beach?' Shaw remembered the dead birds. He remembered the smell of their burnt feathers, the blackness of the smoke as it blew down the beach, their bodies popping as the flames engulfed them. Sonny Fynn continued, enjoying dangling the carrot in front of Shaw's nose. 'You know what caused them all to drop dead out of the sky like that?'

Shaw had considered a weather event could be responsible. Either that or some kind of disease. He kept silent.

'People reported hearing a loud noise, right?' Sonny Fynn said. 'Think about it. Liquor production is time-intensive and risky because it's highly flammable. It has to be heated to high temperatures, right? Liquor stills have been known to explode.'

Shaw shrugged, nodded. He'd never made liquor before, although he supposed there had to be some sort of chemistry involved, and with it, a level of risk.

'Where do you think someone could make a batch of that stuff, without getting caught?' Sonny Fyn asked.

Shaw thought back to the previous morning on the beach. His junior Constable had mentioned something about the steelworks. It was big enough, closed-off enough. 'Are you suggesting the steelworks has something to do with the liquor production?'

'Not the steelworks, genius.'

Shaw's mind ticked over. Mr Barkley had reported a loud, electrical-like bang, but hadn't mentioned where it had come from. An image of the lighthouse appeared in his mind.

Sonny peered at Shaw, edging closer. His voice came in a raspy whisper. 'The White Widow.'

Shaw left the churchyard and crossed the unpaved road. He strode down the hill toward Market Street where a horse stood, attached to a cart loaded with cans of milk. He halted. The driver was nowhere to be found.

The horse's ebony coat reminded him of Missy's hair. A vision of her face, framed by ink-black waves formed in his mind. His stomach dropped as he remembered, again, the previous night at the harbour, and the kiss. The hot shame of it. How could he have completely misread the signs? The lingering gazes, her hand on his. For God sakes, the outright flirtation. Was he so out of touch? He was desperate to see her again. To explain himself.

Shaw approached the animal from the front. It was a fine mare with long legs, and a muscular torso. The horse lifted its face and watched Shaw with shining black eyes. Its ears flicked upright. He extended his hand to the horse's muzzle, and it bent to give it a sniff.

Shaw clicked his tongue, came in close, stroked his thumb across its face. '*Dia dhuit, a chara*,' he whispered, inhaling its earthy scent; a mixture of hay and sweat and leather. The horse cocked its head as Shaw gently rubbed its coarse fur and continued to whisper in Irish.

'*Dia dhuit, cuisle mo chroidhe*.' Hello, my sweetheart.

He rubbed the horse under its neck, just as he used to do to his girl, Silver. She was a bossy mare, but she knew where the lines were. Oh, she would push it as far as she could sometimes, but she trusted that he wouldn't ask her to do anything that would put her in danger. And Shaw, a city man, with no equine experience, had suddenly found himself in charge of this beast of a horse.

Silver was fairly indifferent toward Shaw at first. Self-sufficient and confident. The most he normally got out of her was simply standing quietly with him. But he used to think there was something in that.

Of course, that was before Cambrai. Cavalry units considered horses essential offensive elements, but over the course of the war, they soon realised horses were no match for machine gun and artillery fire. Shaw wasn't part of the cavalry, nothing so grand as that. Once they no longer used the horses on the battlefield, they used them for logistical support.

Horses were better at travelling through deep mud, or over rough terrain. Better than trucks or cars. They were used for carrying messengers and for pulling field guns. They were also used for recovering the dead from No Man's Land. Even though they were just as vulnerable as soldiers at the front. Just as susceptible to shells, artillery fire, mustard gas.

In 1917, the British planned a raid to capture a pocket southwest of Cambrai to relieve pressure on the French. The raid transformed into a fully-fledged offensive, an assault on the Germans' Hindenburg Line. Nineteen British divisions were assembled, supported by hundreds of tanks, and five cavalry divisions.

The tanks ripped through German defences and captured thousands of prisoners. But all the planning and all the resources and all the tanks couldn't stop the weather from intervening. The breakthrough was abandoned when infantry reinforcements failed to show. Five days later, the British had been driven back to where they'd started.

Shaw was part of logistical support, sent to recover the guns. He wrapped Silver's hooves in cloth to reduce noise, then ventured across the line into that muddy, treeless stretch of Hell, dotted with shell holes and barbed wire and festering bodies.

Shaw managed to retrieve one of the guns before a barrage of artillery fire by German troops descended on the road they needed to take to get back behind British lines. Shaw and Silver jumped into a trench and, trapped and starved, waited out the attack.

Stumbling back through No Man's Land, through the mud, rain, and terror, they returned, alive and with the guns, to British lines. After that, Shaw and Silver would spend any time they could together, with her chin resting on his shoulder and nibbling his hair. His bossy girl, she trusted him implicitly. They could read each other without a second thought. He knew exactly how she would react and exactly how to respond to her.

The mare's nostrils flared as large as wooden spoons, suspending Shaw's memory. He whispered to her again and stroked her dark mane.

Through mud, under shellfire, horses brought the British Army food, guns, ammunition. Even though they themselves were starved, sodden, and spent. Without horses, the war would have been impossible. Without them, the British Army would have crumbled. But the British Army knew what they were there for. Shaw knew what he was there for. Those poor devils didn't, did they?

Shaw considered mounting this beauty and riding away, along the coast, along the cliffs. He would gallop south until the land tumbled away and he could sink his feet into wet sand. Away from life, from his past. What if he just disappeared? He considered riding straight to the lighthouse, confronting Edgar Coelho, arresting him. Could Sonny Fynn really have him killed? How would Missy react, knowing that Shaw had a part to play in her grandfather's death?

Dirt crunched as footsteps approached from behind. The horse quivered its lip then let out a loud whinny as its owner approached. Shaw turned to face the man, who stood awkwardly, having interrupted this tender moment, then tipped his hat to Shaw, who nodded and strode away.

Shaw sprung up the stone steps, swung open the wrought iron gate, and passed under the stone archway of Widow's Peak Police Station, stepping through the cool shade of the entranceway into the foyer just as Constable Lou Bowers exited the building.

Shaw reached his arm out to stop the Constable. 'Wait there a minute, would you?'

Constable Bowers's heavy footsteps halted, and he turned to face Detective Shaw. 'Sir?'

Shaw ascended to the top step, into the sunshine. 'You knew Lara Harvey, didn't you?'

Bowers's eyebrows knitted together. 'Why are you asking me about her?'

Shaw placed a cigarette between his lips, leaving it to jolt up and down as he spoke. 'Some of the other fellas mentioned you frequent The Milk and Honey, which is where she worked.' He clicked his cigarette case closed and placed it back in his jacket pocket, not bothering to offer Constable Bowers one.

'Who've you been talking to?' Constable Bowers said.

Shaw lit up. 'No one in particular. So, do you?'

'Do I what?'

Shaw exhaled a cloud of white smoke. 'Frequent The Milk and Honey?'

'What if I do?'

'Well, it's an illegal establishment for one. But I'm more interested in your relationship with the victim. You don't mind if I ask you a few questions about her, do you?'

Constable Bowers took a step up and folded his arms, puffing his chest like a peacock. 'Would it make any difference if I did?'

Shaw fixed his steady gaze on him. 'What was your relationship to Lara Harvey?'

Bowers shrugged. 'Relationship? I ordered drinks from her. She served them up. I paid her.'

'Did you get on with her?'

Bowers looked to the ground, to the street, anywhere but Shaw's eyes. 'I barely spoke to her.'

Shaw nodded, took a deep drag of his cigarette, took his time. 'You never chatted to her? A chat is hardly illegal.'

Bowers's face began to pale. 'Beyond ordering drinks, I never said a word to her.'

'What did you think of her?'

'I don't know. She was pretty, I suppose.'

Shaw gave him a dead look, man-to-man, suggesting there was more that he wasn't telling him. 'You liked her?' he finally said.

Bowers wiped the sweat from his forehead with the sleeve of his oversized uniform. 'I didn't know her. She seemed all right. I feel a bit sorry for waitresses, to be honest. Must be tough dealing with some of the men they get in The Milk and Honey.'

Shaw narrowed his eyes at him. 'Men like Sonny Fynn?'

Bowers's voice came out a little too high-pitched for Shaw's liking. 'Sometimes.'

Shaw flicked his cigarette on the footpath. 'I'd wager Sonny Fynn isn't the type of man who liked other men chatting to his fiancé, even if it were just to order drinks.'

'Where are you going with this?'

'Usually, the killer is someone who knows the victim.' Shaw patted Bowers on the shoulder, a little too roughly to be considered friendly. 'If you can think of anyone else she was close to, Constable Bowers, I'd be grateful for that information.'

Constable Lou Bowers finally met Shaw's eyes and nodded. The spattering of beige freckles emphasised his pallid complexion, made paler by Shaw's piercing blue gaze. Bowers stumbled down the steps and away from the station.

'Watch your step,' Shaw called as he stepped inside and was instantly greeted by Midge.

'Ah, there you are, Detective Shaw. You remember Miss…'

Missy drifted toward him, blank-faced. 'Green.'

Shaw could see she was upset. 'Yes, I remember Miss Green,' he said, taking Missy by the hand. 'Come on. Let's go somewhere quiet.'

18

Sexta-feira

WE drive to the lighthouse.

Detective Shaw dodges the tufts of grass sprouting in the middle of the road. The wind rocks the car violently up here. He pulls up right in front of the tower. Midday sun streams in through the front windscreen.

He looks up from lighting his cigarette, through the windscreen, up at the tower, squinting through the bright sunlight, scrutinising it, wary of it. The smoke curls up in a steady stream, filling the car with a hazy veil. He offers it to me. Not one from his case. The one from his mouth. I accept it and take a long drag. His eyes linger on the lighthouse. I watch him. He glances at the cigarette, still in my fingers. I take another puff and hand it back.

He reaches past me then, so close I smell his cologne, woody and fresh like pine needles and sea salt and I want to lean in and inhale it deeply, but he opens the glove compartment and places a pair of driving goggles in my hand. The leather is worn and soft brown, I rub my finger along the neat seams and smile.

'I've been meaning to give these to you.'

When Shaw speaks, the cigarette dangles languidly from the

221

corner, in that soft cushiony part of his lips. My eyes follow the outline of his jaw as it moves. He is startlingly attractive. His voice, with its Irish lilt, plays like a melody in my ears. My heart flips inside my chest like a fish caught in a net. Only that it is not a fish in a net, it is swimming in wide-open ocean, and my fish heart swims with him in close proximity, it wants to be with him always. Fish swim together to protect themselves from predators. And when I am with him, I feel safe, protected. No predator would dare attack me. I would follow him anywhere.

The car fills with our smoke, his breath. His lean features are disarming, he is impossible to read. His eyes have sunken deeper into their sockets since I saw him yesterday.

He looks at me directly and I realise I've been so transfixed watching his mouth move that I haven't been listening to the words coming out. '…My feelings for you ambushed me and…'

My heart palpitates and I say the words in a rush. 'Your feelings for me?'

He takes a deep breath, sucks air into his hollow cheeks. 'What I'm saying is, Missy, I want to apologise.'

I inhale air and smoke. 'What for?'

He pushes back his greasy coif of hair. 'About last night. I'm sorry.'

'Oh, that,' I say. 'It's fine.' I reach for the door handle, but Shaw stops me.

'No, I mean, I want to explain.' He takes a long drag of the cigarette and holds the smoke in his lungs. Finally, he breathes it out. 'About my wife.'

I try to remain upbeat, carefree. 'What's she like? Your wife?'

Shaw taps the cigarette into the ashtray and leaves it there. He wipes his mouth, looks out the driver's side window, then back at me. 'She was a nurse,' he finally says. He smiles at me. 'That's where we met. On the battlefield.'

I wonder at his use of the past tense. '*Was*? She's not anymore?'

Silence. The wind whistles.

He picks up the cigarette, taps it again, even though there is no ash to tap off. 'No, she errr… she died. Spanish Influenza.'

And there it is. Realisation hits me like a wagon of coal tumbling upon my head. I feel wretched. I feel pity and sympathy but most of all, and worst of all, I feel so, so stupid. I try to find the right words, try to find something comforting to say, but all I can manage is a whispered, 'I'm sorry.'

He nods. 'She… she'd been through a lot. Toward the end, she tried to put on a brave face, but really, she was just… fragile.' He smiles and looks at me from the corner of his eye. 'Probably deserving of a better man. She was beautiful. Funny, too.'

I try to smile but my lip is quivering. 'She sounds nice.'

Shaw laughs half-heartedly. 'She was out of my league, really.'

We lapse back into silence. The wind is awful now. Screaming at us.

I clear my throat. 'No kids?'

Shaw shakes his head. 'Didn't get the chance. The illness saw to that. When she died, everyone always said, you'll get over it. That's the lie they tell you. If you focus on the pain, you continue to suffer. But it's always there, the pain. You learn to live with it. It doesn't mean it ends, but you learn to live with it.'

He smiles at me then, a sincere, shy smile.

'Tell me more,' I say.

'About her?'

I shrug. 'Sure. Or about you.'

'What about me?'

We stare at each other. I look at his eyes, so pale they're almost transparent. He brings his face closer. My breath quickens. I want to trace the freckles on his cheekbone with the fleshy tip of my thumb. A howl of wind makes me jump and Shaw looks through the driver's side window and the moment is lost. He opens the car door and exits the vehicle, and I do the same.

My hair whips my face, and I squint into the briny sea air. We trudge toward the tower, a good distance between us. I drink him in with my eyes, his dark grey pinstriped suit, the way he carries himself, like he holds the world on his shoulders, the straightness of his spine, like he isn't afraid of anything. His charm, his confidence, so disarming. A man who is intelligent, gentle, thoughtful. *A widower.*

I lead Shaw around the cliff side, running my hand along the base of the tower, and walk right up to the edge of the cliff, the wind blowing me back. We stand together and watch the waves breaking on the rocks far below. The cliff is a jagged wall of rock, saltbush clinging to it in places.

I pass my eyes over Shaw, but he has become pale and clammy. I notice his hands are shaking. Gone is the straightness of his spine, his confidence has disappeared. I panic, terrified that he is unwell or maybe dying. He is unsteady on his feet and reaches for me. I take his arm and help him to sit on the grass.

'What's the matter?' I ask. It is difficult to speak because the wind snatches away my voice.

He smiles, unsteadily. 'It's nothing, I just need to get back a bit from the edge.'

I glance at the edge, then back at him. 'Are you afraid of heights?'

He waves away the question. 'Not afraid, no. Just not overly enthusiastic about them.'

'Come on,' I say. 'We have to go over.'

'Just… give me one minute.' He brings his knees up, places his elbows on them and lowers his head in the hole made by his legs. He takes in deep breaths, then slowly exhales. I sit next to him, on the grass, feeling the wind against my face, and watch him perform this ritual. His breathing eventually slows, the colour slowly returning to his face. He looks at me.

'Did something happen? During the war?' I ask.

Shaw breathes the wind deep into his lungs and peers out at the horizon. Finally, he nods. 'We were in a bell tower. Told to shoot any Germans we saw. Right up high, we were, on this precarious little ledge. For five days. No reinforcements. No food. The water ran out. Me and another soldier. I made him swap places with me because I couldn't stand looking at how high up we were. On the fifth day, we got hit by a shell. Hit him right in the face. All his lower teeth knocked out. His bottom lip was torn off. I had to hold on to him, wrestle him basically, to stop him leaping from that tower. I just kept telling him help was coming, help was coming. He'd be all right. After two days like that, he died anyway.'

'You must have been terrified.'

Shaw picks at a blade of grass. He nods. 'Yeah, I was.' He looks me in the eyes. 'But it wasn't a panicky sort of fear. I could feel the urgency. I could feel the danger. But my mind was working because I had a job to do. I don't remember much, really. It was very loud. Then it got quiet. I had this ringing in my ears from the bullets.' He laughs. 'I remember feeling a little bit sad because my Mam was going to find out I had died.'

I stare at him, unable to speak. Unable to fathom the story he'd just told me.

He turns to me, smiles shyly. 'You said I ought to talk about it, remember?'

I study Shaw's face. Could he sense this feeling within me? If he did, could he continue to ignore it forever? I look down at the grass. 'I did say that, didn't I?'

The wind picks up and I motion to the cliff edge. 'Come on, we have to go. The tide will be coming in soon. Would it help if I held your hand?'

Shaw reaches for my hand and interlaces our fingers. He makes himself stand, keeps his eyes from the edge. 'I'll be all right. Just don't let go.'

'Here's the path,' I say. 'I'll go down this side, nearest the edge, so there's no risk of falling.'

He nods.

We step forward, our hands locked together, as if we're on a Sunday stroll rather than going to see a corpse. We find the rocky path down to the bottom. The path is sheer, and the stones are loose underfoot.

'We're perfectly safe,' I say. 'Don't rush.'

We scramble our way to the bottom of the path, onto the sand.

'There, you've done it,' I say, and he smiles at me. I point to where I found the body. Where I found Flea. 'He's over there.'

We trudge along the small stretch of the uneven shoreline, strewn with shells and chunks of seaweed, toward the rock shelf. Waves roll quietly onto the strip of beach and dissolve into foam on the shore. The tide is out, the waves do not yet reach the rocks. Shaw steps up onto the rock shelf then holds his hand out to help me up and we hop carefully over the rockpools around the point.

Standing beside the corpse, I look down at what remains. Shaw crouches to examine the body. The skin on Flea's chest is torn open, and there is a large wound on his neck. His face is almost completely gone. Shaw studies the gash, pauses, looks him over, then turns to look up at me.

My arms fold around my chest, protecting myself from the horror that is left of Flea's body. 'Could it have been an accident?'' I ask. I hope. 'Could he have fallen? Hit his head on the rocks?'

Shaw shakes his head. 'That cut was made by a knife.' He points to the neck, avoiding the torn flesh. 'Serrated, by the looks of it.'

My hand flies to my mouth. 'Murdered?'

Shaw's gaze falls lower, to the legs and the rope that binds them together. He reaches out and carefully traces the line of rope with his fingers, bringing his face closer to the knot.

He speaks, almost whispers, but the wind carries it to me. 'I've seen that knot before.'

I rub my forearms because the wind is biting, even down here, sheltered from the elements. 'Do you think they're connected? Do you think it could be the same killer?'

Shaw's beautiful, cold eyes sweep up the cliffside, to the lighthouse. He nods. 'It's possible.' The wind howls, almost knocking me off my feet. A wave breaks over the lip of the rock shelf. Shaw returns his gaze to me. 'A killer will leave certain clues behind, whether they want to or not. The knife they use, the way they hold it, the way they cut from left to right, or right to left. Whatever it is, it will be the same. That's usually how we know –

the similarities.'

'What's similar about this one?'

Shaw runs a hand through his hair. 'One on the beach and one on the rocks. One seemingly drowned, the other battered and bruised and sliced open with a knife. It's possible this murder was done by a different person, for a different reason but…'

'You don't think so?'

He shrugs.

'Was the killer a man or a woman?' I ask. 'Can you tell?'

'It's difficult to say. The knife has been used with force, but still, a woman could manage to inflict a wound like that. There's nothing under his fingernails. He was probably taken by surprise. But we should leave ourselves open to other possibilities as well. If this is the same killer, we need to know who could have been in the area of both murders.'

'Could the killer be a stranger? Someone who didn't know Flea?'

Shaw nods. 'Perhaps. We can't rule it out. But I still think it's unlikely. Someone with a connection, a motive. Even if it is an irrational one.'

'What do you mean, an irrational one?'

He stands there, slightly slouched, hands in his pockets, his steely glare glazed over, then he looks up, right at me, and he says, 'Lara Harvey was a woman who had a lot of interest from men, so maybe there was someone she was keeping secret about. If so, who, and why?' He gestures to the corpse. 'The same with Flea. What did he do that caused someone to kill him? What did he say? That night at the docks. What was it? Something about the delivery to the lighthouse.'

Waves smashing against rocks intensifies. The rock shelf

slowly disappears as the sea creeps closer.

'We have to go,' I say. 'The tide's coming in. What about the body?'

A wave washes through and sucks back out. The surface of the rock shelf swirls with white water.

'We'll have to leave it.'

'Wait.' A faint shimmer, a glimpse of something glinting from inside the gash in Flea's neck. It catches the sunlight, like a shard of glass or a shiny silver coin. 'What *is* that?' I step closer to Flea's body, bringing my face to the wound. It's wedged in the flesh; I reach in and pluck it out. No bigger than my fingernail, it shimmers in the sun and threatens to blow away in the wind.

Not a coin.

A fish scale.

Shaw's eyes narrow as I hand it to him. He holds it at a distance between the tips of his thumb and forefinger, like it could be poisonous, like it could bite. His face becomes instantly alert, and he looks at me. For a moment I think he's about to say something, but then he folds his handkerchief around it and tucks it away in his trouser pocket. The seawater rushes up around our feet, cold and wet.

'Come on,' Shaw says as he reaches for my hand.

We make our way across the rock shelf, around the point toward the cliff base. The waves surge out furiously, and we clamber across the wet rock surface. Climbing down, I gasp with the shock of cold water. Clutching Shaw's arm, together we wade through, resisting the pull of the undertow. The crest of each wave reaches our waists, and we struggle against the rip current.

At the bottom of the cliff, the water rolls up over the sand. The wind is so fierce and the white water so violent I lose my footing and twist my ankle. Throbbing pain flares in my foot. Before I can register it, the world falls silent, and I am underwater. I try to push up with my hands, but I can't be sure where the ground is and I am quickly running out of air.

Shaw grabs me under my shoulders and pulls me up and toward him. I emerge and water pours down my back. Stabbing pain shoots up my leg as I attempt to stand. He holds me and we scramble a small way up the rocky path, away from the water. My wet hair tangles in the wind and sticks to my face, making it difficult to see. We stay like that, my arms around his waist, my face against his chest, breathing heavily, our legs tangled under us.

We limp up the rest of the path to the top of the cliff, soaking wet and cold from the biting wind. The chafe of my wet clothes and gritty sand makes the climb difficult. At the top, we cling to each other, trembling.

I look back down the way we came. The ocean swells over the rock shelf and Flea's spread-eagled remains are being dragged out to sea by the force of the water. A tear slides down my face and I hurry to wipe it away. My wet hair sticks to my damp cheeks. 'Poor Flea.' A lump lodges in my throat. 'He was my friend.'

Shaw turns to me. The glare of the sun pierces his irises, and it is like I can see into him. Like he is baring his soul to me. He reaches out and, with his thumb, slides the chunk of sandy, wet hair from my face. Out of nowhere, he leans forward and kisses me, full on the mouth. I feel his stubble and I taste his lip rimmed in salt water, and his breath, all tobacco. Something dislodges within me. I feel it. The first time in a long time. Happiness. Joy. Those slippery things I have always been chasing.

He pulls back and I stand, staring at him, my body tingling with desire. The wind steals breath from my mouth, or was it the kiss? He turns, probably to head back to the car, but I draw him back, into me. His muscles tense as I kiss him, hard and long and we give in to it, into each other.

His fingers reach up to touch the back of my head, and now it is my turn to pull away, afraid he will feel the rotting hole in my head. An image floats in front of my eyes, of the hole festering away, with its gelatinous seaweed coming off into my hands in clumps, like grey-green fish-eye jelly. It is rimmed with barnacles and parasitic sea creatures that have burrowed into my mind, blackening my thoughts, making them coil like smoke, making me see things that aren't there.

The memory of the mermaid's hollowed eyes flashes before me. My ribs tighten, sweat slicks my palms, bile churns in my stomach. My thoughts spiral and I lose control of them.

I step away but my mind still spins, the whole world spins. The cliff edge swirls like the churning sea below it, and it rushes up to splash me in the face, just like when the mermaid flicked her tail and sea spray stung my face in the biting wind. I feel light, like a leaf shaken from its twiggy branch, like I could be snapped in half. I put my hand out to steady myself and it's shaking.

Shaw catches it. 'Are you all right?'

A wave hits me then and I am knocked over. At least that's what it feels like. I am aware of a trembling in my legs, the throb in my ankle, and I no longer have the ability to stand. I am suddenly afraid I might fall to the ground.

'Not really,' I say. The snarling wind spins the world around me. The blood from my head rushes to my feet and suddenly I feel so cold, I start to shiver.

He holds my hand tighter, and it is his turn to lower me to the grass. I close my eyes for a second.

'God, your skin is like ice. What's the matter?'

I can't let him see it. I can't let him know that there is this thing, this ugly, rotten, dark secret I'm hiding. Fish always rot from the head and that's what I am, the daughter of a fish, rotting from the head. He would turn away from me in disgust. Just like everyone has always done. And I would be alone, again.

'I don't know,' I say. 'I think I just need to lie down.'

Shaw glances at the lighthouse, then back at me, keeping me upright. 'Your father's right. You shouldn't be spending so much time there.'

I shake my head. 'No. It's not that. I keep having these… episodes. I don't know why this keeps happening to me.'

Although I stare straight ahead, I know he is watching me.

'What happens?'

I take in deep breaths. Deep lungfuls of briny air. 'I hear things. I can hear that seagull screeching. I still hear it, like it entered my head, and I can't shake it out. And then, I hear a voice. I feel like I'm being pulled toward it. I enter these states and I… I don't know where I am. My mind races. I see things that aren't there.' I look at him. 'I saw the mermaid again.'

His frown is full of deep concern. 'You saw the mermaid today?'

I nod. 'It was her. She was sitting right there.' I point over the cliff edge. 'She was sitting where Flea was.'

Shaw holds my face in his hands. 'Tell me what happened.'

I choke out the words. 'I was standing right here. Then I heard… her voice. She called me down to her.' I look into Shaw's eyes. 'But then, it wasn't her. It was… Flea. And he was dead.' I am sobbing now, tears stinging my cheeks.

His eyes search mine. 'What does she say when she calls to you?'

'That I should come to her. That I should join her. Her voice, it gets inside me, and I obey it. I'm scared. But that's not the scariest part. When she calls me… I *want* to go with her. It's as though all my life I've been waiting for her to call me to the sea. It's as though once I'm there, I'll be able to breathe, finally. I'll be free.'

He pulls me into him. My tears and wet face stain his shirt. He rests his chin on the top of my head and holds me there and lets me cry into his chest. When I have run out of tears, he helps me stand, wraps his jacket around my shoulders, and takes all my weight as I hobble toward the car. 'I think it's best we get you home. You need rest.'

Panic washes over me. I cannot risk being left alone with Gust. 'No, I can't go home. My father. Just let me lie down. In the lighthouse.'

'Missy, I promised your father I would keep you away from the lighthouse,' Shaw says.

I flinch away from him. 'What? Why would you do that?'

He comes to me, draws me into him. Our noses touch. 'Please. Not for him. For me?'

My legs are shaking, and my heart is a fish desperate to escape the net. It's flipping like a maniac, not holding back. All I can do is nod. 'Yes,' I say. 'First let me catch my breath, then I'll go home.'

His nose is still pressed firmly against mine, our mouths barely an inch apart. I feel his voice when he speaks. 'Promise?'

'I promise.'

Walking with his arms and his jacket around me to the lighthouse, we heave open the door. I step inside, out of the wind, the pain in my ankle a dull ache, but Shaw makes no move to follow. Terror jolts me at the thought of him leaving.

'Aren't you coming?'

His eyebrows are drawn together. 'There's something…' he stops, as if not knowing how to complete the sentence, then continues. 'There's something I've got to do.'

I remove his jacket and hold it out for him. He shakes his head no. 'You hold on to it. I'll get it off you soon.' He reconsiders, takes it from me, finds the inside pocket and retrieves his silver cigarette case then hands it back. I hug it close. It smells of him. Of smoke and cologne and something else, something inherently masculine.

We stand in silence for a moment or two, staring at each other. Then Shaw reaches out and holds my hand. No squeeze, no stroke. But my hand is there, inside his, for two breaths. He turns and walks to the car, and I watch him. Inside my chest, my heart swells like the ocean. As he opens the driver's side door, he glances over his shoulder and looks back in my direction. My breath catches. He disappears inside the car. Then he is gone.

I still know so little about Detective Ronan Shaw. Apart from the fact I am in love with him.

Friday

At the bend in the road, Detective Shaw took the left-hand fork toward Mount Keira. He drove inland, avoiding the pools of muddy water, until the scrub thickened, and the road began to incline, narrow and turn into an uneven dirt track.

He readjusted his still-damp trousers, drying stiff with salt. His shirt held the faint scent of Missy, and he remembered the softness and warmth of her head against his chest. His heart beat faster thinking about it. It had softened for her. Something he never expected to happen, something he never expected to feel for anyone else. He found himself, even now, longing for her company, thirsting for her smile.

He was hit in the guts by a sudden pang of guilt at leaving her alone in such a vulnerable state. No doubt the shock of discovering Flea's body had triggered her sighting of the mermaid again. He was sure it was shock she was suffering. He'd seen soldiers suffer from it on the battlefield. And off. For a long time after the war, men were prone to any number of symptoms, from headaches and nightmares to violent shaking, hallucinations, and delusions. Yes, it was shock. That's what it was. He was sure of it. But what if it was something else?

Something deeper? Darker?

The Model T inched along the now narrow track, dappled in the yellow glow of afternoon sunlight, and bordered both sides with green ferns and towering gum trees. Over the rumble of the engine, whip birds called to each other, and insects buzzed louder the deeper he drove into the forest. He rolled down the window and took a large gulp of air, thick with moisture and eucalyptus.

Shaw contemplated the facts of the case so far. The fish scale and the rope knot both snagged something in his mind. He wondered who would want to hurt Flea, whether he had got himself caught up in the wrong crowd, just like Lara Harvey. Sonny Fynn was the common denominator here, that was certain, but it didn't make sense for him to have committed either murder. There was no motive. Were the murders even committed by the same man? There were very few signs indicating so. He would need to check Lara Harvey's autopsy report.

What did Flea know that got him killed? He didn't know the name of the supplier of the booze, he said he was just the middleman. But he did say there was something else in the sacks of coal bound for the lighthouse. The man at the docks had no idea when Shaw had asked him. He'd also said that the last time he'd seen Tommy Mathieson, he was wandering off toward Widow's Basin with a tall young chap in a fisherman's cap. There was only one way to be sure. Shaw needed to check the source.

The hill to the Osborne-Wallsend Coal Company was steep and winding, folding upon itself, higher and higher up the mountain. Shaw passed a sign that read *Widow's Peak Coal: Warning No Public Access* and the track opened up to a large open paddock, rimmed by timber fences.

In the distance, nestled into the grassy hillside, stood what looked like a ramshackle structure of beams, with a platform held up by large pylons. Parallel tracks emerged from the structure in all directions, like strands of a spider's web. They converged and sloped away down the far side of the hill.

Shaw parked the Model T Ford at the curve of the vast space, cleared of trees and vegetation. He peered hard through the windscreen and could just make out the entrance to the mine. The timber structure stood over a cave-like hole. Thick beams supported the sides and the roof, and decaying wood and iron supports gave the whole place the feel of a metal scrapyard.

Men with black-smeared faces idled around a large, corrugated-iron shed, and others stood on top of the structure, hauling ropes tied to a pully system. Shaw checked his wristwatch. Almost three pm. He hoped one of them could answer a few questions. Opening the car door, he was hit with the clatter of heavy machinery, the *tap-tap-tap* of a rattling conveyor belt and the clanking of chains. The dry air was thick with the smell of dust and rock and fuel.

Shaw took two tentative steps toward a huge brick chimney, his boots slipping slightly on the shale, and peered at the gaping throat of the earth. Stale air seeped up from underground and he pitied the poor men who were forced to spend hours inside that hole. The dust and darkness prevented him from seeing much, but he could hear water trickling down the walls.

A man passed him, heaving a wagon full to the brim with black shale. His frame was gaunt, but his hands looked capable. Black blotches covered the back of his neck.

'You ever find any diamonds down there?' Shaw called.

The man stopped. When he shook his head, his jowly cheeks

wobbled. 'Coal's the only thing that's ever come out of that hole. Though I s'pose you dig deep enough, you might come across something more.' He made to continue heaving the wagon but Shaw stopped him with another question.

'How deep is it?'

'Three hundred and fifty feet, straight down.'

'So how do you bring the coal to the surface?' Shaw asked.

The man let go of the wagon, wiped his forehead with the back of his hand, then spread his arms wide. 'Men,' he said. 'Mine currently employs three hundred and four. Most of us've been working this mine for generations.'

Detective Shaw offered his hand. 'Detective Ronan Shaw. Mind if I ask you a few questions about the mine?'

The man wiped his grimy hand on a rag and shook Shaw's. A firm shake. 'Alf O'Brian,' he said. 'Of course. Been working this mine all me life. Probably isn't a question I couldn't find the answer to.'

Shaw motioned the wagon Mr O'Brian was carting. 'I noticed the wagons…'

'The skips.'

Shaw nodded. 'The skips, right. How much do they hold?'

The old miner rubbed the filthy rag across his forehead again. 'I'd estimate it to be about a tonne.' He nodded. 'Around about a tonne.'

'And once the coal's loaded, what happens to the skips then?'

Mr O'Brian pointed to the rail tracks under Shaw's feet. 'It's a straight run down the mountain.'

'Then onto the Blue Mile, right?'

'Nope. Wagons go on to the Blue Mile.'

'Not the skips?

'Nope.'

This wasn't going anywhere. Shaw tried a different approach. 'Anyone ever fill the skips with anything other than coal before they send them down the mountain?'

Mr O'Brian shook his head. 'Not to my knowledge. We're paid by the tonne. Paid a rate per tonne for the coal we mine and load into each skip. We throw the small bits aside.'

'Is there anywhere along the incline where anyone else comes into contact with the skips?'

'Clipper boys unclip the empty skips from the haulage rope at a clipping flat located on the haulage roadway.'

'Clipper boys?'

'They're the ones who clip the skip onto the rope at the screening plant.'

'You've lost me again,' Shaw said. 'Screening plant?'

'It's like a pit stop on the way down. Where the coal is loaded from the skips into the wagons. The full skip goes down to the bottom where it's unclipped and taken into the screen house. Then it's turned upside down and the coal falls into a chute and goes down to a large truck on the bottom rail line, before it's loaded into wagons and taken along the Blue Mile to the harbour. Widow's Peak Harbour. That wagon then goes around a loop and comes up and it's hooked on again to the rope and sent back up to the mine.'

'Where is this screening plant?' Shaw asked.

'Screening plant's at the base of the incline.'

'And this screening plant, does it have someone operating it or does the coal go straight through the chute automatically?'

'Out of the skip, the coal gets put into a tumbler.'

'Is that automatic?'

'It's manually done.'

'Someone's there now?'

'Well, they bloody well should be.'

'Can you take me there?'

'S'pose I could. Course, it'll cost you.'

Shaw smiled. 'Oh yeah?' he said. 'What'll it cost me?'

Mr O'Brian's milky eyes met Shaw's. 'How's about a ride down the mountain in that shiny black car o' yours?'

'Done.'

Shaw led the way to the Model T and opened the door for his passenger. Mr O'Brian climbed in, clasping his pick and fork with contorted fingers, and propped them on the seat between them.

'You don't want to leave those at the mine?' Shaw asked.

The old miner shook his head. 'Miners provide their own equipment. I leave these behind, you can bet your last shilling that'll be the last I see of 'em. Cost me a pretty penny these did.'

Shaw turned the ignition and reversed, making his way back along the grass road that lined the paddock. The shadows from the fence were lengthening and he could feel a drop in temperature as the afternoon descended upon the mountain.

'Do you mind me asking what you get paid for your work?' Shaw asked.

Mr O'Brian directed Shaw to continue along the grassy road rather than the track he had driven up on. 'The rate paid to a miner for clean coal loaded into a one point five tonne capacity coal skip is two shillings and nine pence per tonne.'

Shaw descended the incline, along the bumpy grassy road, and kept on driving down the mountain. Caught up in his own thoughts, he didn't see the kangaroo. As he turned a corner, it came out of nowhere and nearly jumped into the side of the car.

Slamming the breaks, Shaw swore so loudly that Mr O'Brian glanced at him. As an immigrant to Australia, the land, the weather, the animals never ceased to astound Shaw. But these creatures, with their muscled hind legs and huge thick tails were like nothing else.

Finally, the screen plant came into view, which looked little more than a shed. Plumes of dust billowed up as chunks of coal tumbled out of a chute into a wagon waiting on parallel rail tracks that sloped away from the screen house and continued down the hill.

Shaw pulled the car to a halt under a tree, and they exited the vehicle. Mr O'Brian waved to the clipper boys, of which there were two. One was carting a wagon down the track, and the other stood idly by, smoking.

'G'day, Bill,' Mr O'Brian called. 'Got a bloke here wants to ask a few questions. You'll help him out, won't you?'

Bill turned and shook Mr O'Brian's hand.

A whisper of small stones tumbled down the chute as Shaw passed underneath. He approached the two clipper boys, stepping into a puddle of fetid water, and felt it ooze under his boot. Bill eyed Shaw.

'Afternoon,' Shaw said. Bill turned away to stretch a sheet of canvas over large boxes, muttering something under his breath that sounded like *Irish scum*. Chains clunked somewhere behind the screen plant.

'You must be the clipper boys?' Shaw said, addressing the man's back.

Bill turned. 'Who wants to know?'

Shaw offered his hand and Bill shook it, leaving the chalky feel of dust on his fingers. 'Detective Ronan Shaw, Widow's Peak PD.'

'Detective?' Bill scoffed. 'Good job, is it? Walking around poking your nose into other people's business?'

Shaw got straight to the point. 'You ever load these wagons with anything other than coal?'

That took Bill aback. An anxious look flashed across his face. It was quickly hidden. 'Don't know what you're talking about. I'm not here to answer your bloody questions. Don't need nobody coming here telling me how to do my job. Bloody detective from the big smoke.' Bill spat into the dirt then stormed off inside the shed.

Shaw looked at Mr O'Brian, who simply shrugged and slapped Shaw good-naturedly on the shoulder.

'Listen,' he said, 'we coal miners are men who've lost fingers, and arms. Men whose bones've been crushed under run-away skips and wagons, men who've lived through leg-cracking explosions. Whose lungs've turned black from decades of breathing in coal dust. Proud as we are, we stand around in shit-stinking holes in the ground and talk about how hard our work really is. When along comes a good-looking fella like you, dressed in your fancy trousers and clean white shirt, well, you can't blame us for not welcoming you with open arms, can you?'

Shaw glanced at his salt-crusted suit and stained shirt. 'Mr O'Brian…'

The old miner held up his hand. 'Let me finish. Maybe it's because you think mining is all bran and no brain. All danger and no art. All stakes and no reward.' They ambled back to the Model T Ford, under the shade of the giant eucalyptus. 'But see it from our perspective: mining's in the blood. So ingrained that a family will send its beloved boys into those shit-stinking holes, even as the father's black-ink cough sets in.'

Shaw opened the car door. Mr O'Brian collected his tools but waved the offer away.

'I'll let you get back to the big smoke. Might just take meself on a nice stroll back up the mountain. Thanks for the ride. It was nice meeting you. Good luck with whatever it is you're looking for.'

And with that, Alf O'Brian strolled back along the grassy road in the shadow of the mountain.

Shaw stood in the last remnants of afternoon sun and smoked a cigarette, noticing, as he snapped his silver case closed, that he was running low. The jarring warble of a magpie broke through the quiet lull of the late afternoon.

Shaw looked up. The glossy black and white bird stared at him with beady, golden-brown eyes from a low-hanging branch. It observed him curiously, as if to say, *what's next, old man?* As if it were suggesting what he already knew; that he'd come to a dead end. He knew he couldn't arrest Missy's grandfather – any hint of suspicion could get back to Sonny Fynn and he wasn't willing to do that, not to Missy.

Shaw sighed deeply as he and the bird watched each other. What's next, indeed. He could chase Mitchell's promotion by bringing in Sonny Fynn but, deep inside, some new feelings had awoken. He had tried to ignore them, but they grew, like whisps of smoke, until they flowed through his entire being. Feelings that were almost frightening in their intensity.

He had once dreamed of returning home to Ireland, a Detective Superintendent. Proving to his parents that leaving

Dublin had been worth it after all. All the sacrifices, all the lives lost. But now, the thought of walking away, of leading a quiet life, switching off from the world, seemed more and more appealing. Finding a faraway corner and living out the rest of his life in relative peace. Maybe a couple of children. Something he didn't get a chance to do with Mary. They just weren't given enough time.

You look for crumbs. When you've got ghosts. When there's grief. You just look for crumbs of happiness. A thousand crumbs make a cake. Focus on those crumbs, then you have a life again. Gather the crumbs together and you'll be happy.

The magpie gave another throaty warble and darted from the branch, swooping past Shaw's face to the grass, right next to his boot. It snatched up a worm and flew away.

Watching the bird disappear behind the treeline, Shaw remembered back to the beginning of the week when he had called Missy a magpie. He had wondered if his behaviour was too familiar, too playful. But she didn't seem to mind. Why *had* he called her a magpie? For stealing the key. The key to Lara Harvey's delivery truck. Without that key, he probably would not have gotten so far along with this case. A sense of quiet settled over him, and in that moment, he knew what he had to do. Shaw flicked the cigarette to the gravel and turned on his heel.

The two clipper boys were now inside the shed, their muffled voices sounding from behind the thin walls. Shaw's mouth was dry, his saliva gritty with dust. He went straight to the large boxes and pulled back the canvas that Bill had covered them with.

It was filled with sacks, similar to the ones that Flea loaded on to Missy's truck. He opened one up and peered inside. Black lumps of coal. He tore it open. Out tumbled more lumps of coal, scattering on the loose stones under his boots. He shook the sack so that more lumps tumbled to the dusty ground. Perspiration dripped down Shaw's neck. He stood and stared into the middle distance. It made no sense. There was nothing here, or at the mine, to suggest that anything other than coal was being transported to the lighthouse.

Shaw turned back to the boxes and dug underneath the top layers of sacks. He reached right down to the bottom sack and wrenched it to the top of the pile. It looked the same as any of the other sacks, but he opened it anyway. It was difficult to tell, but the smell was faintly familiar. Earthy and musty. He shook it and out fell another lump.

But this was not a lump of coal.

This was a potato.

The valley of the mountain was completely in shadow as Shaw found the dirt track and drove the rest of the way down. The scrub thinned out and he reached the paved road back into town.

Something else gnawed at Shaw. He tried to ignore it but the feeling that he was missing something tugged at him. A final piece of the puzzle. Staring through the windscreen, he forced himself to think. He squeezed his eyes momentarily closed and tried to focus. Why would the lighthouse keeper want sacks full of potatoes? It didn't make sense.

Shaw drove to the hospital, pulled up at the rear loading dock. He entered through the back and found the stairs to the basement, following the signs that pointed the way to the morgue. He paused before he entered the room of tile, steel, and porcelain, and the pungent stench of bleach.

From the woman on the front desk, he obtained Lara

Harvey's file. Flipping it open, his eager eyes scanned the pages for the most important details.

Shaw shook his head. He read the pages again. It couldn't be.

The surgeon was just finishing up another autopsy when Shaw stopped him.

'She drowned?' he asked. 'Are you sure?'

The surgeon glanced at the name on the file that Shaw was holding and nodded. 'Lungs were full of salt water,' he said. 'You know, I already telegrammed a copy of this to the station.'

'There wasn't any sign of assault?' Shaw asked.

The surgeon reached for Lara's file and reread it. He pointed to a section of the page with a gloved finger, slightly blood-stained. 'There was a small laceration on her right temple. Some scrapes and bruises to the body, although I don't believe she was assaulted. Probably caused by rocks in the water. But it's difficult to say.'

Shaw pinched the corners of his eyes, then levelled his gaze at the surgeon. 'What do you mean, *difficult to say*?'

'Well, often a body gets bumped around in the water and bleeds, whether or not the person is alive or dead. But with this particular victim, there was no reason to believe there was foul play.'

Shaw sighed. 'Are you fucking kidding me?'

'A little rough water, big enough waves…' The surgeon tucked the file under his arm. 'How was rigour mortis when you found the body?'

Shaw rubbed his forehead and shook his head. 'Complete.'

'Body temperature?'

'Cold.'

The surgeon shrugged. 'The body was found at about six in

the morning, but not examined until that evening. Death probably occurred twelve to forty-eight hours previous.'

Shaw folded his arms. 'So, she was killed before ten o'clock the previous night? Or anytime forty-eight hours before that?'

The surgeon walked away. 'That's as definite as I can be, I'm afraid, Detective.'

Shaw gazed at the ground and shook his head. Not murdered, after all. The surgeon's footsteps stopped, turned back. 'Though there is one other point with this case.'

Shaw looked up. 'What's that?'

The surgeon opened the file to show Shaw a small section at the back of the page. 'Predictably she wasn't a virgin,' he said. 'She was pregnant. About twenty weeks.'

Hot blood rushed through Shaw. 'Jesus.'

By the time Shaw entered Widow's Peak Police Station, it was nearing five pm and the stone floors were slick with water from being recently mopped.

He passed the waiting area and almost tripped on a pair of boots poking out from a bench underneath a large map of Widow's Peak. The boots belonged to Constable Lou Bowers. His awkwardly fitting uniform gave him away.

Shaw noticed red blotches around his eyes. 'Everything all right, Constable?'

Constable Bowers wiped his face with his sleeve. In his other hand, he held a telegram. 'Sorry, Sir. Caught me off guard.'

'Is this about the post-mortem?'

Constable Bowers chewed his lip as he stared at the ground. 'I knew she was pregnant,' he said. 'She told me. We were in love,

Lara and me.'

There it is, thought Shaw.

He sat on the bench seat under the map of the city and leaned all the way back, stretching out his spine, attempting to release some of the tension that had built up that afternoon. That day. Christ, that whole week. He closed his eyes, inhaled deeply, then levelled his gaze at Bowers.

'Can you tell me anything about Lara Harvey on the day of her death?'

Constable Bowers shrugged, his eyes unfocused, gazing somewhere in his memories. 'It was a normal day.'

'Which is?'

'Drive the truck in the morning, work at The Milk and Honey in the evening. I would meet her after her shift, and we would go back to my place.' He glanced at Shaw. 'We'd been putting money aside. Been talking about starting a life together. But she was involved with that mobster, Sonny Fynn. She didn't want to marry him. She was *scared* of him. We were planning to run away, get out of town. Away from this place.'

'So, you saw Lara at The Milk and Honey the night she died?'

Bowers nodded. 'We had an argument.'

'What about?'

'She was upset. She told me she was scared. That arsehole had a hold on her. She was terrified of him. She was stuck and didn't know how to get out. I knew she was getting cold feet. It was him, who killed her, I know it was.'

'Tell me what happened next, Constable,' Shaw said.

'She left The Milk and Honey early. Said she needed to clear her head. I swear to God, if he hurt her… If he so much as touched a fingernail of hers… I'll cut the man's throat.'

'That's a bit much for a pacifist.'

Bowers looked at Shaw, wide-eyed. 'He must've found out about us. It's the only explanation. Why else would she have suddenly started acting so strange?'

'She was acting strangely?' Shaw asked. 'In what way?'

'We'd arranged to meet after her shift. But, like I said, she was second-guessing leaving. Said she needed to speak to someone first. She left The Milk and Honey early…'

'What time?'

'Around eight or nine,' Bowers said, shaking his head. 'I swear to God when I find that arsehole…'

Shaw held out his hand in a *calm down and stick to the facts* gesture. 'Just tell me what happened after you and Lara went back to your place.'

'That's the thing,' Bowers said.

'What's the thing?'

'We didn't. Go back to my place.'

'Where'd she go?' Shaw asked. 'To meet Sonny Fynn?'

'No, she went to the old man. Said she knew where he kept a safe. With a lot of money in it. Something about a trap door. The night she went, she never came back. I waited for her, but she didn't… she didn't show up. That's when we found her, the next morning.' Bowers swallowed, his Adam's apple bobbed up and down like a buoy. 'Washed up on the beach.'

'You said something about an old man?'

'The old man she worked for,' he said. 'The lighthouse keeper.'

Cold water rushed over Shaw's head, right down to his feet. Missy's grandfather? He took him for a bootlegger, but could he really have had something to do with Lara Harvey's death?

'The lighthouse keeper's got a safe?' Shaw asked. 'Where?'

Bowers wiped his nose on his sleeve. 'Under the lighthouse. It's where he hides all his money. I know Lara went there that night. I know she didn't jump. She would never have done that. He must have followed her there. Pushed her off. She couldn't swim. She wouldn't have lasted long out in the water.'

The Greens's house was in one of the old fishermen's huts in Widow's Peak, opposite Widow's Basin. Shaw noted the flaking paint on the outside as he approached, the weathering on the windows.

Augustus Green opened the door and ushered Shaw inside the small and barely furnished room that seemed to double as a kitchen and a sitting room. It was warm and dry, and Gust sat in front of the fire, fishing nets draped over his lap and piled at his feet.

Shaw stood by the fireplace where a row of fish smouldered, filling the room with the intoxicating, musky aroma of land and sea. On the mantle sat a framed photograph of a young woman with long dark hair about her face, similar to Missy. Shaw took her to be Missy's mother, around the same age, perhaps a little younger.

'What's this about?' Gust asked.

Shaw took out his handkerchief from his trouser pocket, unwrapped it. 'An unusual aspect of the investigation, I'll grant you.' He handed it to Gust. 'Can you tell me what sort of fish this is from?'

Gust's eyebrows knitted in concentration as he held the handkerchief open in his palm and ran the tip of his index finger over the flat surface. He picked up the tiny scale. 'Mullet. Blackfish, perhaps.'

'Which?'

Gust held the scale to his nose and inhaled. 'Blackfish,' he said, handing it back to Shaw.

'Blackfish?' Shaw folded the handkerchief and tucked it back into his pocket. 'The type of fish you net?'

Augustus Green picked up a knotted piece of fishing net and started working through the mess of wires. 'We net all types of fish.'

Shaw stared at him relentlessly. 'Blackfish?'

With his knife, Augustus Green cut through a knot using a sawing motion. 'Blackfish, yes.'

Shaw noted the serration along the edge of the blade. He shook his head and smiled. 'I can't figure you out, Mr Green.'

Gust gazed up at Shaw. 'What do you mean, Detective? Are you saying I'm a murder suspect?'

Shaw shrugged, turned his back to Gust and absentmindedly picked up the photograph of Missy's mother. 'Ex-soldier. Trained to kill. We did it often enough. It happened so easily in the trenches. Maybe you forgot yourself. Crossed over the line and couldn't bring yourself back again. Can't flick the switch that easily, right, comrade?'

'That was war, Detective,' Gust said. 'That's what you do. Kill or be killed. But the war is done. Besides, how many ex-soldiers do you think live in this town?'

'Did you know Tommy Mathieson?'

Gust nodded. 'I heard about him. You're asking me about that too? I'm a man who keeps to himself, and here I am, being accused of murdering two people?' He scoffed, shook his head.

'You ought to be sacked.'

'Where were you last night?'

'Is that when he died?'

'You can't tell me where you were?'

'It wasn't me, Detective.'

Shaw slammed the photograph down on the mantle with so much force the glass cracked. He spun around and brought his face close to Gust's. 'How many people know how to tie that knot? You said so yourself. That's the knot of a lifelong fisherman.'

Gust stared at Shaw. 'You really haven't figured it out yet, have you?'

Shaw paced the room. 'Figured what out?'

'There is no Lara Harvey.'

Shaw screwed up his face. 'What?'

Gust smirked at Shaw, enjoying having a hold over him. 'Her real name. She must have changed it when she started working at that underground bar. Her real name was *Laura Hartley.*'

Shaw stared at Gust in disbelief. A string of questions flew through his mind: why would she change it, what was she hiding and, most importantly; 'How do *you* know that?'

Gust shrugged. 'It's a small town, Detective. Been here a long time. Roots run deep.' Shaw shook his head, disbelieving. How could he not have known this? 'They went to school together, Missy and Laura. Missy didn't mention that?'

'No,' Shaw said. His head swam with the realisation that Missy had known her all along. That he couldn't trust her. Was she a liar? He needed answers. He needed to catch his breath. 'I'm sorry.' He was heaving in mouthfuls of air, taking deep, greedy gulps of it. He paced to the chair by the window, sat, and leaned over, rubbing his forehead. 'I'm not… I'm just… I'm trying to put this case together and I can't. I can't.' He laughed darkly. 'You want to know why? I'm worrying about her.'

'Who?' Gust asked.

'Your daughter, Mr Green.'

'Missy? Why? What happened?'

'Something's wrong with her. She says she's hearing things, seeing things, drifting off, spacing out.'

Gust shook his head. 'It's just her imagination. She's always been like that.'

'She thinks it's real,' Shaw said. 'It *is* real to her. Something's really scaring her. It's gotten bad. Really bad.'

'She's always had a tendency toward melancholy. It's in her blood.'

'Open your eyes,' Shaw yelled. 'Can't you see the state she's in? Maybe it's time you consider some serious help.'

'Like what?'

'Like, I don't know, finding out if they have programs at the hospital.'

Gust's voice hardened. 'I'm not sending her to a mental institution.'

'It's not an insane asylum. It's a hospital. A person can only take so much. Christ, we saw it often enough. Men who turned up ready to give hell, who lived through the shelling and the mud and the gas. For months. Years even. Then something in them just breaks. Sometimes they even turned on their own friends, came at them with a bayonet, laughing like a maniac and crying at the same time. Who are we to judge Missy? She's reached her limit, that's all. Everyone has one. She just needs help.'

Gust stood, the bulk of nets tumbling to the floor. His voice filled the small room. 'Talk to me as if I don't know my own daughter? I put my trust in you, and this is the bullshit you spout.'

Shaw held up his hand. 'Sit down, old man,' he spat. 'The fact is, she's not yours. She's not yours and she's not mine. She's her own person, fully capable of making her own decisions. And she's not stupid.'

Gust found his chair and sat down, silently.

Shaw continued, stepping toward Gust, pointing a finger at him. 'What kind of father abandons their child to fight a war anyway? You lost her when you left. And now you're treating her like she's some kind of melancholic child when she's not. And I don't want her to die because I love her, and I can't lose her.'

Gust stared straight ahead. Took a deep breath. 'Where is she? I want to talk to her.'

Shaw glanced around the room, at the doors at the back of the hut. 'She's not here? I sent her home, right after...'

'After what?'

Shaw scratched his eyebrow with his thumb, realising his mistake. 'After I left her at the lighthouse.'

'The lighthouse? I told you to keep her away from that place. Away from him. He's the one who's mad. That light has made him mad.'

Shaw shook his head and cast his eyes at the window, at the line of shells along the edge. It all led back to the lighthouse. 'Do you think he could be responsible? Missy's grandfather?'

Gust sighed deeply. 'He's not a good man, but I can't imagine him a killer.'

'Do you think he could have had something to do with your wife's death?'

Gust stared at the floor. 'Neve?' he whispered.

'They never found the body, did they?' Shaw stood and placed his hands in his trouser pockets, trying to fit together all the pieces of this strange case. 'Can you think of any reason why he would need a delivery of potatoes?'

Gust snorted. 'It's the only thing the man knows how to cook. Stuffs Missy full of them every chance he can get. Breakfast, lunch and dinner. The man's tipped completely off the edge. That's why I don't want Missy there, yet she insists on going there every night.'

Shaw stood and strode to the mantle. He picked up the broken frame. Behind the cracked glass, the black and white photo had shifted slightly, revealing a translucent piece of paper with blue ink.

'Missy was at the lighthouse that night? The night Lara Harvey was killed?'

'I told you,' Gust said. 'She's there every night.'

Shaw tapped out the broken glass, removed the photograph and, underneath, was a neatly folded letter. He opened it. His heart pounded in his chest as he held the letter with shaking hands. For a moment he left his body and floated in the rafters, looking down on himself reading the blue scrawling handwriting.

Come home, or I will show Missy her mother's last words, scratched into the wall in the lantern room.

Shaw rammed the letter into his trouser pocket.

Gust stood and walked Shaw to the door, swung it open and sniffed the air. 'Better get ahead of the storm.'

'What storm?' Shaw said, peering up at the darkening sky.

Seagulls screeched overhead and flapped frantically against the intensifying breeze. The moisture in the air mingled with the stale odour of dead fish and decomposing seaweed. Detective Shaw walked along the pier toward the *Senhora ao Vento*.

Missy, still wearing his jacket, stood at the end, next to the trawler, a barrel of fish at her side.

He watched her. The easy way she moved, her face as the fading light caught it. He studied it, marvelled at it. She seemed sullen. Even more so than usual.

She caught sight of him and smiled. 'Dropping by to see what real work looks like?' She scraped her knife along the fish's side, the shimmering scales flinging about.

Shaw breathed in deeply to gather in all of her and he felt like he was drowning. He repressed a smile. 'How long does it take to do that?'

She shrugged. 'About two minutes a fish.'

With expert motion, she removed the guts of the lifeless creature then scraped away its scales, as if to take from them their sheen, their colour. Blood spattered her sleeve – his jacket – flecks of fish scales flew everywhere.

Missy shook them loose of her hand. 'These things end up all over the place.'

She smiled at him. He wished he could return it. 'Missy, we need to talk.'

She paused, holding the open fish in one hand, her knife in the other. 'About what?'

Shaw sighed. 'I need your help again. I have a lead. It's about your grandfather. I need you to come to the lighthouse with me.'

Missy knitted her brow. 'What about him?'

'It's all connected,' Shaw said. 'Lara Harvey was last seen at the lighthouse before she… died.'

Seagulls circled above them; their wings outstretched. One bird swooped low and landed near a discarded piece of fish guts. It snatched a scrap in its pointy beak. Another landed and ruffled its feathers, elongated its white feathery neck and screeched at its counterpart, angry at missing out. Missy flinched at the sound.

'Are you saying he's a suspect?' she asked.

'I'm saying he's *the* suspect.'

Missy scoffed. She tossed the gutted fish into the barrel and slapped another in front of her. 'There's a difference between believing something is true and having the facts to prove it. It doesn't matter what you think.' She shook her head. 'He didn't do it.'

'We can't rule it out.'

She grasped the fish by its tail and, using the blunt edge of her knife, scraped away its scales. 'Yes, we can.'

'Why are you protecting him?'

The tip of Missy's knife inserted into the fish's flesh like it was butter. Her practised hand moved the blade up along its belly, and with a flick of her wrist, cut all the way to its head. 'He's my grandfather. I'm anchored to the man. Besides, he's not a killer. He just… has a temper.'

Missy spread the fish's body and reached inside the opening. She pulled out her hand and with it, all of the fish's entrails. Crouching down, she dipped the fish in a bucket of brownish water.

'Missy, wait. There's more. It's about Lara's fiancé, Sonny Fynn.'

Missy stood. 'The gangster?'

'He's out for revenge. Wouldn't you rather your grandfather

alive, but in prison, than dead?'

'What are you talking about?'

'I need to arrest your grandfather before anything bad happens to him.'

'Arrest him for what? For murder?' She tossed the fish aside, a little too aggressively.

'Lighthouses are Commonwealth. If we can bring him in now, he'll be transferred to Sydney. To safety. Whether he's guilty or not, it's only a matter of time before Sonny Fynn figures it out.'

'Figures what out?'

'It all leads back to the lighthouse. Dead people in the water. Dead birds in the water.' Shaw gazed into her eyes. He took one step closer to her. 'Your mother in the water.'

Missy stared back; her eyes full of water. 'So, arrest him, then. Why do you need my help?'

Shaw resisted the urge to reach out and hold her. Instead, he reached into his pocket, for a cigarette. He was down to his last one. 'Evidence,' he said as he lit up. He drew deeply, feeling the smoke enter his lungs, and with it, he regained focus. 'We haven't got enough against him. I need to catch him in an act of violence.'

Missy cast her eyes down at the fish guts; a mess of pink and red, deep purple organs, silvery heads, with mouths gaping and blank eyes staring. She shook her head. 'But he's not a violent man.'

Shaw raised his eyebrows. 'Are you sure about that? Why do you think he never told you the truth about your mother's death?' Missy's eyes flicked up to him, then rested on the ground in front of her. 'Why do you think he still hides it from you now? Why do you think your father wants to keep you away from the lighthouse? From *him*?'

She shook her head slightly. 'He won't attack me if that's what you're suggesting.'

'Then you'll have to provoke him. Say something to him, something to unleash his temper.'

The word escaped Missy's lips in a whisper, 'No.'

Shaw reached for her hand, and she looked up at him, her eyes spilling over. 'Look, I know it's not fair to ask this of you, but I wouldn't be here if I didn't think this was the only way. I'm asking you. I'm begging you. I need you.'

Missy pulled her hand out of Shaw's grasp. 'No. *No.* You need to go.' She picked up her knife and scraped the pile of entrails and fish heads to the ground. They landed with a slap on top of Shaw's boots.

Shaw peered up at the sky. The clouds were heavy with rain. He wondered whether to take the next step. He hoped he didn't have to, but this was his last chance. 'Missy, wait,' he said. 'There's something you need to know. While your father was away at war, your grandfather wrote a letter.'

'Oh yeah?' Missy said with feigned interest. 'To whom?'

Shaw levelled his eyes on her. 'Have you ever been up inside the prisms in the lantern room?'

Her mouth was a straight, thin line. Her eyes as dark as the storm clouds gathering overhead. He was losing her; he could feel it. 'What are you talking about? I spent my childhood in there.'

'Ever found anything interesting in there?'

'Like what?'

'Anything.'

'I don't know what you're talking about but if you won't leave, I will.' Missy tucked her knife into her belt and wiped her hands onto her trousers, leaving a smear of red. She bent to pick up the barrel of fish and started off down the timber pier.

'There's a message there,' Shaw called.

Missy stopped. She turned slightly. 'What do you mean?'

Shaw walked after her. He held out the letter. 'I found this,' he said. 'Behind the photograph of your mother. Here, have a look.'

Missy opened it. Shaw watched her eyes read and reread the words written on the page, watched the message sink in.

'He never told you about it, did he? The message your mother scratched into the lantern the day she died? Don't you at least want to see what it says? Whether it answers any of your questions?'

Missy's hands trembled as she held the letter in front of her and stared at its contents. Her eyes glazed over. Shaw pressed further, his voice tight, his jaw tight, his muscles tight.

'I can save your grandfather,' he said, 'but first, I need your help. I need you. Help me do this, and we can end this. Because I know you don't want your grandfather to die. And I can't do it without you.

'You said you wanted to know the truth about your mother's death,' Shaw continued. He pointed toward the hill, glowing iridescent green against the granite sky. 'The truth is right there. In the light. Come on.'

Missy's face had a rawness about it. A raw edge. Her glazed-over eyes found him, focused on him. 'I'm coming.'

20

Sexta-feira

I LEAVE the harbour, close to tears, disoriented, covered in blood and stinking of fish, and climb the hill to the lighthouse.

Tonight is one of those nights when everything feels too difficult. I'm fraying apart like rope. I fight the urge to cry. My temper rises and my mood turns cold. My mind swells like the ocean, I am being swept along with its current.

Just walk, I tell myself, not really fully committed to Shaw's plan. If, on the way, I come to realise I am doing the wrong thing, I can always turn around. If I make it to the lighthouse, then I'll go up to the lantern room. If he's there, then I'll speak to my grandfather.

My thoughts circle back to the letter.

Come home, or I will show Missy her mother's last words, scratched into the wall in the lantern room.

Why have I never seen my mother's last words? I spent my entire childhood in that lighthouse.

The trek up the grassy hill to the tower is harder than ever. A bank of slate-grey clouds is closing in. Far out at sea the rain streams down in huge vapourish curtains. A distant bolt of lightning strikes the horizon, like a white tear down the black pages of a book.

It doesn't frighten me. I like storms. I love when the weather and the sky and the elements make me feel insignificant. It calms me to watch them from my bed in the tower, through the window. Feeling the wind shake and rage and howl. Feeling the tower stand her ground. Watching the dunes crumble and the beach turn to brown sludge.

Hearing Shaw's suspicions, and all that they have brought up, has erased the parts of my life that were easy, happy. I feel thin, translucent, like a jellyfish, with his sting of betrayal. I thought I could trust him. I never should have relied on him, never should have believed he could be the one to bring happiness and joy. Love and protection.

My stomach churns and my thoughts swirl and I feel like I am at the beginning of the end, like this is a one-way spiral down from here. Like the staircase in the lighthouse. The spiral on my shell. In my pocket I finger the shell I saved from earlier. The pain in my abdomen is deep and heavy. I need to let it out. Pressing down as hard as I can against its sharp edge, it pierces through the skin. One big slice on the tip of my finger and the pain flows out of me, with the blood. For some reason, cutting myself and feeling the pain, feeling some kind of release, is somehow good for me. I feel such an intense anger and sadness inside that I cannot express, and somehow opening up this wound on my finger, I am letting the pain show on the outside. Just a little bit.

I am calmer now. The shell and its sharp edge have soothed me, and I regain my focus. If Shaw is right and *Avó* really did have something to do with my mother's death, something he's been hiding from me all this time, then I'm going to find out.

Tonight. Right now.

I bang on the door of the keeper's cottage. No answer. But the air is thick with smoke that makes my nose prickle. His pipe. Unhooking the kerosene lamp, I stomp across the lawn toward the lighthouse. The wind whips my face and stings the saliva on my lips. Something nags at me. Something is wrong. Something is different.

I look around *Avô's* yard in the dark: it is small but well-kept. Short grass and a square plot of vegetable garden butting up to the raw wood fence. I glance at the lighthouse, its base now only a few feet away.

A crash causes my heart to slam against my chest.

I spin around and face the cottage. I think I catch a glimpse of movement through a window from inside, but I shake my head, force myself to keep walking toward the tower. *Don't be ridiculous, Missy.*

My palm is pressed against the door, already heaving, when I realise what's wrong, what's different.

The light is off.

It's well past sunset and the light that is always, *always* turned on right before the sun goes down – even when *Avô* is on his death bed, he still manages to climb the stairs to the lantern room and light the wick – is off.

That's why it looks so different here. I've never seen it so dark before, so completely devoid of light. Someone could come up behind me and I'd never even—

'Need a hand?' His voice echoes from behind, and *Avô's* shadow falls across the door.

The kerosene lamp falls from my grasp and shatters on the stone ground. I can barely speak. I stutter, look around. A wave of relief washes over me and I wipe the sweat from my palm. 'What are you doing?'

He heaves the door open. 'Time to light up.'

'Bit late, isn't it?'

He glares at me. 'You're one to talk.'

Inside, the machinery is ticking, clunking. I peer up into the darkness and we ascend the spiral staircase.

When we make it to the top, we climb the ladder, open the hatch, and emerge through the hole into the lantern room. I go to the window and polish the glass with my sleeve to see more clearly. Layers of dense black cloud have advanced and close in around us. Thunder rumbles.

He gazes through the window, out to sea. 'Wind's changed,' he says. 'Nor'easterly. Dirty weather coming our way.'

Nodding, he steps inside the prisms. I watch as he takes the kerosene and carefully pumps it into the lantern. A match strikes and I hear the *whoomph* of the oil vapour as it ignites.

The lamp glows with the brilliance of a million candles at the touch of that tiny flame. *Avô* yanks on the lever that connects the two weights, and the great beam of light begins to turn in its bath of mercury, illuminating the lantern room. It whooshes past my face, out into the blackness, into the void, revealing every speck of the ocean. We watch it in silence for a few moments.

'I read your letter,' I finally say.

'What letter?' he mutters.

Heat is building, and the light roars around the glass prisms then out across the gallery to the ocean raging below. I retrieve the letter from my pocket and hand it to him.

Avô's eyes become fixed. He squints at the light, then at me. 'Where did you get this? Your father give it to you, did he?' He shakes his head. 'He's a nasty piece of work.'

'Show me.'

His eyes, blood-flecked and as blue as veins, scrutinise me. He sighs, then tells me to look inside the prisms. I rest on the narrow ledge that encircles the inside of the lens and shield my eyes. The rotating light is bright and hot, hissing and spitting, and I feel trapped inside the glass.

Then I see it. At first it appears as drops of water, shimmering in the light. Condensation. The drips tumble down the inner wall of the prisms, into the darkness below. As I stare, the drips dissolve and I realise that they are, in fact, letters. Words. Written in cursive.

I've never seen my mother's handwriting before. They are the tiniest letters I have ever seen, and joined together, scratched into the white paint, in a spiral from the outside, the outer edge, around and slowly circling inwards to its centre, like the staircase here, like the shell.

Blood rushes through me. The prism booms above my head, roaring confusion through my ears. I come closer, attempting to suppress the hundreds of new questions that surge inside me. In as calm a voice as I can manage, I read the words aloud:

If you're reading this, I'm gone. There is something wrong with me. Yesterday I stood at the edge of the ocean, watching the waves. In that moment, I was nobody's daughter. Nobody's wife. Nobody's mother.

The writing quivers and shakes.

Unnerved, I take a step back. I can't breathe. The information I am trying to process undoes me.

Nobody's mother becomes bathed in shadow and light, as if a battle rages for its meaning. I fight the compulsion to read it again, to descend into the greater darkness and keep descending until those words make me sink to their fathomless depths.

The next moments come in a jumble, and I leap from one thought to another. Emerging from the prisms, back into the lantern room, muffled rain now patters the windows.

Avô is pacing outside on the balcony, in the storm, muttering to himself. His shape is there, in the darkness. I go to the window and a flash of silver startles me, his two eyes glare at me. I leap back, then slow my breathing and open the door.

'Tell me what happened,' I call to him.

He steps inside, closes the door behind him. 'Let's go down. I'll make us some coffee.'

The rage that I harbour against myself I turn on him. 'Tell me. Tell me now. What happened to her?'

Lightning splits the sky and shoots into the sea. For an instant, the white crests of a thousand waves illuminate.

Avô inhales a shaky breath. 'She took her own life.'

I feel the blood drain from my face. 'She what?'

My mother killed herself.

When I hear it, something inside shakes loose. I let the thing squirm inside me until my whole body is agitated by it, my arms and legs enflamed by it.

My mother killed herself.

My lungs expand and collapse; a futile attempt at calming myself so that I can understand the words and their meaning. I suck in huge mouthfuls of air, fill my body with it, only it's not air that fills me, it's something else. Salt water. Rage.

'Let's go and sit,' he says again. 'I'll tell you.'

'You told me she drowned.'

'That was what your father wanted you to think. She loved the sea. She could have easily died that way. But she didn't. She took herself to the beach one morning and walked into the ocean. Didn't come back out.'

I shake my head. 'No, that's not possible.'

'She did.'

I peer at him in disbelief. 'I don't believe you.' Freefalling into a nightmare, I lower myself to the floor of the lantern room, gasping. 'Why?'

'*Why?*' he scoffs. 'I ain't the one to tell you the reason why.'

I take three long, slow breaths. A calmness settles over me. As if I have reached the storm's eye. I gaze up at him, at my grandfather, the lighthouse keeper, and I decide, right at that moment, to fully commit to Shaw's plan. 'I'm curious, *Avô*. Why did you keep it from me? All this time?'

'We were trying to protect you.'

'Protect me from the truth?'

'I don't know what you're—'

'Wait. You don't have to explain. I can tell you the whole story. You never liked my father. You tried to convince my mother he wasn't good enough for her. He was only a fisherman after all. But she was young, and they were in love. She didn't listen to you. You, with all your knowledge and wisdom of the world. She went and got herself married, and then I came along. You kept pestering her about it until she finally gave up. You could never admit that to anyone. That it was your fault.'

He doesn't respond for a long time and when he does, his hoarse voice cracks. 'We fought the day she… died.'

'About what?'

'I told her if she wasn't careful, she'd end up just like her mother. I wanted her to have a better life, an easier life, but she acted like *I* was the one who drove her mother off that cliff.'

I pull myself to my feet. 'So you buried her at the bottom of the sea?'

There's an erratic look in his eye. 'Don't contradict yourself, child,' he spits. 'You hypocrite. I might not have done everything right, but I never hurt anyone. I didn't knock up some seventeen-year-old girl and tell her to keep it. Who do you think pays for that hut you've been living in? Certainly not your father. What good is he? The man is blind.'

'Stop lying to me,' I yell.

'I had no choice!' The heat builds in the lantern room and light roars around the windows. It pierces through the glass and out across the wild black ocean, glinting back at us as it goes. 'I was trying to protect you.'

'From what?' My reflection is that of a wild animal. I bash my fist against the glass so hard it shatters and shards sprinkle onto the balcony. Rain soaks me.

'From yourself.' My thoughts spiral into darkness, to the bottom of the lighthouse. *Avô* keeps talking. My heart is pounding so hard in my chest, I almost can't hear him. 'Death comes to those who go looking for it. Your mother, she is no more, but is now, herself, the sea.'

'Stop speaking in riddles. You say the sea took her? You say my father blew her to the Five Islands? I see through you, old man. She came to me. I know why now. I know why she spoke to me. I look into your eyes, and I see. You're nothing but a liar.'

'You spoke to your mother?' he scoffs. 'Tell me, what did she say to you?'

I breathe deeply. 'She warned me. She said I should be afraid of you.'

'Oh, she did?'

The rain battering the roof is deafening.

'I'm tired of listening to your stories and your riddles. It's all bullshit. You sound like a goddamned lunatic. All the while turning this lighthouse into a dirty gin hole. If I hear one more word of a lie come out of your foul, rotten mouth… I'm sick of it, sick of you, you goddamned, drunken, son-of-a-bitch bastard liar. That's what you are. A liar.'

He comes toward me, an urgency in his step. 'Watch your tongue, Missy, you foul-mouthed eel. You're the one who sounds like a lunatic. Raving about sirens, merfolk. What is it you're accusing me of?'

He looks so old, his skin soaked with rain, his complexion pallid and waxy, his fossilised hair slicked across his forehead. My anchor, unmoored. Beyond him, I see the black shadow of the ocean, hear it roaring below us.

I drag in deep breaths. 'The truth is, *Avô*, you killed your own wife and daughter. It was you… It was you who sent them to their deaths. Did you kill the others too? Lara and Flea? The Detective thinks it was you.'

He says the next words quietly, almost to himself. 'Missy, you lying eel. I saw you.'

I won't let him get away with any more lies. 'Tell the truth, *damn you*.'

'It was you who damned us. *You*!' He is shaking now. Purple veins in his forehead protrude, almost through his skin. The storm worsens. Wind beats the tower and I feel it sway, feel the world sway around me.

'You think you're so bloody high and mighty because you live here all alone, the lighthouse keeper that doesn't need anybody? What sort of a person chooses that life?'

'Don't you speak ill of this light, girl. The lighthouse has never failed me.'

Anger rushes out of the depths of me. Completely overpowers me. I'm screaming now. It's easy to decide what happens next. I make the decision because I have barnacles growing on me and I feel dead inside. I want to feel alive. To feel anything. To feel. I only remember certain images. It's too irrational for my mind to comprehend. Nonsensical.

'T'was your mother's own sanity that drove her to the sea. Her mother abandoned us, left us all alone, sent your mother into a deep melancholy from which she never recovered. And then she went and did the same thing.'

'You lied to me, all this time.' My stomach churns. My head is about to explode. The screeching is louder now, louder than it has ever been.

Rain blasts through the broken window.

For a moment, he and I scowl at each other. The hiss and smell of the rotating glass prisms fill the lantern room, illuminates his weatherworn face. I see him sometimes, and then I don't.

Luminous monster.

'Your wife left you, your own child left you, because they hated you. They hated this place – this godforsaken lighthouse.'

He lunges for me. I stumble back to evade him, feel his fingers in my hair as he grabs a fistful of it. The searing heat of pain comes first, then I hear the squelching of seaweed and taste the brine of salt water. The infected wound in my head throbs painfully, and I feel the scrape of barnacles as he tears them from my skull and sends them soaring.

I scream in horror, then take a deep breath for strength. He grabs my arm and I bring my mouth down on his hand, biting through the skin. He bellows. My teeth sink deep into his hand, tear at his paper-thin flesh, and the fine bones snap like I'm biting into a bird. The tang of his blood sours my tongue.

He releases me and I hear him open the hatch door. I lower myself to the lantern room floor. For a moment, I am bathed in ribbons of rain, and I allow myself to be cleansed by them. Cool air washes over me, smelling of ocean. It makes me shiver with cold and fear.

There, it's done. I did it for him, for Shaw.

Now I have no more strength. No more fight left. My mind collapses under the weight of everything. A weight too heavy to bear. I stop taking breaths. My thoughts descend into a deep, black void, where loss and fear drown me.

Detective Shaw is there, I know. Not at first. But I know it is Shaw who picks me up. Wipes the rain from my face. Cleans the blood from my mouth. The quietness of his voice unravels me.

Other constables are there, too. Although I don't remember seeing them. Sometimes those irrational images stream through my head, and, for a moment, I do remember.

Shaw is there. He does pick me up. It isn't my blood. It isn't fish blood.

It is Shaw who leads my grandfather away, marches him across the lawn to the police car. It is he who puts my grandfather inside the car, under arrest, and slams the door.

Then, Shaw comes back.

21

Friday

Waves belted the rocks; the full force of the Pacific Ocean unleashed. Detective Shaw heard them thundering below as he approached the headland, a sound like galloping horses. The wind was getting up, and he struggled against it, toward the lighthouse, rain stinging his face. From the top of the tower, a white shaft of light pierced the night like a bayonet, illuminating thousands of rain droplets.

Rain poured down the hill, and the ground was soaked underfoot. Before Shaw could reach the lighthouse, he slipped and went down sharply, muddying his trousers. Pressing his hands into the ground, he wrenched himself upright. The wind gathered even more pace as he burst through the door and into the cave-like circular room, crunching on shards of glass and a broken kerosene lamp.

The lighthouse roared and shook, as if the wind was inside the tower. It was thunderous. The tower smelled of old smoke and the pungent, oily scent of kerosene. And something else. That familiar, earthy smell.

Several other officers appeared in the doorway, dripping wet and out of breath. Shaw could feel the tension in their bodies.

He spoke to them in a low voice. 'Nobody move until I give the word.'

Shaw glanced up the cast-iron staircase, spiralling to the top of the lighthouse, clenched his fists, unclenched them. The light was lit, but it was too high to see if Missy and her grandfather were still up there.

He lowered his gaze and peered through the darkness, searching the stone floor for the trapdoor to the basement. Outside, a bolt of lightning struck, and, for a moment, the dark room flashed white and the door revealed itself.

Shaw crouched down and lifted it open. He stood back. Before him, a staircase descended into pitch blackness. Striking a match, he held it aloft as he headed down, the walls stained from smoke damage, the earthy smell strengthening the further he descended, as though he was walking into a room full of…

Potatoes.

Just as Shaw had expected. The snag in his brain didn't let up until he remembered what the proprietress of The Milk and Honey had said to him about making bathtub gin from anything that ferments. Including potato peelings.

Inside the smoke-logged basement were barrels and barrels filled to the brim with piles of potato peelings in various stages of rot. He gazed around the room. Other containers were lined up against the wall, their labels for malt, ethanol, and stout.

Along the furthest wall, Shaw discovered a fully equipped distillery with glass bottles filled with different kinds of liquids. He picked one up and brought it to his nose, the alcohol singeing his nostrils.

Constable Lou Bowers appeared behind him out of the shadow, gaping at the sight.

Shaw turned. 'Take samples of these for analysis. This place is sealed, no one comes in or out of here, got that?'

Constable Bowers nodded.

The wind was unnerving, like a wolf howling through the cracks in the curved walls. Shaw's face shot up as the sound of footsteps descending the spiral staircase above them echoed through the room. He pressed a finger to his lips and climbed back up the basement stairs. Silently, he ordered his men outside, and he stood in the dark, listening as the heavy footsteps, wet and squelching, became louder. Closer.

Their echoes intensified, until finally, the lighthouse keeper stepped off the bottom rung. Shaw moved forward, aiming his weapon at the old man's chest.

'Edgar Coelho,' his voice, strong and authoritative, reverberated in the cylindrical room. 'Detective Ronan Shaw, Widow's Peak Police Department. Don't move. You're under arrest.'

Startled, the lighthouse keeper turned in the direction of Shaw's voice. His right hand, dripping with blood, crept toward his jacket pocket. Without hesitation, Shaw lunged, propelling him backward. They hit the floor hard.

Shaw pulled him upright and they faced each other, eye to eye. The lighthouse keeper's cheeks were flushed, the red spreading to his chin and forehead. Shaw's cold blue stare penetrated the old man's eyes, ablaze with conflict. Whatever Missy had said to him, had worked.

Shaw glanced up to the top of the tower. 'Where is she?'

'Leave her be, Detective,' the lighthouse keeper said.

Shaw reached forward and grabbed Coelho's arm. The old man resisted a little, but not nearly as much as Shaw had expected. 'Face the wall,' he said. 'Kneel down. Put your hands up over your head. You're under arrest.'

Edgar Coelho shuffled a few yards away, closer to the curved wall. He tilted his chin up, cleared his throat. 'For what, exactly?'

'Let's start with the illegal production and distribution of liquor,' Shaw said. 'Then we can get to the matter of Lara Harvey and Tommy Mathieson.'

Coelho nodded, seemingly satisfied with Shaw's answer.

Shaw handed the lighthouse keeper over to one of the other officers who led him outside, then stood for a moment in the empty room and peered up toward the top of the tower. A thunderclap filled the chamber.

Shaw clambered up the spiral staircase. As he climbed, the whole tower shook, the rain outside coming down hard. It battered the walls. The long drop to the bottom grew higher, but the adrenaline flooding his body meant he was not inclined to give in to vertigo, to panic.

Reaching the landing, the rain pelted against the small, round window above the bed and drops of water splashed at his feet. It dripped from the ceiling, through the cracks in the wood. He stood underneath the manhole where water streamed through and cascaded down the ladder, making it difficult to climb. Entering the lantern room, his feet crunched on shards of glass that sprinkled the floor. The incessant rain had found its way in, and an inch of water was on the ground, dripping through every crack in the floor.

Shaw scanned the room, then froze. Missy sat propped against one of the large panes of glass, her legs splayed in front of her, her eyes partially open, her lips parted. He rushed to her and crouched over her, turning her face to his. Her chin was smeared with blood.

'Hey, hey, look at me,' he said.

Her eyes rolled back, and it took her a moment to focus on him. He took her hand. It was cold and clammy, her skin pale. She was well into the first stages of shock.

'What the fuck happened here, Missy?'

She couldn't speak, she just buried herself in his lap. He cradled her head. She smelled like an animal, sweaty and afraid. 'It's all right,' he whispered. 'You're all right.'

He lifted her up and carried her like a rolled-up carpet down the ladder, to the landing below the lantern room. He pushed aside a pile of books and helped her to sit on the bed. Removing the soiled and wet jacket, he laid it over the back of the bedhead. Missy looked up at Shaw with bloodshot eyes. Her entire body trembled.

Shaw went to the small desk and lit a kerosene lamp, casting shadows around the room. Sitting on the edge of the bed, he turned to Missy, now in the foetal position, and rubbed her shoulder and arm to get her blood flowing.

'Did you arrest him?' Missy asked, her voice shaking.

Shaw nodded.

Missy buried her face in the pillow. 'I'm going to sleep here tonight.'

'I don't think that's a good idea.'

She turned to him, her face full of venom. 'Why not? The danger's gone, right? You arrested my grandfather.'

Shaw gestured around the flooded room. 'There's water coming in through the roof. The storm's getting worse. Come on, let's go and get dry and I'll make you a cup of tea. You can tell me what happened.'

Missy shook her head, water dripped from the ends of her hair. 'I don't want to talk about it.'

Shaw exhaled. 'Do you want me to stay here with you?'

'No,' Missy said, burying her face in the pillow. 'I don't know. I don't know what I'm supposed to do right now. I just know that, in all my life I've never felt so unmoored. So alone.' Missy sat up; her eyes welled over. 'My mother, she killed herself. *Avó* said there was a sickness in her.' She stared at Shaw desperately. 'And now it's in me. It's taking me…'

Shaw put his hand on hers, her clammy skin, bone white. 'Listen to me, Missy. Whatever sickness your mother had, whatever made her hurt herself, it isn't in you.' Shaw held her face in his hands, peered into her large, soft, doe eyes. Water dripped from the tips of his hair and merged with the tears streaming down her cheeks. 'Whatever happened to her, it's not going to happen to you. I promise. And whatever you need, we can get you help. You don't have to hide anything from me, Missy. Whatever it is, we can work it out. Together.'

He stroked her hair. She flinched at his touch at first, like an animal, wild and unsure. Then she gave in to it and collapsed into him, pushing her face against his chest. Waves of desire pounded into him with every crash of the ocean against the rocks outside. Desire for her, desire to save her, from this place, from herself. He felt heavy with the burden of what he had forced her to do.

'Do you hear me?' Shaw continued, holding her tighter, holding his heart out for her. 'You're not alone anymore. I don't know what my future holds, but I know I want you in it. Everything is going to be all right. We can leave this place, together. Right down the coast, there's a little whaling town called Eden. We can build a place near the beach, ride horses along the shoreline. You can fish as much as you like. At night I'll rub your feet, and we can both fall asleep gazing into the fire.'

Missy sucked in one, two, three silent breaths. The warmth of her against Shaw's chest comforted him and aroused him, being so close to her, finally.

'But something *is* wrong,' she murmured into his neck. 'I feel like… like I'm dying, like I'm already dead. Like I'm decomposing. Something is eating at me.' She leant into him, and he felt the bones beneath her shirt, beneath her skin. He pushed against her. Pushing their bodies closer, hardening against her. 'Because… because I—'

'What is it?'

The storm outside rolled with thunder.

'I want to feel alive,' Missy said as she removed her blood-stained shirt and sat, bare chested, in front of him. His heart hammered as he drank in her nakedness, her slender arms and the curve of her breasts. 'Please,' she whispered, 'make me feel alive.'

Shaw brushed the matted, wet hair off Missy's wet face. 'You're so beautiful. If I keep looking at you, I might do something I'll regret.'

'Close your eyes, then,' she panted into his mouth.

'I don't want to.'

Missy lay back on the bed, shivering with cold. With trembling hands, she unbuckled her belt and removed it from her trousers, then wriggled out of them. Shaw let her unbutton his fly then slid off the bed and shook his trousers to the floor, removing the layers of cold, wet clothes like peeling off layers of skin. He returned to the bed dressed only in his drawers and lay down next to Missy, felt the warmth of her. Painfully warm. Was she feverish?

Shaw brought his lips to Missy's mouth and kissed. Her lips opened and her tongue yielded to his. He cupped her breasts, smooth and as white as limestone. Her nipples hardened under his touch. Missy sighed and parted her legs, pressing herself into him.

'Take these off,' Missy urged.

'Are you sure?'

'I want you with every single part of me,' she told him as she pulled off his underwear. She rolled onto her back and did the same with her own.

Shaw spread Missy's thighs open and moved on top of her. She pulled him closer. He dipped his head to kiss her then caught his breath as his body pressed scaldingly against hers.

22

Sábado

The next morning

THE wind agitates the surface of the ocean. I turn my head to the sound I have caught on the breeze.

'Listen.'

My father quietens, positions his fisherman's cap higher on his head and angles his ear, trying to hear it himself. He hears only the sea. I can tell. He pats my shoulder. 'The wind.'

I shake my head. 'It's gone.' But I don't sound convinced.

The ocean turns from blue to grey. A sudden gust of wind flings spume at me. A fierce spray that stings my skin and spits salt into my eyes. The heavy, heady smell of decomposing plant life assaults my senses. But I'm used to that smell by now. Accepting of it. The same for the pungent smell of fish and brine. I tilt my head to the other side, lower my ear to the water. The ocean rushes in and pats the *Senhora* gently on the belly. Rushes back.

My eyes close in the sun, and I listen. To give in, to let go. The world falls away and I fall away too, into the water, into her arms.

I slip into the sea.

The cold water slaps my face and shocks my eyes open.

My father steps close to me. 'Miss, what are you doing?'

'Nothing,' I whisper.

'The rope.'

He sounds agitated.

I watch the waves, head tilted, as if they have something to tell me. A secret to share. A glint of silvery-green flickers just under the surface. I smile. She is so at home under the waves.

I open my mouth to speak but a noise floats to me first. A shrieking sound, high and piercing, coming to me through the waves, and I know it's her. Her voice calls me. Whistling over the waves and through. One note. Two. Mournful, and haunting, beautiful and—

'Missy.'

Who said that?

I yank on the rope and begin the long pull up from the ocean's depths. It's wet and slimy and there are bits of green algae dangling from it like the slime dangling from the hole in my head. Decomposing plant life but I'm used to it by now.

The muscles in my arms burn from exhaustion because I haven't done this in days, and I feel them wanting to give in, *I* want to give in, but I continue pulling because I refuse to allow that bastard, Gil Sanders, to step foot on my boat anymore.

The slime completely covers the rope now so that it is soft and spongey and suddenly it is not rope but an arm, a long thick tentacle, reddish-brown, dotted with rows of pearly-white suckers. It starts to move, to bend and curl and spiral. It grips me. I feel the pressure tighten on my hand as it takes hold, wraps itself around my wrist and tugs me.

The tentacle yanks me forward and I lose my footing. I collide with the gunwale with enough force to knock the wind out of my lungs. Before I can catch my breath, another gust of wind blows from behind and then I'm overboard.

I am a decent swimmer. The vastness of the open ocean has never frightened me. But this morning, the wind is up after last night's storm and the swell comes at me from all angles. I swallow a mouthful of salt water. Brine floods my throat and nasal passages and then panic takes over.

Waves crash over me and they seem determined to pull me under. I inhale another gulp of seawater, and the weight of the entire ocean pulls me downward. I sneak in one last breath of air and descend, sinking through sunlit layers of water. Under the surface the world is silent.

Something moves around me; I hear little bubbles gush in front of me.

Something slender and pale darts out of the corner of my eye. It could be a shark. I kick my legs, try to swim to the surface, but I am so disoriented that I don't know which way is up. My lungs scream as they empty of air, but drowning suddenly seems like a better option, when compared to being eaten by a shark.

No. Not a shark.

A voice booms and the words are thunder. They undulate through me. I turn and she comes toward me like smoke in the water, her scales patterned like wild tuna, until she is barely inches from my face. Her eyes are cavernous holes, her grey arms unfurling. They wrap themselves around my shoulders, her cold, bony fingers holding me tightly, my lungs burning now, and she pulls me closer to her torn-open chest. I can feel the bones of her ribs.

'Hello, little mermaid,' she whispers in my ear. 'Are you ready to come with me now?'

I turn to her, but I cannot speak. I have no breath.

She presses her mouth to the tender bones in my ear and I barely hear her whisper; 'Did you discover the truth?'

She nips my cheek with her sharp teeth and wraps her fingers around my neck, twists my head painfully. I close my eyes. I don't want to see the water grow dark with my blood. I kick and try to swim away but her cadaverous hands claw at me, pull me back.

I am going to die.

And, drowning, I wonder, do I want to go with her?

Yes, of course. Of course, I do.

More bubbles gush past my ear as the words rush in. 'Don't go up too fast.'

I shoot upward, dragged to the surface, my head breaking through the waves, hauling in gasping breath, choking on air, drinking in huge gulps of it, feeling oxygen burst into my lungs and flow through my veins like opium.

I flounder for the boat's ladder, expecting those cadaverous hands to close around my ankles at any moment and pull me back down. Instead, I feel the strong arm of my father, swimming against the crashing waves. He wrenches me onto the ladder, heaves me upwards, out of the ocean and up the side of the boat, to safety.

Shaking, we collapse on the deck, knocking over a pile of empty wooden crates.

I glance over to him, fully clothed, soaking wet. Panting, he crawls from the gunwale and makes his way through the maze of rusted traps, coils of rope and nets, across the deck, feeling his way with his hands. He stands up with the support of the snottler and gazes off into nothingness, his chest heaving.

He feels the empty space just above the ground, searching for his fisherman's cap, which lays there, just out of his reach, clearly discarded, before he jumped overboard. Before he saved my life.

I pick up his cap, place it in his hands and peer into his pale eyes, milky-white, dead, as far gone as the shell that took their sight, years before. Hugging him, I bury my face into the scratchy, wet wool of his pullover. His heart is beating erratically, as mine is.

'I'm sorry,' I cry.

He pats my head, the way he used to do when I was a child. 'What's happening, Miss? Tell me what's going on.'

I shake my head. 'I think I'm losing my mind. I'm scared. I'm really scared.'

'What is it? Tell me what you're scared of.'

'I'm scared of… of being like her. Like my mother. Of going mad. I know she killed herself. But I don't know why.' I look up at him then, at my father, at his once young and handsome face. 'Tell me the truth. I need to know.'

'The truth?' he says, and after a moment, he nods. 'All right, Miss. The truth. The truth is she *did* walk into the sea. I tried to stop her. In the end, she did it anyway.'

Blood courses through me, the hot sting of anger. 'All those years, a lie? Why did you tell me she drowned?'

'Because she did. You can be angry, but I did my best. I've never kept anything else from you.'

'Why?'

'She didn't say much back then that made sense.'

'Tell me what she said that didn't make sense,' I plead.

'She said it were the mermaids calling to her. And that she was cursed. That's why she couldn't…' He looks down into his lap, tears gather in the corners of his milky eyes.

'She couldn't what?'

He shakes his head. 'I can't. I…'

'She's calling to me. She's calling to me and I don't think I can ignore her much longer. I need to know. So I can stop it from happening to me.'

Gust inhales a shaky breath. Wrings the wet wool of his pullover in his scarred hands. 'All right, I'll tell you. But you are not to blame, you understand?'

'Understand what?'

'After you were born, your mother went to a very dark place. It was like the balance of her mind was… well, unstable. You were only one year old when your mother took her own life. I never wanted you to know.'

'She did that to herself, because of me?'

'What happened was not your fault. You are not responsible for your mother's decision.'

'Had I not been born, she'd still be alive?'

'No, Miss. She was unwell. It was just who she became after you arrived. But you must remember that she loved you. It was just… becoming a mother. There really isn't a way to prepare for the weight of it all. No sleep, keeping you safe, all the while trying to figure out who she was afterwards. Sometimes, she just couldn't handle it. She'd get into these moods, Miss. These dark moods. Unbearable sadness.'

'Why didn't you take her to see someone? A doctor or…?'

'I tried to get her to go to the doctor, but she wouldn't go. She wouldn't let me tell anybody. She forbade me from telling anyone. Missy, nobody knew. Not even your grandfather.'

Gust lowers himself to the ground and rests his back against the side of the boat, bringing his hand up to his forehead. 'Maybe I should've done more. I should've told somebody. But it was because his money paid for our house, put you through school. He wanted you to make something of yourself. Not end up the wife of a fisherman, like your mother. It *is* my fault.' Gust's head drops into his hands. 'It's all my fucking fault.'

I crouch next to him. 'Stop, it's all right. It's not your fault either.'

He is trembling now. 'I'm sorry. I'm sorry I let this happen to you.'

'You didn't do anything.'

'I know. That's the problem. That's always been the problem. I didn't know what was happening. I was just so overwhelmed. We both were. Between the baby, and the boat. And at first it seemed like she loved being a mother. But then the sleep deprivation, and the constant crying and feeding and changing. I started to sense her growing distant. Isolated. Being far away from everyone else. She tried to keep it all inside, but slowly the cracks began to show. I could tell when a bad feeling was coming on. She'd stop eating or sleeping. She'd wake at five o'clock in the morning. I could hear her breathing change in the dark. She'd lie there, so still. If I said anything, if I said, "*Neve, love, are you awake?*" she wouldn't answer, and that's when I knew she was under one of her clouds. I don't know if it was an illness. I don't know if she was going mad, or what, but she'd be so sad.

'How do I help my wife who seemed so determined to endure her ordeal by herself? I told her to go swimming in the ocean.' He half-smiles at me. 'Saltwater cures everything. And then she went to the fucking ocean, and she drowned. And she was gone. None of it made any sense.' A sob catches in his throat.

'Afterwards, whenever I looked at you, I saw her. Broke my heart. You know, your grandmother, she went the same way. Sometimes, these things run in the family. But Missy, falling in love with your mother was the easiest thing I ever did. And having you was the best thing.'

I hug my knees to my chest. 'It's happening to me,' I say. 'I'm blacking out. I lose track of things, of time. I lose minutes, hours. You have no idea how scared I've been.'

'Oh, Miss. I'm sorry. I should have done better. For you. I should have been a better father. I never should have left you. For that, I am so very, very sorry. I never should have gone to war. I thought I would go and come back a changed man, a better man. But I saw things… I saw things in the war, Miss. Things I never told you. Never told anyone. And never will. Christ's sake, I *did* things…' He squeezes his fists tight. 'The more time passes, the more I wonder why. Why did I survive? Why did I get to climb out of those mud pits, when so many others did not? Why did I get to live, get to return home? Get to come back to this?'

I gaze around at the salt-rusted traps, the piles of crates with rotting wood, the blood-stained deck. 'You came back from the trenches for *this*?'

'No, not for this,' Gust says. 'For *you*. I came back for you. We live with the choices we make. That's what courage is. Standing by the consequences of your decisions. And your mistakes.'

I breathe deeply, my chin wobbles, threatening to unravel everything. I blink back the tears that sting my eyes. 'Dad, *please*. What should I do?'

Gust places his hand on mine. 'Endure, Missy. Like we all do. Like we all must.'

My father holds me, anchoring me to the moment.

We head back to the harbour as the glow of the sun breaks the horizon, glittering like scattered seeds of perfect golden light. Leaping fish enjoy our foamy wake.

I steer the *Senhora* between the rocky eyebrows of Widow's Basin and feel the rays warm my bare arms through the cabin windows. A briny breeze pours in through the open door and tousles hair about my face, reminding me of Shaw's fingertips the night before.

Standing here again, in my place at the helm, I am mesmerised by the patterns of the water. Last night's rain has enriched the hue of the harbour to that opaque, turquoise shade of blue. The countless ripples overlap ever inward to shore, and outward to the horizon. A tear slides down my face. I can finally breathe. A calm, light feeling quivers through me.

I wonder if this is what it is to feel alive. To feel hope. Joy. Those slippery things that have always evaded me. Now I, too, have been invited to have those things. Because of one man, one detective. We can have a future together. A future where nobody knows us, our pasts. I wonder if he meant it when he said those things about riding horses in the garden of Eden.

The boat chugs to the pier and I turn off the engine. The silence of the morning is broken but the constant screech of gulls has followed us in from the sea. They hover above like the scavengers they are and wait eagerly for us to unload our haul.

I hop over the side and tie her off. In the next boat, the voice of Gil Sanders rises up, already shouting orders at some other poor sod who agreed to allow him one day's work. He glances at me, and I feel a surging sense of satisfaction when he looks sharply away.

Climbing back on board to help my father unload the nets, I unwind the spool to the creaking and groaning of unfurling chains. The net is slowly lowered to the deck and unleashed. A large pile of fish empties, some flip and flap for their last gaping breaths.

The keener gulls land on the gunwale, waiting for their chance to dive in and steal away with some breakfast. As the peak of the silvery fish mountain slides to the deck, I glimpse something pale and fleshy underneath. I wonder if the net has captured a small porpoise while it was dredging the ocean floor.

But this net has not caught anything like that. My eyes tell me one thing and my mind another. I cannot make sense of what I see. A great weight clenches my chest. The weight of the entire ocean has closed in on it. It is no use describing it to my father. He doesn't see. He wouldn't see. Because he is blind. And because he refuses to see the truth.

This net has caught a body.

A human body.

He is tangled: one arm, white as driftwood, flung severely away from his torso, another rests across his stomach. His legs are twisted in net, like a wooden marionette.

It can't be. He's holding his breath. He's playing a joke. He dove in the water, and he ended up in our nets here and I will reach out and shake him and he shall open his eyes and blink away the salt water and say, *ha! Got you.*

But he is so still.

I kneel down and slide my hand behind his head, feel the dampness of his salt-and-pepper hair and lift his face, trace the roughness of the stubble along his jaw, and whisper, 'Open your eyes.'

But when I lift him, his head is as heavy as a dead weight and his mouth opens and saltwater spills out. His chest isn't moving either and I can see that he is not breathing.

My mind cannot process what is in front of me. I speak firmly now; I am annoyed at him for playing such a cruel joke. I shake him, and it is then that I notice the bruises. Large and purple like some exotic flower, covering him, all over.

I freeze, unable to breathe.

Detective Ronan Shaw. My hope and joy. My future. My love. Dead.

23

Friday

The night before

SHAW and Missy lay side by side, holding hands, their legs entwined. Above them, in the lantern room, the light turned steadily, with its slow, low hum. The lighthouse beam reached in through the window intermittently, casting their bodies in an eerie glow.

Far below them, dark foamy water surged and gurgled across the rock shelf reflecting the midnight sky above. The storm had eased but the raw power of the ocean still filled the small circular room with thunderous noise. When the waves struck the cliff, spray burst upwards. The small round window was open, allowing the salt-scented breeze to rush over their bodies.

Missy curled around Shaw's body, her cold hand touched his chin. 'Can't sleep?'

Shaw turned his face to hers, nestled in his arm. He shook his head. 'No. It's too loud.'

'It's never quiet here.'

'Are you all right?' Shaw asked.

Missy nodded.

'Are you sure?'

'Oddly enough, at this moment, I've never felt surer in my life.'

'What do you mean?'

A cloud must have floated past the moon because suddenly, moonlight spilled through the window and their bodies were bathed in it.

'For the first time in my life, I feel beautiful. Because you are looking at me. For the first time, I feel seen, understood, valued. This past week my whole sense of self has felt… distorted. I've always thought there was something wrong with me, but this week, I… I didn't feel like myself. I've been… irrational. Seeing things that aren't there. Hearing noises, voices, calling to me. I was convinced I was going mad. But for the first time in a long time, I feel like myself again. I can see myself again. I remember myself.'

Shaw was lost in the stare of her golden-brown eyes.

Missy kissed his face and lips. 'I have never felt more me. More embodied and alive. Connected to my body, to everything around me. I am so, so happy. I feel so… safe. Safe to be me. It feels like coming home… an acceptance, of all the parts of me I've always tried to hide. Like a self-expression. It's like what Nietzsche writes in *The Will to Power*. That the will to power is what motivates us all, to become who we really are, to reach the apex of self-expression in our lives.'

Shaw smiled. 'I noticed those books here the other day,' he said. 'It's been a long time since I read Nietzsche, and I don't remember understanding much of what he wrote, but I do remember at the time thinking he had very little understanding of human nature.'

Missy opened her mouth in an exaggerated O shape. '*Beyond Good and Evil* is Nietzsche's crowning work.' She hopped up from the bed and found her copy from the shelf above the desk, then shook it in front of Shaw's face. 'He says more in a single sentence than most other philosophers can say in a chapter… or even an entire book.'

Shaw shook his head and shrugged. 'I'm sorry,' he laughed. 'I thought his views were quite naïve. They were ahead of his time, but still… naïve. His passion is contagious, I'll give you that, but if you take a step back, it's obvious that he had no idea about human nature. Just look at what happened in Europe. It's clear that Nihilism is the key product of the Western world view.'

'How can you say that?' Missy said, crawling back underneath the sheet. 'Anyone who came back from the war would understand all too well the possibility of fighting monsters and becoming one in the process. How great evil can be practised in the name of freedom, of goodness, of defence of the innocent. *"Battle not with monsters, lest ye become a monster, and if you gaze into the abyss, the abyss also gazes into you."*'

Shaw screwed up his nose. 'Even that quote is problematic,' he said. 'The abyss is supposed to be this dark, bottomless space where your worst fears reside. By staring into the abyss, he's saying you're basically waiting for the darkest parts of yourself to consume you. What's the point of that?'

Missy slapped him on the arm. 'That's not it at all,' she said. 'Yes, the mind can be a dark place, but it is as limitless as the universe. The mind *is* the abyss. The search for meaning, for complete self-expression, is to try and fill that abyss.'

Shaw shook his head. 'No, it's a warning that letting your dark side control your thinking can lead to disaster.'

'You're right,' Missy laughed. 'You don't understand Nietzsche at all.'

And then, Missy was on top of him, her face so close to his face. Their arms met, elbow to elbow. She matched her shoulders to his shoulders. Her forehead to his. She pressed down on him as though she were trying to press through his skin, into his blood, his bones. Every sinewy muscle of her taut frame. It felt good, he had to admit, so good. He wanted her, but he also wanted for her to be free to be whatever she wanted.

The sheets tangled around them. Shaw flipped Missy over and held her down playfully. He kissed her neck, his mouth sliding up past her jaw. When he came up behind her ear, he felt something scratch the tip of his nose and pulled back slightly. Something small and shiny glistened in Missy's hair. Confronted with the object, Shaw became instantly alert. He pinched it between his fingers and stared at it warily.

Holding it up for her to see, he said, 'What's this?'

Missy bolted upright. 'What is it?'

There, returning the soft glint of moonlight through the window, was a fish scale. There was no mistaking its type. It was identical to the one they had found inside Flea's neck.

Missy took it from him. She held it in her palm, stared at it, not recognising it. The blood in Shaw's body flowed slowly, like oil. Then she flicked it to the floor.

Shaw thought he caught a glimpse of panic in her eyes. 'Those things get everywhere,' she said.

Shaw opened his mouth to speak but Missy pulled him back into her and led his hand over her nipples. He brought his mouth to hers and they kissed deeply as he fondled her pert breast. He left her mouth and in the near darkness, found her nipple and kissed that deeply too. He licked the skin covering her ribcage, feeling the rise of every rib bone against the tip of his tongue. She took him by the shoulders and twisted her body on top of him, straddling him. With feline exaggeration she stretched her long back to the ceiling, exposing the dark mound of hair between her legs, and pinned him to the bed with her knees, using all her weight to hold him there.

Shaw brought one arm behind his head and watched her through the darkness as she found her rhythm, her breasts bouncing up and down, up, and down, as she grew more urgent.

Her skin shone with sweat, and he felt her wetness against his groin. Very soon he could no longer bear to watch her. His eyes closed as he fought against coming too soon because he wanted her to come first but the rhythm and the momentum was building and the leverage her body was able to create was exhilarating and the feeling of her on top of him was suffocating and the sound of her panting and moaning was almost too much and he felt as though he could almost die from the pleasure of it. Shaw held his breath, and when the air had completely drained from his lungs, when he was on the brink of drowning, he heard her cry out a split second before his own climax.

Missy collapsed onto him, her fast, shallow breaths matching his own. She looked at him and smiled. Gazing at her, as their breathing slowed and their eyes grew heavy, euphoria unspooled its way from his head into his blood stream. He wondered then, why he could feel dread creep its way up from his stomach. The image of the fish scale flashed into his mind. And, as she lay sleeping in his arms, Shaw couldn't stop the thought that Missy's performance was just a way to distract him from it. The thought horrified him. No sooner had it crossed his mind did he push it away.

A dull murmur of thunder rumbled as the storm eased further out to sea. The sky and sea glowed with moonlight.

'We keep this up, I'll end up *in the family way* just like Lara Harvey,' Missy laughed as she placed one hand flat over her stomach. The other rested behind her head; her underarm baring a dark ornament of hair. Shaw turned his face to her, unsure if he'd heard correctly. His eyes narrowed, drilling into her, as she gazed out the window at the inky-blue sky.

'What did you say?' he asked.

Missy turned to him. 'Hmm?'

'About Lara Harvey. How did you know?'

'How did I know what?'

'How did you know she was pregnant?' Missy held Shaw's gaze but said nothing. 'The autopsy report only came back this afternoon. I never mentioned it to you.'

Missy cleared her throat. 'I saw her, the night she died.'

'Here?'

Missy nodded. She bunched the sheet between her fingers, pulled at a loose thread. 'She came asking *Avó* for help.'

Confusion and annoyance crept into Shaw's voice. 'Why didn't you tell me?'

'I… I guess I didn't think about it.'

Shaw propped himself up on his elbows. 'Missy, is there something you're not telling me?' Missy stayed silent, so he spoke again. 'Is there?'

'Yes,' she whispered. 'I listened to their conversation.'

'No. Something else. You lied to me. Your father said you and Lara Harvey went to school together.'

'Why that matters, I don't know. But yes,' she said. 'Laura Hartley. She changed her name.'

'Were you two friends?'

Missy hesitated. 'I didn't have any friends, remember?'

'Did you speak to her that night?'

A pause. 'Yes.'

'What about?'

'Nothing in particular. I congratulated her about being *in the family way*, and she had the hide to make a nasty comment about mothers abandoning their children.'

'Did that make you angry? Did you argue about it?'

'It wasn't like that.'

'What was it like, then?'

'I would hardly kill her because of that. Besides, it wasn't an argument.'

'But you saw her right before she died. Why would you not think to mention that to me?'

Missy shrugged. 'I just… forgot.'

'You forgot?'

'Yes. I closed the door on it.' She paused, looked up at Shaw and smiled. 'Like you do, with the war. Remember?'

Shaw stared mutely at Missy for a moment. He ripped back the sheet, jumped up out of bed, naked, and strode to the shelf. He found a length of coiled rope sitting among the other paraphernalia, picked it up and fell back into bed with Missy, then handed it to her. 'Can you tie a double fisherman's knot?'

Missy stared at him, uncomprehending. 'Why?'

'Just curious.'

Missy eyed him suspiciously but did as he requested. Shaw ran a hand through his hair as he watched her. She twisted the rope end, while she was concentrating on tying the knot, he reached for his trousers and pulled out his cigarette case. He clicked it open. Empty.

'Shit.'

'Wait here,' Missy said, tossing him the rope, tied identically to Gust's, in a perfect double fisherman's knot. 'I have a surprise.'

Missy stood from the bed, climbed up the ladder, to the lantern room. A moment later, she returned and in her hands was her grandfather's pipe. She paused, staring down at it, already stuffed with tobacco. In her hesitation, an expression that Shaw couldn't quite place crossed her face, then she laid the pipe on the pillow. Pulling on her long-johns and shirt, she sat on the edge of the mattress, next to him.

Shaw found his box of matches and lit the pipe, sucking back a few times to get the tobacco lit. He felt a sudden heaviness in his lungs, a building desire to cough. The lighthouse keeper's taste in tobacco was much stronger than his own. Shaw rolled the smoke around in his mouth and blew it out the open window. He offered the pipe to Missy, who waved it away.

'I've got to go,' she said.

Shaw coughed. 'What, right now?'

Missy nodded. 'You don't mind, do you?'

Shaw put the pipe back in his mouth and left it there, then reached out with his hand. Took hers. 'Well, could we at least…'

Missy pulled her hand away. She stood and opened one of the drawers in the desk. 'I need to catch my father before he leaves the harbour.' She pulled out Gust's fisherman's cap. 'I have to give this back to him. I've been keeping it from him. But he deserves it back. He can't fish properly without it.'

Shaw stared at the cap, then back at Missy. Something snagged in his brain. The tall young man in the fisherman's cap. 'You were the last person to see Flea alive, too?'

Shaw let out a hacking cough. He examined the hole in the pipe, smelled the burning embers, then fixed his eyes back on Missy. He picked up on something in her. A detachment. A subtle coldness. There was a moment when he could have asked her what she was doing, what the hell was going on, but that moment passed.

'What is it? Tell me,' he said.

Missy didn't answer for a moment. Then she looked at him and sighed. 'There *is* something I must tell you. Can I trust you with it?'

'I love you, Missy. Whatever it is, you can tell me.'

Missy gazed back at him flatly. She gave nothing back. Unreachable.

'It's difficult to remember. I try not to. I push it down. Deep down.'

A peculiar metal taste had developed in the back of Shaw's throat. He coughed harder, bringing his elbow up to cover his mouth. 'What are you saying?'

'I don't remember killing Flea,' she whispered.

A coughing fit overtook Shaw. He sat up and got himself to the side of the bed. His legs felt wobbly, as though he'd had too much whiskey. He leaned over and spat, pressed his fingers into his eye sockets. 'What are you talking about?'

'I do remember some things. I was standing with him at the edge of the cliff, looking at the horizon. We were standing, talking, and then his body was lying on the rocks with that gash in his neck and my knife, just beside him.'

The coughing did not stop. Shaw began to wheeze. He stared at her in disbelief. A sheen of sweat coated his forehead. '*You* did that to him?'

Missy stared at the ground, shook her head. 'I don't know. I told you, I don't know what's real anymore. I remember the redness of the blood seeping out of him, and, it was as though, as his life left his body, something also left mine. I didn't know what to do, so I pushed him into the water. I thought he'd wash out to sea, or fish would finish him off… I never thought he would wash up…'

A pang slid down Shaw's chest and entered his stomach. He put his hand up to her. 'Wait a minute. I asked you a question.' His voice sounded raspy. He searched her face as though she were a stranger. The coughing and wheezing continued. 'Look at me,' he choked out. 'Missy, look at me. Did you kill Flea?'

But the woman in front of him was gone. The vacant look on her face told him she had left anything rational behind.

'Of course, it was me,' she said dreamily. Her whisper encircled Shaw's throat and gripped, closing off his ability to speak.

He flinched, swallowed, dry and raw. 'Why?'

Missy returned from wherever she had been. Her eyes widened. 'He was on to me.' Panic constricted her voice, high-pitched and irrational. 'That night, at the harbour, you heard him. He knew I wasn't delivering coal to the lighthouse. It was only a matter of time before he found out…' Her eyes brimmed with tears threatening to spill. 'Now you know,' she cried. 'I've done things. Really bad things.'

'We've all done bad things,' Shaw rasped, pulling on his drawers with deliberate effort and moving closer to her. 'It's not too late, Missy.'

Tears streamed down her face. Shaw wiped them away with his thumb. 'You don't understand,' she said. 'I feel like I'm going mad.' She fell into his arms. 'I don't want to be alone anymore.'

Shaw comforted her, kissed her through her tears, even though his head was spinning, his throat burning, his guts churning. 'You don't have to go through this alone. I'm here now, we can get you help.'

Missy gazed into Shaw's eyes. She kissed him on the mouth and turned away. 'I won't be a victim anymore.'

Shaw was hit by a wave of nausea. He shook his head in disbelief. 'Missy…' he paused, not wanting to know the answer to his next question, not wanting to let it escape, but escape it did. 'Did you kill Lara Harvey too?'

Missy turned her face away. 'I didn't mean to kill her,' she said. 'I just wanted to scare her.'

Shaw's breath grew short, the pain and tightness in his chest increased and the coughing worsened. Now his spinning head was starting to throb. 'Why didn't you tell me?'

She leered at him. Spat her words at him. 'You wanted to believe it was my grandfather. All along, you wanted it to be him.'

'But I never thought it was *you* who killed her. Why, Missy? Tell me.' It was difficult to breathe. He was panting. And with every beat of his breaking heart, his head pounded inside his skull. 'Missy?' was all he could utter, his eyes wide with terror. '*Missy!*' he said again, pulling her backwards.

Nausea, chills, headache. Abdominal pain.

Missy shook her head. 'She should have just left. But she came to me. I was standing near the cliff.' Her lips moved into a sort of half smile. She looked at him, kind of… smiling still. 'The moon was so big, so beautiful. If she had just left me there, left me alone, she'd still be alive. None of this would have happened. But she never could leave me alone. All my life, she never left me alone. She was a tyrant. A bully. *"Oh, it's just you, Seaslug,"* she said to me and I pictured her tripping over and tumbling off, there, and then not there. For a wild moment, I imagined what it would feel like, if I pushed her off. But then she did slip.'

'Missy, you're scaring me.' Shaw sat there, dumbfounded, her words curled into him like fishhooks.

A tear streaked down Missy's cheek and dripped from her chin. 'In seconds, she was over and gone and I just froze. I just stood there. I couldn't move. There, and then not there. The afterimage of her, silhouetted against the moon, still clung to my vision. And seeing her slip over the edge, I felt good and happy. It served her right. After what she had said to me. After the way she had treated me. She made my life hell. Every chance she got. I stood, and she slipped. She shouted to me. Called for help. And I just stood. I stood and watched her fall down those rocks and into the ocean. I thought I would see her head pop up and she would swim to shore. Let the woman drive home soaking wet. I didn't know she couldn't swim. How was I supposed to know she couldn't swim?'

'Missy, look at me,' Shaw said. 'I know you're scared. But we have to go to the police.'

Missy bent forward, hugging her knees. 'I know what I did. I know what I am. I am a monster,' she said, barely audible.

'Missy,' Shaw wheezed. 'You speak of monsters. But that's not how the world works.' Missy straightened up and looked at him for a moment, then looked away. 'People aren't good or bad. People make mistakes, they sometimes do bad things. People have good and bad in them. Darkness and light. But by staring into the abyss, you are waiting for those darkest parts to consume you. I know you. You're stronger than that. Don't stare into the abyss. Do not let it overcome you.'

Shaw spluttered into the back of his hand, tasted the metal tang of blood. He looked down in horror to see a dark smear across his knuckles. Like dawn slowly breaking over the horizon, his thoughts battled to understand, tried to keep up with the surge of panic and realisation as he felt his insides tearing to shreds. He looked down at the pipe sitting in front of him, and then like a lock, it clicked. Heat rushed to his face all at once.

Acute exposure.

For a moment he could hear nothing but the thumping of his own heart in his ears. Panic kicked him like a horse hoof to the spleen.

Shaw's clammy hand gripped Missy's wrist and she yanked it away. He fell to the floor, coughing and wheezing. Desperately, he searched her face for answers. He felt his body failing him, his heart slowing, as he slumped on the ground. His vision became hazy in the dark room.

Missy stood, towering over him. 'You think you know me,' she said, as though she was enjoying her power over him. 'You think you love me. You don't. There *is* something wrong with me. I'm not rational. I *do* see things that aren't there. I hear voices. I've always heard them. They call to me. Tell me to do things. Bad things. Evil things.'

'Missy?' Shaw was almost screaming now, although his voice was barely audible, his body fighting to get the words out. He was having a harder and harder time getting enough oxygen. 'What have you done?' His body temperature rose as he tried to remain calm, steady. With each breath, he felt the need to breathe faster and faster. 'What… have… you… *done?*'

He wheezed on the floor, on all fours. He covered his heart with his hand, the burning in his chest. Tried to speak but hacked up blood instead. He collapsed his weight against the bedframe then looked up at her and did not recognise her expression.

Missy rested her dark, sad eyes on him. 'Now you look at me like I'm a monster,' she smiled as she said it, remarkably calm.

Shaw focused on his breathing, dragging in air through his mouth, but felt like it couldn't reach his lungs before it left his body. His insides were ablaze. He blinked, tried to focus on the object in front of him. It was blurry. He reached for it, grasping it on his second attempt. He closed his fist around the lighthouse keeper's pipe and held it up to his face, tapped the tobacco out. A silvery substance spilled onto his palm. His face was reflected, distorted in the droplet.

Mercury.

Shaw gathered his strength and stood on shaking legs. 'I'm not angry, Missy,' he whispered. He felt like he was trying to breathe through mud. Like he was being smothered by it. Back in the trenches. 'We can… get…. you help. There are places… h…h… hospitals, where…'

Missy snatched the pipe from him and tossed it across the landing. It hit the floor, tobacco and quicksilver splattering across the white-washed walls. An agonising silence befell them.

Then, she spoke.

'You know, you could be asleep right now. This could be a dream.' She took a step toward Shaw and he sprang backward defensively. 'You're dreaming that I've poisoned you and it's hard to breathe and you can't wake up.'

Shaw gaped at her, bleeding out his unspoken words at her. Hacking up confusion, anger, and fear with the dark, sticky fluid coming from his lungs. Finally, he stumbled toward the stairs, wondering how it had come to this. After everything he had survived, after all the German shells, all the bullets he had dodged, the trench foot, the disease, the dark and lonely nights. How could he meet his end at the hands of a fisherman's daughter?

Shaw peered over the edge to the bottom of the tower, the deep, dark well of the lighthouse. He couldn't see anything, it was too black, his eyes too blurry. It was all abyss.

'You had a dream about me, and it felt like it was real. But it's only a nightmare. You know all about those, don't you?'

Shaw took the stairs two at a time, eager to get away from her. His chest burned. Amidst his galloping despair, he felt his whole respiratory system giving out.

Missy caught up to him when he had stumbled only a few steps. She reached for him. But as she grabbed his shoulder, Shaw's body twisted in shock. They stood there on the spiral staircase, her arms around him, for one breath. Then, she shoved. His knees buckled beneath him. His foot missed the step below and he plunged away from her, down to the bottom of the tower. And, as he fell through darkness, through abyss, he swore he heard the high-pitched whinny of a horse echo against the curved walls.

Then there was silence. Everything stopped.

24

Domingo

Six weeks later

My father is gone but his bed is disturbed in that way that suggests he's not long left.

Checking his room and the signs of him before I start my day has become part of my routine. My new routine. The one the doctor said would be good for me. To keep my mind ordered, so I know what is real and what is not. I don't go with my father on the *Senhora* anymore. The doctor said I should try not to go anywhere that might trigger seeing her again.

So, after I have stared at my father's unmade bed for a few minutes, I move on to the usual sequence: chickens, eggs, breakfast. The doctor says the protein in the yolk will strengthen my brain. It has been six weeks and still I feel like my mind is weak. Fragile.

Fallible.

I also don't visit the lighthouse anymore. I used to haunt it, like a ghost. It's abandoned now, condemned. All my visits there, all the time I spent there, have started to wither into memory. Like the feeling of salt, drying on skin.

I go out the back door to our small yard, where our chicken coop is. The hens cackle softly, scratching at the ground. Our rooster struts past me in an aggressive circle. Reaching into their feathery nests, I gather three eggs, still warm in my fingers. The hens don't really care if I take their eggs. This used to bother me. It didn't fit with my cherished idea of a hen as a loving, devoted mother. But the fact is, hens are totally indifferent to their eggs. Perhaps they are on to something.

The world is a very cold place. Don't ever trust a soul, Missy.

Those were the warnings of my grandfather. *Avô.* I feel a pang of grief, missing him. Or rather, I miss what I thought he was. And I hate that I caused his arrest. To him, I was a normal girl, innocent, naïve. He worried for my safety, as any grandfather would, yet little did he know how wrong he was. He should have been afraid of me. The world should be afraid of me.

Because here I am, at home on a beautiful Sunday, making breakfast after killing three people, and allowing him to take the blame.

Four, if you count what I did to my mother.

What is wrong with me? I've lost all my joy, my hope. I feel nothing. I don't feel sadness either. Just empty. An empty feeling that I carry with me all day and all night. There must have been a time before I was like this. I can't remember that long ago. Hope and joy are a slippery fish. I can try to hold them in my hands despite their desperate wriggling, but the slick scales keep slipping through my fingers.

I don't remember much about the last few weeks. It feels like I slept right through them. Those black, blank weeks when I could barely drag myself from my own bed. In those moments I have erased from my memory, I sought escape.

Are you capable? Are you physically capable of feeling anything? That is another question the doctor asks during my weekly appointments. To me, the whole question is absurd. There is nothing to weigh it against. I used to feel too much. That was my problem. Too sensitive for my own good. But everyone has their limits. Shaw used to say that. Everyone reaches the point that makes them snap. The question, I have decided, is not really about feeling. The question is, how can I possibly be alive?

And yet…

Standing over the fire, I place the large iron frying pan over the coals. The flames lick the bottom and I throw in a bit of fat and listen to it sizzle. So delicious, like toasted nuts or caramel.

I revel in the solitude of these mornings. Before my father's worried eyes, his milky stare, return from the sea. Ever watchful, even though they see nothing, they can see me. I grab hold of the large spoon and push the bubbles of melted fat around the pan. Picking up one of the perfectly brown eggs, I crack it open on the edge.

My pulse flutters.

The egg leaks a thick brown liquid, and the greyish-purple lump of an unformed baby chicken drops out. My hand flies to my mouth. I notice the veins, its oversized head, its skin so thin I can see its tiny heart and organs, deep purple, through it. I cast my eyes from it, gaping at the bricks at the back of the fireplace, listening to the sizzling oil pop and spit.

The smell is unobtrusive at first, a faint, rotting sweet. But once the heat starts to build, I cover my nose with my arm and bile ferments in my stomach. The baby chicken recoils in the melted fat and a hot spatter hits my cheek.

A wave hits me then. And the bile rises up to the back of my mouth. Suddenly the smell of hot oil is overwhelming, and I retch. The foetus is nothing but a heap of globbing feathers, with closed, purple, bulging eyes, not even shaped like a chicken yet. It looks so wrong, a lump of curdled congealed cells, frying in the hot oil.

Did I kill it by cooking it alive? Now I know for sure: I truly am a monster.

My vision goes hazy, but I know better than to scream. I hold my breath and gather the sick feeling into a tight little fist, a ball of nausea that I can control. I let out the slowest, longest breath as I grab hold of the frypan handle, hold it away from me and carry it through the front door and toss it on the sandy ground. Outside I can hear distant screeching. Muffled, as though there is a flock of seagulls behind a wall.

Back inside our hut, with the door closed, the warm, sweet smell lingers still. Nausea overwhelms me. I press my back against the wall and sink to the floor, drop my head between my knees, gasping for breath. Placing a hand on my stomach, leaving it there, another thought altogether appears in front of me, so clear and so fast it is as though it's been there all along. Terror rises up from inside me, tidal, surging, as I realise what's growing inside me. What's been growing inside me since the night Shaw and I laid together. Another secret to keep buried down deep.

Finally, I can no longer control it and I vomit on my bare feet. It's bile. Acid from my stomach as yellow as the dandelions that dot the grass on the dunes. My heart beats erratically, and I break out in a cold sweat. My throat burns. I want water. I want to be embraced by it, want to feel its cold arms enfold me. I need to fill my mouth with it, my stomach, my lungs, my organs, until every last cell inside me has swollen with it.

Then the truth strikes me. I can't do it anymore. I killed Shaw. It was me. Or I think it was me. In the very last moment I remember, I remember white and silver.

I killed Neve. I killed Laura. I killed Flea. I sent my grandfather to prison.

The memories slice through me like a blade.

Something screeches in my ears, clearer this time. Although I know it's not the mermaid. I know now she isn't real, of course I know that. It was all in my mind. My broken, barnacled mind. I know my mother is gone. But that doesn't stem my wonder.

Then, I hear her. Clear as day. She's calling to me, again. My mermaid. My mother. The woman I killed. I want her back. I'm scared. I don't want to turn out like her, or my grandmother. Abandoning their children. They were right to keep the secret from me. All that time.

My father wanted to protect me from it.

Avô wanted me to face it.

Shaw wanted me to fight it.

But I don't think I want any of those things. I am more attuned to solitude than any of them, but now with Shaw gone, I have no one left. No one even to tell this story to. So, I'll tell it to you. I'll tell it to you, before I take you with me.

I exhale slowly, formulating a plan, then get up off the floor and go to the window, gaze outside, stand there in a daze. My hand rests on one of the seashells that line the windowsill. Without looking at it, I feel the object in my palm. Its weight. With the tip of a finger, I trace the edge of its fine spiral. The smooth surface of that calcified sea creature, the mollusc who lived a thousand years ago, who took in the ocean's salts from the water all around it. Its life long ago ended, but of it, this shell remains. I crumble the shell in my palm, crushing it to fragments.

I know she is not real, of course I know that. I can hear how crazy it sounds. *But*, a voice in my head whispers, *what if?*

The mermaid calls me. There's a tug at my centre. At my womb. And it's coming from the sea. I pick up each of the remaining shells and rocks, one at a time, and slowly fill my pockets with them.

As I weigh my pockets down, I think back to *Avô's* stories about sirens – *sereias*. About what Flea told me of the Yawk Yawks and the Likanaya. All the myths from all the oceans, in the end, they all mean the same thing. Mermaids. Mean. Ugly. Tricky. Luring people to their watery deaths, using their seaweed hair. But then I remember what Flea also told me, about babies being connected to the ocean, about having gills before they are born. And I wonder, perhaps that is where you would rather be. I know it is where *I* would rather be.

I walk outside and follow her voice up and over the hill. Reaching the top, out of breath, sweat makes my thighs slippery. The lighthouse stands alone on top of the headland, blindingly bright. I make my way along the path, covered with overgrown grass, toward the hole in the fence. This place was once pulsating with energy, humming with routine. Now it is all but empty. Barren.

From this spot, the rust-coloured chimneys of the steelworks appear to prick the sky. The black, industrial skyline. The Five Islands clustered off the coast to the east. Five islands with five little mermaids sunning themselves. No sign of my father's boat. Or Gil Sanders, that cocky bastard.

The clouds, motionless, cumulous giants, dominate the pale

blue. They are bright white on top from the strength of the sun and dark grey underneath. Light and dark. Darkness always lurks somewhere underneath, even in the brightest of things. But who could want something so dark, so damaged? Someone that is utterly incapable of joy or happiness? I always knew I had darkness inside me. I thought I could ignore it, push it away. But it kept swimming back to me, kept rising to the surface like mermaid's hair; seaweed luring me into dark waters.

Tears are streaming my cheeks, and the thin skin of my eyelids is chapped, my lips blistering. I let the breeze blow my hair back from my face, let my nose run from the wind, and revel in the beauty of nature and man combined.

Looking down at my hands, I open and close them, considering all that they have done. When I think about how many people I have hurt, everything inside me aches. Everything feels charred and spoiled.

And now I must carry that pain, and also the guilt.

I carry my pain and guilt around with me everywhere. But I confess, it is wearing on me. It's tiresome, a burden. *I* am a burden. I think that the pain and guilt will break me. But it is nothing compared to what I have done. To Shaw. To Flea and to Laura. To my grandfather and my father, too. A thought swims through my mind. If I cannot walk out my pain and guilt, perhaps I can sink it.

Then, I walk.

Beyond the wind-gnarled bushes to the dunes and beyond that, the beach, across the sand and to the shore.

The shore.

Shaw.

Ronan Shaw.

I can't stop thinking that the love between us still exists, even though he no longer does. Freedom. His parting gift to me. Your father made assurances, you see, and in the event of his death, the police would know it was the mobster Sonny Fynn who had orchestrated his murder.

But freedom is no longer what I want. I seek escape. Oblivion. Ambling along the waterline, I search the beach for rocks and stones, bending every now and then to retrieve one and add it to the collection weighing down the pockets of my cardigan.

Then, when I reach the spot where I saw the mermaid, I stand at the edge of the sea. She calls incessantly to me. I can feel her physical presence under my skin with a clarity that mimics the first bloom of love. That electric feeling when you know, without even looking, exactly where your beloved's heart beats.

My quest to find out what happened to my mother has led me here, and now I must undo all my mistakes. Water pools around my boots. It gurgles. The mermaid's voice is insufferably loud, calling me.

Detective Shaw. Shaw.

Shore.

Step away… she sings, *step away from the shore…*

The waves kiss the sand.

Embrace them.

I place a hand over my stomach, imagine the tiny, gilled creature floating in the dark ocean inside my womb. There is water over my boots. See how it washes over them? The silt settles among my boot laces. The froth soaks my trousers, rolled up past my ankles. See how it colours them darker? I go deeper, knee height. The ocean heaves. A wave knocks me sideways, and I take a step back, suddenly terrified. *What am I doing here?*

But the sound of the waves calms me. The water sighs onto the shore around and behind me.

The waves soothe me.

Shhhh. Shhhh.

Soothing me.

I walk further into the ocean. It is cold but there is something reassuring about the feeling. I put one foot in front of the other until the water is up to my cracked leather belt. I undo it and it is taken by a wave, along with my knife.

And then the water is higher. Higher still. My cardigan is wet, the wool impossibly heavy and the stones weigh it down even more. I stiffen with the shock of the cold. My lungs ache with it, they are compressed by it.

I keep walking toward the horizon until the water is up to my neck. I pause. In glimmers, in whisps of thought, in the aftermath of it all, I wonder if she knew all along it would end like this.

I put another foot forward.

Shhh, they say.

The wavesssssss.

AUTHOR'S NOTE

The south coast of New South Wales has an abundance of beautiful coastal towns, many of which boast their own lighthouses thanks to early colonisers wanting the coastline to be "illuminated like a street with lamps", but the setting for this novel, Widow's Peak, will not be found among them. The town, the events, and characters in the story are fictitious.

While *The Woman in the Waves* is a work of fiction, some of the events and characters described in the novel are based on fact.

Mercury poisoning is real and had devastating consequences for lighthouse keepers throughout history, and the women in their lives were particularly susceptible to its effects.

Modern scholars have suggested that it was exposure to mercury vapour, not isolation, that caused lighthouse keepers' erratic behaviours. Mercury is of course highly toxic, and the amount of time keepers spent in close proximity to the lens and mercury bath may have affected the central nervous system and resulted in chronic mercury poisoning. Reports of early lighthouse keeping have suggested that many suffered from confusion, depression and hallucinations, short-term memory loss, incoordination, weakness, confusion, and psychological changes, including manic behaviour.

While not as severe as the Prohibition laws of the United States, there was a period during the early twentieth century that alcohol was banned in the city of Canberra. Not long after the Federal Capital Territory was formed, The Minister of State for Home Affairs, King O'Malley, passed the first ordinance that stated liquor sales be banned. Thus began Canberra's seventeen-year dry spell, which was brought to an end by the "thirsty pollies" in 1928. I have never found anything to suggest that there were bootlegging importations as alcohol was freely available in the nearby NSW town of Queanbeyan.

I have always had a lifelong love affair with and fascination for lighthouses. However, the bones of this story were dreamt up when the world was first plunged into isolation due to the outbreak of the pandemic, when I was pregnant with my second child. In Australia, approximately 15-20% of women are affected by perinatal depression or anxiety. The childbearing years, especially the first few weeks after childbirth, are the peak period for the onset of depression in women. Around 14% of women in Australia experience postnatal depression, which is equal to one in seven pregnant women. For around 40% of those women, the symptoms begin in pregnancy. Despite this number, the negative social stigma surrounding perinatal mental health fuels the harmful effects and can prevent new parents from talking about their experiences.

New and expecting parents who are experiencing perinatal depression and/or anxiety can seek advice and counselling through The Gidget Foundation, Lifeline Australia – 13 11 14, and PANDA National Helpline – 1300 726 306.

ACKNOWLEDGEMENTS

Books are never created by only the person whose name is on the front cover. It takes a community, and it's actually that sense of community that comes from delivering a book into readers hands that gives me so much joy. That blend of talent, heart, and creative thinking is everything to me. I will always be grateful to the unique community that came together to bring *The Woman in the Waves* into existence.

Thank you to the Dharawal people, the traditional custodians of the land that this story was dreamed up and written on. I feel very grateful to live and work on the majestic lands of Dharawal Country. This has been, and always will be, their land.

Thank you to Carolyn Martinez, my publisher, and the entire Hawkeye Publishing team for your unflinching, tireless work and support.

Thank you to the Hawkeye editors, including Lauren Elise Daniels, for your invaluable structural edit, especially with helping me boost this story's tension, momentum and energy, and for unlocking the power of the octopus. Thank you for your continued support of the Hawkeye Manuscript Development Prize. Authors who get to work with you are so fortunate.

Thank you to the judges of the 2023 Hawkeye Manuscript Development Prize for selecting this manuscript as the winner. Literary awards are life-changing for unpublished authors, and this competition in particular has been fundamental to my career. Hawkeye prides itself on discovering quality stories by emerging talent and championing debut authors, and I am so proud to be a part of the Hawkeye family.

My profound thanks to fellow Hawkeye author,

Anne Freeman, for your friendship, and for creating the cover of my dreams. Thank you to Hawkeye crime fiction author, Jack Roney, for your help with my endless detective questions. Your perspectives and expert eye are so appreciated.

Thank you to the judges of the 2022 Book Pipeline Unpublished Competition for selecting *The Woman in the Waves* as the winner of the mystery/thriller category, and to Peter Malone Elliot for your continued support and for suggesting the novel's title, which at the time I was still calling my Lighthouse Story.

Special thanks to Debra Wray for your generous insights, advice and guidance.

Thank you to three authors I truly admire, Lauren Chater, Kell Woods, and Holly Craig, for your generous time and effort in reading and then providing endorsements on the cover of this book. What a dream come true.

Thank you to the 2022 Curtis Brown Creative 6 Month Write Your Novel participants for your support, encouragement, and helping me take a vague idea about a lighthouse and a spooky mermaid and turn it into a novel. In particular, Lindsey Armstrong, who read the whole manuscript more than once and helped me take an unassuming eight-legged creature to something deeper and more horrifying than I could have achieved on my own. Thank you to Rebecca Lewis-Smith, Sarah Lupton, Leanne Quinn, Sophie Stern, Fiona Clarke, Louise Fuller, and Lorna Peplow, who also took the time to read the whole manuscript and provide excellent feedback that improved the story in so many ways.

Thank you to Kelly Sgroi who read an early version of the manuscript and helped me come up with those mic-drop chapter opening and closing lines. My very special beta readers (#betababes) and writing pals, Ike Levick and mermaid sister, Skye Harris. I am so lucky to have you.

Thank you again to Holly Craig and her Writeclubbers. Not only did Holly's insights and feedback strengthen the manuscript, her enthusiasm for writing continues to inspire so many of us to keep going. Writing buddies are essential to any writer and I feel so grateful to have found my community. I don't know what I'd do without all of you. I certainly wouldn't still be writing.

Thank you to the reading community for your time, kindness, and generosity.

Most importantly, thank you to my husband, Adam, for his unwavering support and the nightly cups of tea on the lounge, during which we attempt to squeeze most of our lives between the hours of 8 pm – 10 pm when a lot of this manuscript was written. And to John-John and Matilda, to whom this book is dedicated, and to whom I dedicate my everything.

In this novel, I have drawn on the First Nations' Dreaming Story of the Five Islands, of Mimosa the mermaid, her father, The West Wind, and her sisters. I first knew of this story when I saw a ceramic tile at Belmore Basin in Wollongong Harbour. I lived in the Illawarra for seven years and raised two young children there. We spent much of our time along the beautiful coastline, and this is where a lot of inspiration for the novel came from. I saw the illustration of Mimosa the mermaid, took a quick snap with my phone, then began researching everything about her. The Story of the Five Islands belongs to the Wadi Wadi people of the Dharawal nation. I am sincerely grateful to the traditional owners of the land for sharing their spiritual story which has brought a deeper meaning and connection to the place in which this novel is set.

You can read the story in full, here: Organ, M.K. and Speechley, C., 1997. Illawarra Aborigines-An Introductory History.

ABOUT THE AUTHOR

Camille Booker is an author, editor, teacher, PhD candidate, and literary judge for the Hawkeye Manuscript Development Prize. In 2022 she completed the Curtis Brown Creative 6 Month Write Your Novel Course, during which she wrote *The Woman in the Waves*, her second novel. It was shortlisted for the 2023 Varuna/Affirm Press Mentorship Award and was runner up in the CYA Competition. The manuscript won the Grand Prize of the Mystery/Thriller category of the 2022 Book Pipeline Unpublished Competition and the 2023 Hawkeye Manuscript Development Prize. Her debut, *What If You Fly?*, was longlisted for the Lucy Cavendish Fiction Prize in 2019, released by Hawkeye Publishing in 2021 and will be rereleased as *Code Name Funnel Web* in 2026. When she's not writing, you can find Camille scavenging for sea glass on the shoreline of Dharawal Country, where she resides with her family.

Follow Camille on Instagram @camillebookerauthor or visit her website www.camillebooker.com.

Book reviews can make or break a book. If you liked what you read today, please do consider posting a review on Goodreads or your favourite forum.

The Woman in the Waves is available at www.hawkeyebooks.com.au
and all good bookstores and libraries.

If you enjoyed *The Woman in the Waves*, you'll also enjoy:
Returning to Adelaide and *Me That You See* by Anne Freeman
Rosanna by Annie O'Moon-Browning
New Year's Eve by Sarah Todman
Where There is a Will by Michel Vimal du Monteil
The Truth About My Daughter by Jo Skinner
Big Music by Gillian Wills
And *Code Name Funnel Web* by Camille Booker, coming in 2026.

9 781923 105362